The Presumption

Mitch Turner Legal Thrillers, Volume 3

Dan Decker

Published by Grim Archer Media, 2021.

This is a work of fiction. Similarities to real people, places, or events are entirely coincidental.

THE PRESUMPTION

First edition. July 21, 2021.

Written by Dan Decker.

For my family.

1

"Not guilty." The two best words in the English language, at least if you are a defense attorney. The prosecution had the burden of proof beyond a reasonable doubt, and my client was presumed innocent. The fact the jury had returned so quickly told me there had been plenty of doubt to go around. The jury had barely been gone forty minutes before we were summoned back to court. In my experience, quick turnarounds usually go for the prosecution.

It was nice to see an exception.

It had been a brutal trial, lasting almost four weeks. We'd put three expert witnesses on the stand and had spent days going through tedious bits of evidence. I was certain the jury was bored by the end and would convict because we'd lost them in the mountains of minutia.

I had tried to come up with a memorable slogan for the trial like the one about that glove, but "You must acquit if the blood spatter pattern was beyond the strength of Clyde Peterson to cause," just didn't have a memorable ring.

I'd had no idea what to expect when the jury had come back from deliberations, but I'd been antsy. The judge had reviewed the verdict before instructing the jury foreman to read it out loud.

"The jury finds the Defendant Clyde Peterson not guilty on the charge of first-degree murder."

An audible gasp came from the victim's family. It was followed by a shriek. I didn't need to see who to know it was the victim's mother.

I felt bad for her.

It bothered me that she saw me as a terrible person.

I hoped to change that soon.

I had evidence about the true perpetrator that I'd not been able to get admitted into the trial. Perhaps now the prosecution would take a hard look.

I hoped they did, for the victim's mother's sake.

The evidence had been kept out of the papers by a questionable gag order from the judge, but that was no longer in effect. I was planning to have an impromptu news conference on the courthouse steps. That should put pressure on the prosecution to move.

The judge dismissed us, the bang of the gavel ringing in my ears afterward. At the beginning of the trial I had given us 50/50 odds, but by the end I was fairly confident the jury was set to convict.

It reminded me of the time I had taken a law school estate planning exam and been convinced I'd failed, but had managed to pull an A-. It is sometimes hard to judge your own work.

"You get to go home," I said.

Clyde shook his head, as if coming out of a stupor. "Am I dreaming?"

"Not as far as I can tell."

"I can't believe this. I had just—" He turned and gave me a hug. "Thank you. Thank you!"

"Just doing my job." I stood as I packed my briefcase, glancing around the courtroom. The prosecutor, a man by the name of Tony James Pope, glared at me as he left.

I couldn't help it.

I gave him a triumphant grin, which made him scowl all the more.

He and I had butted heads throughout much of the trial and the proceedings before. He was one of the better prosecutors. He approached his cases from a strategic perspective.

But it was my strategy that had triumphed.

Even without a catch phrase.

"I can't believe I'm free," Clyde said, standing. "This calls for a celebratory lunch. You up for it?"

I checked my watch and saw it was five minutes till noon. I had no better place to be, and my caseload was light at the moment anyway. "Sure, I just have to talk to some people first."

I chuckled when I noticed several reporters badgering Tony Pope. I was too far away to overhear, but I could tell he'd told them he had no comment.

I'll have a comment.

I was walking down the steps of the courthouse a few minutes later when I was stopped by a question.

"How does it feel, Mr. Turner, to get a 'not guilty' verdict?"

I stopped and looked at the reporter, waiting until a camera was shoved in my face. I counted to fifteen while I gave them a smile, my best smile. I needed to give other nearby reporters a chance to get in on the action because I wanted this to be headline news.

"Half baked!"

The woman who had asked the question was taken aback. I went on before she could ask what I meant.

"The true murderer is still out there."

My smile grew as I explained.

I was going to show the judge he couldn't keep the truth from coming out now.

2

I was leaving as Barbara was heading into the restaurant. I had not been paying attention to what I was doing, so the sudden meeting with my ex-girlfriend—almost ex-fiancé—caught me off guard. She must have seen me coming because she had already slowed by the time I looked up.

"Mitch," Barbara said, an awkward expression coming to her face. She quickly glanced around as if looking for somebody and then breathed out a quiet sigh of relief.

Was she meeting someone for lunch?

Another man?

I felt a twinge of jealousy deep inside that I kept from showing on my face. I was still basking in the glow of the 'not guilty' verdict, and I wasn't about to let anything dampen my mood.

Not even a chance meeting with an ex.

Barbara had an expert eye for fashion, and her makeup was usually immaculate. Today was no exception. She was dressed in clothing I had never seen before —I suspected she had engaged in retail therapy since our breakup—and she looked good.

Very good.

"Been a long time, Barbs," I managed to get out in a calm voice, though I found my heart racing because of the unexpected encounter.

Barbs?

I gave her a wry smile, wondering how I would explain the nickname if she called me on it.

Her smile widened, almost as if she were happy to see me. It only lasted for a second, but I was sure it had been there.

I regretted letting her get away, but there was a part of me that assumed it was for the best.

The situation had been complicated, and in the end, she had stopped returning my calls.

"It has." She looked as though she wanted to ask me about the nickname, but then shook her head and muttered something I couldn't catch.

Perhaps it was because I was on a high from court, but I felt like taking a chance. I opened my mouth to suggest we get dinner sometime soon when somebody called out her name.

I didn't recognize the voice, but it was male.

Her awkward smile returned as she turned to acknowledge the approaching man, giving him a friendly wave.

I clapped my mouth shut, the words dying on my lips.

Barbara was an attractive woman and had a lot going for her. It was no surprise she was already dating somebody else. I'd just never expected it to happen so soon.

It'd been six months since things had ended between us. I had yet to go out on a date. I wasn't pining after her. I just wasn't ready yet to move on.

"Mitch," Barbara said as she pointed to the man who had just approached. "This is Thomas. Thomas Guyton."

"Mitch Turner," Thomas said, extending a hand. "I heard on the news you just pulled a 'not guilty' verdict." There was a look on his face that said he knew he was in good with Barbara. He didn't seem concerned about running into her ex. He was several inches shorter than me and wore enough gel in his hair I could almost see my reflection.

At least I'm not the rebound guy.

"Tough case, but the jury did the right thing." I extended my hand, and we shook. The guy gave me a firm grip. I returned it. It looked like we were about to get locked in some sort of macho contest as our muscles tensed.

I wasn't about to back down. The man must have remembered he already had the girl, so he had nothing to prove. He released his grip, an easy smile coming to his face.

I did the same a moment later.

The silent exchange had not gone unnoticed by Barbara, whose eyes had narrowed. She wasn't the type to enjoy two men fighting over her.

I already didn't like this slimy fella. Barbara could do better.

"Don't let me detain you two," I said, reaching back and opening the door to usher them inside.

There was an awkward pause while Thomas waited for Barbara to go first, but she gave him a look that told him he should go ahead.

I hid a smile. Barbara was a master at communicating with just a look.

"I'll give you guys a moment," Thomas said after another awkward few seconds. He entered after glancing at Barbara.

I let the door shut since it was apparent Barbara wanted to talk. Thomas stopped briefly as if he were going to wait for her but then went further into the restaurant, probably to check on a reservation or to ask for a table.

"He seems nice," I said, glancing at his back. "I hope he is treating you okay."

"He is."

"I should get going—"

"Mitch," Barbara said, cutting me off, "I didn't mean for you to learn like this."

"It was bound to happen. I'm glad you moved on."

"Are you?" She gave me a searching look. There was something behind her eyes that told me part of her regretted how things had ended. "Truly?"

"Yeah, sure." I nodded towards him. "You don't want to keep him waiting."

"No, I suppose not." She glanced at me as if she were thinking of saying more but then shook her head and muttered something inaudible.

When she reached for the door, I grabbed it and held it open.

"Don't be a stranger," Barbara said, turning back, just as the door was closing behind her.

Don't be a stranger?

You're the one who didn't return my calls.

The walk back to my office was short.

I supposed I should be glad she had moved on, but I had difficulty believing she would find the type of long-term commitment with Thomas Guyton that she'd said she was looking for with me. There was something about the guy that bothered me, and it wasn't just the fact he was dating Barbara.

It's just jealousy. I chided myself. *Nothing more. She's not your concern anymore.*

I didn't like the thought of him with Barbara, but there was nothing I could do about it. I looked up when I realized I was at the door to my office.

I shook my head, deciding to go for a quick drive to clear my mind and celebrate my victory. I was just opening the door to my Porsche when the front door opened.

"Mitch," Ellie called out, "there you are!"

I turned, surprised she had seen me through the door. She must have been looking for me.

"Everything okay?" I asked.

"You're late."

It took me a moment.

She had texted to schedule an appointment for a potential client while I was at lunch with Clyde Peterson.

"I'll be right there."

I locked my car and followed Ellie inside while putting on my game face.

If I recalled correctly, the potential client had been charged with murder. It was good to already have a new case to replace the one I had just finished.

It was just the thing I needed to take my attention off Barbara.

"Mitch Turner," Ellie said, standing aside so I could see the client who sat waiting in the guest chair, "meet Candy Carlisle."

I had a hard time finding my tongue.

Candy was almost an exact copy of Barbara, from the well-set blonde hair to the way she did her makeup to the designer clothes she wore.

"Pleased to meet you," I said, extending a hand and giving a firm shake, hoping she didn't pick up on my momentary hiccup.

They even have the same purse!

"Come on back," I said, ushering her towards the door with a wave of my hand.

Ellie grabbed my arm as Candy went inside my office. "Where were you? You kept her waiting for fifteen minutes."

"I had something get in the way."

Ellie didn't let go. "Are you okay?"

I opened my mouth to explain to Ellie what had happened with Barbara but couldn't do it. Ellie knew about my past relationship with Barbara.

The two were even friends of sorts or at least acquaintances. I had never talked much with Ellie about my relationships and saw no reason to start now.

I shrugged. "Lost track of the time."

"Don't let it happen again!" Ellie said, frustration creeping into her voice as she pushed me towards my office door.

I gave her a curious look, but she'd already turned away. The response I was getting from her for being a few minutes late was surprising.

It was unlike her.

Something had been going on with her. She had successfully avoided telling me, despite my attempts to figure it out. I had even asked her about it point-blank, but she had refused to say anything.

I needed to learn what was going on, if only so I knew how to interact with her better. I would not take no for an answer again.

Ellie was now back at her computer, furiously typing on her keyboard, avoiding my gaze.

I walked into my office, pulling the door shut behind me.

3

"Ms. Carlisle," I said, once I had taken a seat across from her behind my desk, "what is it that I can do for you?" The resemblance was remarkable. Barbara's nose was more petite, Candy's wider. The hair color was an exact match, as was the style. Candy had a mole just above her lip. There were some subtle differences around the eyes and chin. And some other physical differences as well. But it was like I was talking to my ex-girlfriend.

"I have been charged with murder," Candy said as if the admission pained her. She sat her purse in the empty chair and clasped her hands in her lap, staring at me like she was trying to figure me out.

"Who?"

"My husband," Candy said, her voice catching slightly as if she still could not accept it.

There was something behind her eyes as she spoke, but I couldn't make out what it was.

Grief at his death? Relief he was gone?

I could not tell.

"When did this happen?"

"Four months ago."

I arched an eyebrow. Most clients contacted me right after their arrest. This meant Candy was already represented and not happy with her attorney.

"You're just coming to me now?"

"My other attorney is not working out."

"Who?"

"Karen Brodsky."

"Karen?"

I shook my head, surprised Candy wasn't happy with Karen's service. Karen had been top of my class. She'd studied while others partied. I'd studied too, but I'd had fun as well. Law school is high pressure. If you don't release it every now and again, it comes out in unexpected ways. "You're having a hard time with *her*?"

I had not gone up against Karen when I'd been in the prosecutor's office, so I didn't know what it was like to be across the aisle from her. I ran into her from time to time. We occasionally shared lunch and stopped to exchange pleasantries in the halls of the courthouse. She was well-liked and well-respected by judges and attorneys alike. I was shocked that Candy was having a hard time with her.

"It's just not working out how I'd like."

"Why not? Karen is one of the better attorneys around. If I have a case I'm too busy to handle, I generally refer it to her. Whatever your issues, I can assure you that you are getting quality service."

"Let's just call it personality differences," Candy said coolly, leaning back in her chair as if affronted by the fact I was sticking up for her present attorney.

"Karen and I are friends," I said. "I don't want her to think I'm poaching a client."

"I haven't spoken with her about this, but she'll be pleased to see me go. Our relationship has been difficult. I don't want to get into it more than that."

"If I take this case, you're gonna have to." I let my words sink in. "But we don't have to get into it right this moment. Just give me the details about what happened."

Candy hesitated, and I got the distinct idea she was thinking of picking up and leaving. After a moment, she shrugged.

"I came home late from work. The kids were in bed, sleeping. I found my husband on the couch dead. He'd been shot in the chest."

"Did your kids see or hear anything?"

She shook her head. "Thankfully, no. It appears he got them down to bed before..." She trailed off. "I want you to know I didn't do this, Mr. Turner."

"Oh?"

"It's essential you believe me."

"Look, my clients profess innocence all the time, and I'll tell you the same thing I tell them. I will just stick to the facts and look at the situation as it stands. Your guilt or innocence is almost not relevant. What's relevant is what the prosecution has against you. What the evidence says happened."

"Almost not relevant?"

"If you can convince me you're innocent—and I mean no question, I totally believe you're innocent—I'll go to the mat for you and fight like you're family."

"And if I did it?"

"Then the evidence is usually not on your side, and I almost always encourage my clients to take a plea bargain. Far better that than rolling the dice in court. Why take what you get when you can control the outcome yourself?"

"That's a bit cynical."

"It's practical."

"That is going to be a problem. The facts are against me. They have been made to look as if I killed him." She leaned forward. "There was no sign of forced entry. They had the key or he let them in." Her voice was getting tight now, and I sensed she was doing her best to keep tears from coming. I wondered if they were genuine or fake. "My DNA was found all over him. Makes sense, right? He is my husband. Of course, they also find my DNA all over the place because it's my house. I live there. Lived there."

"You moved?"

She gave me a shocked look. "How could I not?"

"You'd be surprised."

"We haven't sold the house yet for obvious reasons, but the kids and I are in an apartment. Nobody wanted to stay there."

"How old are your children?"

"Fourteen and ten."

"How are they handling this?"

"Their father is dead. How do you think they're handling it?" There was a heat to her tone now, as if she did not like the question. I had asked it to see if I could get a rise out of her to assess her conscience. I wanted to believe she might be innocent but would withhold judgment until after I had a chance to thoroughly review the case.

"When's the trial date?"

"A couple months from now, I waived a speedy trial."

I nodded. "It's not too late to change attorneys mainstream. It will be difficult, but not prohibitively so, like a case I took on once. Let me reach out to Karen. We'll see what comes of it."

"You're gonna talk to her?"

"Yes, professional courtesy."

Candy frowned. "I'm not sure I want you to do that."

"If you want me to take this case, I must speak with Karen first."

Candy was silent for a long time. I thought again she was just going to leave to find somebody else.

"Fine." She stood. "When can I expect to hear back?"

"Perhaps today if I can get hold of Karen."

4

I leaned back in my chair and put my hands behind my head after Candy left. I had a strange feeling about her case but couldn't quite put my finger on it. I wondered if she was a problem client. Maybe it was just a sixth sense that was causing me to be wary. There are warning signs with a problem client, and I was seeing several. I was always careful about clients who came from other attorneys because some clients went from attorney to attorney, trying to shop for a better outcome. Or at least for an attorney they thought was more likely to win their case. It also might be that they didn't like what their attorney was telling them. Or they didn't want to listen to the advice their attorney was giving. Or perhaps their attorney had kicked them to the curb. Regardless of the reason, I rarely had good luck picking up a case midway through.

I liked to be on the ground floor of a new case, going hard at it from the beginning. There are nuances in dealing with prosecutors and courts. It is challenging to come up to speed after the fact because it is easy to miss something significant that never got put down on paper.

Karen would answer some questions, but there would be a limit to how much she would want to help after I took the case from her.

I drummed my fingers on my desk while I considered the matter, making notes on a pad of paper. It would not be a problem to take on the case. I could handle it and several more besides.

That wasn't the issue.

I was concerned about maintaining a good relationship with Karen. Over the years, she and I had passed clients to each other if we conflicted out or didn't have time to do the case ourselves. She had been an excellent source of revenue, and I'd like to think I had done a solid job of returning the favor. The last thing I wanted was to put that in jeopardy.

I also didn't want Karen to think I was desperate and poaching clients.

I drummed my fingers on the desk again. My phone buzzed just as I was about to pull up Karen's contact information.

Ellie.

"What is it?" I asked as I scrolled through my contacts on my computer until I located Karen's number.

"Do you have a moment?" Ellie asked.

I sat back. "Sure. Come on in."

Ellie was soon sitting across from me. She was nervous and pale. If I had to take a guess, she had come with bad news.

Was she going to quit?

She was the best secretary I had ever worked with. I often encouraged her to take the LSAT and apply to law school. She was in her mid-twenties and had a college degree in philosophy. She'd make a great attorney if she went that route. It would be a sore loss for me, but I'd get over it. I made a point of hiring intelligent people, knowing their employment with me was just a stop along the way for them. I was fine with that and planned accordingly.

"I'm sorry if I was ornery," I said to get the conversation going, hoping that I had not done something to make her quit. We'd had far worse blowups, and she was still here.

She shrugged. "No worries. Truth be told, I am feeling off myself."

I nodded and just waited, expecting her to get into the reason for our impromptu meeting. When she didn't immediately get on with it, I refrained from looking at the clock or tapping my foot with impatience.

Was I about to finally learn what had been going on with her?

She looked right through me as if forgetting I was there.

"How is everything?" I finally asked.

"What?" Ellie focused her attention on me.

She swallowed.

"Mitch. I have cancer."

5

I had thought she might be sick and hiding it, but it had never occurred to me it might be something like this. I leaned back in my chair and rubbed a hand on my face. How could Ellie have this problem? She was so young and vibrant.

"I'm so sorry to hear that," I said as I processed the information. "How long have you known?"

"A few weeks." She hesitated. "You might've noticed I've been sick more often. It's taken a while for them to make a diagnosis, but the doctors finally told me I have... cancer."

I noticed the omission but didn't comment on it.

"Are you getting treatment?"

"Chemotherapy starts tomorrow."

"You're just telling me now?" I did my best to keep the surprise from my voice, though I wasn't sure I succeeded. I was completely taken aback. I wasn't angry because she was inconveniencing me—I could get a temp and have her position filled for the meantime—I'd just thought that we had a better relationship than this. I took a deep breath. I went on before she responded. "I'm sorry. I didn't mean to take that tone. I know this is a tough time for you. I just... I just would have expected you to tell me about something like this sooner."

"You'd better be," she said sharply with mock severity. "I didn't want to face what was coming. I've been in denial. It's difficult to swallow. I'm nowhere near thirty, and I have cancer." She shook her head. "I guess in my mind, cancer was always something that happened to older folks. My grandfather died of cancer. My grandmother on the other side had a serious bout, but she recovered."

I opened my mouth, intent on asking her about the specifics but decided not to delve into it. If she wanted to tell me, fine, but I would not pry. I took a different direction.

"How much time off are you going to need?" I glanced at the clock on my wall. "Why are you even here today? You should be home, trying to relax, or doing something fun that you can't do while undergoing treatment."

"Mitch—"

"I'll get a temp in here, and we will—"

"No."

"Excuse me?"

"I'm not going to leave."

"Of course, you aren't going to leave, but you can't—"

"You don't understand me, Mitch. I'm still going to come in every day, at least every day I can, and do my job."

"Ellie, this is just a job. You hardly need to—"

"I made a commitment. I waited until now to tell you because I knew you would try to force me to take time off. I'm not going to do it. I don't need it. I don't want it. I also don't want anybody to know until it's obvious I'm going through treatment."

"Ellie, you have to focus on your health—"

"I am!"

I inhaled deeply. I had not expected an argument over this.

"Ellie, I'll continue to pay you whether or not you come in. If it's about the money—" I tried not to think of what my partner Veronica would say about this. I'd make it work. I had savings of my own if it came down to it. "—don't let it be a worry." I had expected that these words would calm her fears, but she looked more frustrated. "Is there something else going on with you?"

"No." The way she said this made me think that there was something more but that it was best I didn't push it. "I need the job to keep my mind distracted, if that's okay with you."

I nodded. "That's not a problem." I wanted to make sure I kept Ellie happy, but I also had an obligation to my clients to keep things moving smoothly. I also suspected that continuing to come into work was going to be much harder than she expected. She needed a safety net she could rely on, so she didn't feel pressure to come in if she wasn't up to it.

"How about we do this?" I said. "Let's hire somebody, just a temp, to come in and cover for you on the days you cannot be here. Or if you're just having a rough time. I don't want you worrying about work, but I'm happy to have your help whenever you can."

Ellie nodded, the color returning to her face as a quiet sigh escaped her lips. She'd been thinking of suggesting this herself. "Yes, that will work perfectly."

"Are you having troubles with the health insurance company?"

As a small firm, we didn't have the greatest insurance, but we did have a plan. I suddenly regretted the decision we'd made as partners to go with the cheaper insurance company. I couldn't remember what Ellie had signed up for, but I thought it had a high deductible. "Yes and no. They're being nice about the whole thing, so far, but—"

"The deductible?"

Ellie nodded.

"Don't worry about it," I said, a lump forming in my throat. "I'll cover it."

"Mitch, you don't have to do that."

"If you're gonna force yourself to come to work, I'm going to pay for this. End of discussion."

"I don't know what to say."

"There's nothing to say."

"Yes, there is. Thank you."

6

I was stunned after Ellie left my office, trying to understand my emotions as I processed what she had told me. She was too young. It was terrible for something like this to happen to her. She had so much going for her. She didn't need to deal with this. We had exchanged pleasantries for a few more minutes before she had left, but she had still not been forthcoming about what type of cancer she was experiencing.

I wasn't going to ask but couldn't help wonder.

Professional hazard, I suppose.

I let the question go, though it was difficult to do. The thought came to mind that I could hire Winston to search it out, but I didn't even consider it. That would be an invasion of privacy of the highest order.

Questions.

Nagging questions.

I *hated* unanswered questions, but this was Ellie. I owed her my respect. And a lot more.

I turned back to my computer. During our conversation, I'd forgotten about Candy Carlisle and the client intake interview I'd just had with her.

I still had Karen Brodsky's information pulled up on my screen.

I picked up my phone and dialed but hung up before it connected. I didn't have any other appointments for the rest of the day.

I could use a walk.

Ellie wasn't at her desk when I left, so I wrote on a sticky note, explaining I'd be back in about an hour. I stuck it to her computer monitor so she'd be sure not to miss it.

I hesitated and reread my note, hoping that nothing could be misconstrued. I was always careful in my communication with clients, but I let down my guard with Ellie. She got to see the raw and unfiltered me. It worked out pretty well because she didn't take any crap from me. If she had a problem, she let me know. She wasn't one to suffer in silence.

Was the unfiltered Mitch Turner who she needed right now?

Our relationship was not very contentious, but we had the occasional conflict.

I shook my head after I read my note for the third time. I was overthinking this. It seemed fine. If she saw me hovering over her desk, she'd be weirded out.

I left quickly to escape without her seeing me.

I was glad I didn't have to see Ellie again so soon after learning the news. I didn't quite know how to interact with her. It would take some time to figure out.

Should I show greater empathy?

Or should I keep it to a minimum?

She wanted to keep things as normal as possible, but how could I do that while there was this ever-present threat hanging over her head?

I didn't know how I would handle it, but I needed to figure it out.

She needed support. Unfortunately, I'd never been the warm and fuzzy type.

Want me to go to court to fight?

I'm your guy.

Want me to sit beside a bed in a hospital offering support?

You want somebody else.

I also didn't know what to make of her desire to still work while she went through this. There were lots of ways to keep busy and distracted that didn't involve dealing with frustrated clients. There had even been a time or two when she'd dealt with tense situations when angry people had come to confront me because I was doing my job.

I could understand how she wanted to keep busy, but worrying about my client's needs would have been the last thing on my mind if I were in her position.

The realization made me stop.

Would I really be that way?

I shook my head, hoping I never had to cross that bridge. If I did, I expected I'd probably work just as hard for my clients then as I did now.

Maybe even harder.

I'd need something to take my mind off it, too.

Wouldn't I be more prone to mistakes? Wouldn't they be better represented by somebody else?

I finally faced the question that had been dancing in the back of my mind ever since learning of this.

Would it be better for my clients if Ellie just took time off to deal with this?

I didn't know, but I had professional responsibilities to my clients that had to come first.

Something told me that saying any of this to Ellie would be the wrong thing to do.

I was glad to help her out, but I would have to keep an eye on things to make sure it didn't interfere.

I took in a deep breath and tried to let go of the problem.

The air was cool and pleasant. It would be a bit of a walk to Karen's office, but I was happy for the distraction.

I took a circuitous route because a direct approach would have taken me past the restaurant where Barbara and Thomas Guyton were having their late lunch. I didn't want to risk running into them a second time.

The last thing I wanted was for Barbara to think I was spying on her.

I walked into the building where Karen had her law office twenty minutes later.

Karen wasn't part of a firm, preferring to practice solo. That did not mean she worked alone; she had close to ten people on her team that she kept working long hours.

She had built a solid reputation and was kept busy because of it. She had standardized much of her workflow processes, relying on paralegals and investigators to do most of the heavy lifting, leaving her to focus on the high level. She was in a place I hoped to be someday but was a long way from. I needed my partners every bit as much as they needed me.

Her office was on the fifth floor, so I took the elevator up rather than the stairs. I didn't want Karen to think I was nervous by showing up sweaty. I already had a sheen of perspiration on my forehead from the walk over, so I was glad for the elevator ride to calm down my heart rate. I was not looking forward to this conversation. It had the potential to be explosive.

Most lawyers were protective of their clients. I tended to be. I didn't like it when the rug was yanked out from underneath me by another attorney, but it happened from time to time. That was part of why I had decided to have this conversation face-to-face. I also wanted to see her expression when I told her that Candy Carlisle had come to speak with me. I would hopefully glean information from that alone.

I walked through the office door, expecting to see Wendy, the receptionist who Karen had employed before. Instead, I was met by a rough-looking kid in his early twenties who was dressed in a decidedly unprofessional manner. He had his feet up on the desk so that I could see the tears in his jeans. His hair was greasy and went every which way. He wore a black leather jacket that had seen better days, and there was a mustard stain on his shirt. He was out of place in the immaculately decorated office.

I was wondering why Karen had employed somebody who dressed like him until I glanced at the nameplate right next to his worn-out shoes and saw that his last name was Brodsky.

Hubert Brodsky.

I glanced at the kid again and wondered if this was her son.

"Is Karen around?"

"Who are you?" Hubert asked in a condescending tone as he looked up from a magazine he was reading. His eyes narrowed as if sizing me up.

Quite the welcome committee.

"I'm an old friend. We went to law school together. Is she here?"

"She doesn't like people just walking into her office."

I didn't like the tone he was taking with me. Whether this was her son or not, I'd put him in his place. Karen walked around the corner as I opened my mouth. She gritted her teeth when she saw Hubert had his feet up on the desk.

"Mitch!" Karen said, turning to me. "I didn't expect to see you today."

"I was in the neighborhood and wondered if maybe you could spare a minute to catch up."

A curious expression crossed her face. She no doubt knew I wanted to talk about something.

"Come on back."

"Nice meeting you, Hubert," I said as I followed her back, taking note of the consternation on her face.

"Your son?" I asked as we walked down the hallway.

"It's a story."

"Oh?"

"My daughter's son. He thinks he owns the place. I really don't know why I ever agreed to hire him. The clients don't like him. I can barely tolerate him." She did not try to keep her voice down as she spoke. Hubert could likely hear her.

"Why keep him around?"

"I've had some sticky issues recently. He's got a PI license and carries a gun." She shrugged. "He's useful, for now."

We arrived at Karen's office. She pointed to a chair and then shut the door behind me.

"Sticky issues?"

"I had a client threaten to kill me. He was as guilty as sin. He's in prison right now but has a big family. They weren't happy with the outcome."

"You didn't plea him out?"

"I tried, Mitch, I tried. The man refused to listen. The wealthy rarely do. We even took the time—and at great expense, I might add—to put on a mock trial for him. We went through the prosecution's evidence, showing him videos and reading witness transcripts. We went through every last bit of it. After all that, he was still adamant he was not guilty." She paused. "The mock trial took three weeks. The actual trial took two." She shook her head. "We even brought in twelve random strangers to act as a jury. They convicted him with less than five minutes of deliberation. Even then, he still had the audacity to demand we go to trial."

"How long did he get?"

"Life." She let out a sigh. "It could've been worse. At least he didn't get the death penalty. We found some good mitigation experts to use during sentencing to get that off the table."

"If he's angry, it's his own fault."

A mock trial with mock jurors that lasted three weeks? That was expensive. She wasn't kidding when she said her client was wealthy.

"It's just the nature of our business."

I nodded. "I know."

The last time I'd done a mock trial had been in law school. I did my best to prepare my clients, but Karen went the extra mile. She could afford to. Her fees were hefty.

"What can I do for you?" The way she said this told me that she had not bought my excuse for a second. "You didn't come to boast about your 'not guilty' verdict today, did you?"

"You heard about that?"

She smiled. "I saw you talking to the reporters when I came out from a hearing." She leaned forward. "Looked like you were playing with fire."

"I kept everything I said legit."

"I'm sure you did."

"Candy Carlisle," I said to change the subject. I suddenly felt inadequate to take over the case from Karen. I knew Karen had been operating at a different level than me, but I'd had no idea the extent. It was not an emotion I was used to experiencing.

It's not about the money. It's about the brains. We are on par there.

Karen nodded. "I thought it might be about her."

"You referred Candy? She didn't mention that."

"It didn't happen like that." She shook her head. "I wouldn't wish Candy on anybody."

"That bad, huh?"

"Perhaps I'm being too harsh. It's not that she's a bad client. It's just—" She stopped and gave me a look. "This is all off the record, right?"

"Of course."

"She's a pill. She acts like she's my only client. I made the mistake of giving her my personal cell phone number, and I keep getting phone calls from her all the time at all hours of the day and night. She's upset with me because I haven't returned her calls or texts for more than three days." Candy looked at me without blinking. "It's not that somebody in my office hasn't spoken to her. They have spoken to her many times during that time. It's just that she has not spoken to me personally. I have somebody specifically tasked to handle her, but they're not doing a good job. They let her get past them all the time."

"I see," I said, trying to project empathy. Ellie did her best to screen my calls, but I handled everything directly. All of my clients had my personal cell phone number, and none of them hesitated to use it, though I encouraged them to call the office to make appointments to keep Ellie in the loop. I rarely had somebody take advantage of things in the way Candy was of Karen.

"If you want the case, take it."

"I just told her I'd meet with you to talk things over. If we're still off the record, warning bells went off for me during our discussion."

"She knows you're meeting with me?" Karen threw her head back and laughed. "I bet that didn't sit well with her. She thought she could meet with you behind my back. I bet it rankled her when you told her that. She likes to control everything. And I mean everything. It's not that she's manipulative so much as demanding." A toothy smile crossed Karen's face. "Maybe it is time I call her back, see if she fesses up."

"I don't want to get in the way of things. It seems like—"

"To be honest, I'd be happy to see the back of her," Karen said. "At the same time, I have put in enough effort that I don't really want to just walk away from it either. I have mixed feelings about it. Not about her but about the case."

I nodded. "I know how that goes. Our clients aren't always the most sympathetic, but the cases have a way of getting to you."

"The evidence swings against her, big time." Karen leaned back in her chair and swiveled to stare out her window. "However, I'm convinced of her innocence. Just call it a gut feeling. You can get a feel for these things, you know?"

I nodded. "I sometimes get a sixth sense, too." I broke into a roguish smile. "I can't tell you how many times it has been off. Is it just how she's always calling you, or is there something more?"

"She hasn't liked me from day one." She shook a finger. "You want to know what I think? It's because I remind her of somebody she knew in high school. Candy never really left that behind, like most of us do. Her dead husband was a football star. She was the cheerleading prom queen. They figured they had their lives figured out when they graduated and got married. She sees a nerd when she looks at me. She can't believe she's relying on a nerd to get her through this."

I slowly nodded as I thought about what Karen had just told me. It seemed to fit with my impressions of Candy as well. "So, what's your take on the case?"

"I've been encouraging her to think about a plea, but she's refusing. Can't say that I blame her. She's got her two kids; they really don't have anybody other than her."

"No grandparents in the picture?"

"Not really. Candy's mother died at a young age, and she hasn't spoken to her father in years."

"His family?"

"Both dead. Neither has siblings."

"What happens to the kids if she goes to jail?"

"I don't know. I'm doing this more for them than I am for her."

There was some empathy there, but it wasn't nearly enough.

"I ever tell you my dad was in prison?"

"No, what for?"

I shook my head. "Not important. I remember what it's like growing up like that. It's not easy."

"Your mother around?"

"She was back then. She's passed since. Him too."

"I see." Karen gave me a look. "You know what? You might be just the guy for this case. I think Candy might respect you more than she does me." Karen must have seen my eyebrows raise because she went on. "Just because you have been in the papers more than me. She's actually mentioned you a few times." Karen grinned. "Last time she did, I encouraged her to talk to you."

"If I take this case, no hard feelings?" I put up a hand. "Not saying that I'm going to, just wondering where you're at."

"No. None."

I studied Karen, trying to decide if she was holding anything back, but then I finally nodded. "I'm not trying to take it. If I do, it would be for the kids. I don't find her an attractive potential client."

"Do what you have to do." She glanced at her watch. "I'm afraid that's all the time I have for you, Mitch. I have an appointment in a couple minutes.

"Thanks for the chat," I said, extending a hand and giving Karen a firm handshake.

"Think nothing of it."

I headed for the door.

"One more thing. If you take it, watch your back."

I turned. "What do you mean?"

"Candy's litigious, that came up in our civil search. I've been documenting every last decision and discussion I've had with her, concerned she might make a malpractice claim if she doesn't like the outcome."

7

My instincts told me to avoid the case. I almost called Candy from the sidewalk to tell her I would not take it and that I thought she ought to stick with Karen, but I didn't. I continued to analyze it as I walked back to my office.

Candy had not been forthcoming in my discussion about why she wanted to fire Karen as her attorney. She had explained it as personality differences and wanted to leave it at that. Perhaps Candy was eager to avoid painting Karen in a poor light, but what if it was more than just personality differences?

What if they were clashing on how to proceed with the case?

Karen had seemed more than willing to talk, but I knew all too well that there were hidden biases that would not come out in a direct conversation.

I wondered if Karen had been too quick to recommend to Candy that they talk about a plea bargain. Perhaps that was the real reason Candy had wanted to talk with another attorney.

Just because I didn't find Candy sympathetic, that didn't make her guilty of murder. It didn't mean she deserved less than the highest quality of representation.

And what about the kids?

Karen might feel some sympathy for those kids, but she wouldn't understand their situation like I did. She didn't know what it would be like for them to grow up with their only parent in prison. I'd had my angel mother; they would have nobody other than some grandfather who was not around. Candy was heading to prison if Karen's take on the case was accurate.

"The kids," I muttered, "should I do it for them?"

Candy's kids needed their mother.

I was still mulling over the case when I looked up and saw Barbara walking out onto the sidewalk with Thomas Guyton. Panic spiked through me as I realized I should've gone around the long way again. I had just assumed I'd avoided them earlier on my way over, so I hadn't even given it a second thought when I had returned the way I normally would have gone.

I stopped as Thomas opened the door for her so she could get into a cab. He pecked her on the cheek before shutting it. He checked both ways before dashing across the street and disappearing into a building.

I hesitated, thinking of ducking into an alley or around a corner, but there wasn't one close by. It was too late. The cab was already pulling away.

Barbara stared at me as she passed.

Our eyes locked onto each other.

And then she was gone.

It almost seemed to me that there had been regret written on her face.

I hoped for her sake that I was wrong.

8

Ellie was at her desk when I returned to the office. I gave her an awkward smile and was about to pass without saying anything when she motioned me over.

"Please don't let this change anything," Ellie whispered under her breath as she glanced around to make sure nobody was nearby, "treat me like you normally would."

I, too, looked around. Both my partner's doors were shut. The paralegals and secretaries worked down the hallway. Ellie acted as a de facto receptionist for the others, even though that was not technically her role.

I gave a shake of my head. "I wouldn't have it any other way." I was about to ask why she would say such a thing but figured she must have noticed my discomfort.

She gave me a skeptical look. "I know you too well, Mitch Turner. I'm not asking you to be perfect. I just want you to try."

"I promise. Let me know if there's anything I can do."

"It's comments like that you must avoid."

"If other people are around, sure. So what can I do to help?"

She frowned as she thought this over, but then she nodded. "I'm okay for now. I appreciate your concern."

"Anybody call while I was out?" I asked to change the topic of discussion.

"No clients, but I got a call from the court. They rescheduled a hearing. I sent you an email with the details."

"Which case?"

"Anderson. The change is already on your calendar."

"Thank you."

She seemed satisfied as I walked away.

When I got to my desk, I logged into my practice management software and saw Ellie had already entered Candy's contact information and created a case file.

I dialed Candy's number.

"This is Candy," she said after she picked up.

"Ms. Carlisle," I said, "it's Mitch Turner. I met with Karen Brodsky."

"What did she say?"

"We just talked high-level about your case. I don't think she would mind if you switched to me."

Candy snorted. "She'll be happy to see me go."

"I don't know that she would put it like that."

"So you are taking my case?"

"I didn't say that, not yet. You have a skilled attorney. Karen is one of the best. I don't think you're doing yourself any favors by firing her."

"I'm getting rid of her."

"Was there something more than just a personality difference?"

There was a long silence on the other end. "I want somebody who acts as though I'm innocent. I'm not saying you have to believe I'm innocent. I just want you to do what you would for an innocent client. Karen was talking about a plea bargain from the very beginning. She keeps on throwing the evidence in my face. I know it looks bad. I know I should expect a jury to put me into jail; however, I also know I didn't do it. I want to fight tooth and nail. I've seen you get other people out of tight situations. I want you to do the same for me."

"I can't make any promises or assurances. I'll do my best. That's all I can do."

"That's what I want right now. That's what I need."

"Ms. Carlisle, I am going to take your case. The first thing I want to do is meet you at the murder scene."

"You mean my house?"

"Yes."

"I can be there in an hour."

"See you then."

After I hung up with her, my next call was to Winston.

"Mitch Turner," Winston said, "I was just thinking it's been a while since you gave me a case. Tell me you have one."

"You busy right now?"

"For you, no."

I gave him the address to Barbara's house and told him to meet me there in forty-five minutes.

9

It was a nice neighborhood. The sidewalks were lined with tall trees, and the houses were well-maintained. It was a wealthy neighborhood, too, but it wasn't the wealthiest I'd ever visited. If I were to make a call on the financial situation of Candy and her neighbors, I would say they were well off but not well to do. I was surprised Candy had initially gone with Karen, knowing how much Karen charged.

Trying to buy her freedom or fighting to prove her innocence?

I parked my Porsche outside the house, not worrying about it on the street as I got out. The chill air was turning warm, and the sun was out while birds chirped in the trees. I didn't get outside often, so I enjoyed the moment for what it was.

It didn't last long. Winston pulled up behind my car on a motorcycle that seemed to have lost its muffler if it ever had one to begin with.

He nodded as he parked his bike. He approached, holding his helmet in his hand, his cowboy boots slapping against the sidewalk.

"What do we got here?" Winston asked as he looked around the neighborhood, his eyes finally settling on the Carlisle house.

"Murder. My client came home to find her husband shot dead on the couch. The kids were asleep up in the bedrooms."

Winston gave me a curious look. "I haven't heard anything about this in the news."

"This was a few months back. I'm taking it over from Karen Brodsky."

Winston's eyes grew big. "Did I hear that right? She didn't refer this. You're taking it over?"

I nodded. Did he have to act so surprised that a client would fire Karen Brodsky?

I had been fired plenty of times. I'm sure Karen had been too.

"It doesn't seem like the two of them were getting along."

"Don't take this the wrong way," Winston said to me, "you're a good attorney, but if I'm ever charged with murder, Karen would be my first call."

"Mine, too," I said in a chipper voice, hoping my irritation didn't show.

Karen and I are *on par. She's just better funded.*

"You'll pay for it," I added.

"I probably would have to come back to you after I hear her quote," Winston said with a chuckle, "I don't think I could afford her fees."

"I'll have to up mine."

"What about the employee discount?" Winston gave me a dry smile as we walked up to the house.

"You're a contractor."

"Would it help if I did my own investigation?"

"That would double your fee. I'd have to get a second investigator just to check your work."

"Ouch."

I rang the doorbell, but nobody answered. I checked my watch and saw we still had some time before our scheduled appointment.

Just as I was thinking about trying Candy on her cell, she pulled up to the house in a Ford Expedition.

I was expecting a BMW or Mercedes. Perhaps I had the wrong take on her. Maybe she wasn't as ritzy and flashy as she had come off in my office.

Says the guy who drives a Porsche, I thought.

"You guys are quick!" Candy said as she got out of the vehicle. It beeped when she used her remote to lock it behind her.

"We wanted to get a jump on things," I said, without glancing at Winston.

If Winston ever got into legal trouble, he'd be lucky to get my services.

"Have to find the keys," Candy said as she rifled around in her purse. "They're in here somewhere." It took a few more moments, but she finally dug them out and held them up in the air like she had just pulled out a trophy fish. "Here they are."

We were soon standing inside the front door of her house.

She pointed to the left. "I found his body there."

10

A hush fell over us as we entered the room. The atmosphere had been light, almost jovial just the moment before, but it now took a solemn turn. Was it something subtle about the room itself or just the nature of what we knew happened here?

I couldn't say for sure.

I stepped back to observe Candy from the corner of my eye, curious to see her reaction.

Candy claimed to have cleared out that night. I had not asked if she had returned since but made a mental note to ask later.

It was clear the emotions were still fresh for her, even though this had happened several months ago.

What emotion is she feeling?

There was a tightness around her eyes and paleness to her face that showed she felt something intense, but I could not read it from my present angle.

Anger? Fear? Betrayal? Disgust?

The hand in which she clutched her keys was turning white. The jagged metal appeared to be digging into her flesh, but it didn't seem like she noticed.

Did she do it?

I had promised Candy I would act as if she were innocent, but there was no way I could leave that question unanswered as we proceeded with our investigation.

I wasn't one of those attorneys who could pretend their client was innocent when they were actually guilty.

Karen had expressed a belief Candy didn't do it, but she'd been acting as if Candy had.

Those two things didn't align.

For me, it would not have been a simple matter to enter a plea bargain for somebody I believed innocent. Was it just because Karen was jaded from so many years of practicing law? Or was there something she knew or suspected but had not told me?

After several more moments of casually observing Candy, I turned my attention to the room, filing away my observations to examine and categorize later once I had additional context for Candy and her behavior.

The room looked like it had remained untouched since the police had finished their investigation. It was covered with dust and had the stale smell of a place that had not been lived in for some time. There were bloodstains on what remained of the sofa. The cushions where missing, presumably taken as evidence. The forensic team must have decided that was sufficient, otherwise they might have taken the whole couch. I studied the couch, trying to build a mental picture. The room was disheveled and loosely put back together, indicating the police had been through with a fine-tooth comb.

I pulled out my phone and started snapping pictures. Winston did the same. I started with the bloodstains on the couch and worked my way out from there. I walked around while taking pictures, making sure to observe Candy, too, so I had something to mull over later.

I was careful not to include her in any of the pictures. I didn't want to explain to a jury the look she had on her face. I could have taken the pictures and tried to mark them as attorney work product, but why create a potential problem for myself if I could just avoid it?

The emotions were not as pronounced as they had been before, but they were still there. My instincts told me there was an inner conflict going on inside Candy.

Did she do this? Was she now feeling guilty because of it?

Winston and I continued to take pictures.

I soon had what I wanted, just enough to get me started. I'd get the rest from Winston, who was being far more thorough.

I glanced at Candy, slipping my phone back into my pocket while Winston continued to document the scene. The emotions were gone. She had a slight frown, and her face was just a little pale.

She stared at my phone as I put it away, almost as if thinking of stealing it. I hadn't meant to give her the impression I was taking pictures of her, but it was interesting that this had made her uncomfortable.

What is she hiding?

My phone automatically backed up to the cloud. So those pictures were already on their way out of here. If my phone turned up missing, I wasn't going to lose anything.

"Why the pictures?" Candy asked in a neutral voice. "Won't you get those from the police?"

"I like to have my own to compare. It's amazing what shots from different angles can do to provide a little perspective."

She shrugged. "Makes sense, I guess."

There was an intensity in her eyes I could not explain. I was glad we had begun here. I would typically interview a client in my office, but this place had brought out conflicting emotions from deep inside. I was going to kick things off now to take advantage of the situation.

It was a risky move because I would get some raw emotions, but I liked to get the unvarnished truth whenever I could. This was the best opportunity I would get.

"What time did you return that night?" I asked, hoping to come off casual.

"It was after 10:00 PM, probably closer to 10:30."

"You always work late?"

Candy shook her head. "No, I get home between five and six. I'm a graphic designer for a local agency. I had to get a big project done that night for a client meeting the next morning."

There was something she wasn't telling me, but I let it slide for the time being.

"Walk us through what happened when you arrived."

"I entered through the door—"

"Start when you approached the house. What were you driving? What were your impressions as you parked? What did you notice?"

I thought Candy might be offended that I had cut her off, but she closed her eyes as if trying to remember.

"I was in my Ford. The same one I drove here. The lights in the front room were on, which I thought was odd. Raymond liked to go downstairs to catch up on the day's news. We have a projector. That's where I expected to find him."

"The lights were on? Good. What else do you remember?"

"I think that's it, at least from the outside."

"Did you come in through the front door?"

"Yes. Raymond's car was parked, blocking the garage."

"Was the front door locked?"

Candy nodded. "Yes, I remember pulling out my keys to unlock it because I dropped them and had to bend down to pick them up. It was awkward because I was carrying several bags."

"What were you carrying?"

"I wasn't yet finished with the day's work, so I'd brought some of our binders home in a bag. I also had my purse and a briefcase."

"Did anything about the front porch stick out to you as off? A flower pot out of order or missing? Scuff marks on the door?"

"No, nothing like that. I had no idea what was waiting for me on the other side." There was a tightness around her eyes, but I couldn't interpret what it meant. Was she just remembering what it was like to find him? Was she feeling apprehension as she approached the door? Did she have a reason to suspect what she would find?

"Go on."

"I inserted my key and walked inside. Immediately, a smell hit me. It's hard to describe. I just knew there was something wrong. Very wrong."

I nodded. "Did you go into the room?"

"I sniffed the air, trying to puzzle out what it was. I called out for Raymond, but there was no answer. I tried calling for my kids, but they didn't answer either."

"What are your kid's names?"

"Ruby and Travis."

"You're sure they didn't answer?"

"No. Thankfully, they were both asleep."

"I took a step inside. I pulled my keys out of the door and shut it behind me. I have a vivid memory of turning the deadbolt right as I looked into the front room and saw Raymond on the couch." She paused and looked away. "It was obvious from where I stood that he was dead. He wasn't breathing and was covered in blood."

She took a deep breath. "I froze. I just kept myself from screaming. I'm glad I didn't. I would have woken the kids. After the police showed up, I got them out of the house without seeing what happened."

"Did you enter the room?"

"I ran to Raymond." Frustration crossed her face as she relived the memory. "I stopped a few inches back and kept from touching him. Something in the back of my mind told me that I should avoid doing that. I didn't want to risk contaminating the scene." She shrugged. "I don't think it really made much difference. He and I had met up for lunch that day because we knew I'd be working late. He already had my DNA all over him. I gave him a hug and apparently left several strands of hair on him. That's part of why they think I did this."

"You did not touch his body?" I asked, curious that her first response was to protect the crime scene. I would've expected her to resuscitate him or check his vitals.

This was not a normal reaction.

"I did not."

"Why did you think to do that?"

"What do you mean?"

"Most people would've rushed to the aid of their loved one. Instead, you took a step back and thought about preserving evidence."

"I suppose it comes from my dad being a cop. I always heard him tell stories."

"He still on the force?"

"No, different city, different state. He retired long ago."

Karen had suggested the grandfather wasn't in the picture of their daily lives. The way Candy spoke about him made me think there was more to it than that.

"Is there something you're not telling me?" I asked in a calm tone, hoping my matter-of-fact approach would catch her off guard.

Candy's hackles went up. "What do you mean?"

"Was there tension between you and your husband that day?"

Candy hesitated. "Maybe a little."

"Did you tell the police?"

"I didn't think to mention it."

"What was it about?"

"I don't want to get into it."

"We haven't signed paperwork yet," I said. "I haven't entered my notice of appearance. Karen hasn't yet withdrawn. As far as I'm concerned, Karen is still your attorney until these things happen."

"I should talk, or you walk?" Candy asked sarcastically.

"Something like that."

"I'll talk in private." Candy glanced at Winston. He looked up from the pictures he was taking, seemingly oblivious to our conversation. I knew it to be an act, but I preferred to continue the conversation in private anyway.

"Sure."

She walked me back into the kitchen, where we shut the door behind us.

"I don't want you to make more of this than you should."

Too late.

I looked back with unblinking eyes. "I'll be the judge of that."

"That's what I'm afraid of."

"You must tell me the truth. If I'm going to do my job, I need to know everything that happened that day. I need to know about the tension. If there's anything else you're leaving out, please bring it up now. I need to know it all. If I don't, then there's going to be avenues of investigation I won't know about and potential suspects that will be overlooked."

She exhaled. "Several years ago, Raymond had an affair." She waited as if that were enough. I looked at her for a few seconds before motioning for her to continue.

"It's done. That was over with then. As far as I know, he hasn't seen her since."

"But it came up again the day of his murder, and you were reliving old pain?"

"An ex-girlfriend from high school contacted him."

"The one he had an affair with?"

"No, but she proposed he leave me and run away with her."

"Had they been in contact prior to this?"

"He said no."

"Was this intriguing to him?"

"I don't think so," she said a little too quickly, "but he told me about it that day at lunch."

"It sounds like he was forthcoming," I said. "Why was this causing tension if your marriage was fine?"

"He waited two weeks to tell me."

I thought about it. "Was he uncomfortable about telling you, or was he considering her offer?"

"He said he wasn't, but I was wondering. As this wasn't the first time we've had issues, it reopened old wounds when he told me about all of this."

"How'd you meet Raymond?" I asked.

"High school."

"You knew his ex-girlfriend?"

"We were on the cheer squad together."

"Are you friends with her?"

"I was back then. She dumped him. He and I hooked up. The rest is history. She and I were never quite the same after that."

"You saw the diamond in the rough."

"I suppose you could say that."

But she wouldn't.

"Are you happy he's dead?"

11

Candy didn't speak right away. She stared at me with eyes like knives, her upper lip half-raised in a silent snarl. I couldn't help but notice that her free hand was hovering just above her purse.

Did she have a gun in there?

Or a knife?

If two dead bodies were found in her house, the prosecutor's office would have no problem convicting her, regardless of what alibis she might come up with. At that point, surely Karen would have to prevail upon her to enter into a plea bargain, or she'd go away for an even longer time.

I also had Winston in the next room. He was my backup. As a former cop, he would come in handy if things got dicey. Just his presence should be deterrence enough if she was thinking of trying something. This was partly why I had not hesitated to ask the question.

But I didn't think things were going that direction. I trusted my instincts enough to ask because I already knew the answer. We needed to get the truth on the table and get past it, so we could focus on actual issues.

"That's a direct question, Mr. Turner," she finally said after the silence had become uncomfortable.

Through it all, I did not break eye contact. I waited patiently.

"I'm paid to ask them."

I waited in silence again.

Several beads of perspiration formed on her forehead. The keys she still clutched in her other hand were pressed up tight into the flesh of her palm. Her body shifted, and she took a step backward. A very small step.

Her face twitched. She forced a glare to her face. "I thought you said you'd treat me like I was innocent."

Not a denial.

"I promised to act like you were innocent. That's what you asked me to do, and I agreed. I didn't promise to put my head in the ground. I can't ignore what's evident to anybody who's paying attention. Whether you killed him or not is potentially irrelevant to the question. Somebody else could kill him, but you could still be happy he's dead."

"A good point."

"You still haven't answered the question."

"Do I have to?" She licked her lips. "I'm not sure it's good for us to start things off with a lie."

I shrugged. "So don't lie. What you've done already tells me that you *are* happy he's gone. Or at least you were until you were accused of his murder."

"I'm not sure that's how I would put it."

"How would you put it?"

"It's complicated."

"Enlighten me."

"Have you ever loved somebody so much that you hate them?"

"It usually goes the other way around. You hate somebody so much that you become obsessed with them. You can't stop thinking about them. And then you wonder where your affections truly lie. That doesn't sound like what you're describing."

"It's not." She looked frustrated.

"Did you hate him?"

"No, that was the wrong way to describe it. I don't know how to explain it, Mr. Turner. Have you ever been in a long-term relationship?"

I swallowed, her question hitting home. On any other day, I might not have been bothered. It was just because I'd seen Barbara earlier. "I have."

"Was it perfect?"

"Of course not."

"Did you have conflicting feelings?"

"What are you trying to tell me?"

She smiled briefly as if she could tell she'd gotten under my skin. "I think you are starting to understand my point. He and I were good for each other, at least at first. Things changed for us over the years, as I'm sure they do with every couple."

"Was it the affair?"

"It wasn't only that." She stared past me. "It actually didn't affect us all that much. And to be honest with you—" She stopped, hesitating as if she didn't want to go on, but she finally did. "I had one of my own, so I shouldn't really hold it against him." She snorted. "My affair actually happened first. This is why I was telling you it was no big deal. We are both broken people, but somehow we patched things up and stayed together. I was having a bad day that day, that's all. I warned you that you would want to make more of it than you should. Somehow, through all of that, we stayed together. We worked with each other to get past it."

"What changed?"

"It's just that relationships can sometimes be difficult."

"Was he standing in your way?"

"No, not really. Not for anything important."

"Then why are you happy he's gone?" I asked, refusing to back down. I could tell I was frustrating her, but I needed a complete answer to this question, not these cryptic responses she was giving me. I understood what she was trying to say about how relationships are sometimes a mixed bag, but what I saw here went beyond that.

She was trying to downplay it, but I needed to understand exactly what had happened.

"It is complicated. In some ways, it's a bit of a relief, but in most other ways, it's horrible. I miss him terribly. Our marriage survived a lot, and I expected that he and I were going to survive a lot more."

A lie.

"Out with it."

"Are you threatening to walk again?"

I just waited, not answering her question.

"I was mad at him."

"Obviously."

"But not for the reasons I've stated. I had an old flame approach me, too."

"And you were considering it?"

She shook her head. "No. It was several months before Raymond's death."

Something clicked.

"You never told him?"

She looked away, her eyes down. "It was just so ridiculous that I didn't want to bring it up. It is irrational, I know, but I was so mad at him for not telling me sooner, for withholding information for two weeks, when I had been holding back for two months."

"Is that all?"

"No."

"Why are you happy he's gone?"

"He was a suitable husband. We made things work."

"But?"

"I was planning to divorce him, even before he told me about his old high school girlfriend. His death made things considerably easier."

I nodded. "That doesn't mean you killed him."

I didn't blink as I watched her reaction. There was little.

"No," she said in a ragged voice, "it doesn't.

12

Winston stood at the back wall with a flashlight when Candy and I returned to the front room. I wondered if he'd been trying to overhear the conversation that had just happened on the other side between Candy and myself, but dismissed the question when I saw the concentration on his face. While I believed Winston capable of doing something like that, this was different. There was a legitimate reason he was there. The flashlight he used to examine the wall was one of those high-beam lights that fit into a small package. He peered at a specific place as if it contained something of significance.

I frowned as I tried to puzzle out what had drawn his attention, not wanting to disturb him until he noticed our presence.

From where I stood, it looked the same as any other part of the wall.

The back wall was covered with a knotty wood. I cautiously approached. He was focused on a particular knot that looked decayed in the way knots sometimes do.

The knot itself was about an inch in diameter, and bits of the inside were missing. I glanced down at the floor but saw nothing there.

"Perfect timing," Winston said, glancing over his shoulder as he motioned me over with his flashlight. "We might have something."

"What you got?" I looked from the couch to the wall, wondering if perhaps blood spatter or some other residue would've made it that far.

"I think the cops missed something, but I can't tell for sure."

"Blood?" I glanced at Candy. A grimace crossed her face.

She might have been planning to divorce the guy, but she was suffering from a ton of inner turmoil. She would not have been so angry to hear about his old girlfriend if she wasn't.

Was she still in denial?

She might have had an easier time telling me why she was happy he was gone if she had fully processed everything.

Our conversation had been like an onion. There had always been another layer.

Did I get to the last layer?

I studied her before looking back at the knot.

Happy isn't the right word. She's relieved. Another glance at her face. *And also guilty.*

Guilty because she had a hand in it or because she's feeling relieved?

Winston shook his head. "I think it's a bullet."

That piqued my attention. I always liked it when we found something the cops missed.

"How many times was Raymond shot?" I asked Candy.

She shook her head. "I'm not sure. At least twice, possibly more."

"Did you notice empty brass on the floor?"

"I didn't see anything like that, but it would've been easy to miss."

"I won't know what this is unless I pull it out," Winston said, looking over at me, the question evident on his face.

He knew how I liked to work.

He and I had been through this drill before on another case. We had found significant evidence that the police had missed, the literal smoking gun. They hadn't liked it when we called to tell them they had overlooked critical evidence. It had been a disaster for them when it turned out to be the murder weapon. It had almost cost an ex-girlfriend her job. Luckily, we had proven in court that the evidence had been planted after the fact, so she had been spared.

I hesitated.

It was always a touchy situation, calling to tell the cops we had something they missed.

Part of me thought we should call just to have them look at it first, so they didn't accuse us of planting something, but there was also a chance it might be nothing.

I didn't want to have them come over to pull it out, only to discover that it was a nail with the head broken off.

I compromised.

We would cover ourselves in case it turned out to be something significant but would only contact them if it was of value.

"How about I record it on video while you dig it out?" I suggested, taking out my phone.

Winston nodded before pulling out his knife and carefully touching around the sides of the knot, apparently testing to see how embedded the object was.

Something he did must have caused it to shift because I finally saw what had drawn his attention. I could also see why the cops had missed it. It was buried so far back into the knot of the wood that it looked just like the knot itself.

Winston put his knife down on a table beside the wall and reached into his pocket for a pair of latex gloves.

"Almost forgot," he muttered as he put them on.

He brought his knife up again and pried into the wood, knocking loose bits and pieces. He soon had it free.

A nail would not come out that easily.

"That's something you don't find every day." Winston held it up for me to see. "What do you make of that?"

My eyes narrowed. I checked to make sure I was getting this all on camera.

It was indeed a bullet.

13

"Did I catch you at a good time?" I asked Karen Brodsky as I paced around the Carlisle front room, wishing in retrospect that we had called the cops before digging into the wall. I had assumed the chances of Winston finding anything significant were small, so I hadn't even given it a second thought after I'd made my decision to videotape him digging out the unknown object.

Hindsight provides perfect clarity.

I wished I had thought through the problem for a little longer because it was certainly going to be an issue for the prosecution that their primary suspect was on site when we discovered this.

They're never gonna believe it. I shook my head, forcing myself to think through the complexities. *But even if we had called them from the start, Candy has had access to the murder scene this whole time. They will claim anything we find was placed by her after the fact anyway.*

It's what I would've done as a prosecutor.

The thought gave me a measure of peace, even as I remembered Karen's counsel to watch my back because she believed Candy was litigious.

I would make a memo to the file after I got back to my office, detailing everything that happened and my rationale.

I was glad I'd at least had the foresight to record a video, but I was kicking myself for being foolish and overconfident.

This could easily have gone the other way, a little voice said in the back of my head. You *could've called for nothing and had to deal with that instead.*

I took a deep breath and exhaled. I'd made a judgment call, and it had turned out to be the wrong one, but it was time to get past it.

"Yes," Karen said after a moment. It sounded like she had somebody else in the office with her. I thought I heard somebody talking to her in a low voice. "Make it quick."

"Who's the prosecutor on Candy's case?"

"Frank Ward."

It could have been worse. Frank and I knew each other well. There was mutual respect between the two of us, even though we were frequently at odds with each other because of our professional lives. We'd been friendly enough back when I'd been a prosecutor.

"And the lead detective?"

"Bernie Lee."

I almost groaned aloud.

That was a name I had not heard in a long time. I had just assumed Bernie was retired by now. He and I had worked together at the prosecutor's office on several cases.

We had never got along, even while on the same team.

Once Bernie formed an opinion on a matter, he never changed it. Once he had his suspect, he ignored everything else, even in light of new evidence.

He was a good cop otherwise, just plagued with terrible tunnel vision. If he picked the right suspect on the first shot, he usually put them behind bars. But he was wrong often enough that the drawbacks definitely outweighed his approach.

I was not looking forward to any interactions I might have with him on this case.

He and I had not come across each other since I'd left the prosecutor's office, but I wished it could've been anybody else, even my ex-girlfriend Detective Stephanie Gray.

"Thanks," I said, about to hang up.

"You decided to take the case?"

I hesitated, glancing over at Candy, wondering if she could hear Karen. "Yes, I believe so."

"Excellent," Karen said in a neutral voice. "I'll have the files sent over tomorrow."

"I would appreciate that."

My next call was to Frank Ward. I already had his contact information on my phone because he and I frequently dealt with each other on various matters.

The call to his landline went to voicemail. I tried his cell phone. Voicemail as well.

I hesitated. The last thing I wanted was to call Bernie Lee, but I didn't see that I had any other choice. I wanted to get out in front of this so that the evidence was seen as legitimate.

I tried calling the prosecution's office first and got a receptionist.

"Is Frank Ward around?" I asked.

"Can I tell him who is calling?"

"Mitch Turner."

"Let me see." The receptionist put me on hold. I was left listening to classical music. It didn't sound like there had been any recognition in her voice when I told her my name, so it was somebody who had not been working there back when I was a prosecutor.

She came back onto the phone a couple of minutes later. "He appears to be gone for the day. Can I take a message?"

"Just tell him Mitch Turner called and that I would appreciate a call when he has a moment. He has my number."

After I hung up, I searched my phone for Bernie Lee's contact information. I had switched phones several times since we had last worked together, but with the way things were set up these days, I wasn't surprised to find I still had his contact information saved somewhere in the cloud.

I pulled up his cell number and hesitated before punching it. I was about to walk out of the room to take the call before realizing it was probably best I didn't. If I was called on in court to report how we had found this, I wanted to testify I had not let my eyes off it for a single moment.

"Mitch Turner the turncoat," Bernie Lee said when he answered.

I grimaced. It was not the first time I'd been called that. It had a catchy ring, so people remembered it. It also looked like I wasn't the only one who had contact information saved to his phone for somebody long in the past.

Bernie had been a heavy smoker back in the day, and judging by how much raspier his voice was now, he had continued the habit.

"Never thought I'd be getting a call from you, Turncoat," Lee said.

"Bernie," I said evenly with a pause to emphasize the correct use of his name, "you have a second?"

"Why?"

"I am now the lead attorney on the Candy Carlisle matter."

"She finally kicked that old fraud Karen Brodsky to the street? Huh. Don't suppose you're much better. I heard Frank Ward offered her twenty years. Poor deal for the state if you ask me. I hope you guys fight this because we have her cold. I want her to get the max sentence. She killed him in cold blood. Planned it all out weeks in advance. It's all right there in black and white if you know where to look."

"There's two sides to every story." Bernie's opinion of things hardly mattered. It only came down to what could be proven in court. There was nothing to be gained by a testy exchange.

The last thing I needed was to antagonize the man, but I might not be able to help myself. I glanced at Candy, who could only hear my side.

"We're over here at the murder scene looking at things," I said.

Bernie sputtered. "How did you get access to that?" I couldn't answer right away because his question ended in a coughing spell that gave me time to count to ten.

I was remembering just exactly how much I didn't like working with this man.

"We have a key."

"Suppose you probably do, seeing as how Candy killed him in her own home. Her children were asleep upstairs. You know that, right?"

"If you'd stop long enough to listen, I have something to tell you."

Bernie waited.

"We found something you might want to check out."

"What?"

"A bullet."

There was dead silence from the other end of the phone.

"Are you sure?" The antagonism was momentarily gone. Had fear replaced it? I sure hoped so. I wasn't going to cry if he messed up while processing the scene and got let go because of it.

"Dead certain."

"Who's there with you?"

"My investigator, Candy Carlisle, and myself."

"Sheesh, Mitch! You have your client there?" His tone was all attack again, even harsher than before. I could practically see him frothing at the mouth through the phone. "You know how all kinds of wrong that is? And you expect me to believe that you just found a bullet over there, is that it?"

"Come on over. We have to disclose this. It's your job to check it out. We'll talk when you're here."

I hung up without waiting for a reply.

14

It was more than forty-five minutes before Bernie Lee appeared. He came by himself. He drove an unmarked police vehicle that he parked behind my Porsche. As he got out, he carefully scrutinized my parking job as he took a long pull on a cigarette. Just as I had suspected, he had relapsed. He appeared to be looking hard to find something wrong that he could ticket me for. He must not have come up with anything because he finally sauntered over towards the door.

Bernie had gained weight in the intervening years, he had less hair, and it was grayer. He was about a foot shorter than me, but his girth was more than double mine.

I met him as he approached, lighting another cigarette after tossing the butt of the last into the brown grass. He looked a little disappointed it didn't start a fire.

"If it isn't the Turncoat hisself." Bernie nodded towards my car. "Looks like it's paying well enough."

"Bernie," I said through bared teeth.

"How are you liking the wrong side of the law?" Bernie asked as he took a long pull.

"There is no wrong side."

"Of course, there is. Think of all the guilty suspects you've let walk free. If you'd've been a prosecutor, you might've gotten them locked up. Instead, you became a parasite to society."

"Not everybody who is accused is guilty," I said, letting him get a step ahead while I slid out my phone and brought it up after turning it on.

"Are you sure?" Bernie asked with a smirk as he walked inside, not bothering to put out his cigarette. As soon as he was in the hallway, he let out a big puff of smoke while staring straight at Candy, as if daring her to challenge him.

"Another turncoat," Bernie said, taking in Winston. "And the murderess herself."

Winston glared at Bernie but didn't respond. He saw what I was doing.

Candy looked ready to club him. "Can I offer you something to drink?"

I was impressed. Her voice sounded far more civil than mine would have been if a cop had barged into my house while smoking a cigarette and throwing around accusations.

Bernie turned back to me and froze.

"Whatcha doing, Mitch?" He looked at my phone. "Are you recording?"

I made a show of looking down. "What? This?" I gave him my best smile. "I believe you owe my client an apology. Also, we'd appreciate it if you didn't smoke in the house. You can leave your cigarette outside and pick it up when we're done."

Bernie licked his lips but knew I had him. "Sure, I was just having some fun." He stepped outside and put his cigarette on the front step.

"Now that we've got the preliminaries out of the way, how about we take a look at things?"

I made no move to lower my phone while keeping it at an angle to keep Candy out of the video. Bernie looked as if he were going to suggest I turn it off but shrugged before walking back inside.

"What do we got here?" Bernie asked, staring at Candy until she looked like she wanted to hide. She put a hand on her purse.

"Winston was looking at the back wall," I said. I kept the video going. "He discovered something strange. We were not sure what it was, so I pulled out my phone and recorded while he dug it out."

"If you thought it was something real," Bernie's eyes flicked to my phone and then back to my face, "why didn't you call me straightaway?"

"We didn't want to waste your time if it was unimportant."

"Oh, I see," Bernie said in a sarcastic voice. "Well, where is it?"

Winston held out his gloved hand. He'd put it in a bag while we waited. Bernie pulled on a latex glove that he had pulled out from a pocket as he approached. He took the bag from Winston and pulled the bullet out, holding it to the light to examine it.

"Too small," Bernie said thoughtfully, rolling it between his index finger and thumb.

"What caliber was the murder weapon?" I asked, torn between telling him to be careful with it and hoping he damaged it on video. Bernie looked at me like I was incompetent. "I don't have my files yet."

"Ballistics said the bullets that killed him were all 9 mm. Looks like what you got here is .22, but we'll have to send it to ballistics to know for sure."

I studied the bullet. Bernie held it up again with one eye squinting.

"Where was it?" Bernie asked.

"Here," Winston said, pointing to the knot with the edge of his knife.

"Wrong angle, too," Bernie said as he walked to the front of the couch. "The murderer likely stood here." He glanced at Candy. "Isn't that right?"

"My client has a presumption of innocence," I said. "Please direct all comments to me."

Bernie gave me a roguish smile. "Certainly wouldn't want her to confess accidentally to the crime on video, now would we?"

I had to give Bernie credit for trying to turn the situation against us by seeking to elicit an excited response from my client. Or by baiting me. If this video was ever made public, I didn't want to be seen spouting off. I wanted all the attention on Bernie. I gritted my teeth but didn't respond as I looked from where Bernie stood to where the bullet was found. There was a lamp in between Bernie and where the bullet had been located.

"A second shooter?" Winston suggested. It looked like he regretted saying anything in front of Detective Lee, though it was an obvious conclusion.

"Who else did you have with you?" Bernie demanded of Candy, taking a step towards her while also pointing an accusing finger. "Your current lover?" An evil smile crossed his face. "Oh yes, we know about your affairs."

Affairs?

Did he know something I didn't or was he exaggerating?

"I didn't do it," Candy said shrilly, her face growing red. She moved to fold her arms but clenched her hands behind her instead. She was getting flustered, just like Bernie wanted.

I was fascinated by this move, the misbehavior of Detective Lee notwithstanding. Had Candy consciously been aware when she went to fold her arms that this would make her look defensive, giving something else for Detective Lee to read into?

Had she consciously chosen to take a different pose? I was glad I'd had the foresight to keep her out of the video.

"Take a step back," I said to Bernie. "I called you as a favor, from one professional to another professional. Please don't make me regret that."

"Wrong." Bernie took a step towards me now, shaking the bullet. "You were obligated to turn this over. This is not a favor. I owe you nothing."

I took a moment to formulate my response. He owed us basic human decency but saying that would just exacerbate the problem. To get through, I needed to put this in a way he would understand. I needed to help him see a different perspective.

"The way I'm handling this is a favor to you," I said calmly, "because the moment we found this, I was already making plans on how to disclose it in the least embarrassing way possible. It never looks good when cops miss evidence. I know that. You know that. I don't have any interest in pantsing you. I could have called a press conference and handed it over publicly, so your mess-up became public knowledge. Or I could have invited a local reporter to be on site when I did this. I did neither of these things and helped you avoid the headline: 'Experienced and Senior Detective misses an obvious bullet embedded in a wall.' I could also have done other things to make this situation uncomfortable."

Similar to what you are doing to me, I thought but didn't say because the video was still rolling.

"I did none of those things. I didn't even consider them," I said. "Instead, I called and handed it over discreetly. I play fair."

"Since when do scum like you play fair?" Bernie's voice was getting thick. I knew from prior experience this meant he was furious. It looked like my efforts to dampen them weren't paying off. Perhaps it was because I had pointed out that this was a screwup. "Or are you forgetting you are recording this conversation?"

"I think it's time you go," I said. "Please bag the evidence, fill out the paperwork, and then leave."

"You can't kick me out. This is a murder scene."

You guys finished your investigation. You're on private property.

I shrugged. "Stay, that's fine too."

Bernie and I stared at each other before he turned on Candy and thrust a finger in her face. The bullet was curled now into the fingers of the same hand.

"I know you did this. I know it was you. I'm going to prove it." Before we could say or do anything else, he was already stomping towards the door. He slammed it on his way out. Once he was gone, I finally stopped recording.

"Did you get all that?" Winston asked when it was apparent I had stopped the video.

I nodded. "Yep."

"What are you going to do with it?" Candy asked.

"Sit on it for now."

"You could make trouble for him," Winston said. "Just off the top of my head, I can think of several things he did that were against local procedure, not to mention just plain common decency. I'm sure we'll find more when we analyze it."

"I haven't gotten to where I am by willfully making enemies of cops, even if they're making it easy for me to want to do." I held Candy's eyes. "Many are just trying to do their job. It's easy to vilify somebody who's working opposite you, but that does us a disservice. It takes our eye off the ball."

"At the very least—" Winston stopped when I glared at him.

"Having a reputation for fair play is far more valuable than taking every last advantage to stick it to a jerk." I paused for emphasis. "Especially if you're doing it just to stick it to them. That doesn't help our case, not even a little. If it becomes an issue, we have something we can use to back up our claims. Until then, we will not worry about it."

I looked around the room. "What we need is to prove your innocence. We do that? This is all a nonissue."

15

I could tell Winston disagreed with me, but he would wait until it was just the two of us before he tried again to make a case for doing something about Detective Bernie Lee, as he should've done in the first place. My warning glare was hopefully sufficient enough that I wouldn't need to bring up what had happened here when we met in private. He had forgotten we had a client with us when he'd started spouting off. He wasn't used to meeting with my clients and me at the same time.

This was why I usually met with my clients one on one rather than bringing in a team. It never looked good when the team disagreed with each other in front of the client. Disagreements were a part of the process, but they were better handled in a back room.

I didn't regret inviting Winston. He had, after all, found something the police had missed.

I just needed to focus us back on the real issues, not a cranky cop.

Candy looked uncertain but willing to go along with me, at least for now.

"Winston," I asked, "are you all done with your review of the site?"

He nodded. "I noticed that anomaly in the wood and continued through the room before I went back to investigate. Could we keep looking around? Sure. Do we need to?" He shook his head. "Probably not."

"Do you have a place we can sit and talk?" I asked Candy. "Preferably away from here?" I considered dismissing Winston but decided that could have felt punitive after our exchange about Detective Lee. He was now extra motivated on this case because he'd just found something the cops had missed. I hoped now to use that to our advantage in my conversation with Candy. Winston was one of the best investigators I worked with, and a little extra motivation would yield big dividends.

I didn't believe Candy was as innocent as she claimed. Winston was probably in the same place. If we were to put in the hard work required to prove her innocence, we needed to find evidence that proved it, or she needed to convince us. This was her best opportunity.

"Yes," she said, "this way." She took us to the back of the house where she led us into a sunroom. The sun was out, making the room toasty warm. She cracked a few windows before we sat down on patio furniture.

"We need a list of people who you believe could have done this to your husband."

Candy nodded. "I've been racking my brain for months. I've given a couple names to Karen. She's looked into them but has found nothing. We have nothing." She hesitated. "This is part of why I wanted somebody new. I felt we needed a fresh perspective."

"What is the name of the girl who reached out to proposition Raymond?" I asked.

Candy turned pale and looked at Winston. "Does he have to be here?"

I shook my head. "He doesn't. But he's gonna chase down these leads, so it's good for him to hear this from your mouth. If you're concerned about him keeping your confidence, you have nothing to worry about. He is a former cop. I've worked with him for years. We also have a nondisclosure agreement in place between him and my law office. Everything you tell him will be kept confidential."

"If you feel this is best." Candy shook her head and focused on a nearby potted plant as she inhaled. "Her name was Evangeline Brewer."

"Is that her current name?"

"No. I don't remember what it is now. Maybe she changed it back."

"She still married?"

"Doesn't sound like it. She wanted to run away with Raymond, didn't she?"

Winston shifted. I could tell he had questions he wanted to ask. He glanced at me but remained silent.

Good, he picked up on my cue to back off.

"You knew her during high school?" I asked.

She nodded. "Yes."

"Has Raymond had any interaction with her since that time and before this last time?"

"I'm not sure, probably. Social media has changed things. We're connected to everybody we knew in high school, so if she wanted to communicate with him, it is easy to do and keep quiet."

Says one who knows?

"Is that how your ex-boyfriend reached out to you?" I asked.

Candy stared at Winston before nodding. "He instant messaged me."

"What's his name?"

"Do you really think he needs to be a suspect?"

Warning bells went off inside my head. Was she protecting this guy? I would have Winston start with him if I had to push much harder to get the information.

"Everybody who has come into contact with you or Raymond in the past year are potential suspects. We need a list of all the names you can think of. If you have a doubt, please tell us so we can look into it."

"Okay," she said, frowning. She did not seem committed but appeared willing to play along for now. "His name is Ian Mercer."

"Are you connected to either of them on Facebook?" Winston asked.

Candy nodded, the hesitation still clear on her face. "Both. I thought it was odd when Evangeline requested to be my friend, but I couldn't see a reason not to accept it. I mean, it's been years. All that's ancient history. Should have been water under the bridge, right?"

"Tell me the names of all the men you had affairs with," I said casually.

Candy's nostrils flared. "That detective got it wrong. It was just the one time. For both of us."

I shrugged. "Sure. What are their names?"

"Do we really need to get into that?" Candy leaned forward. "It's been years now for both of us. You said you only wanted people we've come in contact with during the last year."

"If we rule out the people you've had affairs with, as well the people you've contacted during the last year, we will have to expand our search horizon. Are you certain Raymond has had no contact with his mistress since?"

"Positive. She moved away. She lives in California. Doesn't have family or any ties here. It's unlikely she had anything to do with this."

I just looked at her.

"Jana Lerner," she finally said.

"And yours?"

"David Washingon. He and I have not spoken in years."

"He hasn't reached out to you since the death of your husband?"

She shook her head. "No."

"Who else can you think of? Who might have had it in for your husband?"

"That's it. That's all I can think of."

"What did Raymond do for a living?"

She looked away. "He was a software programmer. All he did was sit in an office and code or go to the occasional meeting. I don't think anybody there wanted to kill him."

"No friction at work?"

"Nothing beyond normal friction."

"What is normal friction?"

"Have you ever worked with programmers?" Candy asked.

I shook my head.

"They aren't the easiest people in the world."

"Are you saying your husband could be difficult?"

She started to nod but then shook her head. "That's not what I'm trying to say. I'm talking from my personal experience working with other software programmers. I never worked with my husband, nor did I associate with his coworkers. I don't know what it was like to work with him on a professional level. All I know is that programmers can be difficult people."

"So you feel like if there was tension at work, it's just because of the nature of working with a computer programmer?"

"Yes, that's what I'm trying to say. Nothing unusual."

"No work arguments?"

"No."

"Was he a manager?"

"Kind of. He led a group of three people as a team lead. The way he described it to me, he just kept track of them from time to time. He barely ever spoke to any of them. They didn't even work in the same building."

It seemed like a dead-end, but we would check it out before we crossed it off our list.

"Are there any other sources of conflict he might have had in his life?"

Candy was already shaking her head before I finished.

"Did he belong to any clubs?" I asked. "Go to any churches?"

"Do we seem like religious people?"

I shrugged. "I can't make assumptions. I have to ask all the questions, see what shakes out."

"Why does this feel like the worst physical exam I've ever had?"

"It has to be like this if you want me to understand what happened to your husband."

"Clubs, no. Religion, no."

"Friends?"

"A few. Not many. He hasn't seen any of them in months."

"What's the name of his best friend?"

"He doesn't have one."

"What did he do for fun outside of the home?"

"You think we had fun *here*?" She shook her head. "He would go swimming at the local pool. He sometimes took the kids, he sometimes didn't. Occasionally, he'd go drinking with his friends. He'd have a poker night here and there. It wasn't often. He spent most of his time online gaming."

This drew my attention. "Gambling?"

"No. Fantasy land stuff. Computers were his life. He would go to work and bang away on a computer keyboard all day long. He would come home and stay up late doing the same thing."

"Any conflicts from there?" I asked, wondering if there might be a virtual connection to his death.

"I wouldn't know. You would have to ask Karper109."

"Karper109?"

"It is the online player's name. I don't know his name in real life. All I know is that my husband and he would stay up playing till all hours of the morning." She shook her head ruefully. "He probably knew my husband better than I did."

I looked at Winston, who'd already made a note about it.

"What game?" I asked.

"World of Fantasy."

"Is that something you're able to investigate?" I asked Winston, unfamiliar with the gaming community. The name sounded vaguely familiar, but I'd never played it. I didn't know anything about online games. I'd played the occasional game of Halo with the guys next door to blow off steam in college, but that had been rare, and I'd been terrible. I had not played computer games since becoming a lawyer.

"I'm familiar with it. I play some."

This drew a look from both Candy and me.

Winston shrugged. "It's addicting. What can I say?"

"Okay," I said, focusing on Candy. "Assuming that doesn't go anywhere, can you think of anybody else who might have had any reason to kill your husband?"

"No. Not at all."

16

Winston tried to talk to me as we walked out to our cars, but I shook my head and asked him to follow me to my office, where we could talk in private. I didn't want to risk either of us being overheard by Candy, who had told us to go on ahead because she had a few things she wanted to check about the house before she left.

She had seemed a bit shifty as she spoke.

The skeptical part of me wondered if maybe she had seen some evidence left behind that both the cops and Winston and I had missed, but I doubted that was likely. After we had finished our conversation with Candy, both Winston and I had gone through the room one more time.

This time, I had pulled out my phone and recorded a video of the room from every different angle. If there was any evidence that we had missed that she wanted to hide or destroy, chances were good that we already had a record of it anyway. I couldn't think of a reason we needed to stay. The police had already been through the place, and unless there were more bullets buried in the walls, there was no reason for us to stick around. Winston and I had even gone around the room looking at all the knots and hadn't seen anything else.

I decided to give her the benefit of the doubt and assumed she was nervous about being in the home where her husband's body was found.

Winston and I walked into my law office twenty minutes later. Ellie had already gone for the day.

I wished I had somebody I could talk to about what was going on with her because I didn't have the foggiest idea how best to support her.

Barbara would know what to do. I briefly toyed with the idea of calling to get her advice, but I didn't think that was wise after my interaction with her earlier. Even if she took my call, Barbara would probably read more into it than I communicated.

Isn't that what I want?

No, it was best not to go down that avenue. I also didn't want to be seen as taking advantage of Ellie's condition to further my interests with Barbara.

I didn't think that would be my intention, but it could certainly be misinterpreted in that light.

Winston might have some helpful suggestions, but I wasn't about to bring him into it because I didn't know how well he and Ellie knew each other outside the workplace. I didn't want to risk saying something to him and having it get back to her, even though Winston had proven reliable in the past at keeping loaded secrets.

I would just have to figure out how to appropriately support Ellie on my own.

It was frustrating that my ability to communicate didn't seem like it was going to help much in this regard. I couldn't very well argue against the cancer or file a lawsuit to address it. Unless she started having troubles with the insurance company, there wasn't much need for the type of conflict I was schooled in handling.

"What do you think of your new client?" Winston asked after we were seated in my office. Winston wasn't much on small talk and liked to get down to business. He tapped his booted foot impatiently, something I believed was a nervous tic.

"I'm reserving judgment," I said with a coy smile after taking a moment to think about it. I always wanted to believe my clients were innocent, but that rarely ever proved to be the case. I recognized this particular aspect of my psyche and tried to assume the opposite to counterbalance it. This had saved me countless times from fruitless battles because most of the time, it was only a matter of going through the evidence to see the weaknesses in the prosecution's case so we could negotiate a better deal. "What did you make of her?"

"I think she's innocent."

I was surprised. Winston thought everybody was guilty. He was far more jaded than me. It was also unusual for him to arrive at such a decision so early in the case without having reviewed much of the evidence.

Over the years, I'd noticed Winston had some ingrained biases. I suddenly became concerned he might be biased because she was an attractive woman.

Everybody is biased in some way. I was most concerned about people who claimed to be nonbiased because I considered that a red flag that there was some agenda they were trying to keep from me.

It was like the car mechanic who'd told me he was honest.

Why did he feel the need to tell me?

I never went back.

Winston was human, and prejudices came built into the package. It's not like they were all something he could directly control, especially if he wasn't aware of them. I had my own biases, some of which I knew about, and others which I was sure were subconscious.

Whenever I took on any matter, I always tried to look at my potential biases to alleviate the possibility they might influence my view of a case.

Winston tended to think wealthy people were guilty. I'd also suspected he had a hard time looking past a pretty face.

It appeared that might come into play here. I always carefully reviewed Winston's work to make sure he didn't let these potential biases get in the way, and so far, I had not seen direct evidence of them coming into play. I had not yet bothered to talk with him about my suspicions because he did a good job. If I ever suspected they were hampering his ability to handle a case, I might have to mention them.

I was the first to admit Candy was attractive. Her resemblance to Barbara was striking, but they were two different people.

Once I'd gotten to know Candy better, the superficial shock of having a client that looked like Barbara had subsided. It was helpful now that I saw them as two distinct individuals with differing personalities and characteristics. I attributed my awkwardness in that first meeting to my encounter with Barbara just beforehand. If that had not happened, I might not have even made a connection between the two.

"You usually have strong opinions going the other direction," I said while studying him. "You always think my clients are guilty."

He shrugged. "She didn't do this. I'd wager serious money."

"Why are you so sure?"

"Just a gut instinct, I suppose, at least at this point." He gave me a hard look as if he knew what I was thinking. "And don't go getting worried about me being biased. If I find evidence she's guilty, I'll be the first to admit it."

"Just as long as you're aware of the possibility. We'll stick to the facts and see where they take us."

"Of course."

"I want you to start with David Washington. He seems like our best suspect. After you do a thorough background check on him, I then want you to move over to Ian Mercer."

"Any reason you're prioritizing the men?"

I smiled. "Just my instincts, probably subtle biases I should ignore."

"I'll look into them first and then the others, too."

"What about this Karper kid?" I asked Winston. "I don't know anything about this World of Fantasy."

"Karper109, you mean?" Winston shook his head. "It's one of those massive online player games."

"Can you find him?"

"I'll look into it, but that kind of thing can be difficult. I'll see what I can figure out."

"Meaning you're going to go play World of Fantasy tonight?"

He gave me a wicked smile. "And I'm going to bill you for it."

I rubbed my forehead. "Make sure you're actually doing work, not just playing around."

"You're never going to know the difference."

17

I stared into space after Winston left before pulling out a pad of paper and jotting down my impressions from my meeting with Candy. She had been hesitant to reveal their marital infidelities. While that uneasiness could easily be explained as shame or unwillingness to drag their dirty laundry into the light of day, it could also mean she suspected Raymond's death had something to do with their past entanglements.

You would think somebody being tried for murder would want every avenue explored, but I occasionally found that was not the case. There were some things people just didn't want to reveal, regardless of the consequences. I sometimes had to sit down with my clients to talk through the ramifications to get them to recognize the potential risk of not telling me everything.

Candy was headed toward such a discussion if we didn't put together the pieces of what had happened before too long.

She had thrown up a wall when I asked about David Washington, giving us the littlest amount of information she could. She had also been quick to explain Jana Lerner had moved out of state.

I got the sense she had wanted both potential lines of investigation shut down as quickly as possible.

Why?

Especially if there was something there that would get her off the hook?

Resorting to my old standby while I waited for Winston to work his magic, I went to Facebook and searched out Candy Carlisle's profile. I searched through her friends for David Washington but wasn't surprised when I didn't find him.

I tried searching for David Washington but came up with more than a hundred results. I had no way of filtering them by geography except to go through them one by one. Facebook had a wealth of information, but it didn't always make the best research tool if you didn't want to spend the time to filter through things manually.

I had a flash of inspiration and went to LinkedIn to run my search.

Three David Washingtons came up within a thirty-mile radius of my office. Just as I was about to click on the first, I remembered LinkedIn revealed to the user the identity of other users who had recently viewed their profile. I didn't want to tip David Washington off that I was looking into him, so I held back from clicking and examined what little information was shown in my search results.

The first man looked like he was in his early eighties, and while it was possible this had been Candy's lover, I just made a note of his information and profile page before moving on to the next.

The next David A. Washington was a lawyer.

I zoomed in on his profile to see if I recognized him, but I did not. That was hardly a surprise. There were thousands of practicing attorneys in the city. He did estate planning and was a little younger than Candy Carlisle. I bounced over to Facebook to search for his full name and quickly found his profile by matching it to his picture.

It appeared that David A. Washington was single and recently divorced, judging by the fact that he had pictures of himself with three young children at Disneyland. Two looked like twins.

This man was a distinct possibility, but my instincts told me that he was a little young for Candy. She was pushing forty. This David Washington was almost thirty.

I went back to LinkedIn. The next man, David V. Washington, was in his mid-forties. He was a thoracic surgeon and a good-looking guy. My money was on him. I switched back over to Facebook and was able to match his picture within ten minutes.

David V. Washington appeared to be married or had a serious girlfriend. There weren't children in any of the pictures available to the public, but he and his significant other liked to travel. There were pictures of them in Ireland, Egypt, and South America.

I wrote down his information and decided he was the most likely candidate. I put his profile side-by-side with Candy Carlisle. These two looked like a match.

She said the affair ended years ago, but what if that was not the case?

What if it had been ongoing this whole time? And that was why she had seemed to be relieved when she had entered their front room and seen the bloodstains from her dead husband?

Assuming she isn't the one who killed him.

I couldn't get over the way Candy had responded when we had walked into that room. Perhaps she had been nervous, suspecting that I was looking to seeing her reaction, but it just seemed like there was something more to the story than what she had told me. I only partially bought her explanation that she had been planning to divorce Raymond. I needed to figure out a way to get the information if she wasn't willing to volunteer it.

After working on my notes, I took a break and turned my attention to Ellie.

It seemed like I should send her flowers. I had never done that before because whenever something like that was needed, Ellie was always on top of it, telling me about it after the fact.

I snorted when I thought of asking her to send flowers to herself. That just didn't seem right.

I looked up some local florists on my computer, picked one that was well-reviewed, and called them. After placing an order for an expensive bouquet to be delivered to her apartment tomorrow afternoon, I paced around my office, mulling over the information that I had already gathered on the Carlisle matter.

My cell phone rang. I picked it up, intending to let it go to voicemail until I saw it was Karen Brodsky.

18

"Mitch," Karen said when I answered. "I didn't have time for you earlier. I was just about to meet with a client who's gone haywire." She clucked her tongue. "I thought we had everything ready to start negotiating a plea bargain, and at the last moment, he threw in a wrench."

"An indecisive client?" I asked with a snort. "Never had one."

We chuckled. I would never say anything like that to a nonlawyer, but lawyers understood other lawyers. I imagined doctors would talk about their patients who refused to follow directions in the same way.

"I may have got that sorted out by the time he left. He said he was satisfied, but he didn't seem to be. Who knows, maybe he'll come to you?"

She laughed. I was glad to hear her joking around about the Candy Carlisle matter.

"Can I just say it's amazing the kinds of things people think we can do?" Karen said. "Some clients think I walk on water, others not so much. Usually, it comes down to the facts on their case, nothing particularly special that I'm doing.

"This client thinks I should be able to get the murder charge dropped just by virtue of the fact I'm representing him. That's apparently why he hired me. I guess he thought I would have an in with the prosecution and convince them they had the wrong guy.

"I've tried to explain it doesn't work like that and that we need evidence that points to somebody else or clear and convincing alibi witnesses that say he was somewhere else. But he doesn't want to hear it. He just thinks I'm not doing my job."

I knew the type. "I get clients like that, too."

"Anyhow, I figured that now you're the attorney on the Carlisle case, there's a couple things we should talk about."

I checked my email but had not yet received a reply from Candy with a signed representation letter. I technically had not yet entered into the representation; however, I expected to get it back shortly, so I felt no need to explain this to Karen.

"I have a few questions for you, too," I said, "and now's a good time for me as well. I was actually just going over the list of potential suspects."

"You using Winston as your investigator?"

"Yeah, I work with him most of the time."

"I occasionally hire him for minor matters when my other investigators are busy. I've been impressed. He does thorough work."

"He usually gets personally involved in my cases." I thought about earlier. "Sometimes he offers advice when he shouldn't."

"The best ones usually do. How about I go first, and then you can ask your questions afterward? By the way, the files will be delivered to your office at 10:00 AM tomorrow morning. You will notice that we have done an extensive investigation into the people around both Candy and Raymond. Unfortunately, we haven't turned up anybody who looks like a viable suspect."

I tapped my desk in thought. It now made more sense to me why Candy had felt like the case was going nowhere. Karen's team hadn't surfaced any leads. If she couldn't do it with her team of investigators, what were we going to accomplish with just Winston and me?

"Nothing came back on David Washington?" I asked, intending to ask a follow-up question to get the specifics to save Winston the time it would take to dig it up himself.

"Who?"

I hesitated, not wanting to make Karen feel like she hadn't done a good job. "Just a man from Candy's past who may or may not have had a motive to kill Raymond."

"Huh." I could tell this bothered Candy, but I would not volunteer additional information. It was a good sign that I had already found a name Karen's team had missed. Most likely, they had not pressed Candy about her relationship with Raymond prior to his death. They probably hadn't taken her to the murder scene, and even if they had, they might not have noticed any expressions on her face.

"Tell me more about the people you guys investigated," I suggested, hoping that she didn't want to dig into the matter any further.

I could almost hear her thoughts from the other end of the line. On the one hand, she was probably curious to know, but on the other, she wasn't getting paid any longer, so why bother?

"We spent a lot of time going through Raymond's friends," Karen said slowly, "thinking that perhaps there might be something there that would materialize. Raymond had five poker buddies he would get together with, but to be honest, none of them looked the type, and we couldn't find a motive for them anyway."

I was glad to hear this because our efforts to get Candy to tell us about his friends had not been fruitful. After I had dug up the affairs, she had seemed reluctant to reveal much else. It would've taken us a lot of work to find it all ourselves. I was glad they had done the legwork on this already. I would have Winston review Karen's investigation and potentially go back and talk to some witnesses himself to see if anything shook out, but I was happy this part of the investigation had already been covered.

"How long has it been since he last got together with any of them?" I asked, wondering if Candy had told me the truth that it had been months.

"That's kind of the strange thing, they had been getting together regularly every month to play, but in the six months leading up to Raymond's death, they didn't get together one time. At least, they didn't get together with Raymond."

"That is strange."

"It took us the better part of a month to decide we were probably going down the wrong rabbit hole after we had spent considerable resources looking into it, going back and meeting with them several times. We did a thorough workup on each friend and couldn't find many connections between them and Raymond outside of the poker party. None of them came right out and said this, but I got the idea that they didn't want to speak ill of the dead. I don't have any evidence to back it up. I went along on the last meetings with my investigators, and that was my final impression of the situation."

"So you could never satisfactorily explain why he stopped playing poker with them?" I asked, feeling a little frustrated because we would have to do this part of the investigation all over again. It didn't sound like they had made much headway. How could they have wasted so much time and money without coming to any solid conclusions? I was curious to see the background investigations they had run on these five men. What was it about the reports that made them think that none of them had a motive?

"One mentioned there had been a falling out between Raymond and the others. I got the feeling they continued to play without him. Raymond probably offended them, but that's just a guess."

I scribbled down several notes, curious why Karen hadn't found any motives. Anytime I found a place where I had big questions, I assumed there were big answers.

"But you didn't find a single motive?" I asked, not bothering to keep the skepticism from my voice.

"No, it had been six months." Karen's voice was cold and getting defensive. "None of them had come in contact with him since. We couldn't find any form of communication between any of them. It just stopped."

"Strange."

"We looked in other directions." She paused. "That brings us up to the present."

"Thank you for filling me in. That's all good to know."

Karen paused. I could hear papers rustling in the background. "Mitch, I'm sorry to do this to you again, but it turns out I actually have to run. If you have any more questions, give me a holler. The files will be there tomorrow morning."

She hung up.

19

I didn't quite know what to make of my conversation with Karen. It was clear she had wanted to get off the line at the end, probably because my skepticism had been coming through, and she had realized she might have made some mistakes on the case.

I thought back to how worried she had been about Candy Carlisle suing her and wondered if Candy would sue us both if I didn't get her off. I imagined Karen was sitting in her office right now, drafting a memorandum to file in order to protect her in case such a thing ever happened. This reminded me to draft one of my own about the events of the day. It never hurt to be extra careful if you suspected your client might be litigious. It was a professional hazard for all attorneys.

Mistakes and errors in judgment could happen to the best of us. I certainly would not hold anything against Karen unless I got her files and saw they were in shambles. But knowing Karen, I doubted that would be the case. I was likely to get several boxes containing all the research, and I wouldn't be surprised to find it well-organized and color-coded. The most likely explanation for missing the past affairs was that Candy had actively tried to hide them.

She'd only revealed them to me after I had practically bludgeoned them out of her. I'd noticed that she was withholding something and hadn't stopped until I got it.

Perhaps the fact that I was a new attorney on her matter had made her a little more open to sharing something she had thought was a non-issue from her past. I'd also made it clear that I would walk if I didn't like how things went.

But there was another explanation for why Karen might not have pushed Candy too hard. It could come down simply to matters of money. I thought of how much Karen's office overhead had to be with her multiple teams of investigators, paralegals, and associates that she kept running at all times. It could be easy in that type of environment to focus only on bringing in the next billable hour and missing the fact that your client was hiding something.

I didn't really have that problem. Sure, I had my share of overhead, but it was a great deal less than Karen's. I had Ellie and now a temp who I would also have to cover. I would sometimes pull in a paralegal to help, but that was it. Whenever I engaged Winston or another outside contractor, I always billed my client for their services. There was rarely ever any shortfall there because I always required retainers upfront.

I bet that's why Karen missed this. It's a lot of pressure to keep a high-power law firm running.

I would make certain to review the work Karen and her team had done with a critical eye, taking nothing for granted. Maybe after I read through what they had collected on these five friends, I would come to the same conclusion that there was no motive for them, but I doubted it.

I saw things where others didn't.

It's part of what had driven me to go to law school. I'd recognized I had a gift for sorting through details and perceiving the implications, so I had taken advantage of it.

I got up and paced around my office to get the blood flowing, consciously thinking through what I knew about the case and hoping my subconscious would make some connections.

There were many potential suspects already on the wall, but I needed to cross off the primary one.

Candy Carlisle, my client.

I didn't make it far into my first lap around the office before I remembered that I had taken pictures of the murder scene, so I had something to review while I waited for Winston and Karen.

I sat back at my computer and pulled them up.

I went through the pictures one by one, stopping on one that reminded me of her expression. There was no getting past the fact that Candy had been relieved.

Maybe her story explained it; maybe it didn't.

After spinning my wheels for another forty-five minutes, I finally drafted that memo to my file and was just thinking of packing up for the day when there was a knock on my door.

"Come."

I was surprised to see Ellie.

"I thought you left," I said, giving her what I hoped was a supportive grin.

"I just went out for dinner. I'm back to catch up on a few things before tomorrow."

"What do you need?" I asked, leaning back in my chair and motioning for her to take a seat.

"I just wanted to make sure you're really okay with me coming in while I'm going through all this."

"Of course," I said immediately. She studied my face as if searching for the slightest hesitation.

"I'm glad to hear you say that."

"It would be difficult to run this business without you." I gave her a steady look. "But that should never be a reason for you not to take care of yourself or not do things that are right for you. I can make do without you if necessary. I don't want you to feel obligated to stay if you would rather be home or doing something else."

"No." She shook her head. "There is nothing else I would rather do than continue to work here. As long as you're satisfied with this arrangement, I am too."

"I'm good."

"I sent you a list of some potential candidates to fill in. Take a look. I'll have one start tomorrow."

"Thank you."

Ellie stood to leave.

"And Ellie?"

She turned.

"Good luck tomorrow. Let me know if there's anything I can do, even if it's just a small thing."

"I will do that."

I spoke up again as she started walking out. "Do you need a ride to the hospital?"

She shook her head. "I have somebody taking me."

She was gone before I could ask who.

20

The next few days went by quickly. Ellie was in and out of the office, and the new temp—a man by the name of Paul Sampson—was working out okay. I'd only had a few minutes to chat with Paul in passing, but I had learned he was a fourth-year philosophy student at the nearby community college. He was graduating this year and currently applying to law schools.

There was always a part of me that wanted to dissuade anybody applying to law school from pursuing the practice of law because it took the right type of person to enjoy it. Paul seemed like a sharp fella, but I wasn't certain how he would handle conflict. Even though she had no apparent desire to become a lawyer, Ellie was excellent at handling confrontation. It was part of why she was so successful working for me. I attracted that sort of thing.

I was just about to head to court for a hearing on a shoplifting case when there was a knock on my door. Veronica poked her head in.

"Do you have a second, Mitch?"

I glanced at my watch. "Only one, I've got court."

"I'll make it fast," she said, stepping inside and pulling the door shut behind her. "I think we need to bring on another partner."

Our firm had three. It was small but agile.

I liked it that way.

The suggestion took me off guard. "Really?"

"I also think it's time to upgrade our space."

This last one was no surprise. Veronica was always complaining we needed higher-end space to attract better clientele. I disagreed, and so did Tony, our other partner.

At least she's not threatening to leave the law firm again, I thought.

"There's some months we have a hard enough time making the bills work as it is," I said slowly. "I don't know if we should think about getting more expensive space."

"If we pick the right partner, it would be worth it. We might even save money if we get the right person and the right location."

"Do you have somebody in mind?"

She shook her head. "No, I was crunching the numbers last night and looking at various office spaces. If we brought on another attorney, and they had billables comparable to the average of ours, we could make something work that is beneficial to everybody and even cut our costs."

"I don't know, but I'll take it under consideration," I said, snapping shut my briefcase after stuffing a file folder inside. "And now I'm off to court."

"Good luck!"

I took a moment to consider her suggestion after she left.

Tony sometimes struggled to make his monthly commitments, but he was doing better. A couple of big injury case settlements had come in, enabling our firm to build up a buffer. It seemed Veronica wanted to take advantage of that buffer to upgrade our office space. I wasn't so sure this was a good move.

Did I want nicer office space?

Absolutely.

It would be nice to have a location with on-site security, mainly because that had been an issue for me in the past.

But we had made do just fine. I also had the added cost of taking on a temp while Ellie was going through treatment.

I would consider her suggestion, but I didn't think I was likely to agree. I couldn't imagine Tony would either. We had a fourth office that was uninhabited at the moment, so it would make more sense to bring on a fourth partner and keep them there, lowering the overhead costs for everybody. It wouldn't be by much, but it would give us all some extra breathing room.

Just as I was leaving, there was another knock on my door. I half expected it to be Veronica to make one more argument.

"Come on in," I said as I grabbed my briefcase. It appeared the knocker hadn't heard me, so I pulled open the door to find Paul on the other side.

"I know you're about to leave," he said, "but Winston stopped by to talk with you."

"Winston," I said, glancing at my watch as I stepped past Paul. I had to make it fast, or I was going to be late.

"Seems like I stopped by at a bad time," Winston said, falling into step beside me as I headed towards the door.

"I've got court right now, and I'm late." I pushed the door open and stepped outside.

"I think David Washington might be our guy."

I turned back to him.

"You had lunch?"

Winston shook his head.

"Meet me at Miranda's in an hour."

21

My hearing was shorter than I expected, so I arrived early at the restaurant. It was a casual place that encouraged people to just take a seat during the lunch hour, so I found an open table that already had water glasses and sat down to wait for Winston while looking at the menu.

At least I tried to look at the menu. I could not let go of what had just happened. It had been a long time since a judge had steamrolled me like that.

Not only that, the judge had got under my skin in the worst way. And that was what was bothering me the most right now. I couldn't think because I was so angry, but I had to figure out how the judge had got past the usual ice-cold wall of emotion I normally displayed in court. If I'd have known it would go like this, I would've asked Winston to meet me back at my office later in the day instead of at lunch, so I had time to calm down.

I suffered reversals in court all the time, just like anybody else. I usually handled them well enough, but the judge's behavior had really gotten to me today.

I was glad I had some time to collect my wits before Winston showed up. I needed it, or I was likely to snap at Winston if he was just a few minutes late, something he was prone to do for something casual like this.

The judge ruled against me without letting me finish my argument.

That's what had gotten to me.

I saw it now as I sought inner peace. He had attacked my sense of fair play and justice. I would be on the lookout for that type of behavior in the future, knowing it could have this effect on me. I did not like it when I lost control, so I had to remember this lesson.

It was apparent from the questions the judge had asked that he had not read my brief. And to add insult to injury, he had spoken over me half the time without letting me answer his own questions. After he issued his ruling, he had been in such a hurry to leave that he had almost forgotten to dismiss the courtroom. When he realized his mistake, he mumbled something as he left that I had interpreted as a dismissal, though it had not sounded like it.

I only saw it from the corner of my eye, but I could have sworn he'd already been taking off his robe as he went through the door. When I turned for a better look, he was gone.

I'd been angry enough that it was a good thing he'd left quickly because I'd been on the verge of doing something that could have put me in contempt of court.

It was a minor case, a shoplifting matter, but it was going to affect my client for a long time. The least the judge could do was pay attention to what I had to say if he wasn't going to bother to read my brief.

I took a sip of water and let the thought go while I tried to get into the right frame of mind for my meeting with Winston. My thoughts were interrupted when the restaurant door opened, causing the attached bell to jingle.

Winston.

He was early too. He found my table and sat across from me while I tried to let go of my baggage from court. I would have to be careful in our conversation since I was already on edge.

"What do you have for me?" I asked without preamble, realizing afterward that I probably should have started with a bit of small talk, just so Winston didn't figure out that I was having an off day.

Winston gave a small nod as if appreciating how I had skipped the chitchat. He didn't seem to like it and never had much to say.

"David Washington is a piece of work," Winston said as he opened his briefcase and pulled out a file folder that he put on the table in front of us. "Real piece of work."

"You sure you got the right one?"

"No doubt about it. I found our client connected to him on social media."

I looked up from my menu. "I checked her Facebook profile. She wasn't connected to any David Washingtons."

"That's correct. She's not connected to him on Facebook. This is where it gets interesting." He pulled a piece of paper out from the file and slid it over to me, facedown. I picked it up and saw that it was a screenshot of a social media profile. "She has two Instagram accounts. One account has just as many connections as her Facebook account and another smaller Instagram account with just a few followers. One of those is David V. Washington, but he goes by an alias. I don't have any way of checking, but I suspect she has this account so she can direct message him."

"How do you know it's her?" I asked, looking at the profile picture. I would never have been able to tell by it alone because her hair was down, and she wore a hat that obscured her face. It looked nothing like her.

"I'm not gonna get into it, but I have my ways of confirming Instagram accounts details."

"Inside connection?"

Winston shook his head. "I wish."

"Assuming we have the right guy, what did you learn?"

"David Washington is a professional mooch. He makes his way by going from one woman to the next. He doesn't seem to have a permanent place of address, and he has left behind a string of broken relationships."

I nodded. "And you like him for the Raymond murder because?"

"The working theory right now is that Raymond was still jealous and recently confronted him."

"It's odd that he is still connected to her if he likes to love them and leave them," I said. "You don't think he was actually in love with Candy Carlisle, do you?"

Winston shook his head. "Doubt it. It seems like there wasn't much of a relationship, probably a fling for both of them. Perhaps that's part of why he still keeps in touch with her. She didn't have an emotional connection to him, and he didn't have an emotional connection to her. It was just what the other was looking for, and it was safe for them to remain in contact." Winston shrugged. "Candy has some money. He's probably just keeping his toe in the water, so he has a backup source of revenue. From what little I know about the guy, I wouldn't put it past him to blackmail her."

"So David Washington is a player," I said. "He goes from one woman to the next, mooching until they either get wise to him or he tires of them, then he moves on."

"That's pretty much it."

"Does he have any degrees?" I asked, remembering how on his LinkedIn profile he claimed to be a doctor. I suspected now that was fake, based on everything I'd heard here.

"None that I can find. He presents well on social media. On LinkedIn, he identifies himself as a thoracic surgeon. He even has a separate webpage to go along with it. It's actually fairly sophisticated until you examine the details. If he's a licensed doctor, he's not registered in this state or any of the surrounding states. I also wasn't able to find a company registration for his practice. He is not registered here or anywhere in the United States."

David Washington was a character.

Perfect.

It was remarkable the kinds of things criminals could get away with in a virtual world where people didn't always stop to confirm what was presented. His polished online image would allow him to get away with murder. How many millions had he stolen from the women he'd defrauded? The fact his life was so full of provable fraud was concerning.

All of this pushed him to the top of my suspect list, but I wasn't ready to zero in on him as the prime suspect.

He was such an obvious target that it would be easy to miss other subtle possibilities. I had to remain open to all of them.

"Any evidence to suspect that the 'fling' is ongoing between the two?" I asked.

"Not that I can see. I spent a night following Washington. He has a current flavor of the month right now, and boy, are they living it up. If you found his Facebook page, you probably saw all about it. They went to one of the most exclusive and expensive restaurants in the city. I learned from the waiter afterward that they dropped a ton of cash. She's wealthy, and they're traveling all over the place as often as they can, posting so many pictures that it is well-documented. I expect it won't last for long." He shrugged. "But maybe he's finally found a woman whose pockets are deep enough that she doesn't have to ask many questions about his past. Maybe they'll make a serious go of it. Who knows?"

"Criminal history?" I asked, thinking I already knew the answer since Winston had not brought it up.

"No, which is surprising, seeing as how his fraud is right out there in the open and actually quite provable. It didn't take me more than an hour to determine the façade he presents online is a complete and utter lie. All it would take is a bit of online research, and this woman would know exactly who she is dealing with."

I remembered the posts, and in particular, how happy she had looked. I didn't think she would figure it out anytime soon because she didn't want to. She didn't want to ask too many questions when she was having such a good time. Not unless David Washington messed up and left a big clue as to who he really was.

"We know this guy is a fraud, but we don't have any indication that he's committed any violent crimes, correct?" I asked.

"That's right."

"Keep digging into him; see what you find. Have you crosschecked his online activity against the time of the murder to see if he was traveling?"

"A good thought," Winston said, making a note on his phone. "I'll do that today. If it looks like he was out of the country, I'll find some way to confirm that outside of social media just because that sort of thing can be easily faked."

"What were you able to find on Ian Mercer?"

"I've located him on Facebook. Candy Carlisle is connected to him. I should also mention that both hers and Raymond's accounts are connected to Jana Lerner as well."

I nodded. "Candy mentioned they were all Facebook friends. They were in high school together. Sounds like it's pretty common for people to connect with old high school classmates, even if they had some sort of flame for them back in the day."

Winston nodded. "Yes, that is my assessment, too." Winston shuffled some papers in the file folder and brought out a stapled pack of papers that he now referred to. "Ian Mercer lives out of state. It's curious Candy claimed he reached out to her with a proposition." Winston took a moment to turn a page. "He lives in California. He just recently got engaged. He's a divorcee, and his fiancée appears to be a divorcee as well. They got engaged about eight months ago, a few months before the murder."

"So you think Candy Carlisle lied about Mercer?"

"It seems unlikely, given both his geographic location and the fact he got engaged right around the same time Candy claims he was reaching out to her.

Maybe he was having last-minute jitters and just wanted to throw a shot in the dark, but it seems a little improbable."

"Any thoughts on confirming her story?"

Winston shook his head. "Not unless you want me to reach out to Mercer directly. I think at this point, it's safest to just assume she lied because I see nothing else that connects him to this."

"Agreed." Ian Mercer was dropping down the list and would stay there unless something pushed him up.

"Anything on Jana Lerner, Raymond's alleged mistress?" I asked.

"Nothing. I haven't found a connection yet between her and Raymond. Any chance you want to take another crack at Candy to see if you can locate some contact information for Jana?"

"I'll reach out, but it's doubtful she'll be more forthcoming. It doesn't appear she told her previous attorney about any of this."

"Really? She kept Karen in the dark?"

"Yep."

"Why would she want to keep secret people who might have motives to kill her husband?"

I leaned back. "A question I ask myself."

Winston and I exchanged glances. There was more Candy hadn't told us. A lot more. Neither of us needed to say it aloud because it was obvious.

"That's all I have," Winston said, standing, "I don't have time to stay for lunch. I have a previous appointment I am going to be late for."

22

I hesitated as I parked my car outside of Martin's Auto. I actually felt nervous, something I was not accustomed to feeling when meeting with witnesses or even potential suspects. I usually had a case of nerves when I went into court, especially before a big trial, but I was almost never nervous when I interviewed somebody.

It's because I'm planning to catch him off guard.

This approach had a way of blowing up in your face if you didn't do it right.

And I was rusty.

It'd been a long time since I had approached a potential witness in a case without first calling ahead to make an appointment. Back when I was just starting out on my own and trying to keep things cheaper because I wasn't attracting clients who could pay much, I would often do the legwork myself instead of hiring an investigator. Once I had figured some things out about the private practice of law, I preferred to have an investigator help. I usually let them do this sort of legwork for me because of the potential for unexpected conflict.

Most investigators were ex-military or ex-police and had been trained in how to handle tense situations.

I had training for tense situations, too, but mine was for the courtroom.

Abe Martin was the man I was planning to interview. He was the sole remaining owner of Martin's Auto. He had started the mechanic shop with his brother twenty years ago. His brother had since passed away, and now it was just Martin left running the show after he bought his brother's ownership from the widow.

Abe was one of Raymond's poker buddies. He had refused to say much to Karen and her team, but he had been the most forthcoming, revealing there had been a falling out between them and Raymond.

The workup Karen and her team had done on Abe Martin was extensive. When Karen had mentioned to me over the phone that she and her team didn't think he and others had a motive for murder, I had been skeptical.

After I had reviewed the reports of their investigation into Abe Martin, which had come to four hundred pages, I could tell why they felt they could say he did not have a motive.

Once you had a thick stack of paper on somebody, you thought you knew them well enough to make some judgment calls.

Unfortunately for Karen and her team, this was where they had gone wrong. They had allowed the prevalence of too much information blind them to the fact that they didn't know much about Abe Martin even though they knew a lot of facts about his life.

They had been blinded by the noise and missed the signal.

I decided to give it a shot myself to see if I could turn up anything that they had not.

I hadn't yet given Winston the names of Raymond's poker buddies because I wanted him focused on the other avenues of investigation. David Washington was still at the top of our suspect list, Jana Lerner, and Evangeline Brewer were right behind him. Of the people we were investigating, they were the most likely to have killed Raymond. That's where Winston's attention was most needed.

I had decided to look into Raymond's friends myself to see if I could figure out what exactly had happened between them. If I finally got some answers to why Raymond had stopped going to their poker nights, I could probably cross all five off the list because of the thorough investigation Karen's team had already done.

I had not read through every page of the research, but I had reviewed their executive summaries and scanned much of the rest.

There simply weren't many interactions between them and Raymond outside of the poker night to think that there was a motive to kill, not unless something big had caused the falling out.

If, for example, Raymond had won a substantial amount of money from one or all the players, that would be interesting and warrant further research.

Abe Martin was the only one who had revealed anything to Karen's investigators, but he had clammed up after that. Her investigator's notes were fuzzy on whether he had mentioned it in passing and shut up when they followed up at a later date or if he had slipped and then refused to say anything further.

Had he been willing to talk about it initially only to have something change in between interviews? If so, why?

The specifics could be telling.

The investigators had believed the poker boys had stopped talking to them because they'd been too persistent, but I wasn't so sure.

If I couldn't get anything from Abe Martin or any of the other poker buddies, I would reach out to Karen's investigators. But I wanted to try Abe Martin first.

While it was tempting to do what Karen had done and dismiss this as unimportant, the fact all five weren't talking made me want to know more.

I got out of my car, leaving my briefcase inside. I wanted to take a semi-informal approach. I had considered changing out of my suit but had decided against it because some formality might make him take me more seriously. Too much formality might send him running.

One mechanic started towards me. "We don't service those kinds of cars," he said, pointing at my Porsche.

"I'm not here to see a mechanic."

That stopped him short. He gave me a curious look. "You need something?"

"I'm looking for Abe Martin. He around?"

The man shook his head. "He left for lunch about forty-five minutes ago. He's due back anytime. You can wait inside."

"I'll do that," I said, heading toward the waiting area.

There were three people, two women and a man, waiting while their cars were being serviced. The man scrolled through updates on his phone. One woman talked on her phone, and the other flipped through a magazine. I walked over to a wall where there was a picture of Abe Martin and another man that I assumed was his brother. There was a third person in the picture, cutting a ribbon outside a much better kept version of the auto shop than it was today. I didn't recognize the man with the oversized scissors, but he seemed like a local politician. There wasn't a date, but it was at least twenty years old.

If I look hard enough, I'll probably find a copy of this picture in the file. Karen's investigators were thorough. I would give them that.

"I had more hair back then," a voice said behind me. I turned to find Abe Martin walking in as the door shut behind him. "Vince said you were looking for me."

Abe Martin was indeed bald. His hair was going gray. He was of average height and paunchy about the middle. He was almost ten years older than me, which put him just a few years older than Raymond at the time of his death.

"Mr. Martin," I said, "May I have a moment of your time in private."

"Who are you?" Abe asked, looking me up and down, probably wondering why somebody in a suit was visiting him. His eyes narrowed as if a thought had just occurred to him. Was there something else behind his eyes as well?

Fear?

"I'm Mitch Turner. I just have a couple questions I'd like to ask you."

He frowned. "You aren't working with that Karen Brodsky lady, are you?"

"I am not." I hesitated, feeling I should tell him more, but I also didn't want to talk about my client business where other people could hear. "If I might meet with you in private, I will explain further."

"Come on back to my office," he finally said, waving me down a hallway after him. I followed him back to a locked door. He fished out a key and unlocked it before pushing the door open. The place was cluttered with car parts and smelled about the same as a mechanic's garage.

He lifted a carburetor off a chair and motioned to it.

"You can sit there."

The chair had a grease stain that looked fresh.

"Thanks, I'll stand."

Abe sat in his chair and spun to face me.

"Who are you?"

No small talk. No chit-chat. Nothing. And he looked suspicious as well.

It was off to a great start.

"I'm an attorney representing Candy Carlisle," I said, carefully watching Abe for his reaction, wishing somehow that I could get it on video. I was not disappointed.

Abe's nostrils flared, his face turned pale. He balled his hands into fists. "I thought you said you didn't work for Karen Brodsky?" He jabbed a finger at me. "You lied to me!"

"I don't work for Karen Brodsky."

"Brodsky represents Candy Carlisle."

"Not any longer. I'm her new attorney. I just have a few questions."

Abe's eyes narrowed. "I already told her previous attorney everything there is to say."

"If you wouldn't mind, I just have a few follow-up questions."

"Do you have a record of my conversations with Brodsky's investigators?"

"I do."

Abe stood. "I have nothing more to say. You're wasting your time trying to talk to me further about any of this."

"I would just like a moment of your time," I said.

"I am very busy right now, and I have no more time to answer questions I've already answered. Good day."

Abe waited for me to leave his office.

I didn't move, watching him curiously.

I had expected a reaction, but this was beyond anything I had expected.

There was something here. I didn't know what it was, but Karen was wrong to have dismissed it.

I was certain.

If this had just been a simple falling out, Abe would have been willing to talk about it, at least on some level.

But instead, he was flat out refusing to answer questions.

There was a reason.

"If you wouldn't mind just—" I started to say, knowing that I was pushing but also wanting to gauge his reaction.

"I've answered enough!" Abe yelled, cutting me off and walking out. For a moment there, I'd thought he'd been about to attack me, but he must have thought better of it and just left instead.

I had pushed too hard, but I had learned something valuable.

I might not have found a motive, but I had found a temper.

A big one.

I glanced around the office to see if there was anything I might glean about the man that could help answer some questions. Nothing jumped out. I left after another glance because I didn't want him to come back and accuse me of snooping.

Abe was out in the garage talking to one of his mechanics when I walked back into the waiting area.

I watched him as I headed back out towards my car.

I didn't know what it was about this man that had made Karen decide he didn't have a motive, but I didn't like a thing about him.

Something about him just put my teeth on edge.

23

Another person might have been shaken by the encounter with Abe Martin. Not me. The customers out in the waiting area had looked concerned when I had left the mechanic's shop, which was a normal reaction to having somebody blow up on you like that, but I had not felt threatened by Abe Martin in the slightest.

It's just been too long. I'm out of practice.

I smiled.

But it was just like riding a bike.

I thought I had forgotten what to do, but I hadn't, even though Abe had looked ready to attack.

Perhaps that's part of why I had been a little nervous about my strategy. I wasn't as young as I had been back then, and while I still did work out, I was not in as good of shape either.

But none of that had mattered. I had slipped right back into it like a man pulling on comfortable gloves.

It would have been a great thing for the case if Abe Martin had attacked me because it would have given me ammunition to go to the police and tell them they needed to look into this guy for the murder of Raymond Carlisle. But it had not gone down like that, so I was left to run this myself.

Just how I liked it.

My interview with Abe Martin left me revitalized. There was an energy to my step as I got back into my car that I had not had before. This case had suddenly just got a lot more interesting.

There were big secrets.

I got to dig them up.

A part of me had enjoyed confronting people like this back in the day before I started hiring private investigators to do it for me.

It wasn't the fact that I had made Abe angry that was so exhilarating. It was the display of raw emotion that would eventually lead me to the truth.

Truth.

That is what always drove me. Answering questions and figuring out what somebody was trying to hide. That kept me getting out of bed in the morning and doing this job.

There was just something about seeing the reactions yourself firsthand, learning the information as it was discovered, and getting somebody to give up something that they had not meant to that really did it for me.

Have I been missing something by hiring investigators to do this?

I had done this as a one-off because I'd wanted to keep Winston focused on David Washington and the others, but maybe this was how I needed to do things more often going forward.

I would always have a place for people like Winston in my practice. Maybe it was time I did some of the more potentially fruitful and interesting things myself.

Abe Martin might not have answered my questions, but he had given me a lot to think about.

I knew now that it was worth continuing down this path, so my visit had not been a waste.

I considered just heading back to my office but shook my head. That didn't seem like the right call. There was only so much I could learn sitting behind a computer. How many little details had I missed by not getting out on the street and chasing down more leads myself?

I moved on down the list to the next friend. I started looking for a good place to pull off the road to find his contact information. I hadn't thought the meeting with Abe Martin would go anywhere, so I hadn't planned to try another interview today.

There was something here.

Abe Martin's overreaction made it clear he believed this issue to be in their past.

Five friends, I thought. *I'll get at least one to talk, slip up, or accidentally point me to another clue.*

My instincts also told me that I shouldn't quit now, that there might be things I could learn if I confronted some of the other poker buddies before they got their stories straight.

What are the chances they will talk about this over the phone or through text messages?

I shook my head. I certainly wouldn't if I had something to hide. That was one of the first things the police looked at as soon as they narrowed down the list of potential suspects.

If there was something bad here, the poker boys would wait until they could talk in person so they didn't leave behind a record of their conversation.

Unless they're stupid, I mused. There was one mechanic, a dentist, and three software engineers. It didn't seem like a dumb group. If they had conspired to kill Raymond, they would be certain to mitigate the risk of being caught by not leaving behind easily found evidence of their conversations.

I bet Abe is gonna call an impromptu poker game tonight.

Time was suddenly of the essence.

I doubted I could make it to all five today, but could I at least hit two more?

I pulled over to the side of the road and used my phone to access my online notes.

Bill Weaver. He was the next friend.

And as luck would have it, his dental practice was just a couple of miles away. I quickly scanned through the notes I had made about him and got back on the road.

I reviewed my conversation with Abe as I drove, trying to pick up anything subtle. Maybe after my subconscious had time to work on the matter, I would realize something that I had missed.

It happened to me often enough that I relied on it as a crucial part of my strategy for working a case.

Abe had been suspicious as soon as he had seen me. The suit had probably immediately cued him onto the fact that I was a lawyer.

He could also have been worried that I was a detective or a federal agent. Was he looking over his shoulder, expecting somebody in a suit to show up at his door?

Karen's investigators usually preferred to wear plain clothes. Winston did too. They felt it opened more doors to look like everybody else.

What if I'm going up the wrong tree?

What if Karen had done something to Abe to make him shut up? What if there was nothing here beyond he just didn't like the way they had treated him? That was what her investigators had thought.

I pulled into the dentist's office parking lot. I took a few moments to collect my wits. I was getting excited about the case, and I wanted to make sure I didn't run solely on instinct. When I walked in to surprise Bill with an impromptu interview, I needed to be at my logical best, pushing emotions to a back seat.

I reviewed my notes on Bill Weaver again, stopping to ask questions at various points before making a plan.

Regardless of what Bill thought of me approaching him at his dental office, I had a hard time seeing him yell at me in the same way Abe had. He might lose his temper, but he would be careful not to make a scene in front of his patients.

Bill had a reputation to protect as a dental professional and reputations are fragile. Abe could probably get away with yelling at somebody in his back office and not suffer any consequences to his image. Not Bill.

I soon found myself at the reception counter, asking if I might have a few minutes of Bill Weaver's time.

"He is with a patient right now," the receptionist said. Her name was Tina. "Are you a friend? Can I tell him who's asking?"

The way Tina asked if I was a friend made me wonder if Bill's poker buddies sometimes stopped by for an afternoon visit.

Could Bill Weaver be running some sort of criminal enterprise from his office?

It seemed like a ridiculous proposition, but I was glad the thought had occurred to me because it helped me keep my mind open to possibilities. While the scenario was unlikely, it wasn't so far-fetched.

Regardless, it didn't seem to strike Tina as strange for me to show up and ask for a meeting. Another piece of information I filed away to think about later.

"Just tell him it's Mitch Turner," I said casually. "I just need to run something by him really quick."

"I'll pop on back and let him know you're here to meet him." She motioned to the chairs in the waiting area. "Please have a seat."

I sat and looked around.

There could not have been a starker contrast between this waiting room and the one I had just come from at Martin's Auto. The office building was older but nice and also well-maintained.

This room had been recently remodeled. Martin Auto's waiting area had probably not changed in the twenty years it had been in operation.

The magazines were new and from major publishers. There was a place for children to play in the corner. The toys looked like they were cleaned regularly.

The interior design was well done and modern, clearly handled by a professional with exceptional taste. And the pictures combined with the rest of the decor to have a calming effect, the exact ambiance wanted in a dental office.

"He'll be right out to meet with you," Tina said, sitting back down in her chair.

"Thank you."

"Think nothing of it!" She turned to her computer and began typing. Not even a minute later, the door opened, and I found myself face-to-face with Bill Weaver.

I stood, extending a hand.

"Mitch Turner, is it?" Bill said as we shook. "Come on back to my office."

That was easy, I thought. *Why didn't he ask who I am or what I want?*

Does he already know?

Maybe my assumption Abe would not send out a communication was incorrect. Maybe they had a way to send coded messages.

I stared at Bill Weaver's back, trying to figure out what he thought of my presence.

Coded messages? If they are doing that, this thing is much deeper than I thought.

We walked past several patients who were getting their teeth cleaned, down the hall to a door. Bill opened it and motioned for me to go ahead of him.

This, too, was in stark contrast to Abe Martin's office. It was immaculate, well-decorated, and clean. "Have a seat, Mr. Turner," Bill said as he sat in his chair behind a desk, which squeaked when he moved. "What can I do for you?"

I was having a hard time seeing Bill involved in Raymond's murder. He was friendly and didn't seem to have anything to hide.

"I understand you are a friend of Raymond Carlisle," I said. "Is that correct?"

Comprehension dawned on Bill's face. He had not known about me beforehand unless he was a good actor.

"Raymond Carlisle." Bill shook his head. "So sad what happened. Are you with the police?" He frowned. "You know, I talked with a private investigator about Raymond's death several months ago. You wouldn't know anything about that, would you? He was working for the attorney representing Candy Carlisle."

"Actually, I represent Ms. Carlisle now."

Bill nodded as if things were making more sense.

"I don't think Candy did it," he said. "She couldn't do something like that. I suppose I don't know her well; I only saw her in passing a few times at Raymond's house, but she was nice, you know? Pleasant. Not the type you would think capable of murdering her husband in cold blood."

"Did you ever have any private conversations with her?" I asked, glad Bill had been my next stop. I was getting a vastly different perspective of this poker group. Maybe it wasn't a problem with the poker group; maybe it was a problem with Abe Martin.

"Can't say I did. I certainly don't remember them if I did. The only time I ever saw her was at those game nights—a few of us sometimes get together to play poker. She just peeked in to say hello but left us alone after that.

"How about Raymond? You ever hang out with him outside of your poker nights?"

"No, never." Bill raised his eyebrows, suspicion in his eyes. "Has anybody said I did? Is that why you're here?"

I shook my head. "I'm just following up on what Candy's previous attorney learned. I just wanted to visit you myself to see if you had any thoughts about what happened. Sometimes people remember things after the investigators go. I just wanted to see if anything like that happened to you."

"Sorry to say I don't remember anything I didn't tell them. Wish I did, I'd like to see the real perpetrator behind Raymond's death put behind bars. It's a shame they're dragging Candy through all this after losing her husband and having her life turned upside down. I mean, leave the poor woman alone, right?"

I nodded, watching for any tells he was trying to play me. "Do you know anybody who might have had it out for Raymond?"

"No, nothing like that. I also can't say I knew him well. I actually met him through Larry Thompson. He's another one of our poker party. Larry and Raymond used to work together back in the day. Larry left that job, but Raymond stayed if memory serves."

This was all information I knew from the investigator's notes. "So there was never any contention during the poker parties?"

"Goodness no," Bill said, shaking his head as if the thought were ridiculous, "absolutely not. We limited our poker games to $35 a night. Awfully hard to get too worked up about that. We just played for the fun of it." Bill leaned back in his chair. "Once you lose your money, you are out. End of story. It's a hard-fast rule because we want to avoid problems. You lose your money; you're done playing. You can stay and watch, eat some snacks, but you can't get back in."

"So there was never any type of contention between Raymond or any of the others at the poker nights?"

Bill shook his head. "No. Nothing like that."

"Was there any type of conflict outside of the poker meetings?"

"If there was, I was not aware of it."

24

My meeting with Bill Weaver left me unsettled. We didn't talk for long after that. I soon headed out to my car after thanking Tina for helping me to arrange a meeting with him because I didn't know if I would come back. I didn't expect to, but I couldn't rule it out at this stage of my investigation. If I did, I wanted Tina to be just as helpful as she had been today.

I'd been prepared for a contentious conversation when I had gone into my meeting with Bill Weaver. Instead, he had been pleasant and forthcoming. He was either a skilled liar or he had been telling the truth. I couldn't decide which, but I was bothered that I had walked out with a completely different mindset than I had going in.

My experiences with Abe Martin and Bill Weaver could not have been more different. If I had come to Bill Weaver first, I might have stopped there and not bothered to interview any of the other poker players myself, putting it on Winston's task list instead.

The incongruency of the situation nagged at me.

I decided to try one more of the poker buddies to see if he would be a tiebreaker. It seemed Larry Thompson knew Raymond better than Bill Weaver had, so he was a natural next stop.

I was in my car flipping through notes about Larry Thompson on my phone when there was a knock on the driver's side window. I looked up and was surprised to see Bill Weaver standing outside. I immediately turned off my phone and put it down on the passenger seat.

How long had Bill been standing there?

Had he seen anything on my phone?

I tried to remember everything I'd scrolled through but couldn't think of anything I particularly needed to keep secret. I doubted he had seen anything, but it was something to keep in mind.

I was about to unroll my window but then thought better of it. I wanted us to be on the same level if he had something to tell me that pertained to the case.

So I opened my door and got out.

"Sorry to bother you," Bill said. He looked a little nervous, "but I just had something occur to me. It is probably not relevant to your investigation, but I figured I would tell you and let you decide." He took a deep breath. I could tell by how he looked away that he was wondering if maybe he wasn't being a little foolish. "My wife mentioned she once ran into Candy Carlisle." Bill stopped as if thinking about how to word this next part. "Tammy, that's my wife, approached to say hello to Candy, apparently recognizing her from Facebook or something like that. She made some sort of comment about our husbands being friends. I don't know all that was said, but Candy was rude. Tammy came away with an unpleasant taste in her mouth for Ms. Carlisle."

Bill must have noticed my expression because he shrugged. "It's probably nothing. It certainly doesn't seem to relate to your case, but you asked if I'd had any private discussions with Candy, and I haven't. My wife ran into her once, and they talked. That's all, figured I should tell you."

"Thank you, Mr. Weaver," I said. "I appreciate your candor and for telling me about this, even though it doesn't appear to have much relevance."

"I just want to help in any way I can," Bill said, "now, if you'll excuse me, I have a couple of patients in there waiting." He gave me an awkward smile that made me think he regretted coming out before hurrying back into his office.

I didn't know what to make of it. It seemed like an innocuous meeting between Tammy Weaver and Candy Carlisle, but if so, why had Candy been rude?

I got into my car and made a note on my phone to think about it later before pulling up the contact information I had for Larry Thompson. I checked more than once to make sure Bill wasn't coming back out again before leaving.

Ten minutes later, I pulled up to Larry Thompson's place of work.

Unlike Abe Martin and Bill Weaver, Larry Thompson was not self-employed. He worked for a company called Mulvaney Tech. I hesitated about ambushing him at work but didn't want to give Abe Martin or Bill Weaver time to communicate with the others if I could avoid it.

I was unsettled by the different responses I had received from the two poker players.

I needed to determine the truth. The first step was to establish a baseline for the poker players. If Larry was open to my questions, too, I would home in on Abe Martin, considering him to be the aberration.

Karen Brodsky's investigators had focused on Abe Martin, so if my investigation pointed to him, too, that's where I would also put my efforts.

But they got some things wrong. I can't go reaching conclusions prematurely.

I went into the office building and learned that Mulvaney Tech was on the fifth level in suite 502.

I tried to imagine how Larry would respond as I took the elevator up, mentally preparing myself for the abrasiveness I had received from Abe Martin. The notes I had on Larry said he had readily answered questions. There wasn't much else in the file about him, so I assumed the investigators had been satisfied with his answers and moved on to the next potential lead.

I was expecting to do the same thing, though the approach of visiting him at work might yield some interesting results. Karen's investigators had not recorded in their notes where they had met with him. The only thing I had was the date and a brief record of their conversation.

I tried to open the door to Mulvaney Tech when I got to the office suite, but it was locked. A doorbell had a sign that said to ring for assistance, so I pressed the button. A blonde man came strolling up to the door a moment later. He looked annoyed at the interruption. He stopped and stared at me before opening the door.

"Can I help?" His voice was flat, his tone was crisp. He wore ripped jeans and a T-shirt that looked more appropriate for a summer outing than a day at the office. I got the feeling he looked down on me for wearing a suit.

"I'm looking for Larry Thompson," I said with a friendly smile, "he work here?"

The man hesitated before nodding. "One second." A lengthy pause. "You can wait in the lobby if you'd like."

He was already turning to go by the time I stepped inside, striding away at a quick pace as if hoping to make up for the lost time my presence had cost him. There was a receptionist desk but no receptionist. Perhaps she was out, and it bothered him that he had to handle the door.

My eyes were drawn to a television screen hung above the reception area. It cycled through pictures of company employees and advertisements. I learned the blond man was the owner of the small company. He had the audacity to call himself CEO, although this place did not look like it held more than a handful of people.

It wasn't long before Larry Thompson came around the corner. He stopped as soon as he saw me, an unreadable expression on his face.

"Who are you?" Larry asked without making a move to shake my hand or come closer. He folded his arms as he glared at me.

I closed the distance and offered him my hand, which he reluctantly took after a disdainful glance down.

"I'm Mitch Turner," I said. "Do you have a place we can chat in private?"

"What is this about?"

"I'd prefer to tell you when we are alone if that's okay," I said. "If there isn't someplace we can talk here, can we step out into the hallway and find a secluded corner?"

Larry frowned and took a step back as if afraid I was going to assault him. "Am I in some sort of trouble?"

I laughed as I shook my head, hoping to relieve some of the tension. "Nothing like that. I just need a moment of your time if you wouldn't mind."

Larry looked at me through slitted eyes before finally giving a quick nod. "There's a conference room back here. We can chat there."

He turned abruptly and trotted off as if hoping I wouldn't follow. We went down a short hallway and through a door to a small room. It had a round table with four chairs. It smelled like burned popcorn. The furniture looked like it had come from a secondhand store.

"Can you please tell me what this is about?" Larry asked once the door was shut behind us. He didn't make a move towards a seat, so I didn't either.

"I understand you occasionally played poker with Raymond Carlisle."

"Haven't done that in almost a year." Larry's frown deepened as if his worst fears were confirmed.

"Did you know him?" I asked. Even though the answer to this question was implied by what he had already said, I wanted to see if I would get a reaction. Something told me that I would.

A silent snarl formed on Larry's lips. "I just admitted to it, didn't I?"

Admitted to it?

That was an interesting choice of words. Was this a sign of a guilty conscience subliminally rearing its head?

I decided it was as I studied his face.

His tone was way too defensive, too early in our conversation. This was already going much like my conversation with Abe Martin, only a little less hostile. I was surprised I had provoked a reaction so quickly.

My instincts told me that Abe Martin had tipped Larry off to what I was doing, so he was already in a frame of mind to respond like this when I had rung the bell.

If they are hoping to turn me off from investigating them, they're going about it the wrong way. They should have acted more like Bill Weaver.

Maybe Bill Weaver is the outlier.

"Did you know him well?" I asked, reframing my question so it made more sense. My tone said this implication should have been obvious, though I didn't expect him to pick up on my subtlety.

"Only from the games."

Interesting. Was Bill Weaver mistaken about Larry's relationship with Raymond, or was Larry lying?

"I understand you guys met regularly until six months prior to Raymond's death, is that correct?"

"Sounds right."

"But the rest of you kept meeting without him?"

Larry hesitated. "Yes." He answered with reluctance as if he had given up something significant.

"Did he stop coming, or did you guys stop inviting him?"

"I don't remember, to be honest." Larry paused as if in thought. "I think we stopped inviting him, though I don't know for sure. I'm not the one who organized the poker games. You would have to talk to Abe Martin about that." He observed me as he spoke.

So Abe Martin has been talking.

Had he communicated with Bill Weaver before my visit? That changed my view if Bill knew I was poking around ahead of time. Bill Weaver was an excellent communicator, no doubt about that. I would definitely have Winston look into the guy to see what he could find.

"Why would Abe Martin uninvite Raymond?"

Larry shrugged. "I'm not sure that's what happened. You would have to talk to the others. Raymond might have just stopped coming. I never really thought about it. He wasn't a good poker player, so I didn't care. We limit how much money you could play on any night. It wasn't about the money. It was about the fun. Raymond didn't make it fun."

I nodded as if I believed him, though I did not. "What was your first thought when you heard Raymond was murdered?"

"That his wife must've done it." Larry looked happy as if he had said something he had planned beforehand. I doubted he was much of a poker player. He didn't have the face for it.

"What makes you say that?" I asked.

"I dunno, nothing in particular, I guess."

"How—"

"Is this gonna take much longer?" Larry asked, interrupting me. "I really don't have time for this. I also don't appreciate you coming down here to my work and barging in unannounced to ask me questions about things I don't know."

"I just have a few questions," I said placatingly, sensing the end of our interview was close.

"And that's how many I've answered." Larry moved towards the door. "I'm done."

"Were you happy to hear Raymond was dead?"

Larry's hand stopped just above the doorknob as he turned towards me, his hand quivering as his face turned red. He bared his teeth in a silent, feral snarl before he covered them up.

"Why would you ask me that? That's a horrible thing to say."

"You didn't answer my question."

"I will not dignify that with a response. You also didn't answer *my* question."

I nodded. "I'll go first. I asked because you've been hostile to me since the moment I walked in."

"You're trying to pin this on somebody other than your client, aren't you?"

"I never said what I was doing here," I said, not bothering to hide my curiosity.

Larry didn't hesitate because of his slip-up. "I know who you are, Mr. Turner. I've seen your cheap billboards. It didn't take much to put it together."

"I see." I gave him a piercing look. "Are you going to answer my question? I answered yours."

He said nothing.

"Were you happy Raymond was dead?"

"Do you have any reason to believe I would be happy he died?" Larry finally asked through clenched teeth.

"Nothing I can articulate," I said brightly.

"There you go. Now, if you'll excuse me, I really must go."

He was already walking away. I was trying to think of something I could say to detain him for a moment longer when my phone rang. I looked at my smartwatch and did a double-take.

Why is Barbara calling?

I hesitated as Larry stomped away, wondering if I should ask about his poker playing skills.

That probably went too far.

I took out my phone and answered, walking out through the front door of Mulvaney Tech before speaking.

25

"What do you need, Barbara?" I asked as I walked away from Mulvaney Tech, checking over my shoulder to make sure Larry Thompson had not followed me outside. The man had been worked up enough at the end that I would not have put it past him to try something, though I did not think it was a significant risk.

Why was Larry Thompson so angry?

Why had Abe Martin almost thrown me out of his mechanic shop?

And why was Bill Weaver the outlier, portraying a calm demeanor and answering all my questions?

The door clicked shut. I could see through the glass that the reception area was empty. There was still no sign of the receptionist. I imagined Larry Thompson returning to his desk while simmering in his rage. Would his coworkers realize he was upset? Could it be worth my time to track them down to see if I could gain insight into Larry's actions? The CEO who had answered the door would obviously not be any help, but maybe somebody else there might.

Barbara still had not said anything.

"Are you there?" I asked.

I wondered if maybe she had called me by accident and found the thought depressing. I glanced at Mulvaney Tech again and decided I didn't want to have this conversation here, assuming she had meant to call me.

I took the stairs instead of getting into the elevator and risking our connection.

"Barbara?" I said again for a third time without any response.

It's a butt dial.

This was the first time Barbara had reached out since our breakup had been made official. I wanted to maximize the opportunity if she had called me on purpose, though it was looking like an accident.

"Mitch," Barbara finally said, just as I was about to hang up. Her voice was low and quiet and made the hair on my neck stand on end. She was worried. It sounded like she was driving. There was the ticking of her blinker and the crunch of gravel as she made a turn. "Somebody is following me."

I clutched my phone, all thoughts of taking advantage of the situation to renew my relationship with her driven from my head.

"Where are you right now?"

"I'm driving. A gray Honda Civic has been following me for six blocks through two turns." She paused. "I'm sure I've seen it before this week. At least three times."

"What does the driver look like?" I inhaled deeply, trying to calm my heartbeat.

"He is too far away to make out. I'm sure it is a man."

"Can you write down the license number?"

"I don't have a good view. It is several cars back from me right now. I've never seen it closer. They somehow always stay just far enough away that I can't make out the details."

I thought fast about what to do, considering several options and discarding them before settling on one that I thought could work.

"Can you meet me at my office?" I asked as I went down the stairs, taking two at a time while holding onto the rail with my free hand. The last thing I needed was a broken leg because I wasn't paying attention.

"I'm twenty minutes out," Barbara said after a moment.

"I'm twenty-five. Take the long way."

I dashed down the stairs after disconnecting. My heart throbbed in my chest. I wasn't sure if it was more because I'd finally had a phone call from Barbara or because I was worried about her. I was certain both played into it, though I was having a hard time distinguishing between the two emotions. I flew down all five flights of stairs and out to my car, barely remembering anything in passing.

Before her call, I had planned to interview the two remaining poker players, but that was now last on my list.

Abe Martin had gotten to the others anyway, so there was hardly a need now for me to surprise them.

I put my car into gear and tore out of the parking lot, heedless of what anybody might think.

I came to a red light and screeched to a halt. I tapped the wheel impatiently while I thought through the possibilities of who might be following Barbara.

She was a nurse at the local hospital. Perhaps she'd had a patient become obsessed with her.

Then I remembered she had transferred to maternity right before we broke up. That was probably a dead end, though it was still a possibility.

I was the only ex-boyfriend of hers I knew about. She and I had not spent much time talking about our previous relationships, though they had surfaced from time to time. *At least it's a good sign she called me and not her bozo boyfriend.*

The light turned green. I hit the gas, leaving rubber on the street.

The minutes passed slowly, as I made every turn as quick as I could, running lights wherever it was safe and making it back to the office in twenty-two minutes instead of the twenty-five I had promised.

I was lucky I was not pulled over but didn't stop to think about it as I glanced around. Barbara had not yet arrived. I called her on my car's Bluetooth as I parked, dialing the number from memory. It wasn't until after that I remembered I still had her on speed dial.

"How far out are you?" I asked.

"About three minutes."

"I'm here now. I'm going to walk out to the street. I'm going to see who it is when you turn into my parking lot."

"Thank you, Mitch," her voice was quiet. I could tell she was on the edge of panic. It sent a shiver down my back to hear her so afraid.

I pulled out my phone as I got out of my car and ran up the sidewalk toward my building, cutting across the grass to the far side when I got there.

The front door opened.

"Mitch," Ellie called out to me. "Do—"

"Not right out. I'll explain in a moment."

I ran around the back of our building, holding my phone like I was reading the news. In reality, I had pulled up my camera, ready to snap a picture of the gray Honda's license plate.

I looked around but didn't see Barbara approaching yet.

Finally, I saw her.

I twisted my phone and turned in that direction, keeping my head down while lifting my eyes so I could see Barbara. The gray Honda was two cars back. I snapped a picture and then took a dozen more, glancing down at the pictures as I took them. I could clearly identify his license plate in several. I was glad I captured it so easily. I turned after he passed, not caring now if he noticed me. I also switched over to video, rolling footage of the vehicle for as long as I could. I zoomed in on the man, though I didn't expect to get enough to identify him.

Barbara turned into the parking lot. The gray Honda kept going but immediately took a right onto the next street.

I was tempted to run down the street after him, but there was no way I could chase the man down on foot, and I wasn't going to get any better pictures than I already had. I just hoped I had enough information to identify him, so we could take the evidence to the police to get this guy arrested. I wanted to pull up the photos and go through them but headed to the parking lot instead.

I found Barbara parked right next to my car. Her head was in her hands, so she did not notice me approaching.

I tapped lightly on the window with a fingernail, drawing her attention. She tried to force a smile when she saw me but failed miserably.

She opened the door.

"Mitch," she said, "I'm so sorry to call you like this. I know it's not fair for me to do this to you."

"Don't worry about it. Let's talk in my office. We will figure this out."

26

"What's going on, Mitch?" Ellie demanded as I opened the front door. She hid a startled expression when she noticed Barbara was with me.

I gave Ellie a look that I hoped conveyed my desire for her not to ask any more probing questions.

"Just some personal business I must attend to," I said, not wanting to say anything more in front of Barbara. I doubted Barbara wanted other people to know about this situation.

Ellie nodded as if satisfied by my explanation, though I knew she would grill me later for what had really happened.

Ellie and Barbara knew each other tangentially through mutual friends, so it was a good bet Ellie knew Barbara was currently dating somebody else.

Once we were in my office with the door shut behind us, I put my arms around Barbara and held her. She initially resisted my touch but then melted into my arms. That was when I heard a silent sob.

"Mitch," she said in a breathless and quiet voice. "I'm so sorry. I wanted us to have a clean break. That's why I didn't return any of your calls or text messages."

"Don't worry about it," I said, experiencing a rush of memories from when we had dated that I tried without success to put from my mind. "Do you know who that man was?"

She shook her head. "I have no clue. Perhaps it is nothing."

"He followed you for twenty minutes after you called me. That's not nothing. Something is going on. When did you first notice him?"

"Two days ago." Barbara shook her head without releasing me. "I convinced myself it was just my imagination. When I saw him again today, I could no longer tell myself the lie. I didn't know who else to call. That's why I turned to you."

Why not Thomas? I wondered but did not say. I was glad I was the person she had thought of. Perhaps there was something to my guess she still had feelings for me.

"We will get to the bottom of this," I said, "you have nothing to worry about."

"Why are you helping? I didn't think you would take my call."

"This has nothing to do with that," I said firmly. "I always help friends."

With great reluctance, I released her from my arms, knowing that the moment had already passed for me to do it. She was in a relationship with somebody else. I'd had my chance and blown it. Now I had an opportunity to help her. That's what I needed to focus on.

After I released my hold, she stayed a moment longer. Did she want to linger, too?

What was she experiencing right now?

I was reminded of the thought I'd had when we'd run into each other at the restaurant. She was having a tough time letting go. She still was not over me.

I pushed the thought away as I stepped back from her and pulled my phone from my pocket. I set it down by my computer, knowing that the pictures and video I had taken were already uploading to the cloud. I grabbed a guest chair and pulled it around to the back of my desk so Barbara could join me to review the footage.

"I'm getting invited behind the desk," Barbara said lightly, "how often do you do that?"

"Never," I said in about the same tone. I favored her with a smile as I took my seat and motioned for her to sit beside me. I logged in and was soon pulling down the videos and pictures I had taken from the cloud.

"Here's the first pic," I said, blowing it up so we could get a look at the gray Honda Civic.

"That's how I recognized it was him," she said, pointing to the top of the car where the paint had faded, allowing rust to form. "I noticed it two days ago. I thought I saw him yesterday but was not sure. Today, there was no doubt."

"If you thought you saw him yesterday, you almost certainly did. It is safest to assume he is following you all the time."

"But why me?"

"Let's not go there yet. Try to think back to when this first started."

"Oh, Mitch," she said, "I don't think I can do that. I know for sure I saw him last week. I can't think of anything before that."

"Just review in your mind where you've been the last several weeks. Think things through carefully. If you have any pictures you've taken recently, pull them up and see if anything jumps out at you."

"Okay," she said, pulling out her phone, "I'll do that." I resisted the urge to sidle up beside her as she went through her pictures. It wasn't my business, and there were probably pictures of Thomas Guyton on her phone. He was the last thing I want to be reminded of right now.

It was starting to feel like old times.

It was like we had never broken up.

I took hold of myself. I had to guard against these feelings because once we got this sorted out, she would leave, and I would never see her again.

While she was flipping through her pictures, I zoomed in on the license plate and sent a text message to Winston, asking if he could learn what he could.

I zoomed in even further on the picture but could not make out much of the man's features. He appeared to be white. He had either brown or dark-colored hair that was cut close to his head.

"No," Barbara said in a quiet voice, "no, no, no."

I glanced over. "What is it?"

"He hasn't just been following me for a week. It's been a couple months." She held up a picture for me to see.

It was a selfie of her and Thomas. They were at a park. She was pushed up against him.

Barbara pointed to the background.

The car was behind them. It looked empty.

I took her phone and held it up to the picture on my computer monitor, comparing the rust spots. There was no doubt about it.

It was the same car.

"When was this picture taken?"

"Two months ago. Almost to the day."

She was already dating this guy two months ago? She moved on faster than I expected.

I dismissed the thought without entertaining it further.

"All right," I said, "so we've learned that this has been going on for some time, far longer than we thought. Let's now see what else we can figure out about this guy. I pointed to the picture on my computer. "Does he seem familiar to you in any way?" I zoomed in further to give her a better feel for his face though the picture was becoming pixelated.

Barbara leaned in close, brushing up beside me. "I don't recognize him."

I moved onto the next photo and zoomed in again on the head, but it was not that much better than the first. We went through picture by picture. Some were clearer but didn't have a good angle to give us a solid view of the man himself.

I finally came to the pictures of the car from behind. I noticed a spot of rust on the rear of the car that I pointed out. "That will be useful to identify him from the back. Burn it into your memory."

"I'll never forget it."

I brought up the video and pressed play, zooming in on the man. I could easily tell now that his hair was dark brown, though I could make out little else. "You recognize him?"

Barbara shook her head. "Nothing." She looked at me. "Mitch, what am I gonna do about this?"

I opened my mouth, intending to tell her that I hoped to have an identity for the driver soon when my phone dinged with a text message. I picked it up.

"Bad news," I said, "my investigator just got back to me. Those license plates were reported stolen three months ago."

27

Barbara looked like she had just been slapped in the face. "Three months?" She shook her head. "You mean to tell me that this yahoo has been stalking me for three months? That's impossible. That's just when I started dating...."

She trailed off and looked at me. "Didn't mean to get personal on you." She looked at her phone. The screen had turned off, so it no longer displayed the picture of her cuddling Thomas. "I didn't think about how any of this might affect you. I should've gone to somebody else, Mitch." She glanced away. "I just didn't know who else to trust."

I shrugged as if it were no big deal, though, I was happy to hear she trusted me. "I'm glad you called. I'm happy to help."

Barbara studied me as if trying to determine if I was jealous of her relationship.

"Is there some reason you suspect this could be connected to Thomas Guyton?"

Barbara went pale. "I didn't say that."

"You implied it. As soon as you heard that those license plates were stolen three months ago, you immediately thought that this might be about Thomas. If there is not a conscious connection, there is a subconscious one. You must probe it. See where it goes. There is a reason why you said that."

Barbara bit her lip. "I suppose I did, didn't I?"

"What does Thomas do for a living?"

"He's an investment banker."

"Does he have any enemies you're aware of?"

She shook her head. "No. Nothing like that."

"Perhaps it's just the timing," I suggested. "Maybe it's a coincidence."

I said this last part because I didn't want her to believe I was biased against her current boyfriend.

I already didn't like the guy. He had come off smarmy when I'd met him, and the fact her first thought had immediately connected him to this confirmed my worst fears about him.

She nodded. "It has to be happenstance. I can't imagine somebody would follow me just because I am dating Thomas."

Or maybe Thomas is having somebody follow you, I thought. It was an obvious possibility, but I wondered if it wasn't just my jealousy talking. *If that's the case, he's gonna be very interested that you just came to the office of your ex-boyfriend.*

I took my thoughts to their next logical place.

If he was depraved enough to have somebody follow Barbara, what else was he capable of doing? Did he have a bug on her? Was he listening to our conversation right now?

The thought seemed paranoid, but I didn't dismiss it out of hand. I would wait until I knew more about Thomas Guyton before I made a judgment on it.

Until then, I would assume this guy was far more capable of depravity than was apparent.

I would also have Winston look into Thomas Guyton. I'd pay for it myself and never tell Barbara unless I found something interesting.

Isn't that crossing a line?

I shook my head. It wasn't.

Not when the health and well-being of Barbara was involved.

"What are you thinking, Mitch?" Barbara asked, breaking into my thoughts. "I saw you just shake your head. You're thinking something."

"It is not important," I said, "we need to track this guy down. Luckily for us, we have everything we need right here."

Barbara looked at me expectantly.

I was glad she hadn't asked followup questions because I didn't want to lie to her. I also didn't want to tell her what I was planning to do.

"You."

Barbara inhaled. "Excuse me?"

"You're what we need. I'll have somebody follow you to catch him."

28

I made the arrangements fast. Before I knew it, Barbara was heading out of my office. Winston was going to follow her home and run surveillance on her apartment throughout the night.

Barbara had offered to pay for his services, but I insisted that I'd handle it myself.

I walked Barbara out to her car, opened her door, and was just about to lean in to kiss her goodbye before I stopped myself. She looked disappointed that I had not gone through with it. It only lasted for a moment before she remembered our present relationship status. She shook her head and muttered something I didn't catch.

"Thank you, Mitch." She looked up at me. "For everything."

"Think nothing of it."

I wanted to watch her drive away but decided against it just in case we were presently under surveillance. I didn't want to give her stalker further ammunition to think of me as a problem.

I should've let her walk out by herself, I thought as I went back inside. The door opened before I got there.

Ellie was angry. "What was that about?"

"Not now, Ellie. I have a lot on my mind."

Ellie shook her finger at me. "Are you getting involved with her again, Mitch Turner? You aren't gonna break her heart again, are you?"

I was taken aback.

"No."

"You had better not. She had a difficult time after leaving you."

"Oh?" I gave her an expectant look, wanting her to say more.

"You are not getting information out of me. You ran her through the wringer. You don't need to do that twice."

I didn't know how to respond. I wasn't aware Ellie was so well-informed about my past relationship with Barbara. We usually kept our personal lives to ourselves. And while I did know more about what was going on with Ellie, I wasn't ready to exchange in kind. It felt wrong to talk to Ellie about my relationships, though I could not say why.

"Did you have something for me?" I asked gruffly before regretting my tone.

Ellie bristled. "Frank Ward called."

"Which case?"

"The Carlisle matter."

I nodded. "Did he have anything to say?"

"He just wanted you to call him back."

I started to head into my office before I stopped. "Is that why you were chasing me down?"

"No," Ellie said, "it's not important now."

I stared at Ellie, wondering what the issue could have been but decided I was hardly in a position to dig it out if she didn't want to share, not when I had just declined to share with her.

I started towards my office again but turned back. "I don't mean to be all cloak and dagger with you. I'll tell you what's going on at some point. It's just a bit sensitive right now." I ran my fingers through my hair. "And the truth is, I really don't know what's going on myself."

"Are you two getting back together?" Ellie asked.

"No, nothing like that."

Ellie stared at me before nodding. "See that you don't."

Once I had my office door shut, I wondered at Ellie's reaction to seeing me with Barbara.

Surely things had not been so bad for Barbara as Ellie represented?

Barbara and I'd had difficulty nailing down our relationship status or talking about the future, but wasn't that an issue for everybody? Why was Ellie treating me like I had done something horrible to Barbara?

But didn't you? The question came unbidden to my mind. *Didn't you string her along for months, barely paying attention to her, choosing instead to focus on your practice?*

She had been willing to commit. I hadn't.

When I was finally ready, it had been too late.

My phone beeped. It was Ellie. "I got Winston on the phone," she said, "you want to talk to him?"

"Send him through."

Click.

"I'm following Barbara," Winston said, "I'm about six or seven cars back. I don't see any sign of your guy in the gray Honda."

"Anything in the cars around you look suspicious?"

"Too early to tell. I've made mental notes on all of them and will pay attention to any that follow for too long."

"Perfect."

"I also have an update for you on the Carlisle matter," Winston said, "you want it now, or do you want to wait till tomorrow when I'm not driving?"

"Give it to me now."

"We can cross Ian Mercer off the list."

"Why do you say that?"

"I just haven't found any current connections between Candy and him. They may have dated in high school, but they have not communicated since. Maybe we cross him off in pencil in case something pops up to change our minds, but I'm just not seeing a connection. Did you ever ask Candy for a copy of the message she claimed to receive from him?"

"I'll do it today."

"I doubt you'll get it. I've also been through all the information we have on David Washington's travel activities. It appears he was in town when Raymond was murdered. I still like him as our top suspect. Did you want me to visit him?"

"No," I said, "gather more information on him first before we do that. I want to establish a motive before we talk to him." I was finding it difficult to change my thinking from Barbara's situation to Candy Carlisle's case. My gears were stuck, and I couldn't get them to shift.

I hesitated. Now was probably the time for me to fill Winston in on Abe Martin and the poker boys, but I held off. I was certain there was something there, but I didn't have anything to report other than a couple of conversations with some angry guys who appeared to be hiding something.

"Have you tracked down Evangeline Brewer yet?" I asked, remembering another suspect in that line of the investigation.

"Yes, she's here in the city. I have a full workup on her now. I have also confirmed she messaged Raymond as Candy claimed. His email and social media logins were in the notes we got from Brodsky. Perhaps they didn't know what to look for because it doesn't appear they found it. I haven't interviewed Evangeline yet either. Didn't know if you wanted me to do that."

"Send me her information," I said, "let me review what you have before we decide on a next step."

"Will do."

"Let's meet tomorrow while Barbara is at work. Does 4:00 PM work?"

"I'll be there."

"And Winston," I said, "take good care of her for me, will you?"

"Better believe I will, Mitch."

29

My hands shook from all the adrenaline rushing through my body after I hung up with Winston. My heart thundered in my chest, threatening to escape of its own accord. It had been a whirlwind hour. I was feeling overwhelmed by everything I had going on.

I took a deep breath and exhaled, trying to gather my thoughts and understand my emotions.

It's Barbara.

It's my past feelings for her that's messing me up.

I pulled out a small notepad of paper and made a list of the things I needed to get done before the end of my day. Putting it all down on paper helped calm my mind and reframe my focus, allowing me to function.

This business with Barbara was getting to me worse than I had expected. It took me a moment to realize what was bothering me.

I'd been fine when she had been here because she had been safe. But knowing that she was out there with some sicko stalking her made it difficult for me to concentrate or think about anything else. I wanted to catch up to Winston and sit in the car with him all night, keeping watch on Barbara, so I knew she was okay.

But that wasn't my place.

I wasn't trained to do that. And chances were good it would bother Barbara if she found out that I had done something like that.

I already have one stalker, I imagined her saying, *I don't need another.*

No, the best thing I could do was continue to work on my cases so that I would have a fresh mind if any new issues arose with Barbara.

It had never before bothered me before that I was not usually the person doing the actual fieldwork, but I now envied Winston as he sat outside Barbara's apartment looking for signs of this weirdo.

I stood and paced, hoping that would calm my nerves, but it just seemed to agitate me further.

I eventually forced myself to sit at my desk to tackle my list.

My first order of business was to call Candy Carlisle to see if she could produce proof of this communication she had received from Ian Mercer.

I didn't know everything Winston did to track down information, but I doubted it existed if he had not found evidence of recent exchanges between Ian Mercer and Candy Carlisle. Candy didn't answer, so I left a message, asking her to call me back without telling her what I wanted.

I dialed Frank Ward. He answered on the first ring and immediately got down to business.

"Mitch, I heard you picked up the Carlisle case. That right?"

"I'm her new attorney."

"I just wanted to touch base about the upcoming trial." He paused as if expecting me to say something, but he continued when I did not fill the silence. "I expect now that the negotiations I was having with Karen are off the table. Is that correct?"

"What were you guys talking about?" I asked, wondering if this information had been lost in the transition. Detective Bernie Lee had claimed Frank had offered twenty. Karen might have mentioned something about this in passing, but she had not said anything about it specifically.

I could practically see Frank smile on the other end of the phone. My instincts told me he wanted a plea bargain.

He had been a little too hopeful when he asked the question.

Frank was not afraid of going to court, but if he wanted a deal, it was usually a sign there were weaknesses in his case that he was worried about. It was the open and shut cases that he liked to take to trial because it was easy to come off as a hero fighting for justice in those situations. It was much more complicated if the facts were murky.

Karen Brodsky had been practicing as a defense attorney long enough that she should have known this about Frank. Perhaps I needed to rethink my assessment of Karen and her practice. I was not as impressed with her as I had been at the start of all of this. She might have a stellar reputation, but she had missed some significant things in the Carlisle matter.

Of course, it was always easier to come behind somebody and see their mistakes. I would give Karen the benefit of the doubt for as long as I could. But I had referred many potential clients to her over the years because of her reputation. I just hoped it was deserved.

Maybe this Candy Carlisle matter had gone off the tracks because of the supposed personality differences between Karen and her client. That sort of thing happened.

"We were talking about twenty-five years. That sound like something your client would be interested in?"

"I'll run it past her." I hesitated on purpose, wanting to dangle the bait in front of Frank. "But is that the best you can do?"

"Are we renewing negotiations, or are you just shaking the tree?"

"A little of both. I'm new to this case, so I want to keep options on the table, I'm sure you understand."

"Of course, I get it. I'd do the same thing in your shoes. I could probably get down to twenty, but that's if we start talking a deal this next week. After that, it is going to be much more difficult."

"Got it."

I wrote a note about this down on my checklist, so I didn't forget to talk to Candy about it. I would have to be careful in approaching the issue.

Frank cleared his throat. "I hear you're no longer dating Barbara Sampson."

I froze in my seat and leaned back, putting my phone on speaker, so I had my hands free.

This had come out of left field.

Frank and I had never talked about our personal lives. As long as we had known each other, both here and at the prosecutor's office, we had never talked about anything other than work.

"Why did you bring that up?" I asked. A sixth sense told me that something was going on here that I was not aware of.

"Forget I said anything," Frank said as if distracted by something. I could hear papers rustling on his desk.

Why did Frank mention this?

How does he know?

Frank was all business, all the time. If he knew anything about my relationship with Barbara, it was because there was a work connection to it somewhere. Coincidences occasionally happened, but it was just too much of a coincidence for me to believe that Frank had just asked about it randomly on the same day I had learned somebody was stalking her. There had to be a reason he had mentioned it.

Were the police investigating Barbara for a crime? Was the man I had spotted in the Honda a detective, hoping to find evidence to charge her with something?

But would a detective use stolen plates to hide his identity?

That seemed unlikely.

I rubbed my fingers on the side of my head as I tried to think of anything Barbara could have done that they might investigate her for. She was as clean as they came when it came to the law. I had never seen her speed. She had never done illegal drugs, not even one time, not even experimenting a little in college.

She didn't drink, so there was no chance of a DUI.

Why would the prosecutor's office be investigating her?

Unless it has something to do with Thomas Guyton.

A light clicked on.

This was the connection I should have made immediately. When Barbara had learned her stalker had stolen license plates three months ago, her first thought had been Thomas Guyton.

If the prosecutor's office were investigating Thomas Guyton for something, they would know he was dating Barbara. Barbara and I had been together for two years before breaking up. Word did get around about those sorts of things, but Frank and I did not run in the same social circles, so it was unlikely he had come across this information socially.

I closed my eyes. Perhaps Barbara and I had run into Frank somewhere. Maybe I had introduced them. I seemed to have a distant memory of something like that happening. Frank had a good memory. What if he remembered Barbara and then later discovered that she was dating Thomas Guyton because they were investigating him?

"Frank," I said, wondering how much I should push. If it was an active investigation, he wasn't going to say much. Chances were that he had slipped up.

I frowned.

Or perhaps he had mentioned it, hoping to throw me off guard to weasel some sort of advantage in the Carlisle case.

“I should never have brought it up.”

The way Frank said this made me feel like it was something he had planned. I was convinced Frank was trying to throw me off my game.

I tossed out a question to see if I could confirm my theory.

“How do you know that I’m no longer dating Barbara?”

“Nevermind.” Was that satisfaction in his voice? Did he feel like he had successfully baited me? “It’s not important, Mitch. I gotta run. I have another meeting. Let me know what your client says about the offer.”

The line went dead.

30

Things were not making sense. I had learned over my years as a practicing attorney that it was best to treat this like a clue instead of getting frustrated. It was easy to think about in theory, much harder to do in practice. I might never find a satisfying answer to why Frank had brought this up or what had tipped him off to the change in my personal relationship with Barbara.

Frank had been hoping to put me off step, but maybe he had done me a favor.

I had been concerned my jealousy was making me suspect Thomas Guyton, but Frank's comment had given me something more substantial I could point to as a justification to investigate Barbara's boyfriend. It was no longer just my instincts telling me that Thomas Guyton was problematic.

There was no reason for the prosecutor's office to investigate Barbara. She was clean as a whistle and always would be.

Thomas Guyton, on the other hand? I knew nothing about him.

Maybe I should buy Frank lunch, I mused as I did an internet search on Thomas Guyton. The thought made me smile because I could use it as an opportunity to annoy Frank in the same way he had me. I could tell him thanks for the help but not tell him what he had done.

An internet search didn't turn up much about Thomas. I went to Facebook, intending to check Barbara's account, but something stopped me.

Do I want to see what she has posted during the last six months?

What if she had made posts comparing Thomas to me? Maybe there wasn't anything direct, but what were the chances there was something implying her new boyfriend was better than her last?

I would not have normally been concerned about anything like that affecting me, but Barbara walking back into my office again had had an unexpected effect. I couldn't risk letting it affect me further.

I picked up my phone to call Winston to ask him to look into Thomas Guyton when my phone beeped, indicating Ellie was trying to contact me.

"Yes, Ellie, what is it?"

"Candy Carlisle is on the phone."

I took a moment to shift gears back to Candy's case. My mind didn't want to make the jump, but I forced it to.

"Mitch, are you there?" Ellie asked.

"Send her through." I waited for the click. "Candy, how are you?"

"You called?" Candy asked without answering my question. It sounded like she was in a car driving.

"I have a couple things for you," I said looking down at my list, wondering what the best approach would be. I hadn't expected to get an offer from Frank when I called him back, so I had not yet given thought to how I wanted to present this to Candy. My instincts told me I needed to be careful. Maybe it would be sufficient if I laid out the facts as they had happened.

"First, I got a call from the prosecutor."

"What did he have to say?"

"It sounds like Karen was talking to him about a plea bargain." I was about to ask if Candy had been aware of this but decided to just get on with it. "He offered twenty-five but said if we started discussions this week, he might go down as low as twenty."

There was a very long pause on the phone. I made a fist because I knew I had just made a mistake. Perhaps I should have asked Candy to come to the office for this conversation or suggested we meet at a restaurant. Telling her over the phone while she was driving was the wrong thing to do.

"Are you saying I should take this?" Candy demanded. I heard squealing rubber and imagined her speeding through a stop sign or taking a sharp turn. Maybe I should've at least waited until she was done driving to have this conversation.

"No, but as your attorney, I must pass along all offers. It's always your decision what to do with them."

"How many times do I have to say it to you guys! I don't want a plea bargain. I didn't do this. How can you even suggest—"

"I'm doing my job," I said, cutting her off. "I'm required by law to pass all offers on to you. I can't—"

"I don't want to hear anything more about an offer. Do you understand?"

"You can want that, but I still have to tell you."

"Mitch. Can I call you Mitch?"

"Sure."

"I fired Karen because she wasn't doing what I told her to do."

I laughed.

Candy somehow thought she was threatening me. If she walked, I would be just fine, ecstatic even. I was now at a point in my career where the last thing I needed was a cantankerous client.

She seemed taken aback but persevered. "Isn't that what you're supposed to do, what I tell you?"

"No, it's not as simple as that. I have legal and ethical obligations I must meet in addition to representing your interests. Everything I do has to be within the confines of the law. I am legally required to pass along all offers."

"I'll sign whatever I need to sign, just don't tell me about any more offers."

I considered her suggestion but decided against it. Not only was I uncertain whether such a waiver would hold up in court, but it would also be bad practice to ever agree to such a thing, enforceability issues notwithstanding.

"No, I'm not gonna draft up a document like that. Right now, I am hard at work investigating your case, following up on potential suspects who might have done this to your husband, trusting that you told me the truth when you claimed you didn't do it. However, there is always the outside possibility you are lying to me. Or the day may come when there is no better alternative but to consider a plea."

"Mitch—" Her voice was sharp, but I cut her off anyway.

"Candy, listen. If I'm going to represent you, you have to understand how I work. I will do my best to zealously represent you in court. Or in negotiations. I will also do my best to tell you the truth. I'm not going to agree in advance to withhold critical information from you because you feel you aren't in a place to hear it. That is a bad road to go down, and I'm not even going to consider it."

"Mitch—" She was like a pot ready to boil over, but I didn't care.

"I'm not done yet. If you want to go back to Karen Brodsky, that's just fine. If you want to find somebody else, that's fine, too. But as long as I'm the attorney representing you, we will play by the rules. I'm not going to babysit you. I'm not going to sugarcoat things for you. I'm not going to withhold information from you. You are going to get the straight truth every time I feel like you should hear it. Do you understand me?"

Candy was silent for several seconds. "Are you finished?"

Her tone told me that she was indeed thinking of firing me. I would be perfectly okay if she did. I had found some good suspects. I would document them thoroughly for her next attorney to follow up on.

"I'm only half done," I said, digging in further because I didn't like her condescending tone. "I don't know why you fired Karen. I didn't ask too many questions about it because I believe people have the right to an attorney of their choosing. You chose me. That means I'm always going to tell you the truth. If I think we should consider a plea bargain, I'll tell you. If I think we should take it to court, I'll tell you. If I think it's a bad idea to take it to court, I'll tell you that, too. You will always get my full unvarnished opinion. Do you want to know why I took this case in the first place?" I paused, thinking she might try to interject, but she didn't. "I didn't take it for you. I took it for your children. I had to live with a father in prison. It was just part of my growing up experience. I don't want your kids to go through that if you didn't do this."

No matter how terrible of a client you are, I thought, briefly considering saying that but refraining.

I had pushed hard, but I was done.

"Mitch," she said, her voice more composed but still acidic. "I'm being difficult, aren't I?"

I said nothing. I didn't need to.

"I will not apologize. I believe you have the best shot of getting me out of this."

"Great," I said, treating the matter as if it were closed. "On to my next thing. I need proof of the communication you received from Ian Mercer."

"I don't know that I can find that."

Surprise. Surprise.

"Right now, my investigator is telling me there is no proof of any communications between you and Ian Mercer within the last few years. If this is true, it saves me time because I don't have to consider him as a viable suspect any longer. The only reason I was considering him was because of your claim that he reached out, wanting to get back together. If that never happened, you can save me time and you money."

Candy hesitated. I could tell she was thinking it over.

"I am usually quite patient with my clients, at least initially while they are getting over the shock of having their life turned upside down. Many come from difficult circumstances. They are now learning how to face situations they never thought they'd have to face. If you have misspoken or misrepresented this to me, now is the time to tell me."

Further silence.

"And I will not hold it against you—this time. But from now on, you need to be completely forthcoming. If it was a story you just told to explain why you were conflicted about your husband's death, drop it. I need the unvarnished truth."

"I'll find the direct message he sent me. I think it was on Facebook."

She hung up.

31

I walked into my office early the next morning, rubbing my eyes while trying to wake up. It had been a long uncomfortable night. Knowing I wasn't likely to sleep, I had stayed up late working on the Candy Carlisle matter from my home office, hoping that would distract me enough to get some rest, but I'd had no such luck. I had not been the slightest bit tired when I'd finally gone to bed, even though just minutes before I'd had trouble keeping my eyes open while reading reports from Karen Brodsky's investigators.

At one point, I figured I hadn't slept anyway, so I might as well track down Winston to sit in his car so he could sleep. Luckily, I had rolled over instead of giving in to the urge. I didn't want Barbara to come down and see me sitting outside.

I already have one stalker...

I finally dozed in the early hours of the morning. It couldn't have been for longer than thirty minutes, but it was better than nothing. It was obvious I would not fall asleep again when I'd awoken just before 4:30 AM, so I'd gotten ready for the day.

I had pulled through a fast-food joint on my way to work and picked up a breakfast of greasy sausage biscuits and a large Coke. I set them down on my desk but was too antsy to eat.

Everything from the day before had rolled around my mind during the night, but it had been my concern for Barbara that had kept me awake.

I took a long pull on my Coke and forced myself to take out a sausage biscuit. I munched on it.

My phone rang. Winston.

"I have him," Winston said in a quiet voice before I could say anything. "The gray Honda you took pictures of yesterday is back. What do you want me to do?"

I put my biscuit down and tried to think about what the next step ought to be.

"Can you think of any laws he's broken?"

"Stolen license plates."

It was an indication of how tired I was that I had not figured that out myself. "It's enough to at least have the cops arrest him so we can get some identification."

"Precisely. Want me to call them?"

I would have normally agreed, but I was cautious because of my conversation with Frank.

"I have a different idea. I'll call you back."

I leaned back in my chair and took another long sip of my Coke as I thought about my next step. I'd told Winston I'd had a plan, but now that I thought about it, I wasn't sure it was a good idea to go through with it. My instinct had been to call Detective Stephanie Gray to have her facilitate the pickup of the stalker, but what were the chances she was the one running the investigation on Thomas Guyton?

She was one of the few detectives of whom I could say I had a neutral relationship that sometimes bordered on the positive. Most everybody else had a grudge or was prejudiced against me. It wasn't easy being a defense attorney because it was my job to come after the fact and carefully scrutinize the work they had done.

That was not to say Stephanie liked me.

She and I had dated in law school, and it had not ended well. Over the years, the memory of that had faded. Stephanie at least saw me as a person, rather than just a defense attorney who was trying to get criminals out of jail.

I didn't have long to stew on the decision. My instincts told me to call Stephanie, so I went with it. A moment later, her phone was ringing. I hoped I wasn't waking her up. I checked my watch and cringed when I saw it wasn't even 6:00 AM yet.

"Mitch," Stephanie said crisply. From her tone, it was evident she had been awake for some time. "What do you need?"

This was typical of her. She didn't engage in much chitchat, not even when we had dated. She was focused and down to business. These qualities made her a good detective. They would have also made her a good prosecuting attorney if she had decided to go that route. She had once confided in me that she couldn't see herself sitting behind a desk, so it had been no surprise when she had elected to go to the police academy after she had passed the bar.

"I need a favor," I said, trying to remember if I currently owed her one or if she owed me one. I couldn't remember for sure, but it seemed like I owed her. I would now owe two.

"This isn't a good time, Mitch. I'm just finishing up with a scene. What is it?"

"Remember Barbara Sampson?"

"Your girlfriend?"

"Ex-girlfriend, now. She has somebody stalking her. We have located him. He's currently sitting outside her apartment waiting for her to come down."

"What laws has he broken?"

"When Winston checked on his license plates, they came back stolen."

"You want this guy picked up, so you know who to file the restraining order against, that it?"

"Basically."

"I'll send a couple of uniforms."

"Actually, that's the reason I am calling for the favor." I paused, thinking over what I was going to say next. It was a gamble, but nothing ventured, nothing gained. I would probably not have taken this risk for somebody else, but this was for Barbara. I owed it to her to figure out what was going on. "Her boyfriend, Thomas Guyton, is currently the subject of a criminal investigation. I don't want this to become an issue."

There was a long pause on the other end.

"Where did you hear about that?" Stephanie asked as if uncertain she had heard me correctly.

Bingo. I do owe Frank lunch.

I would wait until all this had blown over so he did not connect the dots.

"Don't worry about it. I just don't want it to become an issue. Barbara is as good as they come. She doesn't deserve to be dragged into anything."

Stephanie sighed. "Okay, I'll be there. You have a PI on site?"

"Winston."

"I'll let you know once it's done."

I tried to eat but could not.

Barbara's apartment was fifteen minutes away. If I hurried, I might make it in time to watch Stephanie make the arrest.

I grabbed my Coke and ran for the door.

32

I missed it. I must have arrived just after Stephanie left. The gray Honda was empty, and Winston stood outside the car doing something on his phone. I headed towards him after I parked, wondering what Barbara would think if she noticed me outside her apartment building.

I'm being paranoid, I thought. *She wanted me to catch this guy. That's what I'm doing. It's not weird I'm here.*

Winston put his phone to his ear and turned. When he saw me, he took it down and pressed the screen, presumably disconnecting a call he had just placed to me.

"You just missed Detective Gray," he said, motioning towards the Gray Honda.

"It go okay?"

"Couldn't have gone better. Our perp stepped right out when she knocked on the window. He didn't try to resist arrest. He also didn't have much to say. Stephanie locked the car before she left and said she'd have somebody pick it up." Winston looked around as if checking for an eavesdropper. "That, of course, won't stop me from getting inside if you want to take a peek."

It was tempting.

"You get pictures of the guy?"

Winston handed me his phone. I flipped through a couple but didn't recognize him, though I could tell from his silhouette that it was the same guy who had been following her yesterday. "Can you send me those?"

"Already have."

"Anything visible from outside?"

"No, but I took pictures anyway. I figured you might want them. I sent those to you, too."

"When did he show up?" I asked, stepping up to the Honda while pulling out my phone so I could compare the pictures I had taken the day before with the rust spots on the car. They were a match. There was no doubt about it. This was the same vehicle.

Winston glanced at his watch. "Almost an hour ago."

I frowned when I got to the license plates.

They were different.

Had our suspect noticed me taking pictures of him? Had he stolen new plates, thinking that was enough to hide his identity?

Or did he regularly rotate his plates?

Why drive such a recognizable car if he is smart enough to swap license plates?

This bothered me.

Hopefully, Stephanie would get additional information to shed light on what he was doing.

If she's even willing to tell me what she learns. I may have unintentionally helped her investigation into Thomas Guyton.

Even though Winston had already taken pictures, I snapped a few as well from nonobvious angles, making sure to get the new license plate numbers.

I didn't expect to find anything useful, but I could take pictures now. I couldn't come back and take pictures after the car was towed.

I squatted down beside the car and tried to place myself inside as if looking up through the windshield at the building. He had an unobstructed view of the two windows that belonged to Barbara's apartment. The blinds were both shut, but he would've known she was up if any lights had been on when he arrived. There was now too much light to tell if she was awake.

How often did this guy come?

What did he want with Barbara?

I turned back to the vehicle, hoping to find something that would help me understand why he was doing this, but it was mostly empty. There was a six-pack of unopened beer in the back. He also had a backpack right next to it.

What's in that backpack?

My instincts told me there would be something inside to explain what was going on.

I was looking over at Winston, thinking of taking him up on his offer to break into the car, when I heard somebody approaching, so I waited for them to pass.

I would not normally consider such a thing, but I was worried about Barbara. I was willing to cross some boundaries if it meant we got answers.

While I was glad Stephanie had arrested this guy, there was no guarantee she would tell me what she learned. She would probably tell me this guy's identity so that we could get a restraining order, but it might stop there.

What has Barbara gotten herself into?

"I thought that was you."

Speak of the devil.

Winston and I both turned as Barbara approached. She was fully dressed and even had on her makeup. She was an early riser, something the stalker likely knew. My eyes narrowed. Or had he known she was getting up earlier today than normal?

"Is that his car? Did you guys get him?"

I nodded. "Detective Gray just took him away."

That earned me a look from Barbara, but she didn't follow it up with a question, so I didn't elaborate. She knew about my past with Detective Gray. Barbara could sometimes be the jealous type, but as she was seeing somebody else at the moment, she didn't have room to complain. It was interesting for me to get a taste of her perspective. I had never experienced much jealousy with any of the women I had dated, not until I'd seen Barbara with Thomas.

"Do we know why he was following me?"

I shook my head. "No, I expect Stephanie will question him. She may or may not tell us what she finds. I will get his identity from her so we can get the paperwork put together to file a restraining order."

"Is that going to be good enough?" Barbara asked as she peered inside the Honda. "I can't believe this creep has been following me for three months."

"We don't know that for sure," I said, "all we know is that the original license plates were stolen three months ago and that you have a picture with his car in the background."

I studied Barbara as she examined the vehicle, wondering what she knew about Thomas Guyton.

Did she suspect he was up to something that could get him in trouble with the law? These types of questions could often be just under the surface, waiting for the right event to pull them up.

Was that happening to her? Were there subconscious doubts percolating up?

I wasn't so sure I liked my position in all this. Was I the best person to help? Wouldn't it be smarter for me to have one of my partners do the paperwork? The ideal candidate was Veronica, but I knew she liked to charge through the nose for these things.

It would be cheaper if I handled it myself.

But what about the long run?

I then asked myself the question that I realized had been skimming just under the surface of my subconscious.

What are the chances of further legal complications?

I had confirmed the police were looking into Thomas Guyton, but I didn't know why.

I didn't want to be the man to tell Barbara that her current boyfriend was under investigation for unknown reasons. In fact, if I did tell her, there was a good chance it would get back to Thomas. If he were up to something, he would then lay low or change what he was doing.

And if he was a bad actor, I wanted to make sure the police figured out what he was up to so Barbara didn't make the mistake of staying with this guy long-term.

I would not tell Barbara anything unless I had something concrete and maybe not even then. I didn't want her blaming me for the bad news.

Barbara stepped back from the car. "I see nothing here that answers my questions. Hopefully, Detective Gray will get something out of him."

"Even if not, we will soon know who he is so we can keep tabs on him."

My phone rang. I glanced at my watch and saw that it was Candy.

"I have to take this," I said, "be right back." I walked out of earshot before answering.

"I didn't expect you to answer so early," Candy said. "I was just going to leave you a voicemail. If I had known you would answer, I would've waited until a reasonable hour." A pause. "I found it."

It took me a moment to figure out what she was talking about. The communication I had asked for from Ian Mercer.

"Can you forward a copy to my email?"

"Already sent. It's a screenshot. It was on Facebook."

"I'll take a look." I assumed our conversation was over, but she went on.

"Perhaps we should talk about yesterday," she said. "I'm under pressure. I'm stressed. It wasn't my intention to get worked up. It's just I want you working hard on my case, not thinking you're gonna get me a plea bargain. I know I didn't do this. I want to prove it. I don't even want to think about an offer. If I am convicted, I'm going to fight it with everything I have until the day I die."

"I'm doing everything I can," I said, glancing back at Barbara and Winston, wondering if that was true. Was I letting this mess with Barbara distract me? Was it taking me off my game?

"That's all I ask."

"Were you looking all night?" I asked, stifling a yawn.

"No, I had some things come up. I had to be up early this morning anyway to get the kids ready for school and take care of some other stuff. I knew if I didn't do it now, it would be a day or two before I got to it again. I want you to be like a bulldog who will not let go of this. I don't want to slow you down."

I closed my eyes to focus on Candy's case. Candy had no way of knowing what was going on with Barbara, but perhaps she had subconsciously picked up on my distraction. It had only been for the last day, not even twenty-four hours, but Candy was right about me needing to be a bulldog. That was how I treated all my cases, and I was at risk of not doing it on this one because of what was currently going on with my ex-girlfriend.

Right before all of this had happened, I had been zeroing in on Raymond's poker buddies. Abe Martin's behavior had been unexplainable, and Larry Thompson's hostility was disconcerting. My instincts told me there was something I needed to dig up before I would be satisfied. Now that I had my bearings, I had a few questions for Candy.

"Have any of Raymond's old poker buddies been in contact with you? Did they send flowers or go to the funeral?"

"No. I haven't heard one word from them." Candy paused. I could tell she was thinking about something. "Karen said she didn't think there was anything there. Do you have a different assessment?"

"Too early to say. Did Raymond ever talk about them?"

"No, it was just something he did to relieve pressure. I don't think he ever did anything with them outside of their regular poker night. I always assumed they complained about their wives because he was usually furtive about answering questions whenever I asked."

"Did you know any of their wives?"

"No."

"Did you ever meet any of them?"

Candy thought about it. "I don't think so. If I did, it was certainly unremarkable, so I don't remember it."

"Did you ever, by chance, run into one at the grocery store or someplace like that?"

"If I did, I certainly wouldn't have recognized them. Is there a reason you're asking me these questions?"

"Just covering all the bases. I want to make sure there isn't anything you have forgotten. So you've met none of their wives or girlfriends?"

"Can't say I have. Why?"

"I'm just looking into the poker boys as possible suspects."

"You think one of their wives had something to do with it?"

"No, just following up on a bit of information I heard. Nothing more."

"I assume you're being vague on purpose?"

"Exactly. Let me know if you remember anything at all about his poker buddies. It doesn't matter how unimportant or inconsequential it might seem. Every last bit of information you know might be useful."

"I'll do it, but I don't want you to expect much. I'm pretty sure I won't recall anything."

"I take it you are officially not interested in the prosecutor's offer. I just want to make sure I have that loud and clear before I go back to tell him."

"No. Never. I will not take a plea bargain."

"I will let him know."

33

My sausage biscuits were cold when I returned to the office, so I went to our break room to nuke them in the microwave before returning to my seat to eat. I'd quickly wrapped things up with Barbara and Winston after ending my conversation with Candy. Winston had confirmed he'd still come to my office later for a meeting but had questioned whether it was necessary, as we had just talked on the phone yesterday about everything he had found. He had not had time to pursue any other angles in the case because he had been helping with Barbara. I still needed to bring him up to speed on my investigation, so I asked him to keep the meeting.

Even though I had questions about what was going on with Barbara and the law enforcement investigation into Thomas Guyton, I tried to set them aside, at least until I had more information about the stalker.

I wanted to pester Stephanie for details, but it was best to let the matter rest until she got back to me. The guy was sitting in jail and didn't pose a current threat to Barbara.

That might not be the case for long, so it was best to take advantage of the time I had while I could. It was difficult for me to do, but I needed to get on with my day.

After I jotted down some notes about my investigation the previous day into Abe Martin, Bill Weaver, and Larry Thompson, I turned to the next of the poker boys.

Kyle Rencher.

Kyle was Raymond's old programmer buddy from back in the day. Why had Bill Weaver gotten that wrong? If what I'd learned yesterday night was accurate while reading through the file, it was Kyle who had introduced Raymond to the other poker boys, not Larry.

I pulled up Karen Brodsky's file on Kyle and read through it, hoping to find some background on how Raymond and Kyle knew each other but was disappointed. I was surprised it was so thin, considering that Kyle was the one with the longest connection to Raymond. I had expected to at least find information about their previous shared place of employment.

There was nothing.

I sent Candy a text message asking if she remembered how Raymond knew Kyle. She responded, saying that they'd worked together at a place called MegaCords.

A few internet searches later, I had learned a brief history of MegaCords. It was an online company that sold cords. None of it was likely to be relevant to the case, so I copied what I'd found into my notes and then tracked down Kyle's current employer.

I was surprised to see he was working as a freelance contractor. I found where his office was located from his LinkedIn profile and went for a visit.

If I counted Raymond, four of the poker players were programmers. That seemed a little odd.

Was this a random occurrence?

How did these guys connect up with a mechanic and a dentist from different neighborhoods?

It didn't make sense. I had expected to learn they had something in common that had facilitated the connection, like a church group or a rotary or a shared college experience. Instead, it appeared that they had just somehow found each other.

Candy had said they'd played poker together for years. Maybe it was the sort of thing that had come about naturally over time.

I didn't think Candy would know anything about how it had formed, but I sent her a text asking when I stopped at a light.

I soon pulled into the parking lot of the building where Kyle maintained his executive office. It wasn't yet 10:00 AM, so I wondered if I would even find him at work because many people in his position tended to come in late and work late.

The file had mentioned he was single, so it was a good bet he was not yet here.

Just as I was about to get out, a red Mustang convertible drove into the parking lot with the top down. I recognized Kyle as it pulled to a stop and parked several spaces away.

I considered getting out to talk to him in the parking lot but waited, so I could confront him in his office, where it would be more difficult for him to walk away.

That didn't stop Abe Martin.

I gave it five minutes after he entered the building before following after him.

His profile had specified that he was in Suite 516, so I knew to take the elevator up to the fifth floor.

I was greeted by a receptionist, something I had not expected but was predictable in retrospect. It looked like this entire floor was dedicated to executive office suites.

She smiled. "Can I help you?" She wore a headset and looked like the type of person who was good at multitasking. She had two monitors in front of her and also watched a television screen mounted on the wall that streamed financial news.

"I'm here to meet Kyle Rencher. He around?"

A surprised look came to her face. Did Kyle not have visitors often? I almost asked, but that seemed too invasive, and my long experience as an attorney had taught me never to put pressure on the gatekeeper unless I couldn't avoid it.

"Just one second," she said, "let me see if I can find him."

Right after she spoke, she pressed a button and was immediately talking to somebody else. Judging by her words, she had just received a phone call she had answered on behalf of a person who worked in the executive office space. She had even identified herself as working for the specific company she had answered for.

She got another after she was done with that call. She put up a finger as she glanced at me, giving me a smile that seemed to encourage me to wait patiently while she dealt with the next caller.

After that, I heard her clicking on a keyboard and saw her waiting.

"Kyle," she said, "I have a man out here who is looking to meet you. Do you want me to show him into a conference room?"

She looked at me. "What did you say your name was again?"

There was no point in trying to hide it. He likely expected a visit from me anyway.

"Mitch Turner."

"He says his name is Mitch Turner."

There was a long pause. I couldn't tell if it was because Kyle was trying to think of what to do or if he was giving her instructions.

"This way, please."

She stood and walked briskly away. Her headset was connected to a device she had strapped to her belt so she could take calls wherever she went. She glanced back and motioned for me to follow as she got another call, answering it correctly for a different company. I had no way of discerning how she could tell which company the call had come in for. I was impressed.

She was on the ball. She was juggling a lot at once and didn't appear to be missing or dropping anything.

She came to a conference room and pushed open the door. "Kyle said it would be a moment, but he'll be right in. Make yourself comfortable."

I was about to thank her, but she was already getting a call from somebody else as she walked away. It was rare I felt the desire to poach an employee.

If I had been looking to hire another receptionist, I would have talked to this woman. I expected Ellie to be with me for quite some time. There was no way I would ever let Ellie go, especially while she was in the middle of a health crisis, but I made a mental note to remember this place just in case Ellie ever left my employment.

The conference room was windowless and small. It looked like the sort of room that probably had five or six identical twins on the same floor. I had never worked in an executive office suite like this, but I was familiar enough with how they functioned to know that was probably the case.

"Mitch Turner."

I turned back to the door to see Kyle Rencher walking in. He was short, pale, and wearing shorts. He looked me up and down as if impressed that he was meeting with somebody who wore a suit.

I extended a hand. We shook. He did not seem nervous in the slightest.

"I thought I might meet with you today," he said, pointing at the chairs in the conference room. "Let's get this over with." He said this last part as if telling a joke.

"You had reason to expect me?"

"I spoke with Bill Weaver on the phone last night. He mentioned Candy had a new attorney who was making the rounds." He gave me a curious look. "Only I met with a couple of investigators before, not an actual attorney."

He leaned back in his chair. "What do you want to know?"

"I understand you knew Raymond for a long time. Is that accurate?"

"He and I worked together ten years ago for a company called Mega-Cords. We were both programmers, so it was only natural we met. I don't know that we became friends right away, but by the time I left, we knew each other well."

"So, were you disappointed when Raymond turned up dead?"

"Heartbroken." He frowned. "That's a strange question to ask. Do you think I'm a suspect in his death?"

I gave him a mirthless smile. "I treat everybody like they're a suspect until I know otherwise."

The guy nodded. "Probably the best way to go. I thought about going to law school, but then I discovered coding and found my calling."

"That what you do here?"

"Yep, freelancer. I have done it now for the better part of three years."

"Tell me about your experience with Raymond."

"What would you like to know?"

"For starters, was it you who invited him to the poker group?"

"Yes, I've been playing poker with Bill Weaver and others for quite some time. Bill and I go back to our undergraduate college years. We were roommates. We've had several people come in and out of our poker ranks over the years, but Raymond, Bill, and I were the most consistent for the longest time. It wasn't until recently that we added Abe Martin and Larry Thompson."

"I understand Raymond stopped coming about six months before his death."

"Yes, that's accurate." I watched Kyle's face for any sign of tension, but there was none.

"Why?"

"Unfortunately, you'd have to ask Raymond. It started off slowly. He would miss a game here and there, but before we knew it, he stopped coming altogether." Kyle shrugged. "Maybe he just tired of playing. I don't know. Wish I had an answer. The others wanted an answer to that question, too, and I didn't have one." He snorted. "If I had, it would have saved us all a lot of time because you guys could have been on your way. There would have been no need for follow-up questions. I get it. It's something unusual, so you're trying to figure it out. Perhaps you suspect there was a falling out or something like that. Nothing could be further from the truth. He just stopped coming."

I arched an eyebrow. "It seems like there was a falling out. You know I met with Bill, but I also spoke with Abe Martin and Larry Thompson." Kyle nodded as if he was aware. "My meeting with Abe Martin was nothing less than hostile. He practically kicked me out of his mechanic shop. Why would he do that?"

"He and Raymond didn't like each other. That's gotta be it." Kyle shrugged. "They were frequently at each other's throats. Raymond liked to tease Abe, and Abe didn't take it well. I'm afraid that's all there is." Kyle gave me a smile that made me think it was something he regularly practiced.

I couldn't put my finger on why, but I was bothered by how this was going.

"Larry Thompson didn't seem to care much for Raymond either," I said. "Sure seems like there was a falling out between Raymond and the rest of you guys."

"That's just Larry. He's strange, you know that?" Kyle shook his head. "I've been trying to think of ways to keep him from coming to our poker group for the last two years and have yet to be successful. I don't even care if you tell him that. I want him to know we don't want him coming any longer."

Was Kyle throwing Larry and Abe under the bus to protect himself? It seemed a solid explanation, though I could not logically connect that idea and the facts I knew. I couldn't see any reason they would want to kill Raymond. I also had no way of confirming what went on during their poker nights. My best guess was that they had played high-stakes poker and that things had gotten out of hand. Perhaps Raymond had taken them for much of what they had, and they had erased the debt by killing him.

Was that the cover? Was that the place I needed to focus on to unravel this whole thing?

"Anybody ever put their car on the line during your games? Or perhaps a house?"

"Nothing like that," Kyle said to me with a chuckle. It seemed forced. "We limited our games. It's usually about forty or fifty dollars. We do that on purpose because we want to keep emotions low. It's about having fun, not making money."

"Have you guys ever played for more than that?"

"No."

"Not one time?" I shook my head. "Hard to believe that in all the years you guys got together to play that nobody tried to up the ante."

"It doesn't happen. If anybody ever tried, we would invite them to leave our group."

"So neither Larry nor Abe cared for Raymond. Did Raymond know that?"

"I didn't say Larry didn't like Raymond. All I said is that Larry is odd. Raymond knew Abe had problems with him. He's not a dumb guy. He was one of the best programmers I've worked with. Bill and I got along with Raymond just fine."

"What would you do if you were in my shoes? Who should I look at? Assuming, of course, Candy didn't do it."

"That's an assumption I wouldn't make. I know little about Candy, but I got the idea she was high maintenance and demanding. I don't think Raymond knew what he was getting into when he married her."

"Did you ever meet her?"

"No, I've never even seen her."

"He complained about her to you?"

"No. We rarely talked about our lives at poker night."

That was a flat lie. It had to be. Why else would these guys get together if it wasn't to talk about their problems?

"Did he talk about his wife at other times? Perhaps when you guys worked together?"

"No, he didn't talk about her much at all. I think this is part of why I feel like they didn't have a great relationship. If they had got along, he would've talked about her. It seemed like he was trying to avoid it."

"Do you have evidence that points to her?"

"If I did, wouldn't it be better to give it to the prosecutors rather than her attorney?"

"I don't suppress evidence, Mr. Rencher. I look for the truth."

"And what do you do if you find your client did it?"

"Happens sometimes," I said. "I have rules and ethical obligations to follow that limit how I can advocate for my clients. Do you have something then?"

"I don't have anything. If I think of something, I'll be sure to tell you. I'll just have to trust your ethics are more important than your client's checkbook."

He was trying to ruffle my feathers.

Why?

"Who else would have a reason to kill Raymond?"

"That's a difficult question," he said, "I didn't know him all that well outside of poker night and work. I think I've told you all I know. Any other questions you have are a waste of time, both for you and me. If you think I know anything about this, you are dead wrong."

I studied Kyle. He was hiding something.

Abe is disgruntled when I show up suddenly to interview him. Bill handles me with finesse. And then Larry is hostile, too.

Kyle was trying to smooth things over because several of the others had botched it.

Are they in this together? I wondered.

It wasn't often I came across a conspiracy to commit murder, but that sort of thing happened. The usual murder case involved somebody who lost their temper and let things get out of hand. Or they were on drugs. Or they were drunk. If one of these guys had murdered Raymond, it could also be that the others had agreed to cover for him.

Was the hostility I had experienced in my meeting with Abe Martin a sign of guilt? Was Larry the one who Abe had told first? Had Larry helped him frame Candy after the fact?

What was Kyle's role in all of this?

And Bill's?

"Do you work just for one company, or do you have multiple companies you contract with?" I asked, trying to use a change in my questioning to throw him off guard since he had tried to do the same to me by throwing aspersions on my professional integrity.

Kyle studied me with a frown. "What does that have to do with Raymond's murder?"

"Just being friendly," I said with a casual smile.

"You're trying to mix me up. Don't do that." Kyle leaned forward. "You think I had something to do with this, don't you?"

"Is there a reason I shouldn't?"

Kyle didn't answer for several moments as he regarded me with cold eyes. "It's not every day that somebody comes to my office and accuses me of murder."

"I haven't done that. I told you already I treat everybody like a suspect until I have reason to know they're not. One might ask why you feel the need to confront me as if I have accused you of murder when I've done no such thing."

I gave him an expectant look while lifting my hands, palms up.

He went white.

"I've answered your questions satisfactorily. I have even explained why some of my poker mates may have had issues with Raymond. I have been nothing but forthcoming and honest. I can't believe you have the gall to sit there and think I did it."

I shrugged. "Convince me you didn't. You won't ever see me again."

"That's not how the justice system works. Innocent until proven guilty."

"That is an important principle of our Constitution. If you are tried for Raymond's murder, that can be included as an instruction given to the jury." I worded it like that to see what reaction I would get.

I was not disappointed. It was the closest I had come to actually doing what he was accusing me of doing, and he did not like it.

"If you think I did this, please tell me what evidence you have that says I did."

"Nothing but your demeanor."

Kyle took his hands off the conference table and leaned back as if restraining himself from leaping over. He worked his jaw as if trying to form what he was going to say but was having a difficult time coming up with the words. I almost felt bad for the guy. If I were to ask these questions while he was on the stand and get the same response, it would be easy to make a case to the jury he was guilty of murder, lack of evidence notwithstanding.

"I think it's time you go," he finally said.

"It appears we're getting off on the wrong foot." I leaned back in my chair slightly and put my hands behind my head. "I'm just trying to track down a murderer. I don't have any evidence that makes me think you did it. I just want to figure out who might've had a reason to kill Raymond and frame Candy. That's all I'm doing." I was trying to assuage his concerns so I could continue the interview, but I'd pushed him hard enough that I didn't expect it to work.

"It wasn't me," Kyle said, standing. "I'm sorry, I'd like to continue this pleasant conversation, but I have things I must do."

He bared his teeth in what he probably hoped was a smile.

"Good day," I said, pressing a card into his hands as I stepped outside the door. "Please don't hesitate to reach out if you can think of anything."

Kyle dropped the card and glowered at me before walking away.

34

I couldn't help but think my interview with Kyle had gone better than expected as I walked out to my car. He had probably not expected to become antagonistic, and he was likely berating himself for his mistake. I wasn't sure what I had done to get his mask to slip. I was just glad it had.

Sometimes, I got lucky.

Maybe it was my manner more than my words that had made him feel like I viewed him as a prime suspect. Or perhaps his guilt had gotten to him, and he had read things I had not intended to communicate.

Unfortunately for him, he had just further confirmed my suspicions that there was something here.

I found smoke, I just need the fire.

When the building door opened behind me a second after I walked out, I turned, expecting to find Kyle coming at me with a knife. A short woman dressed sharply in a business suit glanced at me, gave me a small smile, and continued on her way. I pulled out my phone to look up the name of the last poker player while still facing the door, controlling my breathing to get my heart rate back to normal. It would not have been the first time somebody had tried to assault me.

Has this case really gotten to where I need to look over my shoulder? I shook my head. *Or is it just everything going on with Barbara?*

That was it. I was still on edge from the stalker following Barbara.

Seth Roberts.

The file had informed me that Seth worked from home, and that was about it. I didn't know if the other investigators had made it out to chat with him. They forgot to record it in the file if they did. There was almost no other information on the man. Even though I assumed Abe and the others had already informed Seth that I was making the rounds, I decided I might as well finish off the list.

I parked in front of Seth's home fifteen minutes later. It was a two-story dwelling in the suburbs. The front lawn was littered with children's toys, and there was a bench on their front porch.

I found myself hoping this guy wasn't involved in Raymond's death as I walked up the steps. The last thing I wanted was for somebody else's kids to suffer the pain of watching a parent go to prison.

That was my bias coming through.

If Seth had anything to do with it, he should go to prison, regardless of the consequences. If I could prove he had committed the crime, I would do everything in my power to make sure the police had all the evidence necessary to bring him to justice and dismiss the charges against my own client.

A dog barked when I rang the doorbell. A woman with a bandanna wrapped around her head came to the door.

"What is it?"

She regarded me as if I were selling something until she noticed I didn't have anything in my hands. Her eyes widened as she tried to figure out what I was doing. It was clearly an unusual experience for one such as me to knock on her door during the day.

"Your husband around?" I asked with a congenial smile.

"Yes," she said cautiously. "Why?"

"I just wanted to ask a few questions. My name is Mitch Turner."

"I don't think he wants to talk with you."

"Why?"

"We heard you have been going around talking with Raymond Carlisle's old poker buddies. Seth had nothing to do with it. And he's busy right now on a project for work. I'm not going to let you distract him with unimportant questions. Besides, Seth didn't go to their group until after Raymond stopped coming anyway. He never even met the guy."

"If that's the case, my visit will be brief. Can I just confirm that story with him before I go?"

She studied me. Somewhere in the back of the house, a baby started crying. She let out a sigh of exasperation.

"Fine. Wait right here."

She shut the door. I heard her footsteps running to go deal with the screaming child. It wasn't until almost ten minutes later that the door opened again.

Seth was a man of average height in his mid-forties who wore glasses and had a pudgy belly.

"I understand you wanted to talk with me?" Seth asked tentatively. He looked inside as if thinking of inviting me in but then said, "Is it okay if we just chat out here?" He motioned at the bench on their porch. "It might be best. My wife has a lot on her hands."

"Sure," I said, taking a seat.

He hesitated before sitting on his front stairs and turning to face me.

"Your wife tells me that you didn't join Raymond's poker group until after he stopped coming. Is that accurate?"

Seth nodded. "That is true." He looked around nervously as if expecting somebody was eavesdropping on our conversation.

"Why are you nervous?" I asked.

He looked startled and glanced down at his feet as if searching for how to answer.

"I just have a big project I'm on right now for work." He sighed. "I know it sounds bad, but I can hardly even spend a couple more minutes talking to you. I don't even know why you're bothering with me. I barely was a part of their poker night. I only went for one night and never returned."

"Why?"

"They were terrible poker players."

"Really?" That was surprising information.

"I played semi-professionally before I married. Bill Weaver, he's the one who got me an invite to the group, made it sound like they were all a bunch of amateur pros themselves." He chuckled darkly. "I walked away with the entire pot that first night."

"Is it true they limit the amount you can gamble?"

He nodded. "Only $50 or something like that."

"You hear them talk about Raymond Carlisle while you were there?"

He went quiet. "Possibly. They mentioned another guy who used to come. They made a couple comments, but nothing I can attribute directly back to Raymond.

"What did they say?"

"Is it ever going to come back on me?"

"Is it a problem if it does?"

He thought about it, glancing around again. "I suppose not. I haven't seen Bill Weaver in months. I've not seen the other guys since that night."

"Your wife mentioned you heard I was asking questions."

"Bill and I chatted about something last night on the phone. He mentioned it to me."

"So just to be clear, you joined the group after Raymond left, but before he was killed?"

"Joined the group is a bit strong. I went for one night, remember? I don't think they even mentioned his name while we played poker. I didn't even hear it until some investigators came around asking questions."

"What did they say about him?"

"One made a joke about how the last member had not been a good fit for the group. The others laughed. I mean, it's not really much. I just don't want them to think I am talking about them." The answer he gave me was not lining up with the way he had acted beforehand. This was benign at best.

He was not telling me the truth.

"Is there anything else you can remember about those guys?"

"No, nothing you probably don't already know. I could tell you the names of the others, but if you're just getting to me, chances are you've spoken with the rest."

"You still play poker with them?"

He gave me a look. "I thought I already answered that question."

I shrugged.

He shook his head. "No. I would never go again if they invited me. It was the most boring night I've ever experienced in my life. At one point, I suggested we turn a game on for background noise or order pizza, but none of them wanted to do that."

"You think they didn't like you, and they were encouraging you not to come back?"

"Maybe. I certainly never returned." He looked at his watch. "I'm sorry, Mr. Turner, but I've given you all the time I can. I really hope you're able to get this case figured out. If you have questions, feel free to shoot me an email. I'll do my best to answer them, but please don't drop by again unannounced."

He looked around furtively as if expecting to notice somebody was watching us. I glanced around, too. I couldn't help it. He made me feel a little paranoid. Other than an empty black sedan parked down the street, my car was the only other parked on the road.

"You seem nervous," I said again. "Do you have some sort of reason to suspect we are being overheard?"

He laughed while staring at his feet. "Of course not. Why would you think that?"

I studied him. "If I could get your email address before I go?"

35

I got into my car and stared at the black car ahead of me. Was it just my imagination, or had Seth glanced at it several times during our discussion?

It was a Toyota Camry, and to the best of my recollection, it had been there when I first arrived. I hadn't noted it at the time, but I focused on it now. I felt that the substance of my interview with Seth Roberts had turned up little.

I was just trying to figure out why he was so nervous when it appeared he had nothing to hide.

The fact he had been worried to tell me that the others had briefly mentioned Raymond in passing made me pause, too.

I took these as signs that I was on the right track. I would be much further along once I knew the answer to some of these riddles.

I started my car and put it into gear.

My route back to the office dictated that I turn and head back in the way I had come. Instead, I pulled forward while bringing up my phone. I snapped a picture of the black car, confirming I had captured its license plate before driving off.

I got a phone call five minutes later. I didn't recognize the number but answered it using the Bluetooth hands-free feature of my car.

"Mitch Turner here."

"Mr. Turner, this is Abe Martin."

"I wasn't expecting to hear from you. To what do I owe this pleasure?"

"I'm afraid I was having a bad day when you came by yesterday. I must've turned you off me a bit. I apologize. You were just asking questions I had already answered. The truth is, my shop is struggling right now, and I didn't want to take the time to answer your questions. If you have a moment, I'm happy to do my best to retread this ground."

Was he using a speakerphone?

It was difficult for me to tell because I was using my car's speakerphone, which could easily explain the background noise I was hearing.

I took a right turn and turned down a side street. I pulled to a stop, checking to make sure nobody was following me. It appeared I was alone. I switched over to my phone and put it up to my ear to get a better read on what was happening on the other end of the line.

"No worries," I said easily. "Those sorts of things happen. I'm a small businessman myself and know what it's like to meet your overhead every month. I'm sorry you're going through tough times."

"Yeah, it's rough."

There was no doubt. Abe Martin was on speakerphone.

Was he in the same room with Bill Weaver, Larry Thompson, and Kyle Rencher? Were they all sitting around the phone, anxiously wondering how they could best answer questions to throw my suspicions elsewhere?

"Anyhow," Martin went on, "you were asking questions about Raymond's death. You wanted to know about our poker group."

"That's right," I said. "I was curious if there was a falling out between you and Raymond."

"No, although I must tell you that he and I did not get along."

"And why was that?"

"He liked to tease me. I didn't take it well."

"I see." It seemed like this had been spoonfed to him by Kyle Rencher. "I'm sorry your relationship with him was so difficult."

"It wasn't all that bad. He just got under my skin, you know?" Abe chuckled. "Not that big of a deal when you think about it. I probably made more of it than I should have. You dropping by out of the blue yesterday brought some of that back."

A long pause.

I imagined other people in the room urging him to say something more.

"I'm sorry," Abe said with some reluctance.

I heard rustling and the squeaking of a chair. It reminded me of the same noise the chair in Bill Weaver's office had made when I had visited him.

I put my phone back on the Bluetooth hands-free system and pulled out onto the road. I also brought up the navigation on my car's viewscreen and saw that I was about ten minutes away from Bill Weaver's dental office.

If I had to put money on it, I would bet Abe Martin was not at his mechanic's shop.

"How often would you guys play poker?" I asked, barely listening to the answer. I asked him other innocuous questions about their game night. I imagined the others in the room relaxing because it seemed like I was just checking off a list of questions I needed to ask to put the matter behind me. I received several phone calls while I drove but let them both go to voicemail. It looked like Ellie was trying to get hold of me.

She would have to wait.

The poker boys thought they had deceived me.

I soon parked down the street from Bill Weaver's office. I had a view of the cars in his parking lot and his front office door. I noticed Kyle Rencher's Ford Mustang in the parking lot.

Bingo.

Hopefully, I was not that noticeable to anybody leaving the dental office.

Time to turn up the heat.

"What did you say to make Raymond stop coming to your games?" I asked after I switched back over to my phone.

There was a long pause.

I had just drawn the attention of everybody in the room.

"I never said anything."

"My client's previous investigators said you mentioned a falling out. That accurate?"

"No. That is not accurate."

The others in the room were silent.

"Near as I can tell, you're the one who had a bad relationship with Raymond. Isn't that right?"

A long pause. Abe Martin was clearly disturbed by how I had shifted my questioning. I had gone from softballs to asking loaded questions.

The chair squeaked again. There was more rustling.

If there had been any doubt that Abe Martin was not by himself, it was gone now.

"I'm telling the truth. I really don't know why Raymond stopped coming." It sounded like he spoke through gritted teeth. I couldn't think of anything else I could ask that I expected a truthful answer for, so I told him I needed to go.

I then put my phone in video recording mode and rested it on the dash of my car to see what would happen. It wasn't until fifteen minutes later that

I saw Abe Martin, with Larry Thompson and Kyle Rencher, come out of Bill Weaver's dental office.

Looks like all the boys got together, I thought. I recorded until each had gotten into their cars and left.

36

I was elated when I got back to my office because I had made considerable progress in a small amount of time. I couldn't wait to review the video I had taken outside of Bill Weaver's office. I still didn't have any evidence I could present in court, but there was no doubt I was on the right track. They would not have gotten together to help Abe answer questions if they didn't have something to hide.

It was just a matter of figuring out what that was, much easier said than done.

At least I knew where to dig.

That was the hardest part of getting started.

"There you are," Ellie said as soon as I walked in. "I've been trying to get hold of you."

"Sorry. I had some things come up. I'm here now." From the look on her face, I could tell she wanted to chat in private. "My office?"

"That's for the best."

"I let the temp go," Ellie said as soon as we sat. "He wasn't working out. I have a nice law student named Zoey Vern coming in this afternoon. She's an experienced paralegal, as well as a receptionist. She should be able to step into my shoes without a problem."

"Step into your shoes?" I asked, wondering if I was reading the implication correctly. "You make it sound as if you're planning to leave."

"I don't think it's going to work for me to stay here, Mitch. I was hoping I could, but my mind is not in the game. You need somebody who's on task."

"Zoey can help," I said, "but that doesn't mean you still shouldn't come in if you want. I'm going to pay you regardless, and to be frank, I wasn't expecting you to contribute as much as you normally do. I'm okay with that. You said you needed a mental break, so you're free to work or not work however you like."

Ellie burst into tears. I almost fell out of my seat. In all the years she and I had worked together, I had never seen such a display. It was not unwarranted; it was just something she didn't do.

"Mitch, I don't know what to say."

"You're going to get through this. I mean to help in any way I can."

"You're okay if I go?"

"Of course."

"I guess you'll see me when you see me," Ellie said as she left.

I went to my computer and downloaded the video I had recorded outside of Bill Weaver's dental office, which had already backed up to the cloud.

I watched it repeatedly, looking for any clues that might help me figure out exactly what these guys were up to.

Eventually, I had to move on to other matters.

The rest of my day flew by.

Detective Stephanie Gray reached out with information on Barbara's stalker. I also asked a couple of questions to figure out why they were investigating Thomas Guyton, but Stephanie was not forthcoming.

I had originally planned to file the paperwork myself, but at the last moment had asked my partner Veronica to do it. She had agreed and made certain I understood she would not be giving Barbara a discount. I told her to just send the bill to me and turned my attention back to the Candy Carlisle matter. It was for the best I was passing it off because I was too emotionally involved to see things rationally.

When Zoey knocked on my office door to usher Winston in for our 4:00 PM meeting, the elation I'd felt from my earlier discovery had dissipated.

I knew something was going on. I just couldn't prove it. I also hadn't come up with any good ideas on how to find more evidence. It was time to bring in another set of eyes to get a fresh perspective. Once I sat on it for a day or two, I was confident I would have some fresh ideas for next steps.

"We can cross David Washington off the list," Winston said as he sat.

I was now so focused on the poker boys that it took me a moment to remember David Washington had been our prime suspect just the day before. Talking about Washington was the original purpose of our meeting.

It's amazing the difference just a few hours can make. I had thought David Washington was our best suspect until I went to talk with Abe Martin. If Winston could conclusively rule Washington out, that meant we could focus our efforts. I tried hard not to get attached to a particular theory because I never knew when something was going to surface and blow it out of the water.

My gut told me that was not likely to happen with the poker boys, so it was a good reminder to remain open to the possibility.

"What did you find on Washington?"

"I can conclusively prove he was out of town at the time of the murder. Out of the country, to be exact. I thought at first he had posted all of his trips to Facebook, but I found an Instagram account this morning he uses, too, not the same one where he's connected to Candy. I'm not sure why he would post one thing to Instagram and not to Facebook, but that's what he is doing."

"Was he there with a different woman?" I asked. "Maybe he hides the Instagram account from his current flavor."

Winston shook his head. "No, the same one. I couldn't see a reason for his behavior, but I pieced together the timing of the pictures. He was in Italy at the time of the murder."

"Are you sure this isn't just a clever ruse to provide him with a seemingly airtight alibi? I believe social media posts can be scheduled."

"They can, but after I knew where to look, it took just a couple of phone calls to confirm he was out of the country. I even stopped by for a chat with him and his current flavor." Winston paused and gave me a look. I had originally asked him to hold off on doing that until after we met today. I'd even been thinking of doing the interview myself. "Figured you would want it done."

I nodded, glad Winston had taken the initiative to just get this one crossed off.

"If he's no longer on the list, I'd rather know it now than later. So that leaves Ian Mercer, Jana Lerner, and Evangeline Brewer from the list of our original suspects, correct?"

"Yes, that's right. Ian Mercer, we tentatively crossed off with a pencil."

"That reminds me," I said. "Candy sent me a copy of the communication this morning. I've been so busy I haven't yet sent it to you." I turned to my computer and emailed it before I forgot again. "You should have it now. Please see what you can find."

"I've looked into Jana Lerner and not found much that would interest us," Winston said. "She appears to be happily married to her one and only husband with whom she has a child. The baby was born just a few months before Raymond's death. I have a hard time seeing a mother with a baby committing this murder, but I'll continue to investigate her. I have not made much progress on Evangeline Brewer since we last talked."

"While you were chasing down those leads, I followed up on something I didn't think was going to be of consequence, but it turns out there might be something there."

Winston waited expectantly.

"The poker boys."

Winston nodded. "I saw the notes from the previous investigators. I reviewed them and had nothing jump out at me. I saw one had mentioned a falling out, but it was six months prior to Raymond's death. It appeared there were no exchanges between Raymond and the poker boys since."

"That's the guy I met with first, Abe Martin. Our meeting was less than cordial. He practically threw me out of his mechanic shop."

"That's interesting," Winston said.

"That made me want to meet the rest. I have now spoken with each of the poker boys. And of the five, three were hostile."

"Another interesting point."

"Today, I met the last two. One claims to have joined the group after Raymond left. He said he never returned after the first game. Apparently, he found them to be boring and terrible poker players." I made sure I had Winston's full attention. "The other was hostile and even seemed to think that I was accusing him of murder when I had done nothing of the sort."

"More interesting."

"On my way back to the office, I received a phone call from Abe Martin. He claimed he was just having a bad day yesterday and that he now wanted to answer my questions. It appeared he was on speakerphone. I followed a hunch and went to the office of one of the other poker players, a dentist. Abe and two others came out a few minutes after I finished my conversation."

"That's quite a hunch. I can't believe it paid off. What else do you have?"

"Unfortunately, not much more than that. They are trying to throw me off their tracks, and they're concerned about the way Abe Martin originally acted."

"This doesn't sound like a falling out. Where do we go from here?"

"I'm going to turn what I have over to you. I need you to run with it. The trial is a month and a half from now."

"You want me to keep looking into the others, too?"

I nodded. "Keep chasing them down to see if anything interesting pops up." I pointed at my computer, where I had a copy of the communication Candy had received from Ian still pulled up. "It may be Ian's our guy, and there's a different explanation for the poker boys' weird behavior. We won't know until we prove it."

"How do you want me to approach the poker boys?" Winston asked.

I shook my head. "For now, just poke around and see what you can learn."

"Want me to interview any of them?"

"No. They're going to be wary now after my meetings with them. I want them to think they sufficiently explained Abe Martin's hostility."

37

More than two weeks had passed, but I had not made much progress on the Candy Carlisle matter. I was starting to get anxious. It was a month until trial, and I still didn't know how I wanted to present my case. Winston had run thorough background checks on all the poker boys but had not turned up anything that pointed to a motive for killing Raymond. After he did that, I requested he focus his attention on Abe Martin.

Our initial background check into Abe Martin revealed he had been charged with a DUI seven years back. His attorney got him out after just a few months of incarceration. It was Martin's first offense, so they were more lenient.

Winston's deep dive into Abe Martin's past turned up a six-month period Abe spent at a drug rehab center right after he turned eighteen. Winston looked for any related criminal charges but found none.

Winston also tried several different things to figure out why the poker boys were so protective of Abe Martin but had no luck there either.

I had made no further attempt to contact the poker boys. I wanted them to think they had successfully answered my questions, so they would return to their normal lives. I wanted them to start their "poker nights" up again.

If what Seth Roberts had told me was accurate, the poker boys were terrible at poker.

That made me wonder if their poker nights were about something else. Perhaps they had invited Seth Roberts over to act as a cover if anybody started asking questions. They wanted somebody who had actually been to their poker night who could vouch for it. Unfortunately for them, they had not realized just how terrible they were at poker.

I had run different scenarios about what could be really going on at those games but refused to commit to any because I didn't have enough facts to guide my analysis.

I had also looked at the prosecution's case for holes by building a case against my client as if I were the prosecutor. I had not found anything that would amount to a successful defense, but the prosecution's case was largely circumstantial. It was primarily based on DNA that came from Candy's hair. I intended to explain that, but it could easily go either way once it got in front of a jury.

Candy did not have an alibi for that night. She could've been at home killing her husband, or she could have been at work like she claimed.

She had been the only one working late. Her office was small enough it did not keep track of when people entered or exited their premises. There were security cameras on-site at the office building, but all of the footage had been deleted by the time this case landed in my lap.

There was also nothing in Karen Brodsky's notes about the security footage.

I was hesitant to reach out to ask her about it because I knew she was paranoid about Candy Carlisle suing for malpractice.

A legitimate fear I had of my own.

I had an obligation to reach out to Karen, so I opened up my email and sent her a quick message, asking if it was something they had looked into. I normally would have placed a phone call, but I wanted a record of her response in case Candy sued me.

Candy had called Karen frequently for updates, but I barely heard from her. I didn't know what it was, but something about the way I approached things made Candy feel she didn't need to constantly reach out. I hoped it was a sign of confidence that I was handling it.

I got up from my desk and stretched.

I had spent most of my morning reviewing everything we had on the Candy Carlisle matter. I had watched the video of Abe and his buddies coming out of Bill Weaver's dental office but had not had any strokes of inspiration on where to go next in the investigation.

Winston had spent several nights following Abe Martin but had come up with nothing. The man was probably a borderline alcoholic, but that didn't make him a murderer. Winston had followed him into a bar one night. Abe had gotten drunk, but he'd also had the presence of mind to call a cab instead of driving his beat-up truck home.

I had briefly entertained a theory that Abe had confronted Raymond at his home while under the influence. The situation could have escalated into Raymond's murder.

That just didn't seem like the right answer.

If Abe had confronted Raymond while drunk, odds were good, he would have left behind physical evidence.

I paced for half an hour, frustrated that I felt like I was on the right track but had been stopped dead in the water for two weeks.

Winston had made progress with the other leads. We had now crossed Jana Lerner off the list conclusively. There had been no contact between Raymond and Jana since the affair. She had also met and married her husband since that time.

Winston had confirmed the authenticity of the message Candy had forwarded from Ian Mercer. I had a flight out to California next week to meet him, though he did not know I was coming. I also planned to hit the beach and get some sun if I could squeeze in the time.

If Ian could satisfactorily explain why he had reached out to Candy Carlisle, he would soon be crossed off the list as well because we saw nothing else to connect him to Raymond's death. He was far enough away and had enough other things going on in his life that it didn't look like he was the guy who pulled the trigger.

It wasn't an impossibility, just unlikely.

That would just leave the poker boys and Evangeline Brewer.

Evangeline had proven elusive. Winston had done his best to figure out her present location but had not had any success. We had, however, confirmed she had reached out and propositioned Raymond by going through Raymond's social media.

The very fact we could not find anything about her made me nervous that she could be a primary suspect I had been ignoring because my attention was on the poker boys.

When I glanced at my watch, I noticed how long I'd been pacing and headed out of the office for some fresh air.

Zoey stopped me before I got far.

"You have a second, Mr. Turner?"

"Please, call me Mitch." It was not the first time I had asked her to call me by my name, and it would not be the last. My statement went right past without acknowledgment.

"Ellie left some instructions that don't make sense. She told me where to find a file, but I couldn't find it. Do you think it's okay for me to call?"

I checked my watch and saw that it was just a little before noon. "It should be fine. If she doesn't pick up, make sure to leave a message. She should get back in contact with you." I was already heading towards the door before Zoey could ask another question.

I felt like I was on the verge of a breakthrough. I didn't want her to distract me from making it.

My first instinct was to climb into my car to go for a drive, but I chose instead to walk down the street. For some reason I could not explain, I headed to the courthouse. Perhaps it was because the courthouse grounds were well-maintained and would provide a change of scenery. Or maybe it was because the courthouse would be a stark reminder of the approaching trial and my need to push through this wall.

Nothing like a deadline.

As I passed the restaurant where I had run into Barbara and Thomas Guyton, I glanced inside, half expecting to see them coming out. It seemed like the sort of thing that would happen, considering everything that had gone on between Barbara and myself.

I hadn't spoken to Barbara much since the day I'd asked Veronica to file the restraining order against her stalker. Even though I had told Barbara I would pay her legal fees, she had insisted that she handle it and entered into a formal representation agreement with Veronica. I'd run into her one time at the office. I'd been on my way out, and she'd been on her way in. We'd exchanged brief pleasantries, but that had been it.

It was probably for the best, though a part of me had hoped when she had called that things might change between us and that I might be on my way back into her life.

"Hey, mister, you have some change?"

I looked into the man's grimy face and the broken mug he held out. His hair was greasy and long. His coat was torn and dirty.

I reached into my wallet and pulled out a $100 bill that I tossed into his cup.

"Thank you!"

"Think nothing of it," I said as I continued on my way, hoping I wasn't just exacerbating his problems by giving him money.

After I made it to the courthouse, I did a circuit around the building and was on my way back when I noticed a police car pulling up.

I didn't recognize the officer, but when she glanced at me, it appeared she knew who I was because she glared. I smiled and gave her a friendly wave as I continued on my way.

I chuckled quietly. It wasn't that I liked to get under people's skin, but if they weren't going to like me because of my profession, I would not let that hold me back from being civil. It was the best thing for me to do from a professional perspective, even if it irritated them. It also sometimes resulted in me striking up unlikely relationships with people on the opposite side of the aisle, which was always good. I guessed about fifty percent of the police force tolerated me just fine because of my efforts. Perhaps I'd one day get through to her, too.

On my way back to the office, I glanced down the alley where I had once saved a woman from a mugger. I often wondered about the kid who I'd stopped that day. I hoped he had used it as an opportunity to change his ways.

I stopped.

The man who had approached me on my way to the courthouse was back in the corner, leaning up against a garbage bin.

A needle lay on the ground beside him. He let out a sigh.

I curled my hand into a fist, regretting what I had given him. Instead of helping, I had potentially done him harm.

I was just turning away when he convulsed.

Cursing, I ran down the alley.

"Are you okay?"

The man didn't respond as I knelt and grabbed his arm. He was still breathing, but his body shook uncontrollably. I ripped out my phone and called 911.

I gave my location and said, "I found a man on the street. He just injected something and is shaking uncontrollably."

"Can I have your name?" the operator asked calmly.

"Mitch Turner."

"Can you please give me the address?"

I gave it to her through gritted teeth. Had she not heard me the first time?

"Paramedics are on their way." I heard her typing on a keyboard. "Fortunately, they're only a couple minutes out. This man could not have picked a better place to overdose."

Overdose.

The word ricocheted inside my skull as I looked down at the man, trying to think of what else I could do to help while I waited for the paramedics to arrive.

The shaking was getting worse. Drool now came out of his mouth. His eyes rolled up in the back of his head. He started to slide down to the ground. I caught him and was about to put him back in the position he had been before when it occurred to me it might be safer for him to lie down.

I gently maneuvered him until he was on his back.

I turned when I heard an ambulance coming down the street.

Paramedics were soon on either side of me, administering help to the man.

38

After the man had been put into the ambulance and taken away, I stayed in the alley, regretting how I had given him the money needed for a drug overdose. I just hoped it wasn't the last thing he ever did. I didn't want somebody's death on my hands, not even in a tangential way like this.

The paramedics had bagged up the syringe and taken it with them in case they needed to identify the substance.

I didn't know anything about him, and I was unlikely to ever learn anything with HIPPA laws the way they were. It wasn't like I could just go down to the hospital and ask to visit.

I trudged out of the alley, wondering about the sudden twists and turns we experienced in life.

A moment before he had met me, that man had not expected a $100 bill. He had probably hoped for a few coins.

What had made me do it?

I'd pulled that bill out from beside a $20 and a $5. Why hadn't I just given him one of those instead? That might not have been enough to buy the drugs. He could have gotten a meal instead of a trip to the hospital.

Why had he done it? Had he been hoping to relieve pain? Had he just gotten tired of life?

I pondered these questions as I returned to my office and found Karen Brodsky waiting by the receptionist's desk.

"Mr. Turner," Zoey said, pointing to Karen, "you have a visitor."

"Thanks," I said. "Come on back, Karen."

I was painfully conscious of how less ostentatious my office space was compared to Karen's. And for the first time, I found myself wondering if Veronica's idea about new office space had merit. There was something to be said about putting forward an excellent image to impress clients.

Am I interested in impressing clients? Or do I just want to just impress fellow attorneys?

I had met with several other clients since the time Veronica had suggested we upgrade our office space, and I had never once felt like it was not good enough until today. I hadn't given Veronica's suggestion much thought and knew our other partner Tony had not either.

"I got your email," Karen said, her words dripping with venom. "What is this about, Mitch?"

"Excuse me?" I asked. I had not anticipated that Karen was angry when I'd invited her back. I thought perhaps she'd remembered something on the case that she'd come to tell me.

"Are you going to represent her in a malpractice lawsuit, too?" Karen demanded, her face turning red, her hands clenched into fists as if expecting a fight.

"No. Nothing like that. I would never practice that type of law. A shark for the sharks? No, thank you."

"Then why didn't you just call me?"

"I'm—"

"Cut the crap, Mitch. I know how you like to work. I know you prefer a phone call over an email any day of the week because you like to glean other information. You are putting down a trail of evidence in case this case goes sideways, aren't you?"

"You're the one who warned me about Candy suing for malpractice," I said carefully, watching Karen's face. I was glad she had come for a visit instead of calling because it did appear she had something to hide.

"Can I tell you something off the record?" Karen asked after a few awkward seconds.

I hesitated. "If it's about the case, it's probably something we need to have documented."

Karen leaned forward. "Fine. On the record, then. By the time our investigators went to check out her alibi, the videotape had already been deleted. I'm assuming that's what you found as well. Correct?"

I nodded. "Why are you making such a big deal about this?"

"Because it's Candy. Because she called me five times a day. Because I got the sense that if I stepped one foot out of line with her, I was going to hear about it. I don't want her haranguing me about this. My investigators work hard. We didn't get to the office until two weeks after she had come on as a client. Was it my fault they had already deleted the videotape? I had no way of knowing their security video retention procedures."

Karen was more afraid than I thought.

"Two weeks is probably a reasonable time unless you knew the videotapes were going to be destroyed. Put that in a memo and send it over. This is an anomaly. I don't think you're going to—"

"She's not gonna get off. She's gonna look for anything she can do to make our lives miserable. She's gonna sue you. She's gonna sue me. It's going to be a whole can of worms. I never should've taken her on as a client. It was a mistake. I knew it at the time, but I still did."

"I don't think it's as bad as you fear," I said, wondering what I should tell her. On the one hand, Karen was no longer Candy's attorney, so she had no right to know anything. But she might have some helpful insight. "I'm closing in on the true murderer."

Karen guffawed. "I don't believe that for a second. We were at a dead end on that case. You are, too."

I just gave her a knowing look.

"What? Do you think it is one of those idiots they had illicit liaisons with?"

I considered my response. I didn't want to do anything to further enrage her, and I wanted her as an ally.

"You guys were on the right track," I said, neglecting to mention that they'd already decided the poker boys had nothing to do with it. "It's the guys Raymond played poker with. Something is off. We're going to figure out what."

Karen sat up straight. "Really?"

"Yes. I visited Abe Martin. He practically threw me out of his mechanic shop. After that, I met the rest. Most were hostile. All except for Bill Weaver, who was cool as a cucumber, and Seth Roberts who didn't know much. The next day, Abe Martin called, wanting to talk. It sounded like he was on speakerphone. I went to Bill Weaver's office on a hunch. Guess who came out when I was done with that conversation?"

"Abe."

I nodded. "With Larry Thompson and Kyle Rencher."

"So you've got them?"

I shook my head. "We're close. All I know is that they're trying to hide something. The next step is just digging it up."

She thought for a moment. "I'll draft up that memo. I will also do everything I can to help you win this case so it doesn't blow back on us."

"Is everything going okay for you financially?"

My question caught Karen off guard.

"What makes you ask?"

"The fact you have a receptionist who is family." She could hardly do worse. "You're also overly worried about a single malpractice claim."

"Neither of those leads to the conclusion I'm having financial problems.

"They don't?" I raised a skeptical eyebrow.

"Look, Mitch, I gotta go. I'll let you know if I think of anything, but I do think you're on the right track."

Karen left quickly, leaving me to wonder exactly how close my question had cut to the bone. Sometimes, my inner investigator got the best of me, and I asked questions that were better left unsaid.

Back to the poker boys.

I pulled up my file and reviewed it again.

39

Four more days passed without progress on the Candy Carlisle matter. I was entering my office a little before 9:00 AM, intending to catch up on a few things before heading to the airport, when I noticed Barbara sitting in her car.

My first thought was that she was there for me until I remembered she had hired Karen as her attorney.

She opened her door when I stepped out, greeting me with an uncertain smile.

"Have an appointment with Veronica?"

She nodded. "I'm early."

"Everything working out with that stalker?"

"Haven't seen him again."

"What a relief."

We exchanged an awkward glance that was followed by an uncomfortable smile. I thought she was going to say something more, perhaps about the past, but then she shook her head and looked away.

"I don't mean to distract you. I'm sure you have things to do."

"I'm just making a quick stop, and then I'm off to California."

"Really?"

I got the distinct sense she was jealous as if I were going with somebody.

"Nothing like that," I said, "just a business trip. I'll be there two days, three max."

"Business trip in California?" Barbara looked like she didn't believe me.

"Tracking down a witness."

Barbara nodded. I headed towards the door, and she followed.

"It's good to see you, Mitch."

"Likewise."

I was surprised when I walked inside to see Ellie sitting at the reception desk. She had not been around much since our last conversation.

"Mitch," Ellie said, "I got a message—"

She stopped when she saw that Barbara had entered right after me. She gave me a look like she had just caught us in the act.

"Barbara is here to meet with Veronica," I said with a sly smile, stepping out of the way so Barbara could head towards Veronica's office down the hall.

"Good to see you, Ellie," Barbara said as she disappeared. I wasn't sure if she had picked up on any unspoken words between Ellie and me.

"Sorry, Mitch," Ellie said, "I didn't realize."

"Nothing to worry about. What was the message?"

"It was Bill Weaver. He said he wanted you to call him back."

Once I had the door shut behind me and checked my email to make sure nothing urgent had come in, I dialed Bill Weaver. He picked up on the first ring.

I identified myself.

"Thank you for calling me back," Bill said. "Do you have a moment? I know your day is just getting started, and you probably have a big to-do list."

"If it's not long," I said. "I'm heading out of town for a few days."

"Really?" Bill seemed interested in the news, which was the reason I had disclosed it. I had been curious to hear his reaction.

My next call would be to Winston to make sure he paid close attention to Abe Martin and Bill Weaver while I was gone.

Are they about to have their first poker night since I started asking questions?

I decided to sell it.

"Yep, just following up on a lead in Raymond's murder. I have a potential suspect out there."

There was a pregnant pause on the other end of the phone. I thought I heard a quiet sigh of relief.

I was glad I had exercised enough discipline to not bother the poker boys during the last few weeks, even though it had been difficult not to reach out. I had wanted them to think they had put this issue to bed. My gut told me it was going to pay off. I could practically hear Bill's brain working on the other end of the line.

"I believe you had something for me," I said with a big smile when Bill still had not explained the purpose of his call.

"Yes, it was about Candy Carlisle."

Why was he taking so long? Was he wondering if what he had planned to tell me was still necessary?

"My wife remembered another time when she saw her. It was actually right before Raymond was murdered. I think it was a day or two before."

"Okay," I said as if this were significant, though I did not see where he was going.

"She was coming out of a sporting goods store. She was carrying something that looked like a pistol."

Bill is upping the ante.

"Did your wife see the firearm?

"No, it was in a case."

"Do you remember which store?" I asked, picking up a pen to write down the information, so I could follow up on it. I figured he was lying and would not have any specifics, but I would treat it like it was legit until I knew otherwise.

"Unfortunately, no. I talked with my wife for some time. She couldn't remember anything more. To be honest, she might be remembering something that never happened. It's not that my wife doesn't have an excellent memory. It's just, it could've been somebody else."

He's trying to backtrack. He wished he had never called me.

This was excellent.

"This is very helpful information, Mr. Weaver," I said in the best authoritative voice I could muster. "This is really going to help our case. Would you mind if I scheduled an appointment to meet with your wife when I got back from California?"

Another lengthy pause. I don't know what Bill Weaver was expecting, but it was natural for me to want to talk with a potential witness. He had probably coached her to make this claim until he had learned I was investigating somebody else. Perhaps they were getting desperate to know the status of my investigation.

Why?

If Bill's wife is in on it, are any of the others? Abe Martin was divorced and single. Kyle Rencher had a girlfriend. I believed Larry Thompson was married.

"I'm sure she'd be willing," Bill said.

"Excellent. Can you put her on right now?" I couldn't help but smile as I asked. I was delighted Bill Weaver had called.

My patience paid off.

Bill was not expecting this question.

"I'm actually at the office."

I didn't believe him for a second.

"Can I get her number?"

Bill hesitated and then rattled it off as I wrote it down.

"Thank you so much, Mr. Weaver. You have been an excellent help. Please let me know if you think of or remember anything else."

I couldn't help but laugh once Bill was off the phone. I had played the man like a fiddle even though he had called to do that to me.

It had gone well enough I considered canceling my trip to California. I glanced at my watch. I had just a little over two hours to catch my flight. I picked up my phone and called Winston.

"I need you to follow both Bill Weaver and Abe Martin for the next two days. You have somebody that can help?"

"It won't be a problem. You know something?"

"I just got a phone call from Bill. It serendipitously came right as I'm about to fly to California. I took a gamble. I let him know I was going out of town. He seemed happy about it."

"I see," Winston said.

"Let's see what they do while I'm gone. Have any updates for me?"

"I think we should talk to Seth Roberts again. I know you felt he had nothing more to add, and you wanted to give the poker boys some space, but something about the background check was bothering me. I couldn't articulate why until I went back to review it.

"There was a significant break between the time he graduated high school and the time he went to college. It was about four years."

"I remember. We didn't think much of it since he's almost forty. Many people have periods of transition before they decide to grow up and become adults."

"Yes, and sometimes those people spend time behind bars."

"Really?"

"Yep. It didn't come back on our national background check. We didn't know where he was living, so we had no way of checking at the state level. I ran some credit header checks and found an address for him in Iowa.

"When I ran a criminal check in Iowa, it all came back."

"He was in prison for what?"

"Dealing drugs."

"Drugs. Do you think that is what the poker boys are up to?"

"Do you have a better explanation?"

"The thought has crossed my mind. It just seems unlikely Bill Weaver would be mixed up in dealing. I can easily see Abe Martin doing that, and possibly Larry Thompson and Kyle Rencher. Bill Weaver has a lot to lose if he is dealing.

"Can't dentists prescribe drugs?"

"You thinking pain pills?"

"That's the reason Seth went to prison."

I remembered how Seth had told me the poker boys were terrible at poker.

Had that been a subtle clue he had hoped would lead me to the truth without involving him?

40

My trip to California was uneventful. I tracked down Ian Mercer an hour after I landed. He readily agreed to have a conversation, stepping out of the office where he worked to follow me to a little café where we talked. He ordered coffee. I ordered a Coke.

I was convinced he was not the guy after a forty-five-minute conversation.

He readily confessed to sending the message to Candy Carlisle when I asked about it. He then explained his fiancée had just broken up with him when he'd sent it. He had been having a tough night and had reached out to Candy Carlisle in a moment of weakness, even though he knew she was married.

He had held a flame for her during all the years since they had graduated from high school. He was also drunk when he sent the message.

"You can check with Deidra about all this," Ian said, "I told her the whole story. Candy never even replied."

"You and your fiancé are back on?"

Ian gave me a big smile. "It was just a hiccup. Things have never been better. I'm really glad Candy never responded. It could've complicated things."

I studied Ian, trying to decide if he was telling me the truth. In the end, I figured he was.

He had no reason to lie.

Winston and I had already known about his upcoming marriage. From all outward appearances on social media and my face-to-face discussion with him, he was apparently madly in love with his fiancée and had moved on past Candy. I could understand how he'd gotten drunk and sent a message.

As far as I was concerned, Ian was now entirely off the list.

I had not expected to track him down so easily. I had also figured that after I met with him, I would not be satisfied and would want to come back to ask follow-up questions. This was why I had scheduled to stay for a few nights. Luckily, Ellie had the foresight to get trip protection when she'd made my reservations. I canceled my hotel and got a return flight back from California, arriving in Chicago by 8:30 PM.

The first thing I did as the plane taxied was call Winston.

"Any movement from our guys?"

"Nothing yet. I'm sitting outside Abe Martin's place," he said, "and I have another PI contracted to follow Bill Weaver. Her name is Amy Babbitt. I worked with her in the past. She's pretty good."

"Let me know the moment you have anything. Just send me a text."

"Will do."

As I retrieved my car and headed towards home, it occurred to me that now might be a perfect time to visit Seth Roberts. Abe and Bill would likely be distracted. If they had been watching him before, perhaps they would not be so vigilant tonight.

Seth Roberts.

Something told me that he was going to be key to unraveling this.

I drove to Seth Roberts' house instead of heading back to my home as I had planned. It was just a little after nine in the evening when I arrived. I was aware that his children would probably be in bed, so I would be careful about how I made my presence known. I was also curious to see his reaction when he saw me. I wanted to know if he and Bill communicated on a regular basis.

The front lawn of the house was just as messy as before, if not messier. It had been a couple of weeks since the grass was last mowed.

I gently knocked when I got to the door.

A few minutes later, Seth answered.

"What are you doing here?" Seth looked over my shoulder as if expecting somebody was following me.

I smiled. "That Camry that was here last time? The one you kept looking at? I checked it out. It wasn't registered to any of the poker boys or anybody who knows them."

Seth frowned as he hesitated. It looked like he was debating telling me to leave.

"You better come inside," he finally said after a glance over his shoulder to see if anybody had approached while we were talking.

Was he worried his wife might overhear our conversation?

Seth turned on me once the door was shut. "I told you never to come back."

I snorted. "You lied."

"What?" He tried to look surprised, but it came off as fake.

"Tell me you didn't."

"I told you the truth." Seth looked away as he spoke.

"That right there," I said, pointing at his face. "You're acting guilty about something."

"So what if I am?"

"Just tell me the truth so that I can help."

"Help? How are you going to help?"

"It will be a relief to unburden yourself."

Seth studied me. "Have a seat."

I followed him into his living room, where he motioned for me to sit on the couch. He sat in an armchair across from it. "Why do you feel like I lied?"

"Are you admitting you did?"

"No, it's just..." Seth trailed off. "I've had troubles with the law in the past. I have done everything I can to put it behind me. I have a nice family. I have a good job. I have set up a desirable life for myself against all odds. It has not been easy, and I don't want to do anything to put that in jeopardy. You understand what I'm saying?"

"You're afraid that if you tell me the truth, things will go badly for you."

He glanced away. It was a moment before he answered. "Yes. If you felt like there was any hesitation when we spoke before, this is why. I don't know why I'm telling you this now." He grimaced. "I don't like you coming to my home. I don't like you calling me a liar. I've tried to do everything I can to turn my life around."

"I know you went to prison for drug dealing."

"I'm not surprised." Seth got misty-eyed. "I learned my lesson, Mr. Turner. I don't ever want to go back. I don't ever want my family to experience anything like that."

"I understand. I will help in any way I can."

"Do you understand?"

Seth's question was asked in earnest.

"I have never been to prison myself, but I have seen its effects on people. I've seen it firsthand on a daily basis. I'm not here to harm you. I'm here to find justice."

"And what exactly is justice?"

"The right people going to jail."

"And how do you know you have the right people?"

"I don't stop looking until I do."

"You sound more like a prosecutor than a defense attorney, you know that?"

"The roles aren't all that different if you're committed to the search for truth. You're just applying it a bit differently, depending on where you work."

"So you don't represent guilty people?"

I gave him an incredulous look. "Of course, I do. All the time. My job is also to help people navigate the system."

"So you truly believe Candy didn't do it?"

I was taken aback by this question, not by the words but by his tone. It seemed a little desperate like he was holding onto some ragged hope that was being torn away.

Rip off the bandage.

"I don't know what to believe until I have all the evidence in front of me. It doesn't help when people hold it back."

"Like you suspect I have done."

"Exactly."

Seth let out a long sigh. "I don't want to be involved in this. I don't want to be called into court. Can you imagine what a prosecutor would do to me on the stand?" He gave me a pointed look. "Or you?"

"I can't promise you won't be subpoenaed. You just finished telling me how you want to be an upstanding member of our society. One responsibility you have is to make sure justice is done. It is incumbent upon you. It is incumbent upon me. As citizens of this great country, we have a moral obligation to stand up and speak the truth if we know the truth to speak it."

I stared at him.

He refused to make eye contact.

"But Mr. Turner! My family, my livelihood. It is going to all be put at risk. People are not going to believe me anyway. It probably won't do any good. The moment I tell you anything, all eyes and attention are gonna be on me. You're probably gonna think I killed Raymond."

"Did you?"

"No!"

"I promise you that I won't. Not unless the evidence goes there."

"That's the problem. Evidence can be made to dance any way you people want to misread it."

"Are you saying you were wrongly accused when you went to prison before?"

Seth shook his head. "No. I deserved what I got. I'm just saying that I'm an ex-con. An ex-con that could potentially be tied to a group that could be behind the murder of Raymond Carlisle. Do you see what I'm saying?"

"You feel like there's a different standard for you than there will be for the others?"

"Exactly. I have to be very careful."

"You have options."

"What do you mean?"

"You could get an attorney. You could tell him what you know. And then he could communicate to me anything that might be useful."

"I don't trust attorneys." He looked at me. "No offense."

"Did you not like your last lawyer?"

"He was just a public defender. He was too busy to give me the time of day. He was only interested in negotiating a deal, not talking about the nuances of my case. I felt like there were some things he should've brought up, things that could have been mitigating factors in my sentencing, but he didn't have an interest in doing that."

"That's not who I am. That's not what I'm about. I am in search of the truth. I have become convinced you know the truth while we have been talking. You must tell the truth."

"And if I don't?"

"I'll subpoena you. I'll put you on the stand. I'll have you testify in court. I'll make you squirm in ways you never thought possible."

Seth licked his lips. "Is that a threat?"

"No, it's just a tool I have to get to the truth if you refuse to tell me what you know."

"And if I tell you, do I have your word, you'll do everything you can to keep me out of it?"

I hesitated. It was a loaded question. I didn't know exactly how I could go about answering it in a way that would satisfy him.

"I'll do everything I can, but you must understand that I'm not going to hesitate if I need to put you on the stand to prove Candy had nothing to do with Raymond's death."

"Then I think we're done here."

Seth stood.

I remained sitting.

"Let me paint a picture for you," I said, "you get called to the stand. Now I may be nice to you, but the prosecution is going to have an opportunity to cross-examine you, too. I also have to disclose my witnesses ahead of time before I can call you. This means that the prosecution will do a thorough background check on you. They will discover your past. They will make sure to bring it up to humiliate you."

"Again, it sounds like you're threatening me."

"No, I'm telling you what's going to happen. I don't want this to be perceived as a threat. I just want you to understand your options."

"Maybe I do need my own attorney."

"He can't stop you from testifying."

"What about my Fifth Amendment rights?"

"Have you done something you can be convicted of? Or do you just know something you want to keep quiet because you are interested in protecting yourself?"

"Could I get my family into a witness protection program or something like that?"

"As you already have noted, I don't work for the state. I don't know that I could successfully put together something like that. I will certainly try if it is needed, but I can't make any guarantee."

Seth sat back down.

"I want to tell you the truth," he said as he put his head in his hands. "You are very persuasive. However, it's just not as simple as you make it out to be. I just can't take this sort of risk with my family."

I grimaced. His concerns were not without merit. And if he was this afraid of the poker boys, my instincts were dead on about this case.

"Let me just throw out some hypotheses. Perhaps you can enlighten me as we go if there's anything you feel is incorrect."

"I'm not sure how I feel about this."

"They didn't invite you over to play poker. Instead, they made you an offer. They had lost a member of their criminal enterprise, and they wanted you to join them."

Seth said nothing. He just looked on with surprised eyes.

"At this point, Raymond is still alive. So, later on, they decide to kill him for some unknown reason. My assumption is you don't have any knowledge of this, or if you do, it is not direct knowledge. *And* you were not involved in his death."

Seth nodded. "That last statement is accurate."

"On the night they invited you to join them, you didn't play poker."

"I have no comment."

"They reached out to you because of your past, thinking you might have connections or ideas on how they could move their product."

Seth stared at me with cold eyes.

"The product, of course, is illegal drugs. I'm not sure if it's illegal prescription drugs or just regular illegal drugs, but it's one of those things."

I watched Seth with unblinking eyes while I spoke. He had two reactions. He blinked when I first mentioned illegal drugs. He also nodded slightly when I talked about illegal prescription drugs. I believed both were involuntary. I made a mental note as I continued.

"You told them something similar to what you told me. That you weren't interested. That you wanted to live an upstanding life. That you didn't have a desire to get back into that world."

"Again, I'm not commenting on any of this. This is all supposition."

"Next, they agree to let you leave. But they make sure you know not to tell anybody about this. Did they threaten you? Have they threatened you since? Perhaps they gave you some of their product in a traceable way so you would go down, too."

No response, but his face was pale.

"When I start asking questions, you decide to get cute with me. Instead of just giving the story that you and the other poker boys agreed on to explain what had happened the night they tried to recruit you, you said that they were terrible at poker. You did this, hoping it might be a clue that would lead to me figure out what they're doing. Your problem disappears if the drug ring is busted."

Seth looked away. There was something in his eyes as he did, though I could not place it at first. A glint of satisfaction? Pride that he had been so subtle and that I picked up on his clue?

Regardless of what it was, there was no doubt now. It had been intentional.

"I believe I've been fairly accurate."

Seth cleared his throat, looked like he was going to say something, but then said nothing.

"So the question then becomes why did they kill Raymond and not you? Both Raymond and you had knowledge of their criminal enterprise."

"You're going too far."

"Was it because Raymond was going to set up a competitor? Is that what this was about, taking care of the competition?"

Seth looked at me. "It's time you go."

"Can you confirm just one thing?"

"What?"

"Was it Abe Martin who shot him?"

"Go now."

41

I looked around to see if there was anybody watching as I walked down the steps of the Roberts home. Most of the houses on the street had lights on, but they also had blinds down. I studied several of the closest homes to see if anybody might be peeking out but didn't notice anything unusual. There were more cars on the street than there had been the last time I visited, which was no surprise because it was nighttime, and more people were home.

There was one car parked directly across the street. The windows were tinted, so I could not see inside. I studied it as I approached my Porsche, even pulling out my phone and snapping a picture, so I had something to think about later. As I was pulling away, I turned and captured a shot of the license plate just to be on the safe side. I would have Winston check it out, but I didn't expect to find anything interesting.

I expected that the interesting things would happen with Winston and Amy.

I knew I wouldn't be able to sleep because of the questions I now had dancing around my mind, so I returned to my office and drafted a memo about my conversation with Seth Roberts, making sure to mark it as confidential attorney work product.

Most of the thoughts I had suggested to Seth Roberts were things I had been thinking about for some time but had not yet mentioned out loud or even put to paper because I had no evidence. When Seth had been so reticent to talk, I figured I might as well try out my theories to see if any held water.

It was clear from his reactions that I was close, if not dead on.

I dialed Winston.

"Anything yet?" I asked.

"Nothing. I don't think tonight is going to be poker night. It's getting late."

"Stick with them all night. Call me if you need to swap out." I hesitated, thinking of asking Winston to find another PI to sit outside Seth Roberts' home for security purposes, but I decided against it. I didn't want Seth to notice my guy sitting out there and get antsy.

And what were the chances he wasn't involved?

He'd already lied to me once.

"I also have a car I want you to check out." I gave Winston the information, forwarding the pictures I had taken.

"I'll look into it. I won't be able to get to it until morning. Is that okay?"

He must have sensed the urgency in my voice; otherwise, he would not have asked the question.

"That should be fine." I hesitated, uncertain about bringing Winston in on my theory at this point in the case. "I met with Seth Roberts tonight."

"How did that go?"

"He didn't tell me anything, not really. I got the feeling the poker boys threatened him."

"What did you get him to say?"

"Not much. I told him I thought they tried to recruit him."

"A logical conclusion, given what we learned today."

"Exactly. He didn't confirm it, but you should've seen the look on his face. If you had been there, you would have thought the same thing as me."

"Which was?"

"These guys are running drugs."

"Better theory than anything else we have."

Seth had subconsciously shaken his head when I went through the options. "It doesn't look like it's street drugs; it looks like it's pain pills."

Winston growled. "Makes me want to bash their heads against the sidewalk."

The comment surprised me. Winston was notoriously personal. The level of venom he spoke with made me think somebody he knew had been affected by a pain pill addiction in the past.

Maybe even Winston himself had struggled with addiction.

I wanted to ask but refrained.

I had kept from asking Winston many personal questions over the years, and now was not the time to reverse my position.

"Let me know if anything pops up tonight, even the smallest thing. I don't think I'm going to sleep much anyway."

"Will do, but I don't think we should expect anything. Things are very quiet."

42

I was surprised when I woke up on my couch at six in the morning, having slept through the night without waking once. I had sat down for a few minutes to watch the news but must have dozed off. I checked my phone, expecting to have missed a text message or call from Winston, but there was nothing.

I gritted my teeth. I had never been closer to the truth with these poker boys, but I didn't know the next best step. I took a few minutes to run on my treadmill before wolfing down breakfast and showering. It was almost 9:00 AM by the time I got into work.

Ellie was there when I arrived.

"Surprised to see you here so early," I said. "How ya feeling?"

She glanced around as if afraid somebody might have overheard my question. She gave me a warning look when it was clear we were alone.

"I don't want anybody else to know."

"Got it, I remember."

She couldn't keep it secret for long, especially if she continued to miss much more work, but I would provide her as much privacy and space as I could afford. If somebody learned the truth, it would not be from me.

I had just barely sat at my desk when my phone buzzed. "Frank Ward for you," Ellie said, "shall I send him through?"

"I'm ready."

"Mitch, how's everything going?" Frank asked as soon as the line clicked, and he had been transferred over.

"You guys ready to throw in the towel on the Candy Carlisle case yet?" I asked as if it were obviously a mistake for them to have filed charges in the first place.

Frank snorted. "Not unless you have evidence that shows somebody else did it."

I ground my teeth, wishing I had something that would conclusively prove Candy had nothing to do with it. "You'll just have to wait until trial."

"You got nothing."

"Never said that."

"If you had anything compelling, you'd be talking to me about it right now. I know your style. You don't like to wait till court if you can solve the problem before it gets to trial."

"Just when you think you know what I'm up to, I'll turn around and surprise you."

Frank laughed. It sounded genuine. He appeared to be in a good mood. "I just had a meeting with my boss, and to be frank, we'd rather plea this case out."

A silent warning bell went off in my head.

"I think I've made it clear my client is not interested in a deal at this point."

"We'll give her fifteen years."

That was considerably better than his last offer. The last time he had been willing to go down to twenty if we took an offer that week. It had been several weeks since we had turned that down, so I was surprised to see he was coming of his own initiative to make a new offer that was lower than the first. Either there was a weakness in his case, or there was something else I did not yet know.

"I'll tell my client. I don't want you to get your hopes up that the case is going to be resolved so easily."

"Mitch," Frank said. "You know me. You know I don't hand out offers like candy. I'd rather take this to court, but my boss is putting pressure on me to resolve this one because we have other cases that are more time-consuming. We want to nail those, so your client is getting a deal."

"You just want this off your desk," I said as if I didn't believe it.

"Exactly. Please see what you can do. I would take it as a personal favor."

I frowned. It wouldn't be difficult to get the number down further.

This was unexpected.

There weren't any mitigating factors in this case that Winston or I had turned up. Candy could not claim battered wife syndrome or something similar. By all outward appearances, if Candy had done this, she would deserve the max sentence.

The way Frank was acting made me think they had come across evidence to suggest Candy had not committed the crime, but they didn't want to look into it and would rather just take a plea deal to get it off their plate. I hoped that wasn't the case, I thought better of Frank than that, but sometimes the pressures of the job got to people and made it difficult for them to remember that there were real-life consequences on the other end of these cases.

Part of me wanted to throw out ten years just to see how Frank would respond, but I knew my client would have a problem with me doing that. I might have come at it from a roundabout manner in another situation, but not with Candy's case.

I would have to figure out what was going on a different way.

"I'll tell her," I said, feeling like I was repeating myself, "but you need to understand my client says she's innocent. I believe her. I have a hard time seeing her take this offer."

"Just try it out. You and I both know how these things work. They say they're innocent, but suddenly, when the right offer is sitting in front of them, it's harder to turn down. They are ready to tell a different story."

Something is off.

"I'll let her know."

"Thanks, Mitch."

Once I was off the phone with Frank Ward, I felt too antsy to sit.

That's a bad sign. I only just got here.

I glanced at my watch and saw it was way too early for lunch, so I pulled out a pad of paper and started diagraming everything I knew about the case. After I completed that, I flipped to another page and drew a line down the middle. On one side, I wrote, "She did it," and on the other side, I wrote, "She didn't do it."

I listed every fact or piece of evidence I knew and put it into a column to indicate how I thought it went.

By the time I was done, it was almost evenly split. The biggest things the prosecution had against Candy were her DNA, the lack of forced entry, and the fact Candy didn't have a solid alibi for where she was that night. These three things combined to make it look like she could have done this.

The preliminary hearing had occurred before I took on the case. I had read through the transcript but had not seen a solid sign of what Frank believed the motive was. The standard for a preliminary hearing was whether or not there was enough evidence to charge the defendant with a crime, not whether they had actually done it. He had likely kept from making statements on motive to make things more difficult for Karen and now me to poke holes in his case.

What if that's not it?

What if he can't figure out a motive?

I took off my defense attorney's hat and put on my prosecuting attorney cap. As I looked at the case, I realized Frank might have done this on purpose.

They have a motive problem.

Frank could not explain why Candy had killed her husband any more than I could explain how she had not.

A motive problem. Technically speaking, that should swing in my favor when we got to trial because Candy was presumed innocent until proven guilty, but practically speaking, it might not. It was always difficult to predict what a jury was going to do or believe.

I next ran a court search to see which cases had been filed recently by the prosecutor's office, looking specifically for those represented by Frank. I let out a low whistle when I was done. He was currently operating no fewer than twenty active murder cases, which was quite a caseload, considering all the work that had to go into every case. The trials, obviously, wouldn't all happen at the same time. There were several cases where junior prosecutors were officially helping, and he also had separate teams of investigators for each case, but still.

That was a lot of work.

No wonder why his boss was trying to get him to shelve some of his problematic cases.

I smelled blood in the water. They had singled out Candy Carlisle's case for a plea bargain. That meant there was something I didn't know, or they were afraid of what they didn't know.

I had intentionally not mentioned the information I had got from Bill Weaver during my conversation with Frank Ward. I wasn't trying to suppress evidence. I just wanted to be careful in how I revealed it to the prosecution.

I also wanted to check its veracity myself first, so I knew how best to prepare to handle it.

I was sure Bill Weaver and his wife were cooking something up, but the prosecution wouldn't believe that was the case if they could put a witness on the stand who could testify they had seen Candy with something that appeared to be a gun several days before the murder.

Frank might not ask many questions if he was getting desperate.

I reviewed my notes and was surprised to see I didn't have a name for Bill Weaver's wife. I was certain he'd mentioned it, but I had not written it down.

I had to open up Karen's investigator's file before I could locate that information.

Tammy. Tammy Weaver.

I had the number Bill Weaver had given me for Tammy. I remembered Bill believed I was still out of town just as I was about to dial.

I put down my phone.

I'd give it a couple of days before calling.

43

I was sitting at home on the evening of the next day when I got a phone call from Winston. It had been a grueling day; most of my time had been devoted to another client who was having a tough time coming to terms with the fact he needed to take an offer instead of go to trial. I had spent almost two hours with him. He had still not been convinced at the end.

"Bill Weaver is moving."

I was instantly alert.

"Any idea where he is headed?"

"Looks like he's going to Abe Martin's house."

"You still have Amy Babbitt on Abe?"

"I didn't ask her to work tonight since it was a bust the last two nights. I told her that I might call if I needed her, so she's on standby if anything comes up. There's no reason for both of us to sit outside while the poker boys play, but I might call her if he heads somewhere else."

"Don't hesitate." I didn't need to tell Winston we were grabbing at loose ends and any opportunity was something we needed to take full advantage of.

"Just trying to keep costs down."

I normally would've appreciated that, but not on this case. Candy could pay, and we had little else to go on.

"Let me worry about costs, Winston. You just figure out how we nail these guys." I hesitated and then turned off my TV. "I'm going to catch up to you."

"Are you sure that's a good idea? You drive a recognizable vehicle."

"I'll park several blocks away and walk over once everybody's there."

"If you feel that's wise." It was obvious Winston didn't think it was.

I studied my car when I got to my garage. I loved my Porsche, but it did present problems when I wanted to do something incognito.

I trudged back into my living room while pulling out my phone and summoning an Uber.

I didn't want to be without a vehicle, but I also didn't want Abe Martin or Bill Weaver or the others to recognize me.

It took fifteen minutes for the Uber to show. I had already provided him with an address that was several blocks away from Abe Martin's home using the app. We sat in silence while we drove.

Winston was right that it might be a mistake for me to show up like this, but I was just so tired of not making progress. I was tired of being patient and waiting for something to happen.

I was going to make something happen.

If we were to have any chance of breaking this case open, it needed to be soon. Otherwise, I would head into trial with little more than a theory.

It wasn't long before I got out of the Uber and started to finish the last bit on foot.

I sent Winston a text letting him know when I was just a street away. I asked if now was a good time for me to turn the corner. A full minute passed without hearing back.

It didn't take long for it to dawn on me that it was just a little after 10:00 PM, and I was loitering outside somebody's home. I had expected a quick response from Winston, so I was annoyed that he was taking his time. Was he frustrated that I had decided to meet up with him?

Did he think that I was checking up on him, implying he wasn't doing a good job?

It wasn't anything like that. I would feel out if that's what he thought and put the concern to rest. I didn't like it when I had people looking over my shoulder either. I could understand the feeling.

That's not what this was. We just needed a break in this case.

I was here to facilitate.

I pretended to scroll through news on my phone, even though it was an awkward thing to do outside of a random person's home this late at night. I finally started towards the corner, hoping I would receive a message from Winston before I got there.

I didn't. I turned down the street and shuffled forward, putting my phone back in my pocket to not call attention to myself.

I spotted Winston's car when I was seventy-five feet away. He would have spotted me by now if he was paying attention.

My phone buzzed. I pulled it out to see that Winston had confirmed now was a good time.

Nice of him to tell me.

I increased my pace to a normal stride and arrived at Winston's car a moment later. I heard the door locks clicking as I arrived. I assumed he had unlocked the car, so I could enter. I took it as my invitation to just open the door and step inside. Winston picked up his camera, so I could sit down.

I was glad once I was behind the tinted glass of Winston's vehicle. I no longer felt conspicuous.

"Two minutes earlier, and we might have had a problem," Winston said in a neutral tone as if he wanted to suggest it was a bad thing for me to have come but didn't want to say it directly.

"Who arrived?" I asked, unperturbed.

"Larry Thompson."

"Are all of them here?"

"Everybody except for Seth Roberts."

"It will be interesting to see if he shows up."

"Indeed."

Ten minutes later, I wondered if I had made a mistake. I had let my nerves about the case convince me it was best to be on hand to witness the poker night, but there was little to see.

What was I expecting? To see them sell drugs out of Abe Martin's garage?

"Any idea where they normally meet for poker?" Winston asked. "I know the notes from Karen's investigators suggest it was usually Abe Martin's place. Did you confirm that in your conversations?"

"I think it is on a rotation."

Ten minutes more passed. Winston kept looking over at me from his peripheral vision as if he expected me to bail. He was wrong. I would stay until every single last one had gone home. I didn't care if I had to wait until six in the morning.

We waited until 2:00 AM.

Kyle Rencher left first. He was followed by Larry Thompson. It was another ten minutes before Bill Weaver left. Winston started his engine after he was out of view.

"Wait."

"Why?"

"I want to see if anybody else leaves the house." There were other vehicles out on the street. Maybe all of them belonged to the homes they were parked in front of, maybe not. Both Larry Thompson and Kyle Rencher had parked down the street. Bill Weaver had parked in the driveway. What were the chances that another person we didn't know about was a member of this poker gang?

"This is a waste of time. Bill Weaver might go somewhere important."

"Just humor me."

"You're the boss."

Winston was annoyed, but something made me want to stay. I couldn't describe exactly what it was, other than I could feel in my bones that now was not the time to leave.

Winston killed the engine after a couple of minutes, muttering something I didn't catch. It was almost fifteen minutes later, after Winston had given me several lengthy looks and explained we had no way of knowing whether Bill Weaver had gone straight home, when the door to Abe Martin's house opened.

I was surprised to see a woman walk out.

"I was right," I muttered quietly, surprised my gamble had paid off.

"Don't let it go to your head," Winston said, giving me a thin grin as he pulled up his camera and started snapping pictures. She walked down the steps. I didn't recognize her.

"Bill's wife?" I asked.

Winston shook his head. "She would've left with her husband."

"We have a fifth member. They recruited her to fill Raymond's place after Seth turned them down."

"It would seem so."

We watched as she got into a red Acura. I pulled out my phone and snapped pictures of the license plate, and then as an afterthought, made a note as well just in case the picture didn't come through. I would have Winston's photos soon enough, but I wasn't taking chances. This was the first real break we'd had in the case.

I wasn't going to lose it.

"Should we follow?" Winston asked. "Or do you want to go get your car and follow her yourself?

"I took an Uber."

"At least you had the sense to do that."

I let the comment slide.

"We would've never known about her if I hadn't come."

Winston didn't reply.

"Let's follow her."

44

Winston followed her more closely than I was comfortable with. I was becoming concerned she might figure out we were on to her when she turned down a residential street and pulled into the garage of a house. We went straight while I snapped pictures of her home as we passed. Winston turned down the next street and approached her home from the opposite direction.

"She look single to you?" Winston asked as he parked several houses away. He brought up his camera and took pictures.

"Impossible to say. I couldn't see a ring on her finger. It was too dark."

"This is the home of a single lady."

The house was pink. The landscaping was all zero scaping. There wasn't a single blade of grass in her front yard, but there were many flowers.

"You might be onto something," I said as I pulled up the pictures I had taken of her earlier and examined them. They were too dark for me to make out her face.

Perhaps there was another way to figure out her identity. I accessed Karen's investigator's file and used the information within to track down the Facebook pages of the women associated with this case. Abe Martin was single. Kyle Rencher had a girlfriend. Larry Thompson had a wife, as did Bill Weaver. I looked them all up on social media and didn't recognize a single one. It was possible the woman we had just followed might be one of them, but it was not likely.

"Why did she leave after all the others?" I asked, pulling up Abe Martin's profile. I was hoping to find him connected to a girlfriend, but no such luck.

"I don't think there's much more we can learn," Winston said. "It's three in the morning. She's home for the night."

"Agreed. How about we head back over to Bill Weaver's place?"

"Thought you'd never ask." He gave me a thin smile. "What made you want to hang back?"

"They tried to recruit Seth Roberts." I shrugged. "It made sense they would recruit somebody else."

"Good point."

We soon arrived at Bill Weaver's house. We assumed Bill had already returned for the evening after waiting fifteen minutes. I was thinking of summoning another Uber when Bill suddenly pulled up to his house and parked in the garage.

Winston gave me a look. "Wonder where he's been? Don't you wish we could've followed him?"

"It is more important we learned about the woman."

45

I waited for a full hour before I finally summoned an Uber and returned home at about 4:30 in the morning. I was asleep by the time my head hit the pillow. I didn't wake till after 9:00 AM and was in the office an hour later.

Ellie was out, so Zoey greeted me.

"Good morning, Mr. Turner," she said cheerfully, turning to greet me. "How was your evening?"

I gave her a wry smile. "You wouldn't believe me if I told you." I was about to leave it at that but couldn't resist saying more. "I helped my private investigator follow a couple of suspects last night. We had something materialize." I also couldn't suppress a triumphant grin. "Might be about to break a case wide open."

She laughed. "That's great news!"

I was soon sitting behind my desk making notes about the night before when it occurred to me that now might be a good time to reach out to Bill Weaver's wife. I brought up my phone to call her but put it down a moment later. I would visit her instead.

Zoey stopped me as I was walking out. "I have somebody on the line for you, says his name is Frank Ward."

"What does he want?" I asked.

"Says he wants a meeting."

"Tell him I'll meet him at Mike's for lunch at noon. That work?"

"Yes, that does," Zoey said a moment later.

Things couldn't have worked out better. I needed to tell Frank Ward about Tammy Weaver. Hopefully, I'd have a conversation with her prior to our lunch meeting, giving me time to assess her as a potential witness and decide the best way to approach the situation.

I reviewed the events of the night before as I drove. I had initially been excited about this fifth woman—and I still was—but chances were slim she had anything to do with Raymond Carlisle's murder.

I was hoping she would lead me to information about the poker boys that would enable me to prove they were running a drug ring. If I could do that,

I could take it to Stephanie Gray and request she open an investigation into them.

Stephanie Gray. I hadn't thought about her in a while.

Why is she investigating Thomas Guyton?

I had not made another attempt to figure out what was going on. Perhaps it was time I tried.

I thought about calling Barbara while I drove to check on the stalker situation—I still had her on speed dial in my car—but I refrained. It was telling that she had made no move to reach out to me. She wanted to move on. I didn't blame her. She had given me almost two years of her life and had nothing to show for it. I wished her the best.

At least I tried to tell myself that as I parked in front of Bill and Tammy Weaver's house.

I had not gotten a good look at the home in the dead of night, but I now saw that it was a nice place. It was a one-story rambler on a huge lot that appeared to take up most of the available land.

I walked up to the home, taking note of the immaculately kept lawn, the precisely placed landscaping, and how the other houses in the neighborhood had dirty windows from a recent storm, but the Weaver home windows had been recently cleaned.

A dog barked somewhere inside when I rang the doorbell. A woman in workout clothes soon came to the door. She was pretty and greeted me with a smile. She was ten years younger than Bill Weaver, at least.

"Mr. Turner!"

I wasn't expecting her to recognize me. This only further substantiated my suspicion that she and Bill Weaver were concocting a story to implicate my client.

"Tammy Weaver," I said, mimicking the same amount of enthusiasm with which he had greeted me, hoping it came off as genuine.

"Seems like no introductions are needed here," she said with a musical laugh as she swung the door wide open and waved me inside. "I've just been doing yoga downstairs in our workout room. If I would've known you were coming, I would've been more presentable."

"I assume you know what this is about?"

"Yes." She motioned to her front room. "Please have a seat.

The room was immaculately decorated. The coffee table in the middle seemed to be expensive, as did the other furnishings and wall hangings. I expected no less based on the outside of the house. A picture of her and Bill from their wedding day hung in the middle of the wall opposite. I wondered if they had kids as I looked around.

My file said nothing about Bill Weaver having kids, but it was thin. Karen's investigators had quickly dismissed Bill as a suspect and had spent little time digging into his background. I tried to remember if the report from Winston had included information on children and decided it had not. It was the sort of thing Winston would have mentioned.

I sat on a sofa. Tammy took the one perpendicular.

"Should I just get right into it?" Tammy asked brightly, with what appeared to be a genuine smile.

I hid a frown. She would be very presentable in court. Frank would put her on the stand, no question. I wouldn't have hesitated in his position. The jury would believe her just because she was pretty and optimistic. They would have a hard time thinking she could lie.

"If you would not mind."

"I ran into Candy Carlisle at the sporting goods store. It was several days before Raymond was murdered. I remember that for sure."

"What were you doing there?"

She smiled. "I was picking up new exercise equipment. I'd special ordered it, and it had just arrived. I got a message that morning."

"You remember which store this was?"

"Unfortunately, I don't."

I raised an eyebrow. "You special ordered equipment but don't remember where you got it from?"

She gave me an impish smile. I could just imagine her using it to get out of a speeding ticket. "I'm afraid I'm a bit of an airhead sometimes. I went through old credit card bills and found nothing. That means I paid cash. I tried looking for receipts but couldn't find any record of the transaction. I even drove around for a few hours, trying to remember where I had made the purchase, but I just could not remember for the life of me."

"What did you buy?"

"Specialized dumbbells." She held up an arm. "I have puny arms. I ordered them to help me bulk up."

My skin crawled. She was lying, I knew without a doubt. Would Frank feel the same?

"Do you remember what time of day this was?"

"Before noon, I can tell you that for sure. I had just come from my yoga class, which starts at 10:00 AM and ends at 11:00."

"Did you talk with Candy?"

Tammy shook her head. "No. In fact, I have to be honest, I don't know that Candy and I have ever been formally introduced."

I was not surprised by this inclusion. They had spent considerable time thinking about their story and how to present it.

Bill claimed they talked at the grocery store. He must have realized his mistake and is having her backpedal for him.

"Did you see her in the parking lot or in the store itself?"

"She was walking out as I was pulling up. She had this black case. She held it by a handle. It was 5 x 10."

An oddly specific detail.

Was she adding information to convince me?

"I didn't think anything of it," Tammy continued. "I'm sure that if I had recognized the potential for it to contain a pistol, I would've thought to mention it to the investigators when they came around."

"Did you ever talk with law enforcement?"

"Not that I can recall."

That was about to change.

Was Frank going to look at Tammy sideways, or would he just be happy to have another nail to put in my client's coffin? I shuddered when I thought of Detective Bernie Lee interviewing Tammy. He would buy the story without a second thought.

"Did you see any insignia or logos on this black box?"

Tammy shook her head. "I'm afraid I didn't. I really wish I had. If I would've known it would be key to resolving Raymond's murder, you can bet I would have paid closer attention, maybe even pulled out my phone and snapped pictures." She chuckled as if thinking of herself as a spy, and it delighted her.

"Did you see what car she got into?" I asked, wondering exactly how many details they had created and how many were real. It wouldn't be hard for them to figure out the make and model of Candy's vehicle.

"Yes. It was a Ford Expedition. I don't have the license number memorized, but it has a bumper sticker on the back for a yoga place. I don't remember which one. I just remember that there was a sticker.

Once Frank heard this, he would run a quick search and discover Candy Carlisle did, in fact, drive a Ford Expedition. The yoga sticker would seal the deal.

"Did she have anything else? A bag, perhaps?"

"No, not that I saw."

"Do you remember how long it took to get to the sporting goods store after you came from your yoga class?"

"No, I'm afraid I don't."

"You said you saw Candy a little before noon, correct?"

"Yes. Maybe five or ten minutes before."

"Did you linger after you finished your yoga class?"

"No. I usually leave right away."

"So, can we assume it was a forty-five minute drive to get to the sporting goods store, or did you have other places you stopped?"

She paused, looking up at the ceiling as if trying to remember. She might be trying to come off as an airhead, but I was on to her. She was smarter than she wanted to appear. She knew where I was going. It would seem odd that she would drive forty-five minutes to a sporting goods store, the name of which she could not remember, to pick up specialized dumbbell equipment.

"I might have stopped a place or two. I don't remember for certain."

Leaving room to maneuver.

"Can I see the dumbbells?"

She looked crestfallen. "Unfortunately, they didn't work out the way I hoped. I got rid of them."

I almost laughed, it was so ridiculous. "Do you remember what make they were?"

"Sorry, I don't."

"How long did it take for you and Bill to come up with this story?"

It looked like she was going to answer, but then she gave me a flabbergasted look as if I could even suggest such a thing. "I am not lying!"

I opened my mouth, planning to dig into her further, but decided instead to save it for the courtroom.

"Is there anything else you can tell me that might be pertinent?"

It was a moment before she answered. She wanted to come off as haughty and angry, but she just looked scared and confused. She was working hard to cover it up.

"Bill told me that he mentioned to you that I once ran into Candy Carlisle at the grocery store. She was severely put out by something. I'm not sure what was going on, but she was very unhappy. I can tell you that much for sure."

I now understood why Bill had told me that story about Tammy and Candy running into each other. He had been trying to lay the groundwork for this whopper.

Subtle.

"Did you say anything to her?"

"No. She doesn't know me, so obviously, she would not have appreciated meeting me like that."

I hesitated. Bill was indeed using his wife to backtrack from the original story.

"Do you remember when this was?"

"I dunno, a few months before Raymond's death." Tammy shrugged. "Can't say for sure."

"Where did this happen?"

"Sorry, I don't know." She gave me an empathetic look. "I spend a lot of time shopping if you haven't figured it out. It's difficult to remember where I went yesterday, let alone where I went several weeks or even several months ago."

I nodded as if I believed her. "Thank you for your time today."

46

I was nearing the office when I got a phone call from Winston.

"Beatrice Jones," he said as soon as I answered.

"Excuse me?"

"Beatrice Jones. That is the name of the woman we followed last night.

"How did you figure that out?"

"Ran a license plate search, confirmed it with property records. She *is* single, by the way."

I thought he was suggesting I could ask her out until I remembered he had deduced she was single from her landscaping and the color of her house.

"What does she do for a living?"

"You're gonna love this. She's a high school teacher. Theater."

Her house was nicer than I would've expected on a teacher's salary.

"You think she's dealing to her students?"

"That was my first thought too."

"She have a criminal past?"

"Running the search now. I'll let you know what I find."

"Great, thanks, Winston."

By the time I arrived at my office, I had just a few minutes before my lunch meeting with Frank, so I spent that time making notes on my interview with Tammy Weaver. After that, I made a plan for my lunch appointment. I had to disclose to Frank the information I received from Tammy, but I also needed to make sure he called her as a witness.

I felt reasonably confident I had a good strategy by the time I was heading out to my meeting. The restaurant was busy, but they found a table for two within a couple of minutes of my arrival.

Frank was late. I was already seated and had ordered a Coke by the time he showed up.

"Your client ready to make a plea?" Frank asked as he sat.

I shook my head. "You can always make another offer. I'll certainly tell her."

Frank frowned. "I suspected as much."

"What did you want to talk about?"

"I want to give you a preview of my case. I want your client to know exactly what she's going to be walking into the day court starts."

I waited. Frank did, too, as if he expected a comment from me. He didn't speak until the silence became awkward.

"Have you ever wondered where your client gets her money?" Frank asked.

I had my suspicions, but I had never asked outright. I had just assumed the drug money had stopped with either Raymond's death or when he had been expelled from the poker boys.

"How about you tell me?"

"At first glance, we thought it came from her dead husband's job, and to be sure, he made a good salary. However, their real money comes from selling drugs."

It was no surprise to me that Raymond had drug money. I kept my poker face on because I was glad of the direction this conversation was going. Frank thought he was scaring me, but he was going down the path I had come hoping to tempt him down.

"You have proof Candy is involved?"

"Better believe it."

I studied Frank. "I bet anything you have is circumstantial."

"When you have circumstantial evidence of drug dealing and circumstantial evidence of murder, it isn't usually hard for the jury to figure out what happened."

I nodded, choosing to remain silent rather than engaging in a war of words with Frank here and now. I didn't want to risk tipping him off that this was exactly what I wanted him to do.

Maybe I should show some teeth? Isn't that what he's expecting?

I shook my head while frowning. "You have nothing."

"Raymond was deep into drugs, too," Frank said, watching closely for my reaction. I didn't give him one.

The implication was clear, though. Did Candy want her dead husband's name dragged through the mud?

"I expect you guys will want to talk now." Frank acted as though he had just played an ace.

"You should still expect that this will go to trial."

Frank slammed his hand down, almost knocking over his glass of water and drawing attention from nearby tables. It was a moment before they looked away, and he spoke again.

"Trying to do you a favor here, Mitch."

"I recognize that," I said, "and I appreciate it. For another case or a different client, this could be a game-changer in how we approached things. I know my client. She is emphatic she had nothing to do with this. And she is going to do everything she can to prove it."

"She's gonna go to prison for a long time."

"Why don't you want to take this case to trial?" I asked, my tongue getting the better of me. I was glad my instincts had slipped out. This was the type of resistance Frank was expecting.

"Because I have three other trials just like it."

"Working you guys pretty hard, are they?"

"You have no idea." Frank gave me what he must have hoped was a long-suffering smile, but it came off as desperate. "It's crazy how many cases we have going right now. It's like everybody decided to commit murder at the same time."

"I know, right? Why can't they space these things out?" I smiled to show Frank I was joking, primarily because I wasn't sure he could tell unless he had a visual cue. "Things are difficult now. I'm sure they will turn around."

"That's it? That's all you have to say?"

"I don't expect she's going to change her mind, but I'll let you know. There is one other thing I need to tell you."

Frank just waited while he seethed.

"I think you might want to speak to Bill Weaver's wife."

"Who?"

"The wife of a man in Raymond's poker group."

"Why would I want to talk with her?"

Did I have to spell it out?

"Just visit her. She'll tell you an interesting tale. I'm obligated to tell you about it."

"What does she have to say?"

I spoke slowly. "She believes she saw my client purchasing a gun several days before Raymond's death."

Frank's frowned deepened. "Then why won't you guys talk about a deal?"
"It's not up to me. It's up to my client."
"We'll see you in court."

47

I woke up earlier than I normally did when the day of the trial finally arrived. I could not get back to sleep. Eventually, I gave it up and hit the treadmill, running for almost an hour before I showered and had breakfast. It wasn't even five in the morning by the time I was done with all of that.

The last month had sped by, and despite our best efforts, Winston and I had yet to prove that the poker boys were dealing drugs.

There had been one more poker night a few days ago. We had gone with an army of private investigators, Amy Babbitt and three others. Everybody had followed somebody to see if they could find evidence of what was going on, but we had found nothing.

Nothing.

Winston had approached some of Beatrice Jones' students at the high school where she worked, but they had suspected he was a cop. He had not made it far before the conversations had ended. Word had gotten around that some cop was asking questions, so Winston had backed off.

I even had Winston talk to a couple of Bill Weaver's patients to see if anything materialized there, but nothing had.

Whatever these guys were up to, they had done a good job of keeping it on the down-low.

The only spot of luck I had was Frank Ward amending his list of witnesses to include Tammy Weaver, Bill Weaver, Abe Martin, and Kyle Rencher.

I guessed that Bill, Abe, and Kyle had told a story to back up Tammy Weaver's claims. Frank would not have had the time necessary to properly vet them, something I was counting on.

At the last possible minute, I amended my list of witnesses to include Seth Roberts, Larry Thompson, and Beatrice Jones.

I didn't know that I was actually going to call any of them, but I wanted the option to put them on the stand and grill them if I needed to. Frank probably raised an eyebrow when he saw my additions, but I doubted he'd had time to think about it beyond that.

The appointed hour soon arrived. I walked into court with my briefcase, and a fresh bottle of Coke that Ellie had made sure was ice cold. She had come in early to meet with me, an informal ritual that had developed over the years.

The signs of her chemotherapy treatment were showing. It would not be much longer before the rest of the office knew what she was going through. She had transitioned to a wig that was almost an identical match for her hair, but the puffiness in her face was sure to draw questions soon.

"All rise," the bailiff said, breaking into my thoughts.

Judge Cindy Hopkins walked into the courtroom.

Judge Hopkins had been two years ahead of me in law school. I vaguely remembered her from back then. I didn't know much about her from law school other than she had been chief editor of the law review, and she had been famous for the law outlines she had made. I had even studied from a Cindy Hopkins outline a time or two myself.

I'd never had a trial with her as judge, nor had I ever had a case with her when she'd practiced as a defense attorney, and I'd been a prosecutor. The reports I'd heard said she was tough but fair. She didn't seem to lean one way or the other but relied on a strict interpretation of the law in making her decisions. It was about as good as I could've hoped for.

We finished with voir dire and selected a jury by the time lunch rolled around.

"We will come back for opening statements at 1:00 PM sharp," Judge Hopkins said, "and then the prosecution will present its case."

She banged the gavel and dismissed us.

"How do you think things went?" Candy asked, leaning over so only I could hear.

"As good as could be expected," I said. "It's always a crapshoot when selecting jurors. You do your best, but in the end, it's a guess."

Unless you splurge on a pricey jury consultant. But even they only removed so much risk.

I had suggested to Candy that we hire a jury consultant, but she had declined because it was expensive, though I doubted cost was a significant factor. It just didn't seem necessary to her. She was also insisting that I put her on the stand to testify. That's what she was counting on to get out of this. I wasn't so sure that was going to help.

"We're gonna win," Candy said, "the truth is going to come out."

"Absolutely."

After Candy had left, I packed up my briefcase and headed out, too. Winston was waiting for me outside.

"You have anything?" I asked.

"Unfortunately, nothing," Winston said, "just coming to wish you luck. I was in the area."

I glanced around to make sure nobody could overhear me. "We're gonna need it."

I ate a quick lunch when I got back to my office and reviewed my opening statement, tweaking it here and there, trying to envision how the jurors would receive it. That's what today was going to come down to.

My credibility with the jury.

I had to be impeccable in my presentation and skilled in how I handled each and every witness so that the jurors looked at me at all times and thought that I was the utmost professional. I couldn't allow myself to be dragged into persnickety fights. I had to choose my battles.

At 1:00 PM sharp, we were all in our seats.

The bailiff stood.

"All rise, court is now in session."

Once Judge Hopkins was seated, she looked at Frank Ward.

"You may proceed, counselor."

"Thank you, Your Honor," Frank said as he walked to the podium.

"On February 16, just after 10:00 PM, Candy Carlisle claims to have come home and found her husband shot dead on the couch in the living room while their two children were asleep in their bedrooms on the second floor."

Frank paused as if he was himself considering the impact of what he had just said. He shook his head mournfully and looked at the members of the jury.

"That is the story the defense wants us to believe. It is not true. Raymond Carlisle *was* killed, but that's where the truth ends."

He paused for emphasis.

"Candy Carlisle killed her husband in cold blood while their children slept upstairs."

Frank looked at his notepad and turned the page before looking back up into the eyes of the jury.

"Raymond and Candy Carlisle were both involved in drug dealing. Can you imagine running a drug operation from your home? Where your two children live?"

I tensed, wondering if I should object. After a moment of consideration, I relaxed and was glad I hadn't jumped to my feet.

I knew my trial strategy. I didn't want to appear cantankerous or look like I was trying to hide anything.

And they were selling drugs.

Candy wasn't the first unsympathetic client I had ever represented, and she wouldn't be the last.

"The idea is unthinkable," Frank continued, "yet that is what was going on. On top of that, Raymond and Candy had taken lovers."

Another place I could have objected, but it was the truth. If I objected now to something I knew was true, the jury would have a hard time agreeing with my objections later on.

"They were trying to have it all, weren't they?"

Frank was pleased with this last remark, but it didn't look like it played well with the jury. He would've done better to keep sarcasm out of his opening statement.

"We don't know everything that happened between these two, and we might not ever know most of it, yet we do know Candy was planning to divorce her husband.

"Did Raymond threaten her? Did he tell her she couldn't leave because he would go to the cops about their business?

"Unfortunately, we will never know because Raymond is not with us today."

Frank then droned on for twenty more minutes. By the time he finished, most of the jury looked bored.

"Candy mercilessly and skillfully planned and carried out the cold-blood killing of Raymond in the front room of her own home. At the end of this trial, ladies and gentlemen of the jury, I am going to ask you to find Candy Carlisle guilty of first-degree murder."

Frank looked each juror in the eye and then sat down.

"Mr. Turner," Judge Hopkins said.

"Thank you, Your Honor." I approached the podium and turned to face the jury as if I was planning to address them from there. I hesitated and took a step forward before turning to the judge. "Permission to approach the jury, Your Honor?"

"Granted."

I moved until I stood in front of the jury. I still had not said anything to them. I waited for several heartbeats. I wanted to make sure all eyes were on me.

"My client is presumed innocent." I pointed at her. "There sits an innocent woman. It is the burden of the prosecution to prove she did it beyond any reasonable doubt."

I looked at each member of the jury. Four men and eight women, all of different vocational and ethnic backgrounds. It was about as representative of the population as you could get. I didn't have anybody that was particularly worrisome, but I also didn't have anybody that looked like they were for sure going to swing my way.

I had chosen my words carefully. I was being vague on purpose because I didn't want the poker boys to know I was gunning for them before they testified on the prosecution's behalf.

I sat.

It was the shortest opening statement I had ever given. Frank Ward looked over in surprise. He had expected a few more minutes before he called his first witness.

Rule number one. Never let them predict you.

Even the jurors seem to recognize what I had done was unusual. I was known for having brief opening statements, but this time I had outdone even myself. In a profession known for its verbosity, I had chosen to be unusually short.

I had done this for several reasons, the primary one being I didn't want to tie myself to a particular theory. I needed to keep my options open. I still didn't know how I was going to present my defense. I was focused on poking holes in the prosecution's case and looking for opportunities with the witnesses Frank Ward put on the stand.

The judge looked at me curiously as if wondering if I was not adequately prepared. I wondered if my reputation as a lackadaisical law student had gotten back to her. I'd pulled good grades. I just hadn't worked as hard as others had for them. She looked on the verge of saying something but shrugged and turned to Frank.

"Call your first witness, counselor."

"The prosecution calls Bernie Lee to the witness stand."

48

Frank went through the usual questions to lay a foundation for Bernie's experience as a detective and police officer. He started by asking Bernie how long he had been on the force, the cases he had investigated, the jobs he had done. Most of the jury had glazed over eyes by the time we finally got to what had happened on the day Raymond died.

I hid a smile.

Good old reliable Frank. I knew of his tendency to drone on about things that had little relevance to the case and had counted on it in my preparations.

I had managed to present a stark contrast between myself and Frank Ward from the get-go. This would pay dividends the further we got into the trial. It was important to be distinct, memorable, and reliable.

It was not important to say as much as possible. This was a mistake I often saw attorneys make when they presented their cases in court. They wanted to do everything they could, and because of that, and perhaps because of the fear of getting sued for malpractice, they frequently did far more than they should, making things more complicated than they needed to be.

Sometimes, the facts of a case required attorneys not to be brief, but it was rare. And I was yet to find a situation where brevity and a careful choice of words didn't pay off more than making the jury sit back and get bored.

If it was a bench trial where the judge was the fact-finder, it was a different story. You could normally count on a judge to pay better attention and carefully review all the facts and law on a case.

I believed most jurors went by their gut in how they decided.

That's where I came in.

I played to their emotions and instincts.

"Can you tell us what happened on the night of February 16?" Frank Ward finally asked, almost half an hour after Bernie Lee had taken the stand.

One of the jurors stirred—juror number two—as if waking from a nap.

Things were about to get interesting, or so they thought. I never underestimated Frank's tendency to get lost in the details.

"I received a call about a body," Bernie said. "I responded to the residence of Raymond and Candy Carlisle."

"What did you find when you arrived?"

"Police and first responders were already on the scene. Raymond Carlisle was declared dead upon arrival. The coroner was prepping to move the body, and crime scene techs were doing their thing."

"How many people would you say were on-site?"

"Between six and ten."

"Where was Candy Carlisle?"

"She was sitting on the stairs inside her house, the stairs that went up to the second floor."

"Can you please describe how she looked?"

"She had been crying." The tone in Detective Lee's voice made me believe he was trying to appear impartial, and the jury appeared to be eating up every word.

I had to give Bernie credit. He appeared credible, likable even. The jury was going to trust everything he told them.

"Can you elaborate?" Frank asked.

"Yes. Her face was puffy. Her eyes were red." Detective Lee paused as if remembering something. "I caught a faint whiff of onions on her as I passed by on my way to the front room."

My ears perked up. I had seen pictures of the onions that had been found in the kitchen sink but had thought nothing of it. I had certainly not considered that the prosecution would try to turn it into something.

Turns out I was wrong.

"What did you do first?"

"After getting a report and viewing the body, I interviewed Candy Carlisle. I leaned in when I asked if there was a place we could talk privately. This time there was no doubt. I could smell onions. She motioned towards the back of the house where the kitchen was located. As I followed her, I noticed there were chopped onions in the kitchen sink."

"Why did this stand out to you?"

"I've heard some actors use onions to help them cry on screen. I couldn't help wonder if Candy Carlisle had been rubbing onions on her face to summon tears, this—"

"Objection, Your Honor," I said, jumping to my feet. "This is speculation."

Frank grunted. "Your Honor, we intend to show Candy Carlisle carefully planned Raymond's death down to the smallest detail. This is just one of many pieces of evidence we plan to introduce to show things are not as they may first appear."

Judge Hopkins studied me and then frowned at Frank. "I will sustain the objection as it relates to Officer Lee's assumption that Candy Carlisle was rubbing the onions on her face to force tears." She looked at the jury. "This testimony shall not be considered in your deliberations."

Bernie frowned as if he wanted to correct the judge by telling her that he was a detective.

"If there is other evidence to show she did, in fact, do this," Judge Hopkins continued, "that can be presented. Otherwise, Officer Lee needs to keep his speculation to himself."

When Bernie frowned again, I repressed a snort.

Frank looked like he was going to say something else but then gave a small nod. "Do you have reason to believe Candy Carlisle rubbed onions on her face?"

"She smelled like them."

"Can you please be more specific?"

"I noticed the smell came from her face when I leaned in to talk to her," Bernie glanced at the judge. "I wondered why it was so strong."

I glanced at Candy. I couldn't help wonder if this part of the prosecution's theory was true. I had seen firsthand the lack of emotion Candy had surrounding the death of her husband. If she couldn't summon actual tears, she would have wanted to project something when the police showed up, or they would have arrested her on the spot.

Why didn't she just throw the onions down the garbage disposal?

"When you met with Ms. Carlisle, was there anything else that stood out to you?"

"Yes, she did not seem broken up about the death of her husband. The physical signs were there, sure. Her eyes were red. Her cheeks were puffy. It looked like she had been crying. But it seemed she was happy he was dead."

I was again on my feet. "Objection, Your Honor, this is speculation. If there is something concrete, let the detective present it; otherwise, he should leave his suppositions to himself."

"I agree, counselor," Judge Hopkins said, looking at Frank Ward. "The detective needs to stick to the facts. The objection is sustained."

"What was it about the appearance of Ms. Carlisle that made you think this?"

"She was trying hard not to smile."

I frowned but remained in my seat. I thought I knew now what Frank was doing.

"Several times, it seemed she actually did smile, and I'm not talking about just a sly smile, but a big toothy smile." Bernie Lee hesitated. I could almost hear him adding the words, 'as if she was glad she finally got the guy,' but Bernie looked at the judge and clapped his mouth shut.

Judge Hopkins wouldn't suffer nonsense like that. Frank Ward and Bernie Lee might have tried it with another judge but not with Judge Hopkins.

She had a reputation.

I leaned back and studied the jury from the corner of my eye. Frank Ward knew what he was doing. He'd known I would object to Detective Lee's responses, yet he had still asked the questions anyway. I'd stopped objecting when I figured out what he was up to.

What was he trying to accomplish?

I didn't want it to appear as if I were trying to hide something from the jury, but I also wanted to make sure I defended my client's rights.

I figured the jury believed everything Detective Lee had said anyway, even the things they had been instructed to disregard. I needed to be careful in how I exercised my client's rights going forward.

"What did you do next?"

"I didn't make it far into my interview before we were interrupted by an officer. One of Raymond's children had woken up."

Subtle.

Would it have been too hard for Detective Lee to say one of the Carlisle children?

"Which one?"

"The older girl. She tried to come down, but an officer was placed at the top of the stairs in case one of them woke. We wanted to prevent the children from seeing the carnage in the front room. Candy Carlisle became distraught upon hearing the news her daughter was awake and immediately went to her child."

Bernie waited. I could tell this had been planned ahead of time. That was the one thing about detectives and prosecuting attorneys. They worked closely together when building a case. I could usually tell when things had been choreographed. It's not that I blamed them, but Frank was probably walking the line that prohibited an attorney from coaching a witness on their testimony.

"What did you find significant about this?"

"It was the level of emotion she showed. When talking to me before hearing this, she appeared giddy, just trying to hide a smile," Lee glanced at the judge and then at me as if afraid I would object. I'd been thinking about it but had decided to let this one slide because I'd already made my point with the jury about how Lee was speculating. If I harped on this anymore, it could also make the jury sympathize with Lee if I came down on him too hard. I would just have to wait to hammer Lee in my cross-examination.

"She seemed almost calm before she knew her child was awake. Her demeanor completely changed upon hearing the news. She went from hiding smiles to being worried."

"Can you please describe how you could tell she was worried?"

"She clutched her arms to her chest. She frowned. Worry lines etched her face."

Etched, seriously?

"Did you follow her?"

"Yes, I was concerned about the child myself. The scene in the front room was not something any child should see, let alone one that involved her father. I followed Ms. Carlisle up the stairs to where an officer stood with the child. The child was in tears. Tears now flowed easily from Ms. Carlisle, too. I suspected this was because she could empathize with the plight of her child at having lost a parent more than she felt the loss of her own husband."

I hesitated about whether to object. I was tempted to let it slide after glancing at the jury but then decided to try something else.

I slowly stood and held my hands out as I looked at the judge. "Objection, Your Honor, the witness is speculating again." I kept my voice quiet, but my words clear.

"Sustained."

I made a show of carefully sitting down, even adjusting my chair before I did. I did not want to appear overly aggressive.

I hoped I had succeeded.

I glanced at Candy and was surprised to see her eyes were glistening. It was natural to feel empathy for a child. Perhaps Detective Bernie Lee's assessment of my client was dead on again. Maybe she really had felt nothing until she saw it would have a profound effect on her children.

"What did you do after Ms. Carlisle talked to her child?"

"It was clear Candy Carlisle would have nothing further to say. She was too concerned with consoling her child to continue the discussion we had started. I went back to examine the murder scene."

"Where was the body?"

"Lying on the couch face up, arms spread. My first thought when I saw him was that he had been shot standing up and fallen to the couch afterward. I thought this because of the awkward angle of his body on the couch and the way his arms were positioned. It didn't appear he had been settled into a comfortable position when he was killed."

"How many times was he shot?"

"Four."

"And how many shell casings did you find in the room?"

"No brass was found."

"Was the murder weapon found in the room?"

"No, it was not."

"Did you find it in the house?"

"No, we did not."

"Did you find any of the bullets?"

"Not personally," he glanced at me. "I received a coroner's report that said two bullets were found in the victim's body. The crime scene report showed two more were found in the couch."

I could have objected, but that was all going to get admitted later as evidence anyway.

"Were there any other bullets found at the scene?"

"Yes, one."

"Can you please describe the way it was found?"

"I received a call from Ms. Carlisle's attorney, Mitch Turner." I could feel all eyes on me. I kept my focus on Bernie without glancing around. "He told me they had found evidence at the murder scene. I came over to investigate it immediately."

Only after I convinced him.

"What did you find when you arrived?" Frank asked.

"I found Candy Carlisle, Mitch Turner, and their private detectives in the front room. Apparently, Mr. Turner had met with Candy to discuss the death of her husband at the scene of the crime. During their investigation, they noticed it in the back wall."

"Did you confirm there was a bullet?"

"Yes. I did.

"What did you do with the bullet?"

"I bagged it as evidence and sent it to ballistics for analysis."

"Why did you guys miss the bullet?"

"I don't know. You would have to ask the crime scene techs." Bernie Lee shrugged. "The bullet was a different caliber than that used to kill Raymond Carlisle. It was smaller in diameter and found embedded in a knot of the decorative wood on the back wall. They were not looking for a bullet that size. Perhaps that's why they didn't notice it."

"What did ballistics determine?"

"This was a different bullet than the one used to kill Raymond Carlisle. The bullet used to kill Raymond was a 9 mm. This was a .22."

"Did you think this was significant?"

"Not at the time. It wasn't until later that we discovered the drug angle in this case."

"Objection," I said, standing, "if the prosecution has evidence about a 'drug angle,' it would be appropriate now to submit it; otherwise, it is prejudicial."

This was a strategic move on my part to emphasize this point.

Frank didn't know how much I was counting on the 'drug angle.' I wanted it introduced as soon as possible because this was where I would focus my attention. I wanted it put into the minds of the jury at the outset of the trial. Far better if it was put there by Bernie Lee and Frank Ward first. It would make it easier for me to build on later. Frank didn't know what he was walking into.

"That was my next question," Frank said without glancing over.

"Overruled," Judge Hopkins said. "You may continue with your questions."

"Can you please tell us how drugs figure into this?"

"One of the things we found strange about the Raymond and Candy Carlisle household was how they appeared to have more money than we could account for either of them earning. He was a programmer. She is a graphic designer. At first, as in many investigations, this did not seem to be significant because we were more focused on tracking down the murderer.

"With time, it became obvious something was going on that needed to be investigated. We followed the money. It turned out the Carlisles had been depositing thousands of dollars in cash into their accounts on a regular basis."

"Can you give me an example?"

"Sure. On February 8, this is before Raymond was killed, Candy Carlisle deposited $4,000 into their bank account. All cash."

"How do you know it was Candy Carlisle who made the deposit?"

"We reviewed bank footage and receipts."

"Did you find any other such deposits?"

"Yes. On January 26, Raymond Carlisle made a deposit of $5,000 in cash."

"And would you say this was indicative of the deposits you found?"

"Yes, it was."

"What made you think this was related to drugs?"

"That's the first thought I usually have whenever I find somebody depositing large sums of money, unfortunately," Bernie hastened to add as if expecting an objection, I had shifted in my seat as if I were about to stand, "we found actual drug paraphernalia in the Carlisle home, too. One plus one."

"When did you find that?"

"After the .22 was turned over to us by the defense and after we started investigating the money, we executed another search warrant on the house."

"What were you expecting to find?"

I could have let it slide but chose not to. I wanted Frank to feel resistance. I wanted him to tack into the wind.

"Objection, Your Honor," I said, standing slowly, "speculation." I kept my demeanor and tone pleasant for the jury's benefit.

"Sustained."

"Please tell us what you found at the house, Detective Lee," Frank said.

"The first time we went through the home, we did not find any evidence of drugs. On our return visit, in Candy's bedroom, we found medicine bottles that did not have Candy Carlisle's name."

"Can you please explain what you mean?"

"Candy Carlisle had in her possession prescription medicines for which she did not have a prescription."

"What evidence did you find of drug dealing?"

"The medicine bottles were found in a box. There were a lot of them. It was far more than one would expect a person to have if they were keeping them for themselves."

"Did you find any evidence of transactions?"

"Not directly, but we did find $40,000 cash under the bed."

Candy stirred beside me. She swore that the only time she had ever been back to the house was the time she had showed Winston and me around. She claimed to know nothing about the drugs or the money.

"Did you check under that bed on the night Raymond was killed?"

"Yes. There was nothing."

"So approximately three months after Raymond's death, Candy Carlisle somehow found and stashed $40,000 cash under her bed, along with a box of illegal prescription drugs. Is that correct?"

"Yes."

"Let's return to the crime scene on the day of Raymond's death," Frank Ward said. "What else about the scene stuck out to you?"

"There was no sign of forced entry. I examined the door myself. Raymond Carlisle let whoever killed him into the house or the killer had a key."

"Thank you, Your Honor," Frank Ward said, "I have no further questions for this witness at this time."

49

"Counselor, you can start with your questions," Judge Hopkins said. "We may stop for a small break in an hour."

"That's fine, Your Honor," I said, heading to the podium with my notepad. "How are you doing today, Detective Bernie Lee?" I kept my voice light and tone easy.

"I'm fine, Mr. Turner."

I gave him a smile. He glowered back.

He probably figured that I had just tried to bait him into using his nickname for me.

I considered other questions that might elicit such a response but decided against them for now. If he slipped and called me Turncoat in court, great. Otherwise, I would not dwell on it.

I had more important things to do.

"You testified earlier that Candy Carlisle appeared to smell like onions on the night of her husband's death. Are you sure that's what you smelled?"

"Yes."

"And you suggested she smelled this way because she rubbed onions onto her cheeks to make her cry, correct?"

"Yes."

There were several directions I could go with this to sow doubt in the minds of the jurors.

"Have you ever eaten food that was heavily flavored with onions, perhaps at a steak restaurant or some such place?"

"Yes."

"Do you recall ever smelling your clothes the day afterward?"

"Yes."

"Did they smell like onion?"

Detective Lee hesitated. This was such a common observation that there was no way for him to get around it. He shrugged. "That sort of thing happens."

"Is it correct to say onions have a strong smell?"

"Yes."

"And that smell can linger, correct?"

"I suppose so."

Did you ask my client what she had for dinner?"

"No."

"Isn't it possible she could have had something that was flavored with onions?"

"Perhaps."

"And isn't it possible that the onions you thought you smelled on her face were really onions from her breath because of what she ate for dinner?"

"I don't think so."

"How can you tell the difference between somebody's breath and the smell of their cheeks?"

"I know what I smelt."

I frowned. "Perhaps we should blindfold you and have you smell two people, one who ate onions and one who rubbed onions on their cheeks. Should we put on a demonstration?"

"Objection, Your Honor," Frank said. "This suggestion is spurious."

"The witness claims to know the difference. Let him prove it."

"Overruled."

"Shall I send somebody for onions and two volunteers, Detective? Or do you want to revise your answer?"

Lee didn't respond.

The judge cleared her throat. "I believe you've made your point, counselor."

"Did you see my client rub onions on her face?"

"No."

"Did anybody check my client for onion residue on her face?"

"No."

"Did anybody think to collect the onions from the kitchen?"

"No, we did not, but we do have pictures."

"Did anybody check my client's fingertips for the smell of onions?"

I asked this in such a way as to make it seem like a ridiculous suggestion.

"No, of course not."

"Is there any way to know if Candy Carlisle chopped the onions and left them in the sink?"

"No."

"Isn't it also true that there was a crockpot in the kitchen?"

"Yes."

"Isn't it conceivable that whoever chopped the onions might have been planning to place them into the crockpot with other ingredients to simmer through the night?"

"I suppose."

"To sum up, you have testified you have personal first-hand knowledge that onions are smelly." I almost couldn't say this with a straight face, but somehow, I did. "Correct?"

Detective Lee only nodded. His mouth was one thin line.

"And that there is no evidence Candy Carlisle rubbed onions on her face?"

Detective Bernie Lee was getting angry. "You're trying to twist my words."

"You're the one who opened the door to this speculation. I'm just carrying it through to its natural conclusion, don't you agree?"

Detective Lee didn't respond.

"Isn't it most likely that whoever was chopping up the onions might have been planning a meal for the next day?"

"Objection," Frank Ward said, "calls for speculation."

"Sustained." Judge Hopkins looked at me. "I believe you've made your point twice, counselor. Please move on."

"Thank you, Your Honor." I focused on Detective Bernie Lee. He was fuming. His face was turning red, but I wasn't done with him yet, not by half. "You mentioned you executed a second search warrant on my client's home. What was the basis of the search warrant?"

"The financial deposits."

"Was it based on anything else?"

"No."

"And when you searched the house, did you find anything else of interest?"

"No. The only thing we found that was different this time was money and drugs under the bed in the master bedroom."

"Did it look like the house had been lived in since you last visited?"

"I couldn't say."

"But you did just testify that nothing else was different, correct?"

"Yes," he said through clenched teeth.

"It's reasonable to assume if the house had been lived in, things would have changed, correct?"

"I don't know that I would say that."

"Did you check the kitchen sink?"

"Yes."

"Were the onions still there?"

"Yes, they were."

"Did you guys collect them this time?"

"No. We did not."

"If the house was still lived in, don't you think the onions would've been cleaned up?"

"I don't know."

He lost credibility on that one. It would've been better for him to admit that I had a point.

"Did you check to see if the house had been broken into since you last examined the door locks?"

"I don't believe we did."

"So you didn't have the crime scene techs examine the front door lock before you opened the door?"

"No. We did not."

"Did you check for fingerprints on the lock or the door or anywhere thereabouts?"

"No."

"And you didn't check any of the other locks either?"

"No."

"Did anybody answer the door when you knocked for the second search warrant?"

"No."

"Do you have any evidence that my client was currently living in the house at the time you executed the search warrant?"

Bernie didn't answer and glanced over at Frank Ward as if expecting him to get him out of this.

"Detective?"

"No, I don't have any way of verifying if your client was currently living at the home. How about we put her on the stand, so you can ask her?"

He is getting touchy.

I refrained from smiling, keeping my face dead serious.

I held his eyes. It would not have been improper for me to ask the judge to instruct him to only answer my questions, but I wanted to keep the focus on him and me. "When you went into the bedroom, did it look like the bed had been touched since the last time you had been there?"

"Hard to say."

"Did you examine the bathroom?"

"We did."

"Did it look like the bathroom had been used since you last visited?"

"Again, hard to say."

I shifted my questioning because I felt like I had sufficiently made my point.

I didn't know how else I was going to get information on the trial record that Candy had no longer been living in the home without putting her on the stand.

I wasn't sure I wanted to do that, although Bernie had successfully planted that idea into the minds of the jurors, and she might end up looking guilty if she didn't, regardless of any jury instructions to infer otherwise. Hopefully, what I had done already was adequate, but I would think about other things I could do.

"You also mentioned you felt my client was happy her husband was dead."

Bernie shifted. He looked more comfortable now. "Yes, that is how she appeared to me."

"You said she seemed to be smiling. Did you take a picture or record a video?"

"Come on, counselor, would you really expect me to do something like that?"

"How hard would it have been to pull out your phone?" I said, taking mine out from my suit pocket and snapping a picture. Click. "Wouldn't that have been the smart thing to do if you wanted us to believe you? You formed a snap judgment on the spot that she seemed happy, so why didn't you pull out your phone to record her?"

"I didn't think of it at the time."

Bernie looked less comfortable now.

"Did you talk to any of the other officers on the scene? Did any of them share your opinion?"

"Objection. Hearsay."

"Withdrawn."

It had been a tactical move on my part and a gamble, too. It would be interesting now to see if Frank put anybody else on the stand to testify whether she seemed happy her husband was dead.

"You have also admitted her face was raw, and her eyes were red as if she had been crying. These two things don't coincide, wouldn't you agree? Had she been crying, or was she happy?"

"I explained that by telling you about the onion smell."

"Did you or did you not see her rub onions on her cheeks?"

"No."

Detective Lee looked ready to explode.

I hesitated. The jury didn't know the real Bernie Lee.

Not like I knew him.

They didn't know he was a man with a short fuse. They didn't know he called me Mitch Turner the Turncoat whenever he saw me.

And they didn't know he never changed his mind once he reached a conclusion, regardless of what additional evidence came to light.

"When I called to tell you that we had found a bullet in Raymond Carlisle's living room, did you believe me?"

"I thought at first you were playing a joke."

"Have I ever played a joke on you before, Detective?"

He didn't answer for a long moment. I wondered if there was something I had forgotten.

"No."

"When did you believe I had told the truth?"

"When I saw the bullet."

From the look on Detective Lee's face, it was apparent that he knew exactly where I was going. I had subtly reminded him that I had taken a video of his visit to the Carlisle home.

That was enough.

"Did you ever find any evidence that my client had been dealing drugs?"

"The money. The drugs."

"Did you look for fingerprints on the drugs?"

"We did."

"And?"

"Her fingerprints were not found."

"Did you check the money?"

"Yes."

"And?"

"No fingerprints were found there either."

"The only connection between my client and the money and the drugs was the fact that they were found in her master bedroom. Correct?"

"Yes."

"A room which was untouched since the day Raymond Carlisle died?"

"We don't know that."

"Did you find evidence that things had been moved around?"

Detective Lee was silent.

"Did you ever see her with the drugs or the money?"

"No."

"Did you ever find a witness who saw her with the drugs or the money?"

"No."

I had hoped to get a bit more emotion from him at the end, but perhaps I had gotten him angry enough. I had also poked enough holes in Bernie Lee's testimony that I could stop here.

"No further questions, Your Honor."

50

"We will break for a fifteen-minute recess," Judge Hopkins said, looking at the clock, "and then pick up again."

The judge banged the gavel.

"Did you see how angry he was?" Candy asked in a whisper while leaning over. "You really ruffled his feathers."

I grimaced. She was missing the point.

"That's because I was poking holes in his testimony. He didn't like that. Hopefully, the jury noticed the flaws in the things he said."

"Oh, they noticed." Candy smiled as she left. I was not as optimistic as my client.

I made some notes on my pad of paper about how the questioning had gone. I wasn't particularly pleased, but it could have gone worse. It was a solid step forward.

"Do you have a moment?" Frank asked, looking around. "Can we talk outside?"

"Sure." I packed my stuff in my briefcase, locked it, and left it on the table.

We found a quiet corner.

"Still fifteen years, but she is up for parole after seven," Frank said, glancing around to make sure nobody could overhear.

I was surprised at this offer because I didn't feel like either of us had the upper hand at this point.

"I'm feeling like a broken record, Frank."

"Your client did this. I'm offering you and her a favor. I'm thinking of the children."

"So am I," I said. "I'm grateful for the offer. She's just not going to take it."

"Convince her, Mitch. I've seen you convince people to do things they never thought they would do."

"That's quite a compliment."

"I'm not sure it is," Frank said as he walked away.

I didn't make it far before Bernie Lee stopped me.

"What were you trying to do in there?" Bernie demanded.

I gave him an innocent look. "What do you mean?"

"You made me look like a fool."

"I had to clean up your testimony. I wouldn't have to do that if you would just stick to the facts."

"You and I both know she was happy her husband died. Your client is going to prison for a long time."

Not if we take Frank's offer.

Apparently, Frank hadn't consulted with Bernie Lee about the offer he had just made. I wondered what Bernie would think.

I wasn't so sure Candy shouldn't take it. The poker boys had done a thorough job of keeping things on the down-low.

I caught somebody looking at me from the corner of my eye. When I turned, I was surprised to see Tammy Weaver.

The way she hovered out here made me think Frank intended to put her on today.

Was she going to be his next witness?

I couldn't wait for the chance to question her on the stand.

Bernie growled.

I couldn't afford to waste more time with him. I wanted to review my questions for Tammy before court was back in session.

"I'll see you, Bernie."

I didn't wait for his response, but it couldn't have been the worst thing he'd ever said to me. There were too many around who might have overheard for him to say something like that.

Judge Hopkins looked at Frank Ward once court was back in session. "Please call your next witness."

"The state calls Tammy Weaver to the stand."

I was glad I'd had forewarning about what Frank intended. A large part of my case hinged on what happened next.

51

After Tammy was sworn in, Frank asked a few questions and then got right into the meat of the matter.

"How did you know the victim Raymond Carlisle?"

"My husband, Bill, was in a poker group with him."

"You met Raymond before his death?"

"Yes."

"Was he ever over at your house?"

"Yes, the group had a rotation, switching houses depending on the month."

"How many years did your husband play with the group?"

"I couldn't say, at least four or five, possibly more."

"When did Raymond join?"

"He was there from the beginning. Bill, Raymond, and a few others started the group."

"Did you have much interaction with Raymond?"

"No. I might have seen him in passing as the guys got together, but that was it. I never saw him outside of that."

"How many times would you say you saw him over the years?"

"I don't know, probably a dozen or so."

"Did you ever meet his wife Candy?"

"No, I don't know that I ever formally met her."

"But you knew what she looked like?"

"Yes. I saw pictures of her on social media."

"Did you ever see her in person?"

"A few times."

"Can you please tell us about the first time you saw her?"

"Yes, it was at the grocery store." Tammy stopped and gave Candy a look before continuing. "She was at the customer service desk, yelling at the person behind the counter."

I froze.

I clearly recalled the first time Bill Weaver had told me about this supposed incident. I had thought it was completely unremarkable. He had certainly not included this pertinent detail.

Neither had Tammy.

Were they feeling their way forward as they made up stories? Had Bill thrown this out with vague details? And then had he and Tammy worked on it afterward?

What other embellishments was I going to hear today?

I settled in, expecting Tammy to take us for a ride. I needed to relax, so my subconscious was paying attention. My best ideas during trial usually came from there. I glanced at Candy from the corner of my eye. She had gone still and wore a stern expression on her face.

"Yelling?" Frank asked.

"Yes, it was pretty bad, too. I couldn't make it all out, but what I could hear made me want to hide from her just in case she knew who I was."

I stood. "Objection, Your Honor. What is the relevance of this?"

"Counselor?" Judge Hopkins asked Frank Ward.

"If you wouldn't mind giving me a little leeway, it should quickly be apparent why this is relevant."

"Hmmm," Judge Hopkins said thoughtfully as she studied Candy. "I'm going to allow the questions, but you'd better get there quick."

"Yes, Your Honor."

"Could you hear what the conversation was about, Miss Weaver?"

"No, but Candy was worked up. She was swearing and pointing her finger at the customer service clerk aggressively."

"Objection, hearsay."

"Sustained, the jury will please disregard the part about the swearing."

"Where were you when this was happening?" Frank asked.

"I was checking out."

"How far were you from the customer service desk?"

"Probably about twenty to thirty feet."

"Was there anything else?"

"Yes, she shook her fist at the customer service desk and screamed."

Was a scream hearsay?

Tammy had not made any mention of the words Candy allegedly said. Tammy either had a thorough knowledge of the rules of evidence, or somebody had carefully prepped her on her testimony.

I let it go.

The jury was paying careful attention. Some had skeptical looks. They would be far more critical by the time I was done with Tammy.

I kept my face still. I saw where this was going. Frank was taking an awful risk putting this story out there. I didn't know if Frank had thoroughly investigated Tammy and the poker boys, but he should have thought twice before doing this. It would have been better to just focus on Tammy's testimony about the supposed gun purchase.

He is grasping at straws, I thought, *if he wants to include this in the trial record.*

First, he made a low offer. Second, he put an unvetted witness on the stand who was lying through her teeth.

What else was he going to do?

"Can you please describe how the poor customer service attendant looked?"

Poor?

I shook my head. It wasn't worth the objection.

"The woman behind the counter was pale and stepped back."

"Did she look afraid for her life?"

"Objection!" I stood. "Who is testifying here?"

"Sustained. Please don't put words into your witness' mouth."

"Yes, Your Honor."

Frank looked down at his notepad. I didn't have a clear angle on his face, but I could have sworn he had briefly smiled.

It was a tactic.

He had put the idea into the jury's mind, had me object to it, and then if I was reading things correctly, was now going to move on to something else. He had just wanted to plant the idea with the jury.

"Let's talk about the second time you saw Ms. Carlisle. When was that?"

"A few days before the death of Raymond Carlisle."

"And where did you see her?"

"At a sporting goods store."

"Can you please describe to the court what you saw?"

"I was parking when I saw Candy coming out. She was carrying something in her hands."

"What did she have?"

"It was a plastic box. It had a handle at the top."

"Why did you think this was significant?"

"My husband Bill is a firearms enthusiast." Tammy smiled faintly. "He owns several. I was with him when he made some of his purchases. I recognized the type of box a new firearm comes in. That is what Candy was carrying."

I wanted to object but decided I'd wait until it was my turn to cross-examine her. I was going to make Tammy rue the day she got on the stand to perjure herself.

"I have no further questions for this witness."

52

"Counselor, your turn."

"Thank you, Your Honor." I approached the lectern. I took a few moments to arrange several things on the podium in front of me. I had a notepad with my questions. I placed my phone down beside it. And then I put my watch right beside that. Finally, I set a pen down beside the pad of paper.

I did this deliberately to build tension and because I wanted all eyes on me.

"Mrs. Weaver, thank you for being here today," I said, giving her my toothiest smile. "Can you please tell us more about the poker nights your husband likes to play with his friends?"

Frank had opened the door.

I was walking in.

There was a microscopic hesitation on her part. She had not expected me to ask about this. I noticed Frank looking at me curiously.

"What would you like to know?"

"How often would they happen?"

"I don't know, perhaps every month."

"And you said they rotated houses frequently?"

"Yes, they did."

"Did you ever walk in on any of their poker nights?"

"Occasionally, I might bring in treats or something for them. They looked like they were always having a good time. They limited the amount of money they could bet, so it was more about the game than the winnings."

"Did they ever do anything outside of poker night together?"

"Not that I can recall."

"So there was never a night where they all got together with their wives or girlfriends?"

"No. Nothing like that."

"No family barbecues together?"

"No."

"The only thing these guys ever did together was poker night, correct?"

"Yes."

"And the only thing they ever did at those poker nights was play poker, correct?"

"Yes."

"Would you say your husband was a skillful player?"

She smiled. "I couldn't say. I've never played with him. Poker isn't my thing."

"Can you tell us who came to the poker nights?"

"Sure. There was Abe Martin, Larry Thompson, Kyle Rencher, and Raymond Carlisle."

"Over the years, were there any other poker players?"

"I don't know for sure. I don't think so."

"Does the name Seth Roberts mean anything to you?"

She shook her head. "No. It doesn't."

"How about Beatrice Jones?"

"Never heard of her."

"Is it true Raymond stopped coming to the poker nights?"

"I don't know. You would have to ask somebody else."

"I see," I said, picking up my pen to make a note on the paper in front of me. I took my time. When I looked up, I saw the judge was on the verge of telling me to get on with it.

"Do you know if they ever did anything illegal at these poker nights?"

"Not that I'm aware of."

"Did they use illegal drugs?"

"I highly doubt it."

"But you didn't go in there often, so if they did, you might not know about it, correct?"

"I suppose not, but I really don't think they did. I would've seen evidence. I never saw my husband or any of the others high."

"Is it possible they did things other than poker?"

"Sure, but that's what they got together for."

"Don't you think it's strange they never did anything together outside of poker night?"

"No."

"I mean, you never met any of the other wives or girlfriends attached to these men, did you?"

"No."

"So it seems like it was strictly about the poker night. There weren't outside relationships. It was almost like a professional get-together, would you agree?"

"I don't understand what you mean."

"It was almost like a professional monthly gathering of some sort, a monthly get-together of people talking shop. Do you think that's what it was?"

"No."

I nodded as if I believed her, but my skepticism was written plainly on my face.

"You said you saw Candy at the supermarket, apparently yelling at some 'poor' person behind a customer service desk. Do you remember the location of the grocery store?"

"No, I don't."

"Do you remember the name of the store?"

"No."

"Do you remember if it was a chain grocery store?"

"No, I don't."

"Do you remember anybody else in the grocery store you can identify who could also testify about what you witnessed?"

"No."

"So there's no way for us to independently verify that this ever happened, correct?"

"I suppose you could put Candy on the stand and ask her."

I ignored her suggestion.

"We just have to take your word for it, correct?"

"I suppose so."

"Do you remember what day this happened?"

"No. I don't."

"Time?"

"No."

"Now correct me if I am wrong, but it is the same story for the sporting goods store, is it not?"

"I'm sorry. I don't understand what you mean."

"Do you remember the day you supposedly saw Candy at the sporting goods store?"

"I already said it was a couple of days before Raymond was killed."

"Was it two or three?"

"I have no idea."

"Could it possibly be four or five?"

"I don't know."

"And do you remember the location of the store?"

"No, I do not."

"Was it a chain?"

"I don't recall."

"Do you remember what time of day this was?"

"Just before noon."

I could have kicked myself. It would've been better not to ask a question for which I knew she had an actual answer to keep with the theme.

"But just to be clear, you don't remember the date, the location, or the name of the store. Do I have it right?"

"Yes."

"Could you describe the box she was carrying?"

"It was a plastic box."

"Do you remember the color?"

"I dunno, black or blue or something like that."

"Was it black or was it blue?"

"I don't remember."

I frowned. "When we met, you told me you thought it was black. Have you changed your mind?"

"No. It was black."

I paused. "So it was not blue."

"No, it was not."

"Were there identifying logos on the box you believe you saw Candy carrying?"

"I don't recall."

"Let me just make sure I have this right. You believe you saw Candy at the grocery store appearing to make threatening statements to the person behind the customer service desk. However, you did not hear those statements. You also don't remember the name of the grocery store or even where it is located. And you don't remember the date or the time this happened. Did I *remember* it all?"

She nodded. "That is correct."

My sarcasm was apparently lost on her.

"You also believe you saw Candy a couple days before Raymond's death. You don't know if a couple means two, three, four, or five, or something altogether different. You are also, again, unable to remember either the name of the store or its location. Is that correct?"

"I am certain of one thing. She carried a box that contained a pistol."

"You don't remember what brand?"

"No."

"Did you see a pistol?"

"No."

"How do you know there was a pistol inside?"

"I just know."

"Why should we believe you are telling the truth?"

"Because I am."

"Would you say you have a good memory?"

She hesitated. She probably knew where I was going.

"I think it's about average."

"Would you say it is better than average?"

"I don't know."

"Do you expect us to believe that you remember a few supposedly incriminating details but no real concrete facts that would allow us to confirm the veracity of your story, on this day that was two or three or four or five days before Raymond died?"

"I don't know how to answer that question."

"Do you remember what Candy was wearing?"

"No."

"Have you ever taken illegal drugs, Mrs. Weaver?"

Her face went white. She clasped her hands in her lap, and her knuckles turned white, too.

"Are you going to answer the question?"

"I don't know how to answer. That's just such a ridiculous proposition."

"It seems you don't want to answer. Is that accurate?"

"No, I have not used illegal drugs."

I doubted the jury believed her. I had done a thorough job of poking holes in her testimony. Unfortunately, I had not yet elicited some of the information I wanted to get from her, and I didn't see a clear path to it.

"Have you ever taken illegal prescription drugs?"

"No."

"Did your husband ever go over to the Carlisle home?"

"Yes, of course, he did. They had poker night there sometimes."

"How often would you say he went over?"

"I don't know, half a dozen times over the years. They tended to favor our house or Abe Martin's place, but they had a regular rotation."

"How late into the night would they play?"

"I don't know. Bill would usually get home way after I had gone to bed."

"So if he came home high, you would never have known about it?"

"Objection, Your Honor, he is badgering the witness. He has already asked, and she has already answered."

Judge Hopkins looked at me. "I think you've pushed hard enough, but the witness will answer the question. Overruled."

"I suppose it is possible."

"One final question. If we looked at your financial records, would we find unexplained cash deposits in your bank account?"

"Objection! Relevance."

"Withdrawn."

53

"Mr. Ward," Judge Hopkins said, "we have thirty minutes before I was planning to shut things down. Do you have a witness you want to put on? Or would you prefer to wait till morning?"

"I'll wait till morning, Your Honor, if it's all the same to you."

Judge Hopkins turned her attention to the jury and gave them instructions before dismissing them. Afterward, we had a few items of business, and then we were dismissed.

"Frank made an offer today of fifteen years," I whispered to Candy. "Possibility of parole in seven. Just wanted you to know."

She looked affronted at the very suggestion, but I didn't have time to hold her hand.

I packed my briefcase and left, even though it looked like she wanted to talk to me about it.

I had hoped to get Tammy to slip up on the stand in a way that would have led me to the poker boys' illegal activities, but it had not worked.

Overall, I figured the score between Frank and me was tied. Whenever that was the case, I assumed I was running behind because I believed the jury tended to favor the prosecution when things were even.

On my way out of the courthouse, I noticed Tammy Weaver standing by a tree, typing into her phone. She glared when she saw me. I gave her a friendly smile and wave before I went on my way.

I was halfway back to the office when my phone rang. I pulled it out and saw it was Winston.

"I have something small," he said. "I was digging into Seth Roberts' past, trying to figure out why they might have been so interested in recruiting him, outside of his obvious past experience, and I discovered Seth spent time at a rehab known as Spring Lake Recovery.

"Not surprising," I said, continuing to walk. "What's the relevance?"

"This is something I cannot testify to in court, understand?"

"Got it."

"And there's no way you should ever repeat this to anybody. This is just information to help us figure out what's going on."

"I get it."

"Seth Roberts was at the rehab place with Beatrice Jones."

I stopped. "They were in rehab together?"

"Yes. I confirmed they were both there at the same time."

"What is the significance of this from your perspective?"

"I don't know. It's just too great a coincidence that the poker boys recruited her after failing to recruit him."

"It might just be a coincidence."

"There has to be a reason. It just doesn't make sense unless there is a connection. I just don't see what it is."

"I'll give it some thought."

I continued on my walk back.

My office was deserted. It was nice to have the place to myself. I sat my briefcase down on my desk but couldn't bring myself to sit. I felt the need to get out and do something. I just couldn't decide what it was.

I was glad my cross-examinations of Detective Bernie Lee and Tammy Weaver had gone well enough.

But it's not a tie, I'm behind.

My phone rang. The number was blocked. I almost let it go to voicemail but decided to answer at the last moment.

"It's Mitch."

"I need to talk to you."

"Barbara? What is this about?"

"Mitch—" I heard footsteps on the other end of the line and a door shut. "I'm sorry, I have to go."

54

I sent Barbara a text message, asking if everything was okay. I texted the number I had for her, hoping it went through.

She responded right away.

"I'm fine. Talk later."

I called Winston. "Can you do a favor for me tonight?"

"Maybe."

"Can you track down Barbara? I don't want you talking to her. I just want to know where she is and if she's okay."

"Mitch, I'm not sure about this. This doesn't sound like a good idea."

"I just need you to do it."

"Why? What's going on?"

I took in a haggard breath. "I just got a phone call. She said she needed to talk and then hung up before explaining. It sounded like somebody was approaching when she did. I just texted. She texted back, saying we can talk later."

Winston hesitated. "I'll let you know what I find." He disconnected.

Had I made the right call?

Part of me wanted to figure out what was going on myself, but I knew it was a risky thing to do.

I was biased. I had no way of knowing what I might find or how I would react to it. I trusted Winston would make a better decision if he found something needed to be done.

There's nothing you can do if she doesn't want to talk to you.

Sending Winston over was already too much.

I slumped down in my chair, pulled out my pad of paper, and started writing down every scenario I could think of to explain why the poker boys had recruited Beatrice Jones after Seth Roberts had turned them down.

At the end, I had nothing.

55

I woke up in bed and checked the clock. It wasn't even two in the morning.

I was wide awake.

I knew I would not get back to sleep. I checked my phone for a text message from Winston but didn't have one. I had sent him a text, asking if he had found Barbara before lying down in bed. I had expected to hear back right away but had fallen asleep while waiting.

I got dressed and went down to my car, intending to go to Barbara's apartment. I was halfway there before I realized I could be making a serious mistake.

I could be horribly overreacting.

What if Barbara had called to tell me that she was thinking of breaking up with Thomas Guyton?

Maybe Thomas had walked into the room right after she called, so she had ended the conversation.

There were all sorts of benign reasons to explain what happened. My mind had naturally gone to the worst one, probably because of the stalker.

Instead of going to Barbara's apartment, I went over to Abe Martin's home and parked down the street, so I could keep an eye on the place. I wasn't expecting to find anything. I was just hoping that being in proximity to Abe would give me ideas I might not have otherwise.

When I first interviewed him, he had been angry, practically throwing me out of his mechanic shop. The next day, he called up and apologized profusely, trying to repair the damage he had done. When I had met with Kyle Rencher, he had acted as if I were accusing him of murder when I had not.

Since that time, none of the poker boys had made a single misstep.

Maybe I'm chasing the wrong people?

We still had Evangeline Brewer as a potential suspect, but she was a waste of time. Winston and I had both completed our investigation into her and decided she wasn't a good fit for the murder.

Was that just my bias coming through?

I needed to figure out what the poker boys were up to. I just didn't have a way of doing it.

I left Abe's place a few minutes later. On my way back home, I swung past his mechanic shop.

I was surprised when I arrived to find that the lights were on. I quickly circled the block and parked down the street in a place that gave me a view but was far enough back that nobody would notice me.

The garage door opened. A dark SUV pulled out. I saw Abe Martin and Bill Weaver just before the door shut again.

I snapped pictures of the SUV, making sure to capture the license plate number.

Once I confirmed that I had the license plate, I backed out with my lights off. The last thing I wanted was for Abe or Bill to see me sitting outside.

I took a route that I hoped would put me back on track with the SUV. I had the license plate, but I also wanted more.

There was no doubt I had just stumbled onto evidence of the wrongdoings I'd been looking for.

I might not have taken it upon myself to follow them under other circumstances, but I was willing to take the risk if it meant I walked into court with something better today than I did yesterday. I held my breath for the few minutes I was out of view of the SUV. I let out a sigh when I finally had eyes on it again. I almost didn't dare speak or move as I contemplated what my next best move should be because I was afraid it was an apparition that would disappear the moment I did.

I checked my clock. It was just a little before three in the morning. I dialed Winston.

"You're up early," he said.

"How's Barbara?" I asked.

It took him a moment to respond. "She's fine. She's at her apartment."

"Alone?"

"Mitch," Winston said. "You're pushing it."

"This is important."

"Yes."

I let out a sigh. It was nothing then.

"I found something," I said, slowing to put more distance between the SUV and myself.

"What are you doing up this late, Mitch?"

I could tell from his tone he was worried I was doing something foolish.

"I was sitting outside Abe Martin's shop when I noticed an SUV pulling out. I followed it."

A brief pause. "You did what?"

"I'm tracking it now."

"You're not trained for this sort of thing, Mitch."

"I'll be fine."

"These guys already killed one person to protect their secret. You don't think they won't kill again?"

He had a point.

"I'm several blocks back."

"Yes, but it's the middle of the night. They will notice any car. They do these things now because there's fewer people around, so it's easier to spot if somebody is following them."

"A good point. How about you come meet me? I'll peel off. You can follow them."

"Double my normal rate."

"Done."

I gave Winston instructions on where I was and where I thought we were heading.

"I'll catch up in less than ten minutes. Stay back. If they stop, you just keep driving. Got it? I'll find them."

I couldn't help but chuckle at Winston's concern after we disconnected. I was not worried. I was far enough back that it was unlikely something would happen.

I was just relieved to finally make progress on this case.

When I approached the next street, I checked all ways before proceeding into the intersection, even though the light was green. I imagined a truck coming from nowhere and slamming into me. Winston had made me paranoid that something like that could happen.

I checked my rearview mirror to make sure nobody was following me. It appeared I was alone. I now understood better why Winston was concerned. There had been a few cars in between me and the SUV when this had started, but the SUV and I were now the only ones on the road. I slowed even further. I was far enough back that the driver could not recognize anything about my car. They would see my headlights, and that was it.

But perhaps it was better I throw them off my scent.

I pulled up the navigation on my car and saw that after the next turn, the road did not have another intersection for half a mile. I took the turn. I sped as I went around the long way, hoping I wasn't about to lose the SUV. It was a risk, but Winston had gotten to me.

It was not long before I circled back and connected up with the road. I came to a stoplight, prepared to turn back out, just as the SUV passed. I then turned and followed. Perhaps they had figured out what I'd done, but likely not.

A thought occurred to me.

I had just given the SUV driver a clear look at my car.

A very distinctive car.

How many Porsches were on the road tonight?

I'd been happy about my move before, but perhaps it had been a foolish thing to do. I got a phone call from Winston two minutes later. "I can see you. I have eyes on the SUV. Back off."

"I don't see you."

"I'm here. Take the next left and go to your office. I'll meet you there.

Winston hung up.

I took the turn, but then, out of an abundance of caution, I took a circuitous route with many turns, just to make sure there wasn't anybody following me. I didn't think there was, but I had not been trained for this sort of thing. I made sure I locked the front door once I was inside my office building. I even pulled out a Glock 19 that I kept in my desk drawer. I set it on the desk just in case there was a problem. It wasn't the first time I had faced mortal danger as a lawyer, and it would not be the last. I didn't expect anything to happen, but it was late. I had just done something risky, especially considering how recognizable my car was.

The doorbell rang an hour later. I peeked my head out and had an unobstructed view of the front door window.

Winston stood outside. I returned to my desk and put the pistol away because I didn't want Winston knowing just how paranoid he had made me.

"The plot thickens," Winston said with a thin smile as he walked inside. "I followed them to a place called Mount Pleasant."

"Mount Pleasant?"

"It's a rehab center."

"Are you sure?" I asked.

"No doubt about it."

"Is it the same rehab center Seth Roberts used?" I asked, wondering if the name had changed.

"No. It's a different one altogether."

"Think these guys are using a rehab center as a front for their drug operations?" I asked. Just the thought sickened me. Rehab was supposed to be a place of hope and new beginnings.

"What better way to get in contact with the customers and recruit dealers?"

I already hadn't liked these guys before, but this thought made me ball my hand into a fist.

"See what you can find out about Mount Pleasant. Take a long, hard look. You should probably investigate the other, too."

"The poker boys were looking for competitive intelligence when they offered Seth Roberts a position."

I nodded, glad to see he was following me. "If one rehab center is a front for drugs, why not two?"

56

It was a little after five in the morning by the time I got back home. I was way too worked up to think about sleeping. I hit the treadmill and started my day out with a Coke before I even sat for breakfast. I was in my office before 6:30 AM. Even though Ellie usually came in early every day I had a trial, I wasn't expecting her today. I figured she'd made the effort to meet me yesterday but that I wouldn't see her through the duration of the trial.

I had just sat at my desk when I got a call from Candy.

"I'm hoping I didn't wake you." It was not a question.

"I'm awake."

I considered telling her about the break in the case but decided against it. I didn't know how much she knew about Raymond's drug operations. I wanted us to be face-to-face when I told her what I had found, so I could see her reaction. I had asked about the money and drugs under the bed before the trial had begun. She had denied they were hers.

I didn't know if I believed her.

"I couldn't sleep all night," Candy said. "Do you think I should take this offer?"

"It's up to you. I can't tell you what to do. You know your situation." I tapped my finger on the table. "How about you come into my office, so we can talk about it. Can you be here by 8:00 AM?"

"I'll be there."

I prepped my strategy by reviewing the witnesses Frank had put on the stand the previous day and how I thought they had done.

I was surprised Tammy Weaver had been his second witness. I had expected she would come towards the end after he went through law enforcement.

Why did Frank do that?

It was obvious he wanted to get the idea of Candy buying a gun in front of the jury as soon as he could. He knew his case was circumstantial. But he also knew Tammy had credibility problems, as I had pointed out during my cross. People believed what they wanted to believe. If the jurors decided they believed Tammy Weaver, it would be difficult for me to get them to come back from that.

Perhaps that had been Frank's strategy.

He'd been trying to make a first impression right after he had Detective Bernie Lee present the evidence about Raymond Carlisle's murder.

The judge had given Frank half an hour last night to stick another witness on the stand, and he had declined. Was that because he wanted the jury to go home and think about how Candy had been seen with something that looked like a weapon?

He had given them little else to think about during the night.

It wasn't long before the doorbell rang, and I showed Candy into my office.

"Want a soda?" I asked. "We have a coffee machine back there if you want. You'd have to make it."

"I'm fine."

"Were you involved with Raymond's drug business?" I asked once she was sitting across the desk from me in my office.

Candy stared. She swallowed. She looked away. And then made eye contact with me again.

"Not directly, but I was aware of it."

"Did you know that the poker boys were involved?"

"How much do you know, Mr. Turner?"

Her question could have taken me off guard, but it didn't. It was obvious there was still vital information she had held back.

"So you didn't know that's what the poker boys were doing?" I asked.

I could see her hesitation.

"I'm your lawyer. Whatever you tell me remains confidential."

"I don't know the specifics of the day-to-day. I only knew high-level things."

It was clear this was not the full truth.

She was neck-deep.

"And the poker boys?"

She licked her lips. "The poker boys were all involved."

"Why didn't you tell Karen Brodsky about this?"

Candy hesitated. "I'm not sure. It's obvious in retrospect the poker boys are good suspects."

"It's because you're still getting money from them, aren't you?"

Candy hesitated.

"How's the money being transferred?"

Candy didn't answer again.

"You have not once pointed to the poker boys this whole time that you have been under investigation for murder because they're still paying you Raymond's cut of the business. Is that correct?"

"Mr. Turner, this is a tricky situation."

"No, they framed you for murder. You shouldn't be accepting money from them."

"It is not as simple as that."

"Enlighten me."

"Raymond had the relationship with the distributor."

"Did you take Raymond's place?"

"In a manner of speaking."

"It is either a yes or a no."

"Yes, I suppose I did."

"Why did he leave the poker group?"

"He was squeezing them for more money."

I just waited, making it clear I expected her to go on.

"The other guys did not have a relationship with the distributor. Raymond did not think he was being paid his fair share. He backed out of the group for a time."

"Until they killed him."

"No, he started working with them again, but he didn't trust them enough to be alone with them ever again."

"We have a clear motive for murder."

"You can't tell anybody about any of this."

"Excuse me?"

"Mitch, this distributor, he is not a pleasant man."

"Tell me about him."

"He's brutal. If one of his downstream distributors has a problem, he just takes care of it. Doesn't matter who dies. It is not uncommon for a downstream distributor and his family to go missing."

"Are your children safe right now?"

"Yes. I dropped them off at school this morning."

"Has he made any threats?"

"He doesn't have to."

"How do you know it was the poker boys who killed your husband and not the distributor?"

She hesitated, but the jig was up. "We all would have died if it was the distributor."

It was time to play my next card. "How does Mount Pleasant play into all this?"

Candy's eyes grew big. "How do you know about Mount Pleasant?"

I just shrugged.

"You cannot tell them."

"Just tell me what you know."

"You misunderstand me. You can't tell anybody you know that name. I'm not gonna say anything more. You're messing with things that are dangerous."

"I recognize that *now*. It would've been better if you had been honest with me from the beginning. There are things we could have done to keep it from getting this far. We could have gone to the prosecution and worked on a witness protection program for you and your kids."

Candy shook her head. "It wouldn't work. The last family that went into protection were all killed."

"You have proof this happened?"

"Well, no."

"A story told by the distributor?"

Her lack of response was all I needed.

"If we went to them now—"

"No. If the distributor is brought to justice, somebody else will take his place. The next distributor will clean house. That means all questionable downstream distributors are removed from the food chain."

I stared at Candy. "What is the name of your distributor?"

"I'm not gonna tell you."

"Would you tell me in exchange for how I know about Mount Pleasant?"

Candy considered it but shook her head. "As much as I want to know how you know, I can't. If I even utter that guy's name, he'll find me."

"He doesn't know everything."

"He comes close."

"Let's talk about your plea bargain."

"You said I could get out after seven years?"

"That's no guarantee. It's just a possibility of parole after seven years."

"I think I'm gonna take it."

"Who's gonna take care of your kids?"

Candy stopped. "My father. I can track him down. He would do it. I know he would."

"You don't know the first thing about him, do you?"

"No."

"You really want him looking after your kids for the next seven to fifteen years? Where will they be when you get out?"

"I don't know, Mitch. I don't know. I just... The fact you're already onto the truth is concerning."

"What did you think was going to happen?"

"I don't know."

"You were protecting the poker boys. That's what this comes down to. And because of that, you're now at risk of going to prison for the foreseeable future, maybe even for the rest of your life."

"You think I don't know that?"

I stared at Candy, trying to figure out this knot. I had seen some difficult situations before, but never one quite like this.

I almost liked it better the day before when I hadn't known what was going on, as frustrating as that was.

"Seth Roberts. What do you know about him?"

Candy smiled. "They were trying to go around me. It didn't work. Seth turned them down."

"Does Seth know the distributor?"

"I don't believe so, not directly."

"What happens to you if they do that?"

"I'm no longer a problem. I don't have a place to push my supply. I can't make my payments. They know all that."

"The distributor cleans up?"

Candy nodded.

"Tell me how Mount Pleasant works."

"No."

"I'm on your side. I'm probably the only person who will ever be on your side. You are not making the most sympathetic client right now." I held her gaze. "You wanted me to put you on the stand, but there's no way I can do that now."

"Why not?"

I was happy to hear there was some fire behind her words. This woman needed to fight, and she'd have to fight on multiple fronts. I would help her where I could, but there were limits to what I could do.

"Frank Ward will talk about this for the rest of the trial if he catches wind of it. His entire theory is that you are a drug dealer. Everything you have just told me proves that. If he can prove this to the jury, they will assume you killed your husband."

"But I didn't. That's not how this is supposed to work."

I shook my head. "Doesn't matter, especially if the details come to light.

"What are we gonna do?"

"I have no clue." I gave her a tightlipped smile. "But we do everything we can to figure this out."

"Are you going to tell Frank Ward that I will take the deal?" The way she asked told me that she hadn't yet made up her mind.

"That's not my decision. I will if you tell me to, but if not, I'm going to keep fighting." She opened her mouth, but I cut her off. "Take some time to think about it. This trial's got a few days. You don't have to decide now."

"Did Frank say how long the offer was good for?"

"The offer is probably good as long as we keep on an even footing with the prosecution. If things start to swing Frank's way, that's when you should get worried."

She nodded.

"One last question. Do you know a woman named Beatrice?"

"Who?"

57

I didn't have long after Candy left before I needed to be in court. I was glad I had taken the risk to follow the dark SUV. That had led Winston to Mount Pleasant, which had, in turn, given me the key piece of information I needed to get Candy to tell me what was going on.

I didn't know yet how I would get her out of this, but I finally had an accurate lay of the land. Understanding the facts and what had been going on behind the scenes was crucial for me to untie this and keep my client out of prison.

And alive if fortune smiles on us.

I packed my briefcase and headed towards the break room to grab a soda when I saw Ellie at her desk. She had my usual bottle of Coke ready.

"You didn't think I'd forget, did you?" Ellie asked when she saw where I was going.

"I just expected you had more important things to worry about."

Ellie smiled. "What could be more important than this?"

"Almost anything else. Thank you."

I tried to decide what I should tell Winston on my walk over to the courthouse.

He would have useful insights, but it might be safer for him not to know everything that was going on.

If I were Winston, I'd want to know.

These guys were more dangerous than we had thought. I pulled out my phone and sent Winston a text.

"Watch your back. We don't know what we're dealing with yet."

Winston responded. "Explain?"

"I'll fill you in later. Just act like we have the Mafia following us." There was a limit to how much I would send over a text message.

I put my phone away as I walked up the steps of the courthouse, went through security, and was soon sitting at my place a few minutes before the start of the trial. Candy joined me a couple of minutes later.

She was pale.

I could tell she was giving Frank's offer serious thought.

"Things are gonna be okay," I said.

"How do you know?"

"We don't stop fighting until they are." I gave her a smile as the bailiff stood.

"All rise. Court is now in session."

58

"You may call your next witness," Judge Hopkins said to Frank after we had taken care of some housekeeping matters and the jury had been seated.

Frank positioned himself at the podium. "I call Philip Dixon to the witness stand."

I was familiar with Dixon but had never come across him before this case. He was a crime scene technician who had developed a bit of a name for himself because of his analysis and ability to process a crime scene thoroughly. I had expected more from his lackluster report. Perhaps he had drafted it on a bad day.

Philip took the stand and was sworn in. Frank went through preliminary questions, asking Philip about his background.

"Can you please describe what you found when you entered the Carlisle's front room?" Frank asked fifteen minutes later.

"I found the deceased, Raymond Carlisle, semi-prostrate on the couch. One hand hung off the edge. His other was beside him. He was dead, presumably from the four gunshot wounds in his chest.

"Did you find empty brass in the room?"

Philip shook his head. "No. I did not."

"Did you find any bullets in the room?"

"The coroner found two bullets in the deceased's body. We found two bullets in the couch. Detective Lee later entered another bullet into evidence, too."

"Were you able to identify the caliber of the bullets?"

"Yes, at the time, I identified them as 9 mm; ballistics subsequently confirmed this. Detective Lee's bullet was a .22."

"Can you tell us about your examination of the room?"

"The room was carpeted. We did a trace analysis and didn't find anything unexpected."

"Can you elaborate?"

"It did not appear there had been any outsiders in the home based on the trace evidence found on the floor."

"And by this, you mean?"

"We didn't find any unknown DNA."

Philip was subtle in how he had answered these questions. It was calculated to make the jury think there weren't discrepancies. I would pull those out during my cross.

This is the rockstar crime scene tech?

I wasn't impressed.

"Did you find any other significant residue?"

"No, we did not."

"What else did you find?"

"We did a fingerprint analysis. We found Candy Carlisle's fingerprints on the victim's shirt buttons."

Another carefully worded statement.

"What DNA did you find on the victim?"

"We found hair from the defendant, Candy Carlisle."

"Where did you find it?"

"We found it on his shirt, as well as on his pants."

"Did you find DNA from anybody else on the victim?"

Philip shook his head. "No, we did not."

"I have no further questions for this witness."

I could tell from Frank's smile as he turned back to his seat that he was satisfied with how his questioning had gone.

"Your turn, counselor," Judge Hopkins said. I approached the witness stand with only my notepad. My questions for this witness would be far fewer.

"When you say you didn't find DNA on the victim other than that from Raymond's wife Candy, are you neglecting to mention DNA from the children?"

"No. We did not find any DNA from the victim's children."

"Really?" I let that sink in. "You didn't find any hair from their oldest female child?"

"No. We did not."

"Doesn't she have hair down past her shoulders?"

"I don't know."

"And you didn't find any hair from the other child either?"

"No."

"Did you find any DNA from the children inside the room?"

"No. We did not."

I frowned. "Isn't that something you would expect to find?"

"The evidence is what the evidence is."

"The children are probably in that room every day. Isn't it natural that the children—especially the older girl—would have shed hair on the couch and on the floor?"

Philip shrugged. "It wasn't there."

"How do you explain the absence of something we would expect to see?"

"I think you're asking me to speculate."

Frank stirred but said nothing.

"Did it look as if someone had freshly vacuumed the room?"

A light dinged on in Philip's eyes. "Yes, in fact, it did. There were marks on the carpet as if a vacuum had recently been run over it."

"Did you try to identify what vacuum had been used?"

"No, I did not."

"Did you check the Carlisle vacuum for remnants of DNA from their children?"

"No, we did not."

"Why not?"

"We saw no need."

"How would you explain that there was no DNA from the children?"

I didn't expect to get the same line about speculating, especially since I had now slow-walked him through this. I hoped the jury would see that this should have been obvious and would doubt his other analysis.

"I assume Ms. Carlisle must have vacuumed earlier in the day."

"The children had been home since Ms. Carlisle had gone to work. Surely at least one might have gone into the room. Wouldn't they have left something behind?"

Philip shrugged. "I guess they didn't."

I waited for a moment to emphasize my next question.

"Did you find evidence the couch had been recently vacuumed, too?"

He furrowed his brow. "Meaning?"

"Did you see any signs left behind by a vacuum on the couch?"

"Not that I could see. The couch itself is made from a fiber that wouldn't have a telltale trail after it was vacuumed."

"So other than the DNA from Ms. Carlisle—her hair—did you find anything else on the couch?"

"No."

"Did you look under the cushions?"

"Yes."

"And?"

"Nothing."

I hesitated and put an expression on my face as if I found this curious. "Do you mean to tell me that you did not find any crumbs underneath the couch cushions?"

"We did not."

"And," I said, "you didn't find any DNA from anybody else either?"

"No. We did not."

"You testified you found Ms. Carlisle's DNA. What was the source of her DNA?"

A nonchalant glance at the jury. "Hair, skin."

"No blood?"

"No."

"Let's talk about the victim's body."

"I'm not the coroner, Mr. Turner."

"Indeed not, but I have a question a layperson such as yourself should be able to answer."

I repressed a snort.

Rockstar.

Mr. Dixon frowned when I referred to him as a layperson, but he has set me up, so I had taken it.

"Did it look like Mr. Carlisle's hands had been restrained?"

He shrugged. "How could I tell?"

"Were there red marks on his wrists?"

A momentary pause. "Yes."

"And what would you say was the reason for those red marks?"

"Objection," Frank said, "calls for speculation."

"Sustained."

"Was there any DNA found under Raymond's fingernails?"

"No."

I moved as if to go but then turned back. "One final question. Did you find any of the DNA from the victim in the room?"

"Sure. We found blood on the couch. And on the floor. And on the walls."

I nodded. "But what about his hair?"

"We did not find any of his hair on the floor."

"Couch?"

"No hair on the floor or the couch."

"I have no further questions for this witness."

59

Frank Ward was now back at the podium. "The state calls Tonya Wood to the stand."

The new medical examiner.

I had not yet met her. I'd read through her report. It was well written and had some insights that weren't obvious from the data.

Tonya entered from the back of the courtroom. She was a pretty blonde woman who appeared to be a few years younger than me. She wore glasses and had a stern expression that made me wonder if she were nervous.

Was this her first time testifying in court?

After she was sworn in, Frank started his questions, asking her to describe her credentials and laying the groundwork for her later testimony. He didn't ask outright, but I was increasingly certain this was her first trial based on some of her answers.

He had her describe Raymond's wounds in painstaking detail, projecting diagrams up for the jury and having her walk through everything she had found.

"And what would you say was the cause of death?" Frank asked two hours later.

"Pulmonary failure as a result of wounds from the four bullets."

"Thank you. Your Honor, I have no further questions for this witness.

"Counselor?"

"I have a few questions."

"Thank you for being here today, Ms. wood," I said with a pleasant smile, hoping to put her at ease. "Can you please tell us about the condition of Frank's body at the time of his death?"

Tonya looked confused. "It was full of holes—"

"My apologies. Would you talk about his general health?"

"I would describe it as average. What do you want to know specifically?"

"Was he in good enough shape to say go for a run?"

"I doubt he could have run a marathon. He had extra weight around the middle. He wasn't obese, but he wasn't fit either."

"Did you find evidence of illegal drug use?"

"No. The toxicology report came back clear."

"Is there any way to know if he had prior illegal drug use?"

"Yes, there are some ways, and we found nothing like that."

"Did he have scars from needle marks on his arm?

"No."

"Did the toxicology report come back clear for alcohol and prescription drugs too?"

"Yes, we checked for all of those things."

"In your professional opinion, he was in his right mind at the time of his death?"

"I don't know that I can say that. I will say he was not under the influence of drugs or alcohol at the time he died."

"What did you put down in your report as the time of his death?"

"I put it between 7:00 PM and 10:00 PM."

"You testified he was shot with a 9 mm. Did you find evidence he had also been shot with any other caliber?"

"No, the only bullet wounds we found came from a 9 mm."

"So you're confident enough to say that he was not shot with a .22, correct?"

"That is correct."

"I have no further questions for this witness."

Frank stood as I moved toward the defense table. "Your Honor, I have another question or two, if you don't mind."

"Proceed."

"Ms. Wood," Frank asked, not moving to the podium. "Can you conclusively say that Raymond never took any illegal drugs?"

"No, I cannot. I can only say that his body did not show signs of habitual drug use."

"In other words, he could have experimented in college or even taken illegal drugs occasionally later in life, and you might not have been able to tell, correct?"

"Yes, that is correct."

"I have no further questions, Your Honor."

Once Tonya Wood had been dismissed from the stand, Frank called his next witness.

"I call Bill Weaver to the stand."

60

Bill Weaver entered the courtroom, drawing all eyes. What would we hear from him today? This was the man who had not had a second thought about involving his wife in this trial. Tammy Weaver had been called to testify and perjure herself because of Bill Weaver's lies.

I remembered well that initial conversation I had with Bill. I'd almost walked away thinking he could have had nothing to do with Raymond's death. He was an upstanding member of the community. A respected dentist. His practice appeared to be thriving.

The guy had been clean.

But then he had stopped me just outside of his office to tell me that his wife had run into Candy and had a bad experience.

I couldn't stop thinking about it. It had been a strange thing to do. What had he been hoping to accomplish? Had he feared we were onto him and wanted to point the finger at Candy in response? Was he hoping to persuade me that she was guilty, so I was more likely to push for a plea bargain?

At the time, it had seemed unimportant. It wasn't until later that further "details" had come out about the encounter.

I was doubly glad I'd stalked Abe Martin and seen Bill Weaver hiding out in the mechanic shop in the middle of the night.

I would not let him off easy.

Frank Ward started his questioning after Bill Weaver took his oath.

"Can you please introduce yourself to the ladies and gentlemen of the jury?"

"Yes, I am Bill Weaver. I was a friend and associate of Raymond Carlisle."

"How exactly did you know Raymond?"

"We met through a monthly poker group."

"How long ago would you say that was?"

"Approximately five or six years."

"Was this a group you started?"

"Yes, with some others."

"Did you invite Raymond?"

"No. He was invited by Kyle Rencher. He's actually the one who formed the group, the brains behind it, if you will."

That was a strange way to put it.

Was Bill laying the groundwork to serve up Kyle on a platter if things went south?

"What did you think about Raymond when you first met him?"

I thought about objecting as irrelevant but decided against it. I didn't know where Frank was going with this line of questioning, but I found it interesting, and it presented potential opportunities for me to come back and ask additional questions on my cross-examination. I wanted Bill Weaver to sing like a canary, and to do that, I wanted him comfortable answering all sorts of questions.

Judge Hopkins glanced at me as if expecting an objection, but I intentionally folded my hands on top of the table and leaned back to make it clear I wasn't going to.

"I thought he was okay. He was a decent player. I don't know that I'd say I knew him well enough to say anything more than that."

A non-answer.

"You played poker with Raymond approximately twelve times a year for the last five to six years, is that correct?"

"Yes, give or take."

"By the time of his death, you knew him pretty well. Did he seem like an honest person?"

Another glance from the judge, but I was willing to let Frank have it without a fight. It only fed into my case if Frank could present Raymond as a drug dealer.

"I'm not quite sure how to answer. I mean, during poker, the whole idea is to bluff."

A quiet murmur came from around the courtroom. I noticed several jurors smiling.

"Point made." Frank smiled as if he had not thought of this himself, though I was certain there was a reason he asked. I just couldn't tell what it was at this point.

"Was Raymond good at bluffing?"

"Would he have been just an average poker player if he was?"

Another round of laughter. This time, there was a touch more merriment.

Bill Weaver hid a smile.

Something about the guy struck me as off.

He had made me feel comfortable when I had walked into his office for a surprise interview. I had expected a hostile and antagonistic conversation similar to what I experienced with Abe Martin, but it had been nothing like that.

Is this man a sociopath?

Did he have the ability to read people and play to them?

"Did Raymond ever talk about his work?"

I didn't glance at the judge but was sure she expected an objection.

"Yes, actually, quite a bit. He and Kyle Rencher worked together. That's how Kyle and Raymond got to know each other. I heard a lot about the company they were working for in those days. Eventually, Kyle moved on to something else. I believe Raymond stayed for another year or two after that. I'm not sure what he was doing at the time of his death."

"Raymond was a software programmer, is that correct?"

"Yes."

"Did you ever have any reason to suspect Raymond was a drug dealer?"

I had not expected Frank to ask such a direct question so early in his examination of Bill Weaver.

My eyes narrowed. A positive answer would open the door to opportunities.

"To be frank, yes, I did."

I hid a triumphant smile. I'd hoped to get here with Tammy, but I'd take Bill.

"What made you think this?"

"It was the things Raymond liked to talk about. He talked about how he liked to experiment in college. He talked about how he thought marijuana should be legal. He talked about an LSD trip he took once."

Frank glanced my way as if surprised I hadn't made a single objection. I liked how it made him uncertain.

"Doing drugs is different from selling drugs, isn't it?" Frank asked.

"I would suppose."

"What was it about Raymond that made you think he was actually selling?"

"He was open about how in college he did some light drug dealing."

Candy stirred and leaned over. "Raymond refused to touch the product, just in case you're wondering, and he didn't deal in college."

I nodded and made a note on my paper. It was for the benefit of the jury, too, so when I got to my cross-examination of Bill Weaver, they would know Candy had helped inform some of my questions.

I wasn't hearing anything unexpected.

I was surprised at how open Bill Weaver was in talking about this. I had wondered if he might be, but I had not expected it because I would have thought he would want to distance himself from a known drug dealer as much as possible.

It was a risky maneuver. It would play into my hands if I could make it work just right.

"College was two decades ago. What makes you think that he was still dealing?"

"He would talk about it in a wistful sort of way, you know what I mean?"

"Can you please provide an example?"

Again, Judge Hopkins looked at me. I wasn't about to object. Her eyebrows rose when our eyes met, but I gave a small shake of my head.

Her eyes narrowed. I wondered if she knew Bill was only helping my case.

"Sure," Bill said, "there was a time in college he talked about fondly. He was running out of money but had a stash he had purchased for his own use. He was proud of how he'd made a handsome profit when he'd run into a desperate person with a nice car."

"He traded the car for the drugs?"

"Yep, and then sold the car."

"Did he ever say or do anything in your presence to make you think he was actively selling drugs?"

"It's the little things that stand out the most. There was the time he seemed desperate for money and wanted us to raise the limit we had on our poker night to $2,000. I think he would've been willing to risk offending us all to make some extra money that night."

"Was he having money problems?"

"I don't know, maybe at that point. Now let me be clear, this was several years ago. Things have changed. Or at least they changed right before he died."

"Can you provide an example?"

"Yes, he kept wanting to raise our betting limit, but for a different reason. I think he wanted to flaunt how much money he had. He would often say we ought to play high stakes poker, suggesting the buy-in should be $50,000."

"$50,000? Did the rest of your group have that kind of money?"

"No way!" Bill laughed. He got a few chuckles. "Nothing like that."

"Did anybody else want to raise the amount you guys were gambling?"

"No. Never. And certainly not in the sums Raymond kept talking about."

"Was there anything else that made you think Raymond was dealing drugs?"

"I talked about the money. I talked about his history dealing in college. He continued afterward, too. I can't think of anything more about Raymond."

"What about Candy?"

Bill looked right at her. "Apparently, that's how they met." The look on Bill's face challenged her to testify and say otherwise.

I hesitated. I'd wanted to keep this out of court, but the door was now open. I could object, but the fact of the matter was that she was involved in dealing. I could lose credibility with the jury if the truth was fully disclosed. It was time now to pivot my strategy.

"Dealing or doing?" Frank asked.

"It sounded like it was a fluid situation."

I chanced a glance at Candy out of the corner of my eye, hoping the jury would not notice. She was pale and gripped her hands together, turning her knuckles white. I couldn't tell if she was angry because it wasn't true or because a personal secret had just been spilled in court.

Could be either.

"You know when?"

"I believe they met sometime after college. A few years after."

"Raymond told you they were dealing drugs?"

"Objection, Your Honor," I said. "Mr. Ward is asking for hearsay."

"Indeed, counselor." Judge Hopkins' tone was cold, telling me that she suspected I was up to something by waiting so long to object. "Sustained."

"No further questions for this witness."

61

"We can either break for lunch early," Judge Hopkins said, looking at me, "or you can get started with your questioning, and we'll have a late lunch. Choice is yours."

"Let's go now, Your Honor," I said. "Everybody needs a break. We'll start fresh when we come back."

"Court is dismissed."

I leaned towards Candy and lowered my voice. "Anything else you want to tell me?"

She looked shocked that I had posed such a question in public. Perhaps she'd forgotten that she'd just told me that Raymond never used the product. I'd spoken no louder than her, and the room was now less quiet.

"Is there a place we can talk?"

Ten minutes later, we were both back at my office. Ellie was gone, so I asked Zoey to run out and get sandwiches for both Candy and myself, telling her to pick up something for herself as well.

Candy burst into tears once the door was shut. "I'm going to prison for a long time, aren't I?"

"Not necessarily." I leaned back and put my hands behind my head. "I think things went pretty well."

"You do?"

"The one thing I have been having trouble proving was that the poker boys were dealing drugs. It wasn't until this morning that I stumbled upon Mount Pleasant. You finally leveled with me after I told you." I placed my hands on the desk and leaned forward. "You are the key to unraveling this, Candy. If you don't start talking and providing actual evidence, you could go to prison for a long time. If you can provide what I need to put these guys away—"

"But they've already presented me as a drug dealer." She looked up from her hands. "You already know that's what I am."

"You're not a murderer. It's a big distinction."

"Are you judging me?"

I snorted. "I don't have the time or luxury while I'm working a case. If I thought you had actually murdered Raymond, I would push you towards a deal. It's only because I think you are telling the truth about not killing him—if not everything else—that I am not doing that."

"I'm so glad you believe me."

"Don't be. I'm not the one who matters. It's the jury who matters." I let my words sink in. "And that's where you come in. It is time to put all your cards on the table."

"But they already think I'm a drug dealer."

"Which is perfectly fine if we can prove they are all drug dealers, too. Pots and kettles."

"Okay."

"What can you provide as evidence?"

"Well, obviously, we don't keep records, now do we?"

"You never recorded a video of them? Did Raymond?"

She hesitated. "I don't think so."

"Did Raymond have a computer you didn't have access to? Any files you never reviewed?"

"Raymond had his home office, but the police went through it. I don't know that they would have found anything I missed."

"So you found something?"

"No. I went through it after Raymond died, fearing they might come back. I didn't find anything."

A lie. I was certain.

"Can I get your keys?"

She nodded. "What are you looking for?"

"No idea."

Candy took her key ring out and pulled several keys off while I dialed Winston. He answered on the first ring.

"Are you ready to tell me what's going on?"

It took me a moment to remember the cryptic text I'd sent him.

"We can't get into that now," I said, "I want you to get over to the Carlisle home. You can stop by my office and get the keys. I'll leave them with Zoey."

"What am I looking for?"

I put the phone on speaker. “You’re now on with Candy, too. Where should Winston look?”

62

"You may all be seated," Judge Hopkins said. She looked at Bill. "I remind you, Mr. Weaver, that you are still under oath."

"Yes, ma'am."

The judge turned to me. "Are you ready, counselor?"

"Yes, Your Honor." I approached the podium and set my notepad in front of me, putting my pen beside it. "Mr. Weaver, did you have a pleasant lunch?"

"I suppose I did."

"Can you please tell me more about your poker games?" I asked with a friendly smile.

"Sure, what would you like to know?"

"What time did they start?"

He shrugged. "I dunno, typically around eight or nine in the evening."

"Did you guys switch venues, or was it always the same house?"

"We mixed it up."

"How often would you host at your place?"

"A few times a year."

"How late would they go?"

"One, sometimes two in the morning."

"That's an awfully long poker game if you're gambling with so little money. Why so late?"

"We played with coins."

"Would you say that you became a skilled poker player over the last six years?"

He gave me a big smile. "You'd have to ask the other players."

"Did you win more often than not?"

"I won my share. The others, too. It wasn't about winning or even about the game. It was just about getting together with the guys."

"Would you say you guys became good friends?"

"Yes, I'd say that."

"The type of friends who'd invite each other over for barbecues?"

Bill hesitated, seeing what I'd backed him into. "We didn't go for that sort of thing."

"Really? Why not?"

"We were a disparate group of guys. We didn't run in the same circles, so it didn't make sense to get together with our families for a Sunday barbecue."

I nodded. "Would you describe yourself as better than the others?"

"If anything, they're better than me." Bill beamed at the jury, but they weren't buying it.

"Were you friends with *any* of them outside of the poker group?"

"Not really. I would occasionally take my car to Abe Martin's mechanic shop, but that was it."

I gave him a steady look. "And when was the last time you were at Abe's shop?"

"Probably six months ago or so."

I wanted to ask if he had been there that morning, but I had no way to contradict him if he lied, which I knew he would.

I also didn't want to tip him off that I was on to his operation, not yet.

"Have you ever been to the places where your other poker buddies work?"

"No."

"Have they been to yours?"

"I don't believe so."

"You've never given any of them dental work?"

"No."

"Nothing like that ever came about as the result of a losing hand?"

"No, I remind you we didn't gamble for much."

I nodded. "Tell me more about how poker nights would unfold."

"Not much to say. Everybody would show up. We had the buy-in. We kept a big box of coins we would use to change the cash into coins, and then we'd start playing."

"Like a little casino."

"Sure, if you want to call it that."

"Did you guys have food?"

"Yeah, we had snacks."

"Did you guys ever do any illegal drugs?"

"No." Bill was emphatic. It was the first time I'd seen him show emotion on the stand.

"Did anybody ever bring any illegal drugs?"

"Not that I was aware of."

"Would you consider Raymond to be an outlier of your group?"

"What do you mean?"

"Your testimony earlier was that he did drugs, and you suspected him of dealing. Did he fit in with your group because others did, too?"

"No. None of the rest of us ever dealt or did drugs. If they did, they didn't talk about it."

"You never experimented in college?"

"It's been so long. I think I tried marijuana, but I don't remember for sure."

"Not cocaine?"

"No."

"Heroine?"

"No."

"Meth?"

"No."

"And you never did any drug dealing in college?"

"No."

"Not after college?"

"No."

Bill watched me carefully. Was he afraid that I knew something? We had looked into Bill Weaver's past and found no incidents of drug usage or dealing that had made it onto public records. It appeared there was something he was concerned about.

Smoke.

Where was the fire?

"Did your wife Tammy ever do any illegal drugs?"

"No."

"Did you guys meet while drug dealing?"

"Objection, Your Honor," Frank said, standing, "this is spurious. The defense has no basis for a belief in any of this."

"Mr. Turner, tread carefully," Judge Hopkins said, "but I will allow the witness to answer. Overruled."

Frank sat down, looking like he had walked into a trap.

"Please answer the question, Mr. Weaver," I said.

"No, we did not meet dealing drugs." Bill was losing his composure. I was onto something. I just didn't know what. Nothing in his background report suggested where they had met.

"Can you please tell us how you met your wife?"

"I'd rather not get into it if it's all the same to you."

"Why not?"

"It doesn't seem relevant."

"Your Honor, I object," Frank said, standing. "This line of questioning has little to do with the matter at hand."

"Overruled. The witness will answer the question," Judge Hopkins said. It must have been clear to her, too, that I was onto something.

"How did you meet your wife?"

"I met her after college."

It was a nonanswer. I glanced at the jury. I bet they thought the same thing.

I nodded slightly, taking a moment as I considered my next best move. It was clear I had found a touchy subject.

I looked up. "Was it by chance in rehab?"

Bill turned white and rocked back on the witness stand while glaring at me. He opened his mouth and then shut it again.

"Yes," he said through gritted teeth, "that is where we met."

I arched an eyebrow. "Were you working at the rehab center?"

"No."

"What were you doing there?"

"I was a patient."

"Why were you a patient?"

"I had an addiction."

It was like I had to pry the words from his mouth. He glanced at the jury. He looked worried.

"What was the name of the rehab center?"

That drew Bill's attention. He now suspected I was on to something significant.

"I don't recall."

I hesitated, wanting to try out the name Mount Pleasant, but refrained. "You mentioned you had an addiction. What was it?"

"I am an alcoholic."

"You experimented with alcohol and marijuana but never tried other illegal drugs?"

"Yes, is that so hard to believe?"

"Why were you so hesitant to tell us about where you and your wife met?"

"I didn't think it was relevant. I didn't think it was any of your business."

"Was your future wife there for the same addiction?"

"Yes."

"Were you telling the truth when you admitted earlier you never did drugs apart from your marijuana use?"

"Sure."

"How long were you in rehab together?"

"I was there for approximately nine months; she was there for three. She came in after I got there and left before me."

I nodded. "How did this experience change you?"

"It made me never want to experiment with drugs or alcohol again."

"Objection, Your Honor. I know you're giving counsel leeway, but this has really gone on long enough. Mr. Turner is asking these questions to embarrass the witness."

"I assure you that I have my reasons, Your Honor," I said. "They will become apparent in due course."

Judge Hopkins studied me and then turned her attention back to Frank. "Sustained. Mr. Turner, I suggest you get on with it."

"Sure thing, Your Honor." I looked at my notepad. None of these questions had been on it. I had not even suspected there would be something hidden here. It had been pure instinct that made me ask how he met his wife.

I had not known it was such a touchy subject. And I was also convinced we still didn't know the whole truth.

"Mr. Weaver, did Raymond ever stop coming to your poker nights?"

"Yes, he did."

"When?"

"Six months before his death."

"Why?"

"I don't know. You'd have to ask him."

"He didn't tell you or any of the other poker players why he stopped coming?"

Frank stirred but remained seated.

"No, he did not."

"Did he ever communicate with you after that?"

"No, all communication stopped at that point." There was something on Bill's face. He glanced at me, and I could tell he was concerned about something, but I couldn't say what.

How did Raymond put the squeeze on them? I wondered. As soon as I had the chance, I would text Winston to ask him to look for a burner phone in Raymond's home office.

"Let me make sure this is clear. After that last poker night, Raymond never returned, and you never asked why. Is that accurate?"

"Yes."

"And you're certain you never spoke to him again?"

"Yes."

"Or communicated in any way?"

"Yes."

"Did you ever enter Raymond's house after that day?"

"No, I never did."

Another glance at me. Another worried look.

Was it Bill who had hidden the drugs and cash in the Carlisle master bedroom?

"And you're certain Raymond never told any of the others why he just stopped coming to the poker night?"

"Objection, calls for hearsay."

"Sustained."

"You're positive you don't know the reason he stopped coming?"

"I don't."

I nodded. "Could a falling out explain his absence from the poker group?"

"No. He just stopped."

"Do you know if any of the others ever reached out to him?"

"No, I don't."

"What did you do when Raymond stopped coming?"

"We kept meeting. We kept playing. The pot was smaller, but that was okay."

"Did anybody comment on his absence?"

"I'm sure we mentioned it."

"Isn't this all a little strange?"

"How do you mean?"

"If I was part of a poker group, and somebody stopped coming without a word of explanation, I would've at least sent a text message or placed a call to see how they were doing. Why didn't you?"

"We didn't. I don't know what else to say."

"I thought you were friends?"

Bill hesitated. "We weren't that good of friends. As I already mentioned, it is not like we did Sunday barbecues."

"Would you say your relationship with Raymond was purely professional?"

"How do you mean?"

"Like you guys were in business together or were coworkers?"

"No, it was nothing like that. We were friends."

"I see." I nodded but kept my face dubious. "I'm done with this witness, but I reserve the right to question him again."

"So noted."

I studied Bill Weaver as he left. He stared right at me as he passed.

I smiled at him, but he just frowned.

He looked very worried.

63

"The state calls Abe Martin to the stand," Frank Ward said after we had taken a five-minute break. I was curious why he had called Abe as a witness. If I had been in his shoes, I'd have avoided calling Abe unless I had no other option. I didn't know what he was hoping Abe would prove.

"Can you please tell us about your relationship with Raymond Carlisle?" Frank asked once Abe had been sworn in and identified for the record.

"Sure. We were poker buddies."

"How long did you guys play poker together?"

"I dunno, five or six years."

"Would you say you knew Raymond well?"

"Yes."

"Did it seem like Raymond had money?"

"Yes, it did. There were also times when he seemed hard up for cash. They never did last long."

"Did Raymond ever offer you drugs?"

Abe hesitated and glanced around the room before putting his attention back on Frank.

"Yes, he did."

"What kind of drugs did he offer you?"

"Prescription painkillers."

"Did he say where he got them from?"

"No."

"Did you take them?"

"Yes."

"How often would you buy drugs from him?"

"I don't know, a few times a month."

"And you played poker with him, too?"

"Yes, that's how we met."

I studied Abe. I had not expected this testimony. I didn't believe a single word of it, but I'd also have a hard time disproving any of it.

Perhaps that's what Frank wanted.

Or more likely Bill Weaver.

Is Bill making Abe clean up his own mess?

I hesitated, wondering if my strategy was going to play out. They were doing a solid job of painting Raymond as a drug dealer, but I had not yet made the segue from Raymond to the other poker boys.

I settled back in my seat, studying Abe Martin while Frank continued his questioning, going through dates and times and places where Abe had apparently purchased drugs from Raymond.

It wasn't long before Frank announced he had no further questions.

I went up to the podium.

"Good afternoon, Mr. Martin," I said, "how are you doing?"

"I'm fine," he said gruffly. Bill had prepared him for the third degree, and he was scared.

"When did you first take illegal drugs?"

"I didn't take drugs until Raymond offered them to me."

It was a nice touch to make it seem like Raymond had brought Abe over to the dark side.

I raised my eyebrows. "You never once tried them, not even in college or high school?"

"No, I never did."

"What was it about Raymond's offer that made them so appealing to you?"

"I was going through a hard time in my life." He paused. "I was going through a divorce."

"I'm sorry to hear that. That must've been difficult."

"It was."

"Raymond offered them to you out of the goodness of his heart?"

"Something like that."

"Were you aware Raymond was dealing drugs prior to this?"

"Yeah, I heard him mention it. He liked to talk about the glory days of college. He did some dealing then, though I believe most of his time in college was spent with recreational drug use himself."

"Did he ever offer anybody else in the group drugs?"

"I don't know, he offered them to me on the side."

"Did you ever get together with Raymond outside of the poker group?"

Abe hesitated as if uncertain. "No, not really. It was just afterwards. We had just played a game at my house, and he hung around to talk. He asked me questions about my divorce, and then he offered me a free sample. After that, I was hooked."

"So you have no direct knowledge of him selling drugs to any of the other poker players?"

"You would have to ask them."

"Was there ever anybody else around when you purchased the drugs?"

"No."

"Did you ever tell anybody you were buying drugs from Raymond?"

"No."

"Did you keep any evidence of these transactions?"

"How do you mean?"

"Did you ever pay with a check?"

"Of course not. It was all cash."

"Did you keep any of the drug vials?"

"Gone, long ago."

"Do we have anything other than your word that you bought these drugs from Raymond Carlisle?"

"No."

"Would you consider yourself an honest person?"

"Yes."

"Did you ever get together with any of the others outside of poker night?"

"No, not really."

"Did any of them ever come to your shop?"

Abe hesitated and acted like he'd remembered something.

"Yes," he said, "sometimes they would bring in their vehicles. I'd give them a price break, ten percent off."

"Do you have evidence that any of them have been to your shop? Could you provide it if requested?"

"I might if I looked hard enough. I probably have receipts."

"And you're sure you never got together with any of the others outside of poker night?"

"I never did."

"Have you ever been to Bill Weaver's dental office?"

"I never have."

"Are you sure?"

Abe hesitated. "Yes."

"Do you remember that you called me the day after I came to visit you at your shop?"

"Yes, I remember."

"Do you remember where you were when you called?"

Abe was sweating. "No, I don't."

"Is there any chance you were at Bill Weaver's dental office?"

"No, none whatsoever."

"Did you have anybody else in the room when you called?"

A bead of sweat dripped down the side of his face and fell onto his shirt. "I was all alone."

I smiled.

Time for the kill.

"Are you certain?"

"Yes."

He was pale. His face was covered now in sweat.

"I could have sworn I saw you coming out of Bill Weaver's dental office just after you finished talking to me. You weren't alone. Do you want to change your story?"

Abe didn't answer.

I pulled my phone out of my pocket. "I made a video. Would you like to see?"

"No."

"Do you want to amend your answer?"

"I just remembered. I *was* at Bill Weaver's office."

"Who else was with you?"

"Bill Weaver, Kyle Rencher, Larry Thompson, and myself."

"Were you talking to me on speakerphone?"

"Yes."

"Why were you all together?"

"I don't know."

"Were they helping you answer my questions?"

"I don't know."

"Was it because you feared I suspected you had something to do with Raymond's death, and you were keen to keep my interest off of you and your poker group?"

"I don't know."

"Isn't it a fact that the poker boys are a front and that you guys are running drugs?"

"I plead the fifth."

I studied him. "I have no further questions for this witness."

64

I kept my composure as I sat. Frank gave me an evil glare. I had struck a blow, but it was not unrecoverable.

"Counselor," Judge Hopkins said to Frank, "would you care to ask any questions on redirect?"

"Not at this time, Your Honor."

Judge Hopkins looked at Abe Martin. "You are excused."

Judge Hopkins studied her notes as Abe left and then looked at me. I held her gaze until she turned her attention back to Frank.

"We have several hours left, Mr. Ward. Would you like to call your next witness?"

"If I could request a fifteen-minute recess?"

She looked between Frank and me. She probably thought Frank wanted to make an offer.

"Make it twenty." She banged her gavel.

"That was quite the display," Candy whispered.

"We're not there yet," I said, lowering my voice. "I impeached him, and he all but confessed the poker boys are running a drug ring, but we have more to do."

"What's the problem?"

"We have to show now that they were more likely to kill your husband than you."

"We've made progress."

I nodded. "Considerable."

I looked at Frank, and he nodded towards the door.

"I'll be right back."

I followed Frank outside and down the hallway until we found an empty corner.

"You set me up, Mitch."

"How?"

"You're the one who told me about Tammy Weaver. She led me to Bill Weaver and Abe Martin. None of them have been good witnesses."

I snorted. "Don't blame me for your failure to prep adequately. I had an ethical obligation to tell you what she told me. Was there a way around it?"

Frank glared at me.

Even though I had disclosed the information, hoping he would call Tammy and some of the poker boys to the stand, I had no way of knowing he would actually do it. And I was required to disclose what I knew.

My intentions were not relevant.

"Ten years, possibility of parole in five."

I shook my head. "Frank, you have the wrong person."

"She did it. You just muddied the waters enough that I have no choice but to offer a plea deal that is beyond reason."

"I believe my client when she says she didn't do this." I jerked a thumb over my shoulder towards the courtroom. "You realize what you have back there?"

He didn't answer.

"I all but got Abe Martin to confess that their poker night is a cover for a drug operation."

"So?"

"Isn't that significant?"

"Not unless you give me the smoking gun."

I shrugged. "I don't have that."

"Then you're between a rock and a hard place."

"Not me, you. I want you to think back to when this case first landed on your desk. If you had known then what you know now, would you have still pegged this murder on Candy, or would you have taken a hard look at the poker boys?"

Frank didn't hesitate. "Let me know your answer."

He walked off. I meant to follow but didn't make it far before Bernie Lee was right in my face.

Again with this guy? Are they playing good cop/bad cop?

"What are you doing in there?" Bernie demanded.

"Bernie. Good to see you."

"You're gonna get her off."

"Are you still sure she did it?"

"Absolutely."

"Where's the murder weapon?"

Bernie sputtered.

"What's her motive?" I asked.

"She wanted to take control of the whole operation. They were planning to divorce, and she didn't want to split it with him."

I raised an eyebrow. "If they were running a criminal enterprise, it's not like they would've gone to court to get that split up."

"My point exactly. There was no other choice but to do what she did. It was going to be one or the other. Candy moved first."

I shook my head. "You got this all wrong. You should take a hard look at Abe Martin. He didn't confess on the stand, but he came close."

"Maybe for dealing drugs, not for murdering Raymond Carlisle. It is circumstantial at best."

"Everything is circumstantial," I said on my way into the courtroom.

And that was the problem.

65

"Your Honor," Frank Ward said once we were back in session, but before the jury had been brought back in, "we have made an offer to the defense. We would like to give them the rest of the day to think about it."

"Counselor?" Judge Hopkins looked at me.

I hesitated as I stood. Candy stirred beside me, but I didn't look at her. I didn't need to.

I wouldn't mind catching up to Winston to see how things were going at the Carlisle home, but if Frank was in a bad enough spot to make this surprise move, the best thing I could do was to proceed with the trial.

I also had my reputation to consider. It could be perceived as reasonable for Frank to make this request. I didn't immediately see a way I could deny him this without looking like a jerk.

A thought occurred to me.

"We're happy to take the rest of the day, but as I have already made obvious to the prosecution, my client isn't willing to talk about a plea bargain at this point." I saw Candy nodding out of the corner of my eye.

Judge Hopkins looked at Candy. "Ms. Carlisle?"

"Yes, Your Honor."

I touched Candy on the shoulder and motioned for her to stand. She stood abruptly.

Judge Hopkins smiled pleasantly. "Is this true? Are you not interested in an offer?"

"No, Your Honor. I know I didn't do this."

Judge Hopkins frowned as she looked between Frank and me. She glanced at the clock on the back of the courtroom wall. "I want to see counsel in my chambers. Now."

A few minutes later, we were both in the judge's chambers.

Frank kept glaring at me as if I had intentionally pantsed him in court. I couldn't see why he felt that way when I had made it clear from the beginning my client had no interest in a plea bargain. He had made a ploy, and I had taken the wind out of it by just telling the truth.

It was well within my rights to do so. I didn't have to back him up.

"What is the offer?" Judge Hopkins asked Frank.

"Ten, possibility of parole in five."

Judge Hopkins looked at me. "That's quite the offer, Mitch. You can't convince your client to take it?"

"She says she's innocent. She's been adamant from day one."

Judge Hopkins gave me a look. "Are you sincere in this belief, Mr. Turner?"

I smiled. "Does it matter what I think? My job is to zealously represent my client." My smile grew. "I'm also not gonna convince her to take an offer if I feel like there's a good chance she could walk away." I nodded at Frank. "If he's ready to dismiss the charges, there's no need for us to talk about an offer."

"And why would I do that?"

"Because your case is based on circumstantial evidence."

"What about Tammy Weaver's testimony?"

I chuckled. "It hasn't even been five minutes since you accused me of setting you up by telling you about her." I looked at the judge. "During the course of my investigation, I learned that Tammy believed she had seen my client purchasing a weapon several days before Raymond's death. I was under obligation to tell him. He is claiming now that I used it to set him up because she had no concrete details, her husband was a dud, and they led him to Abe Martin who just perjured himself." I looked at Frank. "You can't have it both ways."

"Mr. Ward, I believe Mr. Turner is correct. He had an ethical duty to tell you."

I kept a smirk from my face. "The question we need to now answer is whether Frank has enough of a case to continue forward. If he doesn't, he can dismiss the charges and start looking for the true murderers."

"What is your theory of the case, Counselor?" Judge Hopkins asked.

"If Frank agrees to dismiss all charges against my client with prejudice, I'm willing and ready to talk. I will give him every single shred of evidence we have uncovered in this case."

"Frank?"

"I'm not there, Your Honor."

She nodded. "Here's what I'm going to do for you guys. It seems like you're in a bad spot, Frank. It seems like you're in a better position, Mitch.

I'm going to order you both to put your heads together and see if you can talk this through."

Frank and I glanced at each other before looking at the judge.

It was an unusual request.

"I just made it clear my client's not interested in an offer, Your Honor."

"And we're not interested in looking at anybody else for this."

"And the truth is still out there." She must have realized what she had said because she broke into a smile. "My apologies for getting philosophical on you guys, but we have a dead body, and we need to make sure we send the right person or persons to prison. That's my job, and at the end of the day, it's both of your jobs, too, as officers of the court." She tapped her finger on her desk. "If you guys aren't willing to sit down and talk about it together, I'm happy to facilitate."

"I think we can manage," Frank said.

I nodded. "Of course, Your Honor."

66

After a brief discussion out in the hall, Frank and I decided on my conference room. Once I was done with him, I pulled Candy aside and gave her a hurried update before asking her to come back to my office. I wanted her on hand if I needed her. I didn't think I would, but it couldn't hurt.

I called Winston as I walked back to my office. He picked up on the first ring.

"Didn't expect to hear from you till later, on break?"

"We got out early for the day. I impeached Abe Martin, and Frank is having a hard time dealing with it."

"Poor guy."

"Have you found anything?"

"No. I've been through the office, and now I'm just searching the basement to see if there's anything hidden in a nook or cranny somewhere."

"Keep it up. We've got to find something." I glanced around to make sure nobody was listening and took a chance. "The word I have is that Raymond was putting the squeeze on the poker boys. If we can find evidence of him doing that, we might just be able to finish this."

"I'll see what I can come up with."

Five minutes later, I walked into my office and stopped dead in my tracks. Ellie sat at the reception desk. She had tears running down her face.

"Want to talk?" I asked, pointing to my office.

She nodded.

"What's going on?" I asked once we were inside.

"Prognosis is not good."

"It's not in remission?"

She shook her head. "They say I might not have long to live if things don't turn around fast. There's one more test to know for sure, but I got a bad feeling about it."

"I'm so sorry. Did you get a second opinion?"

She shook her head. "No. I don't see the point. I've never felt worse in my life."

I did something I had never done before. I came around from behind my desk and pulled a chair up beside Ellie. I sat and put my arm around her. "You'll get through this."

"How?"

"I don't know. I'll do whatever I can."

"There are so many things I wanted to do. There's so much I needed to do."

She glanced at me. I had the strangest feeling there was something she wanted to tell me. I opened my mouth to ask what it was, but something stopped me.

"What can I do for you, Ellie?" I asked instead.

The awkward moment passed.

"Nothing. There's nothing anybody can do."

"You shouldn't be alone tonight," I said. "Do you have anybody you can stay with?"

Ellie nodded. "My sister. I think I might spend the night at her place."

"That's a good idea."

Ellie stood.

"Let me call you an Uber."

"Thank you."

After she had gone, I sat at my desk, racking my brain for ideas on how to help.

It was not long before there was a knock.

"Come."

Candy stepped inside. "I don't mean to disturb you, but there isn't anybody out here. I thought I'd just let you know I'm here."

"Have a seat."

I pulled out my notepad and looked across my desk at Candy. "Are you ready to tell me the rest?"

"You still feel like I'm holding something back?"

"Do I have a reason to believe you aren't?"

"I suppose not."

"We need evidence of the communications between Raymond and the poker boys. If we have that, then we have a powerful motive to show they murdered them."

"I don't even know how Raymond was carrying out the negotiations in the end. It was face-to-face at first, but then I got the idea that neither of them trusted the other long enough to be in the room together."

"Who was he negotiating with?"

"Bill."

"I have Winston at your house right now. He went through Raymond's office and found nothing. He's also poking around the basement. Is there any other place he should look?"

"He can try the shed out back, and maybe the attic.

I pulled out my phone and texted Winston both suggestions.

"What are you thinking, Mitch?"

"We had a victory today, but the war's not over. Frank is going to regroup and come back strong unless we can help him see the light and decide he should chase the poker boys."

"What are the chances of that?"

"I would say not good."

"Why?"

"He's devoted months to putting you in jail. He won't stop unless we hand him solid evidence he cannot ignore."

There was a knock on the door.

"Come."

It was Frank. "I'm ready whenever you are, Mitch."

"I'll be right there. You know where it is?"

He nodded.

"There's a break room in back. Feel free to get something."

"Thanks."

"Stay put."

I grabbed a blank notepad and went to the conference room.

67

"Why do you think the judge wanted us to meet?" I asked Frank once we were both sitting around the conference room table. I had grabbed a Coke from the fridge, which I now opened. It wasn't until after I had sat that I realized somebody must have just put it in because it was lukewarm. I was too thirsty to care.

"It's clear she wants you to convince your client to take my offer."

I snorted. "She wants you to look harder at the poker boys. What do you really have that says Candy did this?"

"Her fingerprints are on his shirt buttons, and her DNA is all over. There aren't any other prints at the murder scene."

"Don't you find it strange that nothing else was found in that room?"

"Maybe she vacuumed and dusted."

"If she killed him, wouldn't she want everything left untouched to muddy the waters?

"What do you want me to say? Do you think the poker boys took time to clean up after they killed Raymond?"

I shrugged. "Or before. There were those red marks on his wrists. They might have held him somewhere else while they cleaned. They next killed him and then framed Candy."

"That's crazy. Candy cleaned up really well that morning."

"Yeah, she went to the extra trouble to wipe up all the fingerprints and clean up any DNA, so it was obvious she did it. Think about it, Frank. The children were home. They didn't find any DNA or fingerprints from the kids in that room."

Frank shrugged. "Maybe they didn't go in there. Maybe if they did, they didn't leave anything behind."

"The teenage girl has a full head of hair. She would've left something if she'd so much as sat down on the couch."

"I don't think this is getting us anywhere."

"So it is your belief, because there's DNA evidence on the couch and on the victim, that Candy did it, even though there is nothing else that points to it. You don't even have a real motive."

"She wanted control of the business."

"Can you prove Raymond was a dealer? Can you prove *they* were selling drugs? Your key witness committed perjury."

Frank was silent.

"I caught Abe Martin in a lie. That's all you had. Bill Weaver had nothing other than rumors and speculation. His wife's testimony was little more than that, too."

"I noticed you weren't objecting to most of that." His eyes narrowed. "Why?"

"Rumors and speculation are all you have."

Frank shook his head. "The DNA and prints tell the full story."

"She's his wife. There's lots of ways she could have gotten hair on him and prints on his buttons. Maybe she did his laundry. Maybe she laid out his clothes. Maybe they met for lunch, or he gave her a hug on the way to work. Maybe he brushed his hair with her brush. I'm just getting started."

"What do you have that says your client didn't do this?"

"The second shooter."

"We talked about the .22 bullet. You heard what the medical examiner said. He was not shot with anything other than a 9 mm."

"I said second shooter, not second killer."

"You think one of the boys got excited and fired off a shot early, is that it?"

"Or had terrible aim?"

Frank growled. "Do you have to be contrary to everything I say?"

I smiled. "Force of habit."

Frank let out a deep breath. "I admit I find your theory about the poker boys interesting, but it is all circumstantial."

"So is your case against my client."

"If I were to dismiss the charges against Ms. Carlisle, do you have anything substantive you can give me?"

I hesitated. It was tempting to bluff and say I did, but I knew I didn't. Unless Winston magically turned something up in the next few hours, I had little but conjecture, too.

"I thought not. What if I make Candy a better offer?"

"If she'd done this, Frank, we would've started negotiating weeks ago, and you wouldn't be making better offers."

"You think all your clients are innocent."

"You know that's not true. Let's consider our options, shall we?"

Frank scowled but remained silent.

"Option one. You dismiss the charges against Candy, and I help you investigate the poker boys. Option two. You go to court tomorrow. I make you look like a fool. You regret ever bringing this case, and we revert to option one."

"Option three?" Frank asked with a wry smile.

"There's only two."

"Option three," Frank said. "We go back to court. I wipe the floor with you and Candy. I don't need Abe Martin's testimony to convict. What did you prove today anyway? Did you prove the poker boys were selling drugs or that they killed Raymond or that Candy is innocent?" Frank shook his head. "No. You did not."

Frank stood. "She's guilty. By the time I'm done, the jurors will know it. This has been a waste of time. I'll see you in court."

68

I sat at my desk after I sent Candy on her way, trying to think of anything to help Ellie. It was a difficult situation, and I couldn't think of a single thing. I didn't even know her sister's address so I could send flowers.

I sent Ellie a quick text message of support before heading to my car and going to the Carlisle home. I realized on my way over that I had said something to Frank that could be significant.

If the poker boys or somebody else had cleaned up all the DNA in the front room, whoever killed Raymond Carlisle still needed a way to frame Candy.

The prosecution was basing its case on Candy's hair. If the room had just been vacuumed, there was way too much left behind from just a single encounter. Even if Candy and Raymond had fought—there were no signs of a struggle—it still couldn't account for the amount of hair.

"Hairbrush," I said aloud to an empty car.

I had suggested to Frank that perhaps Raymond had used her brush.

What if the killers had used hair from her brush to plant evidence at the murder scene?

I slammed my foot down on the gas.

69

Winston met me at the door when I arrived at the Carlisle home. I ran up to the master bedroom and went into the bathroom. I pulled on latex gloves before I started going through drawers, looking for a hairbrush. I found several combs and lots of other hair things, but I didn't find a single brush.

"What are you looking for?" Winston asked.

He must have noticed the look on my face and followed me.

"Hairbrushes."

It took him a moment. "The DNA came from somewhere," Winston said, nodding. "That room had nothing except for Candy Carlisle's DNA. How did it get there?"

"Exactly," I said. "There's nothing here."

"Maybe she took her hairbrushes when she left?"

"I should have thought of that." I pulled out my phone and dialed Candy.

"Surprised to hear from you so soon, Mr. Turner." It sounded like Candy was in her car.

"When you left your home, did you pack a bag?"

"No, I just left. I couldn't stand the thought of returning. I just bought us all new things. I didn't go back until the day I let you in."

"Do you own a hairbrush?"

"What kind of question is that? I have lots of brushes."

"How many brushes did you have in your bathroom?"

"I don't know, probably four, maybe five."

"I can't find a single one."

"That's strange."

"It is suspicious your brushes are missing."

"I told you I didn't do it."

"You're sure they were here?"

"I don't see where else they could be."

"Let me know if you think of anything." I hung up without waiting for a response.

I turned to Winston. "Somewhere in this house is evidence Raymond was negotiating with the poker boys for a better deal. We must find it."

70

I let out a sigh when I looked at my watch and saw it was past midnight. We had been through every conceivable place in the house and found nothing. I had gone through Raymond's office twice myself, knocking on walls and shuffling things around. I was becoming convinced Raymond had left nothing behind to document his activities.

I was sure we were missing something significant but could not begin to say what it was. I had been through the basement. The attic. The backyard. The shed in the backyard.

And found absolutely nothing.

Winston sat down with me at the kitchen table. "What about Raymond's phone?"

"It was never found."

"That's a shame."

"The prosecution disclosed a report from his carrier. I went through his text messages and call logs. Nothing."

"That's not the only way to communicate. There's many encrypted communication apps."

"I just assumed we were looking for a burner phone."

Winston shook his head. "How paranoid was he? If they tracked down the numbers, there would be a record for the cops."

"You're saying he used an app on his phone that was destroyed by the poker boys?"

"Most likely."

I banged the back of my head against the kitchen wall. "There has got to be something."

I considered Winston's idea.

It didn't ring true.

I had a hard time seeing Raymond trust his communication to something that could be tied back to him. Sure, some of these apps claimed to be encrypted. Some even claimed they wouldn't turn things over to the government.

But at the end of the day, there was a digital trail that could be followed.

"I don't think he used an app," I said to Winston. "A burner phone is safer. He could buy it with cash, and nobody could track it back unless he made mistakes."

Winston shrugged. "A burner phone is what I would use, but we don't know his reasoning."

"Let's go through it one more time. There has got to be something. Cut into walls if you must." I stood. "I'll be in the master bedroom."

I took the stairs two at a time, trying to force my mind to think by exerting myself physically. My breathing was labored at the top, and my heart rate had picked up.

There's something. I just have to find it.

The first thing I did was check under the bed. I next flipped the mattress up and against a wall while probing it for a telltale bulge. I examined the sides for slits.

Nothing.

I hadn't expected to find anything, so I was not disappointed.

I went through the room inch by inch. Both Raymond and Candy had nightstands. I pulled them back from the wall so I could peek behind. I checked all the drawers.

I thought I felt some friction when I pushed the bottom drawer of Raymond's nightstand back into place. None of the other drawers had any friction. I pulled it out and pushed it back.

Friction.

I gently maneuvered the drawer until I had pulled it out of the nightstand. I turned it over.

A burner phone was taped to the bottom.

71

My hands trembled as I held up the nightstand drawer. Tape had partially covered the bottom runner.

I didn't want to let the phone out of my sight. I was afraid it might disappear. Holding the drawer like a venomous snake, I went downstairs. I found Winston going through the office for probably the tenth time. He had actually cut a hole into a wall.

He glanced up from where he was crouched on the floor, peering inside. "Thought I heard a rattle back there. Nothing."

"Bingo," I said.

Winston looked up again. "You found it?" His eyes narrowed when he saw the drawer.

"I want you to do the examination in case I need to put you on the stand."

"Sure thing. Can you show me where that came from?"

We retraced my steps to the master bedroom, where I pointed out the nightstand. I carefully set the drawer on the floor.

"How did you find that?"

I shrugged as I pointed to the tape on the runner. "There was friction when I pushed it back in. I took it out to see what might be causing it."

"How many have been through this room?" Winston asked. "And we all missed it."

"It wasn't until my third time."

Winston pulled out his phone and took pictures before he gently removed the burner phone, leaving the tape in place.

He turned it on and started pressing buttons. "Just going through the text messages.

He swore.

"This is it. This is everything we need."

"You sure?"

Winston nodded. "I'm not just talking about proving they're drug dealers."

"Neither am I."

Winston looked up. "They threatened him."

72

I still didn't sleep well, even though we had found the burner phone. When I woke at 5:00 AM, I didn't have the energy to hit the treadmill. I was exhausted and knew this race was nowhere near finished.

I would have called Frank first thing to tell him about the discovery if I had thought it would do any good, but he would not see the evidence the same way I did. Each of us was biased towards our own perspective.

It wasn't like I had a smoking gun.

All I had was proof they had threatened Raymond because he had been squeezing their operation to make it difficult for them to work.

I had asked Winston to go through the other contacts on the phone to see if we could discover the distributor's identity, but Winston had answered quickly.

"Only one contact."

I showered, ate breakfast, and was in the office before 6:00 AM. Winston had worked through the night to provide me with transcriptions and pictures of the messages, which I now went through. After that, I made the necessary arrangements to disclose the file to Frank Ward.

I could have followed it with a phone call to see if he was ready to change his mind on dismissing the charges against my client, but I didn't think he would, so I didn't waste my time.

I proceeded like the trial was still going to happen as planned.

I walked into the courtroom five minutes before 9:00 AM. I didn't have my typical bottle of Coke provided by Ellie, but that had not been a surprise. I had stuffed a couple of cans from the break room into my briefcase before dashing out the door.

Candy sat beside me after I was set up at the defense table.

"We found it," I said, leaning in, "the burner phone."

A surprised look crossed her face. "Are you sure?"

Was there something behind her eyes?

"It was in your master bedroom. It was taped to the bottom of Raymond's nightstand drawer."

She wishes she found it.

Would she have turned it over to me?

I suspected I knew the answer.

"I have a complete transcript of all the messages. We can prove now that Bill and the others were all involved in the drug dealing."

"That's good, right?"

I nodded. "They threatened him."

Candy let out a huge sigh. "Problem solved."

"Hardly." I shook my head. "I know Frank well enough to know he will not dismiss the charges based on this alone. We need to find the murder weapon or other hard evidence before he'll think about it."

"Are you kidding me?"

"Look at it from his perspective. He has invested countless hours in proving you're the one who did this. Unless we hand him something he can't argue with, he's not gonna buy it."

"I can't catch a break."

"This *is* a significant break. It's gonna make an enormous difference. We're just not there yet."

"If you say so."

"I should also warn you that Raymond does not shy away from talking about the distributor in the text messages."

Candy frowned.

My gut told me there was another burner phone Raymond used to communicate with the distributor.

What are the chances Candy has it?

I opened my mouth to ask, but the bailiff stood.

"All rise. Court is now in session."

I glanced at Candy from the corner of my eye as we did.

She was afraid.

I had expected as much. The texts about the distributor were going to be a problem.

Raymond referred to the distributor throughout the messages, even making it sound like he was on their side and that he was trying to work with the distributor for them. I expected that if we found the other burner phone, it would be nothing of the sort.

The distributor would not be happy when all this became public knowledge.

Raymond had been playing these guys, pure and simple. They hadn't liked the game, so they killed him to try to get around him.

Do they have the missing burner phone?

Judge Hopkins sat. "You may be seated. Mr. Ward, do you have any updates for us before I summon the jury?"

Frank shook his head. "No, Your Honor, I do not. We are ready to call our next witness."

She frowned but said nothing more until after the jury had entered. "You may proceed."

"The prosecution calls Kyle Rencher to the witness stand."

I was surprised by this move. Hadn't he learned his lesson with Abe Martin? I would have thought he'd avoid the rest of the poker boys like the plague.

"Can you please tell us what you do for a living?" Frank asked Kyle after he had been sworn in and answered a few preliminary questions.

"I am a software developer."

"Who do you work for?"

"I freelance."

"How long have you been doing that?"

"Approximately two years."

"Are you familiar with the victim, Raymond Carlisle?"

"Yes, he and I used to work together."

"How would you describe your relationship with Raymond?"

"At first, it was good. There were no problems. We worked together daily, we got along well, and usually saw things the same way."

"Did that change?"

"Yes, during the last few years, Raymond's behavior became erratic."

"Can you give some specifics?"

"He would call, occasionally making statements about things that didn't make a lot of sense. For example, one day, I got a phone call. He was panicking. 'What's wrong?' I asked. 'She's coming for me,' he said."

I didn't hesitate. "Objection, Your Honor. This is hearsay."

Frank didn't miss a beat. "This goes to the victim's state of mind, Your Honor, and the declarant is also unavailable."

"Overruled."

"Did Raymond say who was coming for him?"

"Objection, Your Honor, hearsay, again."

"Your Honor, please see my previous arguments. This is also an excited utterance. I would put Raymond on the stand if he were here to testify, but he's not.

The judge frowned. "Overruled. The witness will answer the question."

"He wouldn't say who."

"How did you interpret this?"

"Objection," I said. "Calls for speculation."

"Sustained."

"Did you ever learn what that was about?" Frank asked without a pause like this had all been carefully choreographed.

"No, I never did."

"Did Raymond ever approach you to sell drugs?"

Kyle nodded. "Yes, multiple times, in fact."

"Did you ever buy from him?"

Kyle shook his head. "No, I never did."

"What kind of drugs was he selling?"

"Prescription painkillers, if I am not mistaken."

"Did you ever see these drugs?"

Kyle nodded. "Yes, I did. One time, he left a vial with me. A free sample, I think. I returned it and told him I didn't want it."

"Did you get a close look at the bottle?"

"Yes, I did."

"Did you question Raymond about it?"

"Yes."

I was poised for an objection until I looked at the jury. Half looked bored. Several appeared as though they didn't know what was going on. I sat back in my chair. I already knew the judge would overrule me anyway.

"Did you think about turning Raymond into the police?"

"Yes, but I just felt bad for the guy. I knew he was in a difficult marriage."

"Objection," I said, "the witness lacks personal knowledge."

"Sustained."

"Do you have personal knowledge of their problems?"

"There was one time I witnessed an exchange between Candy and Raymond."

"Can you tell us about it?"

I leaned forward.

"They were arguing. I'm not sure what it was about, but I overheard the word 'drugs' and 'money' several times."

"Objection, Your Honor," I said, "hearsay."

Frank cleared his throat. "I remind the Court Raymond Carlisle is unable to testify himself."

"Overruled."

"When did you hear this?"

"Candy came to a poker night. Raymond went out to meet her. I went to the restroom. I heard something, so I peeked out the window and saw them arguing. I was a little concerned for Raymond, so I cracked the door to see if I could overhear what they were saying."

"Your Honor," I said standing, "any conversations overheard between Raymond Carlisle and Candy Carlisle are privileged."

I had debated whether I wanted to bring this up as soon as I had figured out where this was going. It was a stretch, and I didn't want to look like we were hiding something, but I didn't know how far Kyle was willing to perjure himself.

Was he about to testify that Candy had threatened Raymond?

I couldn't discount the possibility out of hand. Something like that would be highly prejudicial and difficult to challenge without having Candy testify. It was better to get in front of it and just hope I could clean up any fallout afterward.

There had been enough pressure from the other witnesses that I had to give serious thought to putting Candy on the stand. It was a tremendous risk because I didn't know what she was going to say, and I was fairly certain she wouldn't hesitate to perjure herself if she thought it was necessary.

Both were problems.

"I believe the counselor is correct," Judge Hopkins said, "unless you can think of an exception for this testimony to be included?"

"You should hear the probative value of the testimony before reaching a decision," Frank said, glancing at the jury. He'd said this to make it appear like it was something substantial when it might not be.

The judge glanced at her watch. "I will excuse the jury for a fifteen-minute break. I'll also clear the courtroom while we hear the witness' testimony."

Frank addressed Kyle a few minutes later. "Can you please tell us what you overheard?"

"I overheard Candy threatening to kill Raymond."

My mind started working fast. Frank would try to find an exception to bring this into the trial, and I needed to keep it out.

"What did you hear specifically?"

"Candy said he would one day go to bed but never wake up."

"Are those the exact words?"

"As near as I can recall."

"You mentioned earlier that you overheard the words 'drugs' and 'money.' Did you hear anything specific?"

"No, Candy raised her voice when she made the threat but then lowered it after that."

"Do you have anything else to say on this topic?"

Kyle shook his head. "No."

Frank faced the judge. "As you can see, Your Honor, this goes to the heart of the matter. It provides the defendant's motive."

"Counselor?" Judge Hopkins said, looking at me.

I stood. "Your Honor, it is vitally important we protect the sacrosanct marriage relationship. Besides that, I believe this witness is committing perjury." I looked right at Kyle as I spoke. "Or did you forget you told me that you never saw Candy Carlisle in person?"

Kyle frowned.

"Your Honor, may I ask the witness additional questions?" Frank asked.

"Go ahead."

"Why did you frown?"

"I was trying to remember. My encounter with Mr. Turner was not pleasant."

"Can you describe it?"

"Sure, he barged into my office and accused me of murdering Raymond Carlisle."

I couldn't let that stand. "That's not what happened, Mr. Rencher."

He looked like he wanted to say something more but snapped his mouth shut.

Judge Hopkins looked at me. "Do you have evidence to support your claim?"

"Yes, in fact, I do, Your Honor." I glanced at Kyle. "I'm not sure that now is the proper time to disclose this. I recommend either dismissing the witness or meeting in chambers for a discussion."

"Mr. Rencher, you are dismissed for now. Please leave the courtroom."

Once he had gone, I continued.

"Your Honor, last night, my private investigator and I uncovered a phone that Raymond Carlisle used to communicate with Bill Weaver."

"There is no evidence that the Bill Weaver referred to in the messages," Frank said, "is actually the Bill Weaver testifying in this courtroom."

"Your Honor," I said, ignoring Frank, "the messages prove that Raymond, Bill Weaver, Abe Martin, Kyle Rencher, and Larry Thompson were all part of a poker group that wasn't really playing poker. They were running drugs.

"In addition, Your Honor, Bill Weaver made an explicit threat on Raymond's life. It's right there in black and white."

"Have you disclosed this information to the prosecution?"

"Yes, I disclosed it first thing this morning after I had a transcription. The prosecution is now in possession of pictures of the text messages as well as the transcript itself."

"Frank, have you had a chance to review this new evidence?"

"Yes, Your Honor, I have, and to be honest, I believe that while this does show that there was illegal activity going on between Raymond and others, it is hardly adequate proof—"

"Can you verify that these messages were sent to the Bill Weaver who has testified in this case?"

"We have not yet received the phone. I would need to have forensics take a look."

Judge Hopkins looked at me. "Let's assume we can prove this phone is undoubtedly connected to Bill Weaver and the others. What happens next?"

"We have solid evidence the poker boys were selling drugs. And we know Bill Weaver threatened to kill Raymond Carlisle. This threat was made three weeks before Raymond's death."

Judge Hopkins nodded. "There is no doubt the others were involved?"

"Raymond was trying to create a trail of evidence in case something happened. He references everybody by their full name in the text messages, including Bill Weaver."

"Mr. Ward?"

"I think counsel is doing quite the dance here," Frank said. "He found some evidence. Yes, it might impeach some witnesses. It might not. Maybe it implicates them all in a drug ring; however, we cannot ignore the DNA evidence found on Raymond Carlisle's body. Defense counsel also appears to have forgotten the real reason we are here is to discuss his objection to Kyle Rencher's testimony."

"I have an answer for the DNA at issue as well," I said, ignoring Kyle Rencher for the moment. "We noticed when we were in the Carlisle home yesterday that there were no brushes in the Carlisle master bathroom. As you have probably noted, my client likes to look put together and spends time, money, and effort pursuing such things. I asked her how many hairbrushes she had. She informed me that she had no less than four, probably five. I could not find a single one in the bathroom. It doesn't take much to conclude that the people who set the frame for Candy used hair from the brushes to plant her DNA all over that room."

"An interesting theory," Frank said, "but it is just a theory. What we know for sure is that Ms. Carlisle's DNA was found in that room. It was on Raymond's body."

Judge Hopkins looked at Frank and then turned her attention to me. "Do you have any other evidence that ties the poker boys to Raymond's death?"

"Not as yet," I said, "but we did just find this phone last night. I am sure if we had additional time, we would—"

"And there it is, Your Honor," Frank said, "a delay tactic. Things are not going well for him here in the courtroom, so he—"

"Things are actually going great for me. I impeached your witness yesterday. Furthermore, you are the one using delay tactics—"

"And you turned evidence over to me just this morning that incontrovertibly proves Raymond was a drug dealer, thereby sustaining my theory—"

"And if you had a shred of common sense—"

"Enough, gentlemen," Judge Hopkins said, breaking in. "I recognize both of you are under a lot of pressure. Pressure to deliver a guilty verdict, as well as pressure to do the opposite." Judge Hopkins stared straight at Frank. "You and I have had a lot of cases together. You're a great prosecutor, but you're like a bulldog. Once you get something in your teeth, you don't let go, even if other evidence comes to light that indicates maybe you should."

"And you, Mr. Turner, you and I have never had a case together, but I'm familiar with your reputation."

I smiled. "All good things, I hope?"

"I'm going to leave it at that," Judge Hopkins said with a wry smile.

Frank scowled.

"Your Honor, I move for a mistrial," I said. "The new evidence we have disclosed shows that many of the prosecution's witnesses have a significant bias in the outcome of this case. Kyle Rencher has likely committed perjury today. The testimony he has likely fabricated unfairly prejudices the jury against my client. Even if we can't show the witness is perjuring himself, we do know that he testified as to a privileged marital communication, which is grounds in and of itself. It was hearsay and privileged. The substance of the testimony is such that it will simply not be enough to instruct the jury to disregard it."

Judge Hopkins didn't answer right away.

"I'll take it under consideration. I highly recommend, Frank, that you take a hard look at your approach to this case. We will adjourn until noon. Maybe I will declare a mistrial, and you gentlemen will have to go back to the drawing board. Maybe the second time will be the charm, who knows?"

"On what grounds, Your Honor?" Frank demanded. "Surely, you aren't buying what Mr. Turner is selling? The victim and the defendant were having a heated conversation in public. There was no expectation of privacy. The excited utterance exception clearly applies to this issue, too. The testimony should not be stricken from the record. Furthermore, Mr. Rencher should be allowed to testify as to the threat the defendant made against Raymond

Carlisle. Finally, if Mr. Turner wants to challenge Kyle Rencher's testimony, let's put him on the stand and see how he fares."

"That won't be necessary. I will review the new evidence and the trial transcript. I will let you know of my decision at noon. Do either of you have anything more to add?"

"No, Your Honor," I said.

Frank shook his head.

"You guys have a little more than two hours. I suggest you make wise use of the time as shall I."

She looked at Frank before departing.

73

I glanced at Frank after the judge had gone, wondering if he would want to meet, but he didn't even make eye contact as he left.

The judge had all but told him to dismiss the charges.

"What's going on?" Candy asked.

I spoke in a normal voice because we were now alone, the bailiff having just walked out. "Judge Hopkins believes Frank made a mistake. She's giving him time to fix it."

"Will he?"

I shook my head. "Not unless something miraculously comes to light over the next two hours."

"What do we do now?"

"Come back at noon." I packed up my briefcase. "It's time you tell me the full truth, Ms. Carlisle."

"I told you to call me Candy."

I looked right into her eyes. "Do you have the other burner phone Frank was using to communicate with the distributor?"

"You shouldn't talk to me like that here." Candy glanced around the courtroom, anxiety written on her face until she saw we were alone. "You shouldn't talk to me like that at all. How do you even know about that?"

Bingo.

I leaned in and whispered. "I know there was another phone. I know you have it. You said you are worried about the distributor. I might be able to keep him from coming after you, but you must level with me."

She didn't respond.

"If you don't give me that phone, I'm not gonna be able to do anything to protect you."

"What if I have things handled?"

"You are planning to continue in the business?"

"I'm not gonna answer that question."

I shook my head. "You're in too deep. They're not trying you for the drug charges today. At some point, they will, especially if you walk on the murder charge."

"What do you recommend?"

"Let's take a walk."

74

We walked in silence for some time. I initially headed towards my office but then angled toward a park. I was hoping to find children on the playground, but it was empty. Instead, I found a bench where we faced the swings and then sat down.

"You and Raymond were risking a lot," I said, turning to look at her. "You want to know why my father went to prison?"

"Why?"

"Because he wasn't thinking about me."

"Meaning?"

"You have a chance to give up this life."

"You don't understand," Candy said. "The distributor does not let his contractors just walk away. The only way I get out is if I die. I have no choice but to continue on with the business."

I studied her. "The distributor isn't the real problem. You aren't willing to walk away. Are your graphic design skills not enough?"

Candy rolled her eyes. "My expenses far exceed my salary."

"What about your kids?" I asked, turning to look at the swing set, hoping our proximity to it would evoke emotion in her.

"What about them?"

"They're going to know the truth one day."

"No, they won't. Raymond and I took precautions. The children know nothing about our business. They never will."

"They will." I shook my head. "You think you can hide things like this, but you can't. The truth always comes out, one way or another. Truth is like that. Truth wants to be found."

"Not if you do a good job hiding it."

"Look, I know you have additional evidence you are withholding, but I don't know why. It will help get you out of this mess. It's either fear or greed or a combination of those keeping you from doing this. Are you hoping we can prove your innocence in a way that doesn't wreck your business? Is that what this is about?"

"You know nothing about me."

"You're right, I know hardly anything about you, but I do know a lot about people like you. You think you're the first criminal I've represented that thinks they're smarter than the law?" I shook my head and laughed ruefully. "Some of the smartest criminals I've seen have gone to prison."

"They made dumb mistakes."

"And what do you think all of this is?" I asked. "You made dumb mistakes. Raymond made dumb mistakes. If you guys hadn't been doing the things you were doing—"

"None of this would have ever happened? Spare me the lecture. Are you able to get me out of this, or are you not?"

I ignored her scorn. "That's exactly what we're talking about. I'm also trying to help with your distributor problem. I need you to give me everything you have on them. Once I have that evidence, I can make an assessment as to whether it will be useful for the trial and how we can resolve the situation."

"And if I don't?"

"If we successfully beat the murder rap, they'll come after you again for the drugs."

"If I get off on the murder charge, I can handle the drug charges."

"No, you can't. You're sunk on those."

"I have a good attorney."

"I'm done with you after this case."

Candy was quiet as she processed this. "Once I'm exonerated of the present charges, certainly they won't come at me again so soon? They will have learned their lesson, won't they?"

"Have you not been paying attention? Frank knows you're dirty. He'll try to get you one way or another. That's what this case has turned into, a trial about the drugs. That's been my primary defense strategy. I needed the drug information to come out because the poker boys have done a good job of hiding it. I have done little to suppress any of the drug evidence. I've even encouraged it. We have all but admitted Raymond was dealing drugs."

Candy sat there quietly.

Had I finally gotten through?

"You did this on purpose. You set me up."

"No. That's what I'm explaining to you. The truth wants to come out, and I don't try to hide the truth. You must give me what you have, so I can unravel this situation."

"They'll kill me. My children, too."

"Level with me. Tell me everything. There is a way out, we just have to find it." I nodded towards the swings. "You remember when your kids were young enough to play on those?"

"My youngest still is," Candy whispered.

"Right now, they're innocent. Right now, they look on you and your dead husband as heroes. That's gonna change when they learn the truth about their parents. The only thing you can do between here and there is course correct."

"I hear what you're saying. I just don't think I can make it happen."

"Give me the other burner phone. Tell me who the distributor is. Tell me everything you know about his operations." I leaned in. "I will handle the rest."

"Let me think about it."

I shook my head. "This is not just an opportunity for Frank to reevaluate his case. It's an opportunity for you to reevaluate your life."

"You have something in mind?"

"If I can go to law enforcement and give them the name of Raymond's distributor, then we have something to talk about. We'll work something out you can live with. It might be they are already investigating this guy. It might be you could provide the final evidence they need to shut his op down and lock him up. You mentioned you wanted witness protection. This is how we get it."

"I don't know—"

"There's nothing to know. You're in a bad spot. You said it yourself. You either must sell drugs, or you and your children die. Do you expect your children to carry on in the family business if something premature happens to you? What happens to your children then?"

"I don't know." Her voice was barely a whisper.

"Let's make a third option."

Candy swallowed. It was time to push her over the edge.

"Do this for your children."

"Guyton."

The name struck a chord of fear deep within me.

Could it be Thomas Guyton?

I couldn't breathe. "First name?"

"Marc. His name is Marc Guyton."

75

It was lucky for me that Candy was so overwhelmed by the emotions of the moment that she did not recognize the shock I likely had on my face.

"And you're sure about his name?" I asked. It couldn't just be a coincidence that law enforcement was investigating Thomas Guyton and that her distributor's name was Marc Guyton. I didn't need to see a family tree to know that the two would be related.

She nodded. "Yes. I have never met him, but Raymond did. Guyton likes to work from an exclusive country club. Raymond was never a member; however, he visited sometimes after receiving an invite from Guyton. He didn't tell me anything about the visits, but I got the idea they were not exactly pleasant, if you know what I mean."

"The burner phone?" I asked.

She hesitated before reaching into her purse and pulling it out. After another pause, she gave it to me.

"You had it on you this whole time?"

"What else was I to do with it?"

I shook my head, unable to believe she had been walking around with this core piece of evidence just in her purse.

"Is this all?"

"It's all right there and here," she reached into her purse and pulled out a flash drive. "Raymond made copies of all his text messages. The distributor requires they switch to new phones every year or two.

"Is that what's on here?"

"I don't know. I never looked at the drive. There should be some videos, too. The phone has instructions from the distributor for the last year."

"Does it identify Marc Guyton?"

Candy shook her head. "No, but Raymond met him in person. He didn't know the guy's name at the time, but he tracked it down. I'm not quite sure how, but he was serious about doing it."

My heart sunk. "You have no way of proving Marc Guyton is the distributor?"

"I didn't say that. Not by a longshot." Candy gave me a weird look. "I don't think you recognize just how paranoid my husband was. Before he died, he made videos implicating not only Marc Guyton but also all of the poker boys. Those are on the drive."

It took me a moment to compose myself.

"And you've been sitting on this the whole time?" I had to stop from saying more. Now was not the time. "This changes everything."

"Is my family going to be okay, Mr. Turner?"

"We'll see what we can make happen."

Candy stood. "I'm suddenly famished. I need an early lunch. I'll see you back at the courtroom."

76

I was filled with a sudden bout of paranoia after Candy left, the likes of which I had never experienced in my life. I had not thought the case would go this way. I had never expected that Thomas Guyton could be tied to the distributor.

I glanced over my shoulder as I left the park, convinced somebody could have followed us and overheard our conversation. I had thought myself clever for taking her to a playground to talk about her children, but I should have gone back to my office where I could have guaranteed our privacy.

The first thing I would do upon my return was figure out Marc Guyton's connection to Thomas Guyton. I would watch the videos on the flash drive right afterward.

I called Winston as I walked. "My office. Ten minutes."

I didn't even wait for an answer before hanging up and quickening my pace. It was all I could do not to run.

Was this why Detective Stephanie Gray was investigating Thomas Guyton? Was his family part of a criminal syndicate?

I knew deep in my gut that there was some truth to the supposition.

The reception desk was empty, probably because I was scheduled to be in court all day, and Ellie had thought I wouldn't need Zoey.

I stopped after I entered my office.

There was no going back after I knew the connection between Marc Guyton and Thomas Guyton.

I sat down.

The first thing I did was look up Thomas Guyton on Facebook. I found he was connected to somebody named Marc Guyton.

It was all right there in the open.

Sometimes, that's the best place to hide.

I plugged the flash drive into my computer. Before looking at any of the contents, I immediately copied it to my hard drive and encrypted the folder with a password. I pulled out three spare thumb drives I had in my desk drawer and made more backups. I put one in my office safe and stored the others in my briefcase. I would drop one off at a safe deposit box I kept at a local bank after court today if I got the chance.

It was only after I had done those things that I finally turned to the video files.

I opened the first one to find Raymond talking into a camera, presumably his smartphone. I twisted in chagrin as I watched Raymond implicate each of the poker boys, going into great detail about the drug operations, how Mount Pleasant was involved and then revealing at the end that he had been threatened in person by Bill Weaver. All the other poker boys had been there. The video implicated everybody.

"She has some nerve," I said.

"Who does?" Winston asked, walking into my office.

I looked up. I was about to chew Winston out for opening my door without knocking until I realized that I had left it open.

Cursing, I moved past Winston and shut the door so fast that I slammed it.

"Candy."

I shook my head and cursed again. "We've got a problem."

77

"We've got a problem," Winston said twenty minutes later after I had briefed him on what I had learned from Candy, and we'd watched both videos from the thumb drive.

"Say it again."

"What are we gonna do with this?"

"I don't know. I have to be back in court in forty-five minutes. That's not nearly enough time to sort this all out or put together a cohesive strategy. And on top of that, I'm worried about Barbara."

Winston nodded. "I'll get right on Marc Guyton."

"Did I tell you Stephanie was investigating Thomas Guyton?"

"Are you serious?" Winston gave me a frosty glare.

"We must avoid hasty decisions. I need some time to think. I want to unravel this, but it has to be in the right way; otherwise, we risk a lot of things. The Carlisle children hang in the balance. Barbara hangs in the balance. Candy hangs in the balance."

Winston nodded.

I grimaced. "Three of those people are innocent. The fourth one might not be guilty of murder, but she's not innocent."

"When are you going to tell Frank what you found?"

I shook my head. "I don't know."

"Surely this will change things."

"The video is damaging to the prosecution's case," I said, "there is no way around that, but remember, this is Frank Ward."

Winston nodded. He knew exactly what I was talking about.

"I'll probably have to take this all the way through to the completion of the trial. I have to get an acquittal so that Frank takes me seriously."

I sat at my desk after Winston had gone. I played both videos one more time.

I then picked up my phone and made a call.

78

I was a ball of nervous energy when I walked back into the courtroom. While Winston had not yet found a definitive link between Thomas Guyton and Marc Guyton, I didn't need one to know it was there.

Perhaps it was paranoia. Maybe my wires were getting crossed. But I wasn't willing to take the risk that Barbara wasn't dating a relative of the distributor.

And there was also the pesky little fact that Detective Stephanie Gray was investigating Thomas Guyton.

There was a reason.

It's connected, I thought. *It's all connected.*

I almost did not notice when Candy sat down beside me because I was so focused on thinking through the situation. When I glanced over and saw she was there, I did a double-take. She was a woman wracked with guilt and fear.

Had I finally got through to her?

Or was she just afraid that the evidence she had turned over to me had sealed her fate?

The last thing I wanted to do right now was to be back in court, pushing through another day of trial, but I didn't see a way out of it, not unless I was willing to reveal to the judge and Frank Ward the hand I had just been dealt.

Something I was not yet ready to do.

Judge Hopkins was soon seated, and court was back in session. The jury had not yet been brought back in.

"I have reached a decision," Judge Hopkins said, glancing at Frank without looking at me. "I will allow Kyle Rencher's previous testimony to remain on the record. I will also allow him to testify on the matter we were discussing in private earlier."

I stood. "Your Honor, I hardly think—"

"I made my decision, counselor, after carefully weighing your arguments. They were almost persuasive, but we must let the jury hear the testimony. They can decide who they believe."

"Your Honor—"

"I will entertain no further discussion on the issue, counselor. Your dissent is noted for the record."

I hesitated and then sat down. There was nothing more I could do about it. Frank looked like the cat who had just got the canary.

"If there is nothing else, I will summon the jury."

The jury took about five minutes to enter and get settled.

"You may call your witness back to the stand now, Mr. Ward."

"Thank you, Your Honor."

This was not how I had expected the judge to decide. I'd had her persuaded during our meeting earlier. What had happened in the two hours since to change her mind?

Frank didn't bother to hide a smug look as he approached the lectern and called Kyle Rencher back to the stand. Frank resumed his questioning after the judge reminded Kyle he was still under oath.

"Before our break, we were talking about an argument you overheard between Raymond and Candy Carlisle. Can you tell us what you heard?"

"Yes," Kyle said. He was sitting up straight in his chair with a smug look on his face, too. He glanced at me.

"Candy threatened to kill Raymond Carlisle. She said he might not wake up one day."

"I never did!"

I turned at the outburst from my client.

The judge banged her gavel. "I will have order in my courtroom!" She focused her attention on Candy. "You will have an opportunity to testify, should you choose. That will be the right place to speak in my courtroom. Do you understand me?"

Candy nodded.

"You may answer audibly for the record."

"Yes, Your Honor, I do."

A part of me was glad for Candy's mistake, but the judge had just increased the pressure to have her testify.

"What did you think about this at the time?" Frank asked.

"I didn't think anything of it, to be honest. I figured she hadn't meant it. Sometimes, people get worked up about something and say things they don't mean."

"Do you think that was the case here?"

"Objection," I said, standing, "calls for speculation."

"Sustained."

"I have no further questions for this witness, Your Honor."

I took my time to gather my things and move to the lectern because I was trying to calm down. Things had not gone in the way I had planned.

I took a deep breath and tried my best to put it aside while setting my stuff down on the lectern.

"Mr. Rencher, it is a pleasure to see you again," I said after I was ready. "Can you tell us where you were on the night Raymond was killed?"

"Yes, in fact, I had a poker night that night."

"With Bill Weaver, Larry Thompsen, and Abe Martin?"

"Yes."

"Did anybody see you there besides the other members of your poker group?"

Kyle shook his head. "No."

I nodded. Part of me wanted to continue to ask questions about this, but I figured I was not in the right frame of mind to pull it off, so I moved in a different direction.

Kyle was easily offended when I didn't even accuse him of murder.

I can take this guy.

"You mentioned earlier you saw my client outside where you were playing poker on a different night. Do you remember whose house that was at?"

Kyle thought about it. "I'm sorry, I don't recall."

"Do you remember what day this was?"

"No, I don't. I might be able to figure it out from my calendar. I might've recorded that I had poker night. It wasn't long after that that Raymond was killed."

"How long after?"

He shrugged. "I don't know, a month or two?"

Gotcha.

I nodded agreeably. "Did Raymond ever stop coming to your poker night?"

Kyle froze as if he had just remembered something. "Yes, he did."

"What was the space of time between his death and the last poker night he attended?"

Kyle swallowed. He looked trapped. "Six months."

I frowned. "I'm confused. You just testified you saw Candy at a poker night 'a month or two' before Raymond's death. You also testified Raymond stopped coming to poker night six months before he died. Surely, both statements can't be true?"

I let it sink in. "Isn't it true that you lied about seeing Candy at poker night and that you made up the threat she supposedly said to Raymond?"

"No. I didn't. What I meant to say was that it was one of the last poker nights we had with him there. After that, the next thing I heard about him was that Candy had killed—"

"Were you there at Raymond's death?"

His face was getting clouded, just like the day I'd interviewed him. "What do you mean?"

"You just said Candy killed Raymond. Did you see this firsthand?"

"No, of course not."

"Then how do you know if she killed him?"

"I guess I don't. I just assumed, didn't I?"

My next question was risky; technically, I already had enough, but I wanted more.

"You showed an emotion on your face when I asked if Raymond stopped coming to poker night. Can you please describe what you were feeling?"

"I realized I made a mistake."

"You weren't feeling trapped in a lie?"

"No. I was afraid because I didn't want my mistake to be misconstrued." He was trying to clean it up. He was saying the right things, but his tone wasn't helping him.

It was helping me.

"How do you expect the jury to believe you?"

"I told the truth."

"Was there a falling out between Raymond and the rest of you poker boys?"

"I'm not sure. He just stopped coming."

"Did you meet with the other poker boys prior to this trial to agree on what your testimony would be?"

"No, of course not."

"Have you ever been into the Carlisle home?"

"Yes, I think we played poker there once or twice a year."

"Have you ever been into the Carlisle master bedroom?"

"No. I never have."

Kyle was turning a shade of pink. He didn't like the implication. I was getting to him. I just hoped the jury could see it.

I needed more.

"Have you ever been into the master bathroom?"

"No."

"Were you in the Carlisle home on the night Raymond died?"

"No, I never was."

He spoke through gritted teeth.

"What do you mean by never was?"

"I meant to say that I was not there that night."

"But you have been there before, correct?"

"Yes."

"Did you find anything interesting in the Carlisle master bathroom when you were looking for Ms. Carlisle's hairbrushes?"

"No—" Kyle stopped. Sweat covered his face.

I broke into a smile.

"I'm sorry," he said, "I don't believe I understood the question."

"How many hairbrushes did you find?"

"None— I mean, I didn't look for any."

"So you were in the master bathroom on the night Raymond died?"

"No, I've never been into the bathroom."

Kyle was trying to cover up his tracks, but it wasn't working. Everybody in the room knew it.

Everybody, except for Frank Ward.

"Isn't it true that you're who Bill Weaver sent up to the Carlisle bathroom to retrieve the hairbrushes so that he could pull off hair to plant on the victim?"

"Objection, Your Honor," Frank said. "He's badgering the witness."

"He just doesn't like the answers I'm getting."

Judge Hopkins frowned.

I studied her.

Kyle had slipped up several times now.

She knew what was going on.

"Sustained. Counselor, please keep your questions focused and on point."

My anger was gone. Judge Hopkins' words had poured cold water on it. I could blame her or treat it as an opportunity to up my game.

I turned back to Kyle.

He was mine.

"Isn't it true that when I interviewed you in your office, you told me that you had never before met or even seen Candy?"

"I don't recall ever saying that."

"Are you sure?"

Kyle frowned. "Yes, actually, I do remember now. I did tell you the truth. I didn't actually see Ms. Carlisle. I just heard her."

"Do you expect us to believe that you were just passing by a window and heard the two of them arguing but didn't look out?"

"Yep, it's the truth. I actually ducked down below the window because I didn't want Raymond to think I was spying on him."

"And you didn't peek out when you opened the door to listen to their conversation?"

"No, I just opened it a crack, so I could hear. I could not have seen them from my angle at the door."

"You still don't remember where you were playing poker that night?"

"No, I do not."

"But you seem to remember a lot of details about this supposed conversation you overheard. Why is that?"

"It was a memorable conversation."

"So you *were* able to make out *all* the words?"

"I meant to say that it was a memorable incident."

I wasn't certain that the jury was buying this, but I couldn't take the risk. I needed more.

"You said that when Raymond offered you drugs, he left a free sample. You didn't take one?"

"No, I never did."

"Have you ever used illegal drugs?"

"No."

"Have you ever used pharmaceutical drugs that were not prescribed to you?"

"No."

"You never smoked marijuana?"

"No."

"Have you ever been checked into a rehab center?"

"No."

"So you were never checked into the rehab center named Mount Pleasant?"

A long pause.

"No."

"Do you remember where you were playing poker on the night Raymond Carlisle was killed?"

"We were at Bill Weaver's house."

"Did anybody other than the poker boys see you there that night?"

"No, not unless Tammy Weaver popped her head inside, but I don't remember."

"What time did poker start that night?"

"I don't know, probably around about 10:00 PM."

"How far is it from Bill Weaver's house to the Carlisle home?"

"Maybe a mile."

I nodded as if I thought this was very significant.

Kyle was now a dark shade of purple.

He feels like I am accusing him of murder again.

"Did Raymond have any last words before he was killed?"

"Objection, Your Honor," Frank said, "he's badgering the witness."

"Sustained."

"Your Honor," I said, "it's a fair question."

"Please move along, counselor."

"Did you get angry when I interviewed you at your office?"

"I don't recall."

"Did you accuse me of accusing you of killing Raymond?"

"I don't remember."

"Do you recall anything I said that made you feel like I had accused you?"

"I think it was more your tone. You weren't as direct then as you are today."

"So you *do* remember?"

"It just came to me."

"Would you describe Raymond as a friend?"

"Yes."

"Did you mourn his death?"

"Yes, I did."

"Do you own a firearm?"

Frank jumped to his feet. "Objection, Your Honor. Relevance?"

I faced Judge Hopkins, giving her my most indignant glare. "This is a murder trial, Your Honor. The victim was shot. The weapon is yet to be found. If the witness owns a weapon, I'd say that's highly relevant."

Hopkins hesitated. I raised an eyebrow.

"Overruled."

I didn't bat an eye. "Please answer the question, Mr. Rencher."

A very long pause. "Yes."

"What caliber?"

"I have a .22 pistol."

"Have you ever fired it?"

"I've taken it to the range a few times."

"Do you still have it in your possession?"

"Yes, of course, I do."

I studied Kyle, trying to decide if he was the source of the unexplained bullet in the Carlisle front room. My question had been a shot in the dark. I wouldn't have known the difference if he'd lied. For a brief moment, I closed my eyes and imagined Bill standing in front of Raymond with a 9 mm pistol. I imagined Abe, Larry, and Kyle all there, too.

Abe had proven himself a hothead, but Kyle was volatile in his own way.

It was either Abe or Kyle.

I would have guessed Abe was the man who fired off the shot that missed, but perhaps it was Kyle. Maybe Raymond had known just how easily Kyle could get hot under the collar. Maybe he had attempted to press the same buttons I was trying to press today.

"Would you say you're a good shot with your pistol?"

"Yes." He was getting touchy again.

"Would you say you hit what you aim at?"

"Yes."

"You never miss?"

"Rarely."

I was close. I just needed to push this guy over the edge.

"Was there a reason Raymond apparently felt like you could use a free drug sample?"

"I dunno, you'd have to ask him."

"Were you going through something difficult, such as a breakup with a girlfriend?"

"I don't remember."

"Maybe she dumped you?"

He went white in the face.

"You know nothing."

"Was Raymond feeling sorry for you?"

"No."

"Is that why he was giving you free drugs?"

"I have no idea." Kyle was even paler now.

"Are you lying about this?"

"No."

"Are you lying about the conversation you overheard with Raymond and Candy?"

"No."

"Are you lying about never going into the master bathroom of the Carlisle home?"

"No!"

"Are you lying about where you were when Raymond died?"

"No!"

"Were you there when Raymond was shot?"

"I wasn't there!"

"Did you shoot your own pistol at him?"

"No!" Kyle screamed his answer, jumping to his feet while shaking a fist.

The judge banged her gavel. "Mr. Rencher, you will address the court in a calm voice and remain in your seat."

"Did you miss when you pulled the trigger?"

Frank jumped to his feet. "Objection, Your Honor, he is badgering the witness. Again."

"Withdrawn. No further questions for this witness, Your Honor."

I sat down.

79

The courtroom was now silent, a stark comparison to how it had been just the moment before. I was glad for the contrast.

Judge Hopkins studied Kyle Rencher, her skepticism evident. I hoped the jury noticed.

I had scored points on this witness. I hadn't dragged out a confession, but I'd come close.

Had I done enough that Frank would have a hard time cleaning it up on redirect?

I was surprised the judge had sided with me on several of the objections. When it had counted, she had let me continue my questioning.

Had I done something to make her angry? Was that why she'd been so short before? I tried to remember but came up with nothing.

"Redirect, Mr. Ward?" Judge Hopkins said.

"Yes, Your Honor."

Frank took a moment to gather his thoughts before he walked up to the lectern. "Mr. Rencher, did you have anything to do with the death of Raymond Carlisle?"

"No!" Kyle's voice was sharp, and his face was still red.

"Why did you get so angry on the stand just a moment ago?"

"I didn't like the implication that I did."

"That's the only reason?"

"Yes."

"No further questions, Your Honor."

It was anybody's guess if the jury had bought it. I certainly hadn't.

I didn't think Judge Hopkins had either.

It was difficult for me to read the expressions of the jurors. Had they seen through Kyle Rencher's lies, or did they accept his explanation that he didn't like to be accused of murder? I'd tripped him up enough on the stand that I didn't think they would believe him.

"The witness is excused," Judge Hopkins said. "Mr. Ward, you can call your next witness."

"The prosecution rests, Your Honor."

I stood. "Your Honor, I move for a directed verdict."

Judge Hopkins frowned and glanced at the jury. "Ladies and gentlemen of the jury, we're going to take a short break."

We waited for the jury to exit.

"Mr. Turner, what is the basis for your motion?"

I could tell the judge was already considering it.

She knew Kyle was lying.

"The prosecution has failed to prove its case, Your Honor. Each of the witnesses Mr. Ward put on the stand failed in their essential purpose to show that my client killed Mr. Carlisle and that she intended to kill him. There is insufficient proof my client had anything to do with this. The only things that tie my client to Mr. Carlisle's death are the fact his body was discovered in the Carlisle home, and my client's hair was found at the murder scene.

"The location of the body is circumstantial. There was too much hair from Ms. Carlisle found at the murder scene, especially because there was no DNA from anybody else. The only plausible explanation is that it was planted. There is no way that a jury can conclude beyond a reasonable doubt that Candy killed Raymond.

"Furthermore, the prosecution has failed to show intent. There is no need for a defense because, as a matter of law, the prosecution has failed to provide sufficient evidence to meet the elements of first-degree murder."

"Mr. Ward?"

Frank stood. "Your Honor, the defendant's case is on shaky legs, and Mr. Turner knows it. The defense is in a position where they must put Ms. Carlisle on the stand. He wants to avoid letting me take a crack at her."

Judge Hopkins frowned.

"The prosecution makes another good point," I said. "Failing a motion for a directed verdict, I also move for a mistrial. As Mr. Ward has pointed out, an expectation has developed during the course of this trial that Ms. Carlisle will testify. This is prejudicial. Several of the witnesses practically demanded it, and you, yourself, made a comment to that effect earlier, thus building the expectation."

"The defendant was out of line!" Judge Hopkins said. "I don't believe my statement has prejudiced the jury, Mr. Turner. Neither do I believe that the statements from any of the witnesses arise to a level of prejudice to justify declaring a mistrial. Your second motion is, therefore, denied."

I opened my mouth, but the judge continued.

"I need to give some thought to your motion for a directed verdict. I cannot decide that one off the top of my head." She looked at the clock. "We will take a thirty-minute recess while I review the motion."

She slammed down the gavel.

80

I looked at Frank once the judge had gone and nodded towards the hall.

"Sit tight," I said to Candy, "I might need you."

I didn't stop to explain why before I followed Frank out into the hallway. He meandered around, even though we passed several places where we could have had a private conversation.

Frank finally found a corner he liked and then turned on me. "What was that about? You're in rare form out there, you know that? I thought you were one of the good guys."

I blinked. *Good guys?*

"Just doing my job, Frank."

"You're making it look like Kyle had something to do with this when he didn't. You're trying to do that to all the poker boys."

"Are you certain they didn't?"

"Absolutely!"

"I've found new evidence that I have not yet disclosed to you."

"Holding back, are we?"

"Hardly. It just came to light during the break this morning. I must tell you, it is not good for your case."

"What is it?"

"A video." I paused. "From Raymond Carlisle. Actually, there are two videos."

"What does he say?"

"He made a record of his interactions with the poker boys. He documented that they threatened to kill him." I made sure I had Frank's attention. "He says at the beginning, he's afraid they will kill him and that he made the video, so they don't get away with it."

"That's nothing." Frank's voice faltered. "How do I know it's not faked?"

"You will see the truth if you look—"

"The truth is Candy did this."

I shook my head. "You found Candy's hair on her husband. That's not an unusual thing to find. And there was way too much. It was planted. Your witnesses all have credibility problems. The jury isn't going to buy what you're selling."

"We'll see about that."

"Frank, I'm trying to help you. You haven't seen the video. It's damning."

"Send it over. I'll take a look."

"I'll do that," I said, pulling out my phone. "And I'll show it to you, too."

He looked about to object but must have changed his mind.

"Just play it."

I played the video. Frank was stoic to the end. He looked at me when it was over.

"It doesn't get rid of the DNA we found on the victim."

"But you have no motive." I waved my phone. "This gives you motive. The poker boys tried to coordinate their testimony, but they all made mistakes. Every single one slipped up on the stand. None of them have any credibility. If the judge rules against my motion, I'll put my witnesses on the stand, and I'll show this video. What do you think that's going to do to your case? It's going to eviscerate it. It would be far better now to save yourself the embarrassment and just dismiss these charges. Charge the poker boys for this murder. Think of it as a four for one."

"No."

Frank walked away.

I had done my best to convince him. There was little else I could do to spare him what was coming. I looked around for Bernie on my way back to the courtroom, expecting him to confront me like he had the last two times Frank and I had stepped out for a private conversation in the hallway.

"What was that about?" Candy asked once I was in my seat.

"I was trying to get Frank to see reason, didn't work."

"Did you expect it to?"

"No, I was just hoping." I smiled. "Don't worry. We about have this one in the bag."

I checked my phone for a text message but didn't have one. We still had twenty minutes.

I pulled out my phone and made a call.

"Is it a go?"

I listened and hung up after saying, "Let me know when you do."

"What was that about?" Candy asked.

I didn't answer.

Twenty minutes later, the judge was back in the courtroom, and court was back in session.

"I deny your motion, counselor," Judge Hopkins said without preamble. "But I gave it considerable thought."

"Thank you for your consideration, Your Honor."

There was only one thing left to do after the jury was seated.

"You may call your first witness, counselor," Judge Hopkins said to me.

"I call Candy Carlisle to the stand."

81

A hush fell over the crowd. It was the moment they had been waiting for. I hoped my play didn't backfire. I had no other choice but to put Candy on the stand and walk her through everything that had happened.

Everything.

I hoped the jury believed her.

I was going to ask Candy hard questions. And she was going to tell the truth. I had told her ahead of time that if she did not, I would stop and turn her over to Frank because I would not suborn perjury.

We didn't need her to lie.

We only needed the truth.

I checked my phone one more time but still did not have the text message I was looking for.

I was playing with fire until I had it.

I began my questioning after I had settled in at the lectern, and Candy had been sworn in.

"Ms. Carlisle, can you please tell us about your relationship with your husband?"

"It was strained."

Good, she didn't hesitate.

"What do you mean?"

"We were planning to divorce."

"Why?"

"I don't know that either of us felt much romantic love anymore."

"How long had it been that way?"

She shrugged. "I don't know, a year or two?"

"Did you meet with a divorce attorney prior to your husband's death?"

Candy nodded. "Yes, he knew that, too."

"Ms. Carlisle, did Raymond deal drugs?"

"Yes."

I paused to let that sink in and glanced back at Frank. He was smiling.

It wasn't going to last.

It had been one of Frank's central contentions that Raymond had been a drug dealer. He thought I was making his case for him.

I had asked this question on purpose, not only to get it out of the way, but I wanted the jury to see Candy was being brutally honest and holding nothing back.

I glanced at the jury and slowly took in a deep breath.

"Can you tell us where you were on the night Raymond was murdered?"

"Yes, I was working at my office."

"Was there anybody else there who can testify you were there?"

Candy shook her head. "No, unfortunately not."

"Are there any access points that record comings and goings that can show you were there?"

"No."

"Are there any security cameras at your office?"

"Yes, there are, but the video was deleted before investigators could get to it. It's only kept for two weeks."

"Is there any other way to prove you were at the office during the time of your husband's death?"

"No, there's not. I can show you the work I did if that helps."

I nodded. "Perhaps it might be for the best."

"Objection, Your Honor," Frank said. "We have no way of knowing that she is telling the truth."

"Your Honor, it is the sole province of the jury to make such a determination."

"Overruled."

Candy opened up a manila envelope that she took out of her purse. "I work for a marketing agency. That night, I was working on these graphic designs." She pulled the first one out and held it up. It was an advertisement for some company I'd never heard of that sold energy drinks.

"Did you do all of that yourself?"

"No, I did the layout and the text. The illustrations you see were ordered from contractors, and we used stock images for the rest."

"Approximately how long did this take you to assemble?"

"This piece? An hour. I worked on it earlier in the day. I finished it that night, then worked on the next." She pulled out another sheet of paper and held it up for the jury to see.

"And how long did this one take?"

"This one probably took me about thirty minutes. It was a little easier now that I had the template from the previous one."

"Was that all you did?"

"No, I did five more." She pulled each one out and held it up in succession.

"Your Honor, I move to admit all of this as one exhibit. I believe we are on Exhibit A for the defense."

"Any objections, Mr. Ward?"

"None, Your Honor."

"The motion is granted."

"Ms. Carlisle, what time did you leave the office?"

"I left at approximately 9:50 PM."

"How long does it take for you to get from the office to your home?"

"Approximately fifteen to twenty minutes."

"What time did you arrive at your home that night?"

"About 10:05."

"Did you go through the front door?"

"Yes."

"Doesn't your house have a garage?"

"Yes, but Raymond had parked his car in front of it, blocking both spaces, so I didn't have a way to get in without moving it. I was too tired to do that, so I just parked on the street."

"Was it typical for Raymond to park there?"

"No, he usually parked in the garage. It was very unusual that he parked his car blocking both spots."

"How many years were you married?"

"Fifteen."

"And during the fifteen years that you were married to him, did he ever park his car in front of the garage to block both spaces?"

"No."

"Isn't it a possibility that because you guys were about to go through a divorce that he was being passive-aggressive?"

"No, Raymond was not passive-aggressive. I think deep down, he still cared for me, just like I still cared for him. The marriage had lost our romantic spark. It was really going to be more of a perfunctory matter, not a bitterly contested divorce."

"What happened when you walked in the door?"

"The first thing I noticed was that the door was unlocked."

"Was this strange?"

"A little. Raymond is good about locking the door. He is concerned for our children because of his side business." Candy frowned. "He was always very concerned for the safety of our children."

"What was the first thing you noticed upon walking into your home?"

"The smell. Something smelled off." She shook her head. "It's difficult to describe, but I knew something had gone very wrong."

"What did you do next?"

"I looked for the source. We have two rooms off the entryway, one on the right, one on the left. The one on the right is a dining room. I glanced in there but didn't see anything. I went to the one on the left. That is where I found Raymond."

"What was your first thought when you saw him?"

"Honestly? My first thought was that we didn't need a divorce anymore. I know that sounds callous, but I'm just telling the truth. My next thought was how terrible this was going to be for my children. Part of me felt relief, perhaps, that I didn't have to go through a divorce. Of course, that was an irrational thought. The tangible benefits of my children having a father around would've far outweighed any discomfort caused through our divorce."

"I'm surprised you're being so honest about your thoughts. Why is that?"

"Excuse me?" Candy looked surprised. "I'm under oath, aren't I?"

"You could've told us how devastated you were to see your soon-to-be ex-husband lying dead on the couch. You could've lied about that, and we would have never known. Why didn't you?"

"Because that's not the truth."

"What did you do next?"

"I called the police."

"You didn't try to resuscitate him?"

"No. He was dead."

"How could you tell?"

"There was so much blood. He wasn't moving. He wasn't breathing."

"How long was it until the police arrived?"

"I don't know, it felt like forever, but it was probably less than ten minutes."

"What did you do during that time?"

"I sat on the stairs."

"Why there?"

"Because if my children tried to come down, I wanted to intercept them and get them back upstairs."

"Did either one of them come down before the police arrived?"

"No, neither one did, thankfully."

"Did you go into the kitchen?"

"No, I did not."

"Why were there onions in the sink?"

"I don't know. I didn't even know that there were until I heard Detective Lee testify about it."

"Is it possible Raymond was cooking something?"

Frank stood. "Objection, calls for speculation."

"Sustained."

"Did Raymond like to cook?"

"Yes, he did."

"What types of things would he make?"

"A variety of things. He liked to use the crockpot. It is my assumption—"

Frank was on his feet again. "Objection, Your Honor. Speculation."

"Sustained."

"Did Raymond cook with onions?"

"Yes, he loved them."

"How did he use the crockpot?"

"He'd put something in the night before."

"Can you tell us, Ms. Carlisle, why Detective Bernie Lee felt like you were not sufficiently shocked by your husband's death?"

"I was shocked! I was devastated after it sank in, more for my children than for me, but for me, too. Raymond and I had shared many years of happiness together. I was not happy to see him die, as Detective Lee surmised."

"Do you remember your conversation with Detective Lee?"

"Yes, I do."

"Can you describe how he made you feel?"

"He made me feel like I was guilty of killing my husband, even though I had nothing to do with it."

"How did he do that?"

"His questions all centered on how I could have done it. He never once expressed any sympathy for me and the sudden plight I found myself in."

"Were you relieved when an officer came to tell you that your daughter was awake?"

"No, I was horrified. I did not want my daughter to see Raymond in that position."

I nodded and looked at my watch. I was not yet past the point of no return, but I was getting close.

I did a double-take.

I *had* received a text message but had not felt my watch vibrate when it came in.

I glanced at the message and hid a smile.

My next move was risky, but I needed to make it. Luckily, my insurance plan had just come through.

"Ms. Carlisle, were you involved with your husband's business dealings?"

Candy nodded. "Yes."

"Ms. Carlisle, let us be very clear on this matter. You were helping your husband deal drugs, correct?"

"Yes."

82

I had everybody's attention, from Judge Hopkins, to Frank Ward, to the jury, to those in attendance. They all hung on every single word from Candy's mouth. It wasn't often somebody confessed to crimes in open court. Frank had no doubt hoped to get my client to admit to this. The fact I had requested the confession probably made him squirm in his seat, wondering what I would ask next.

A glance at him confirmed this. *He's angry I brought it out of her myself.* It took away some of the punch from the drama he was hoping for.

"Why do you admit to this?" I asked after I'd let the silence grow.

"Because the truth needs to come out."

I nodded. "Who supplied the drugs?"

Candy didn't answer right away. She gave me a cautious look. She did not yet know all the specifics of what I was working on behind the scenes. I had just told her to trust me and that I would take care of it.

I felt bad for her, but I wanted the judge and jury to see this. I wanted them to empathize with her struggle.

"Ms. Carlisle?" I said a moment later after she had still not answered. I was glad to see how hesitant she was. I would use this in my closing statement to illustrate just how afraid she was of the distributor.

"A man by the name of Marc Guyton."

Candy's voice was quiet. She held my eyes as she spoke, afraid to look at anybody else. I didn't dare blink or break her gaze, willing her forward.

I was her lifeline.

She had made this step, trusting that everything would be all right because I had made her a promise. Even holding onto that hope, she paled as if afraid the truth would kill her.

It could not have gone better if I had scripted it out myself.

"Ms. Carlisle, you seem afraid right now. Can you please tell the court why?"

"Marc Guyton is dangerous. The very fact I'm here testifying puts my family in danger."

"Why tell the truth?"

"What choice do I have?"

"It may comfort you to know, Candy, I received a text message a few minutes ago. Marc Guyton has been arrested, so have many of his associates."

Relief spread across Candy's face. She muttered something under her breath I could not make out. I couldn't tell if she had just cursed me or mumbled a prayer of gratitude.

"Objection, Your Honor," Frank said. "Was there a question in there?"

I bit my tongue while Judge Hopkins looked at Frank like he was daft. The guy was not reading the room.

It was clear this was not a charade. The judge and jury were looking at raw, unfiltered emotion from my client as she dealt with a situation.

"Overruled."

"How did things work?"

"The distributor, Marc Guyton, provided the drugs. Raymond channeled them to a group called the poker boys."

"Can you please be specific by who you mean when you say the poker boys?"

"He would give them to Bill Weaver, Larry Thompson, Kyle Rencher, and Abe Martin. The poker boys."

"What would they do with them?"

"They would sell through a variety of outlets."

"Did they sell direct?"

Candy shook her head. "As I understand it, no. They had multiple ways they recruited street-level dealers to push the drugs."

"Does the name Mount Pleasant mean anything to you?"

She grimaced. "Yes, it does. It is the name of a rehabilitation center."

"Why are you familiar with it?"

"It is one of the places used to sell the drugs."

"It seems unusual that a rehab center would be the focus for a drug distribution operation. Are you sure?"

Candy nodded. "It came with clientele and dealers already built-in."

"Who owns Mount Pleasant?"

"One of the poker boys, I'm not sure which."

"Objection!" Frank stood. "Speculation. Let the defense submit evidence if they have it."

"Sustained."

"Did they deal drugs at the center?"

"No, that happened off site."

Another hush had fallen over the courtroom.

This, more than any other revelation, was one I had been concerned about bringing forward, but I wanted to paint a complete picture of the poker boys.

Using a rehab place to sell drugs was bad. I imagined several of the jurors just had their stomachs do backflips.

It was risky to reveal this because it could blow back on my client, but I wanted it all on the record. It would give Candy greater credibility when I pointed out in my closing statement that she had held nothing back.

I looked down at my notes to give it a moment to sink in.

The poker boys were using a rehab center to sell drugs.

If that wasn't evil, what was?

If they were capable of that, what more could they do?

Murder?

Those were all questions I wanted the jury thinking.

"Is that the only rehab center you are aware of that the poker boys were using?"

"No, there were at least five more."

"Can you name them?"

Candy rattled them all off.

"Ms. Carlisle, you have just admitted in court under oath to a variety of different drug-related crimes. You also have admitted to knowledge of a variety of different drug-related crimes."

I paused to make sure everybody was paying attention.

"Ms. Carlisle, did you kill your husband?"

"No."

"Did you have anything to do with the death of your husband?"

"No."

I nodded. Frank stirred, drawing my eye. His teeth were clenched. I was certain a part of him believed her, but he was too set on his course to change.

"Do you brush your hair?"

"Everyday."

"How many brushes did you have in your bathroom?"

"I dunno, probably four or five."

I took my time to turn the page of my notepad to the next set of questions. I wanted to make a clean break between my last line of questioning and my new line of questioning.

"Earlier today, Ms. Carlisle, you gave me two things. What were they?"

"A flash drive and a cell phone."

"Let's talk about the cell phone first. What was the cell phone used for?"

"Raymond used it to contact the distributor, Marc Guyton." She said his name with a little less fear.

"Did he use it to contact anybody else?"

"No, he did not."

"And how did Raymond contact the distributor?"

"Text messages."

"Do you have a record of those text messages?"

"Yes, I do."

"Even from previous phones?"

"Yes."

"How far back?"

"I have a record for the last year on the phone. It's backed up to the flash drive, too. The flash drive contains an additional five years of messages."

"Does Raymond ever refer to the buyer by name in those text messages?"

"No, he never does."

"How do you know then that Marc Guyton is the distributor?"

"Raymond told me."

Frank went to his feet. "Objection, hearsay."

"Why would Raymond lie to his wife on this issue?" I asked. "And as the prosecution has also pointed out, Raymond is not here to testify. This should be treated as an excited utterance." It was a stretch. I wasn't sure the judge would buy it.

Surprisingly, Judge Hopkins hesitated. It didn't matter if she sustained the objection. Frank knew it, too. His case was sunk. He just refused to accept it.

"Overruled."

"What else was on the flash drives?"

"There were two videos."

I pulled a spare flash drive out of my pocket and held it up. "Your Honor, I would like to have this marked as Defense Exhibit B."

Frank was on his feet. "Your Honor—"

Hopkins cut him off with a wave of her hand. "Can you provide some foundation first for the videos?" She nodded at Frank. "Have these videos been disclosed to the prosecution?"

"Yes, I will, Your Honor, and yes, I played one of the videos for Frank out in the hallway, and he has copies of both. He has also received a copy of all the messages from the flash drive."

"Is this a problem, Mr. Ward?"

"If it pleases the court," I said quickly, "it's not my intention to refer to any of those text messages at this time during the testimony today, so Frank should have adequate time to review them before they are introduced in court."

"Proceed then, counselor."

Frank was still standing. "Your Honor, I object to these videos. We have no way of knowing if they are genuine. For all we know, they could be a deep-fake. Video manipulation technology has gotten quite good these days."

"But not that good, Your Honor," I said. "Anybody ever see that sci-fi movie where they tried to bring an actor back to life? It was only semi-believable because the fans wanted to believe, even then, there was a lot of criticism. If Hollywood with such great resources can't do it, how can we expect that somebody with far less knowhow and resources can?"

"Overruled for now. You may show the videos after foundation has been laid, assuming that is sufficient."

"Thank you, Your Honor." I turned back to Candy. "Have you seen the videos?"

"I have."

"Did you help make the videos?"

"Yes. I held his phone while Raymond spoke."

"I'm confused that they're just now coming to light, Ms. Carlisle. Can you explain why you held these back?"

"I was hoping we could resolve the murder charge against me without having to bring them forward, primarily because I was afraid of what Marc Guyton would do when these were made known to the public."

A solid answer, but Frank wouldn't let it go at that, so neither would I.

"Why were you afraid?"

"I did not see the images myself, but Raymond told me about photos Marc Guyton's people had shown to him of those who had crossed him. They were not pretty images."

"Objection, hearsay."

"Excited utterance," I said. "Goes to the victim's state of mind."

"Overruled."

"Did Raymond have a copy of the photos?"

"No, he did not. He does, however, reference these in his video."

"Did Raymond give you a copy of these videos before his death?"

"No, he did not."

"How did you locate these videos?"

"I checked our safe deposit box after Raymond's death. I found them there."

"Where did you find the distributor's phone?"

"I also found that in the same safe deposit box."

"How long was it after he died before you checked the safe deposit box?"

"It was approximately a week later."

"That's a long time to keep evidence in your possession, Ms. Carlisle. Why didn't you turn it over to your attorney sooner? Are you sure it is just because you were afraid of Marc Guyton?"

"Yes, that is the primary reason."

I waited. "And?"

"Because I was planning on keeping the business going."

"What changed your mind?"

Candy hesitated but finally said, "I want out of this life."

"Is that sufficient foundation, Your Honor?"

Hopkins looked at Frank. "Mr. Ward?"

"I renew my previous objection."

"Overruled, Mr. Ward. You may submit the flash drive as Defense Exhibit B, Mr. Turner."

"With your permission, Your Honor, I will connect my computer up to the courtroom projector, so we can view both videos."

"Yes, you may proceed, counselor, to show the videos."

I went back for my computer and took it to the lectern, connecting it up to the courtroom system. The bailiff lowered the projection screen while I was doing this. I brought up the first video and pressed play, motioning to the bailiff to shut off the lights.

Raymond appeared on screen. Ironically, he sat on the same sofa where his body was discovered.

"My name is Raymond Carlisle. I have been involved for the last six years as a middleman dealing drugs between Marc Guyton and a group informally known as the poker boys. This group consists of..."

I watched the jury's faces while they watched the video. Raymond talked about how he feared for his life. He talked about how the poker boys had threatened him multiple times. He talked about how he made this video because he wanted them to go down for his death if he was killed.

It was probably the most persuasive thing I had ever seen in court. By the time the video ended, I even saw one jury member wiping a tear out of her eye. Raymond had finished with a message to his children.

I was surprised that the juror could summon a tear for somebody who had been putting so many people's lives at risk to make money, but I wasn't going to question it.

"Ms. Carlisle," I said, "do you remember when this video was made?"

She nodded. "Yes, it was recorded approximately four weeks before Raymond was killed."

"Your Honor, may I now present the next video?"

"I object, Your Honor," Frank said, standing while glancing warily at the jury. The crying juror was no doubt something he had noticed, and he wanted to avoid aggravating the damage the video had done to his case.

"On what grounds, Mr. Ward?"

"I've viewed both videos. The first is adequate for us to get the idea. The second one is redundant."

"Your Honor," I said, breaking in, "I think it's vitally important that both videos are shown. These are Raymond's last words. He doesn't have an opportunity to testify here in court today because it was taken from him. Let him talk about who he thinks killed him."

"Overruled, Mr. Ward."

I brought up the second video and played it. This was a more recent video. He said again that he had received more threats from the poker boys, and then he ended the video by telling us the date.

It was three days before he died.

I looked around the courtroom after the bailiff turned back on the lights.

It was deathly silent.

I hesitated. When I had made my earlier motion for a directed verdict, I had not really thought the judge would buy it. I had been surprised when she had given it careful consideration.

I had been close to convincing her before. I'd got the distinct impression when she'd issued her ruling that she had almost sided with me.

What are the chances?

"Your Honor," I said, "I renew my motion for a directed verdict."

83

Judge Hopkins turned to the jury. "We're going to take another break here, ladies and gentlemen."

She looked at me once they had gone.

"Counselor, please make your argument."

"Yes, Your Honor." I doubted I would ever deliver the closing argument I had prepared. I would pull some of that into this.

"Your Honor, the only evidence that ties Candy to this crime is the fact that her hair was found on the murder victim and at the murder scene. Her fingerprints were also found on the victim's buttons. We have since discovered that the hairbrushes she kept in her master bathroom are missing. It was my intention to put my private investigator on the stand, so he could testify about this point, but I can tell you that I found firsthand all these brushes were gone. Her prints were likely left when she folded her husband's clothes.

"The prosecution cannot prove Candy killed Raymond. The only piece of evidence is explainable. He would have her DNA on him just because they lived in the same house.

"That she was framed is further substantiated by the fact that nobody else's DNA was found in that room. The Carlisle's have a teenage daughter and a young son. I imagine they shed hair all the time. It is concerning that law enforcement did not find any of their hair in that room.

"Why not?

"We don't know. It is reasonable to assume that the poker boys, in their efforts to frame Candy Carlisle, thoroughly cleaned the room, wiping it down for fingerprints as well as vacuuming for other DNA that might've been left behind the last time they played poker there.

"Furthermore, the prosecution has failed to prove intent. They have not provided one single shred of evidence to indicate why Candy could have done this.

"On the other hand, we have now provided incontrovertible proof from the victim himself—made three days before his death!—that the poker boys were threatening to kill him.

"They made good on their promise.

"The facts as we know them speak for themselves. The prosecution, well-meaning in their efforts, has charged the wrong person for this crime.

"The prosecution lacks sufficient evidence to overcome the presumption of innocence. No reasonable trier of fact can find for the prosecution as a matter of law. I, therefore, move for a directed verdict. We should stop wasting court time and state resources pursuing somebody who has not committed the crime to seek out those who did.

"Thank you, Your Honor." I returned to my seat.

"Mr. Ward?"

"Your Honor, there is no substantial evidence that shows the poker boys had anything to do with this. All we have is this video that came forward at the eleventh hour. It purportedly shows Raymond testifying the poker boys were behind his death.

"We have not had an opportunity to examine this video, but technology has gotten good at faking these things. With just a small sample of home videos from Raymond Carlisle, is it possible that Candy commissioned these videos herself?"

Frank shrugged. "The timing is rather suspicious and fortuitous for the defense. It is also highly unusual for us to be considering a directed verdict at this point in the trial.

"The prosecution has proved Candy was in the room where Raymond died. Her DNA was found all over the victim.

"Why *was* there so much hair? The defense would have you believe somebody took it from some hairbrushes." Frank shook his head. "This defies reason, Your Honor. Raymond and Candy got into a physical altercation. Raymond ended up dead and was covered with the defendant's DNA at the end.

"The master bathroom has sat empty and unused in the months since Raymond's death. How are we to know what happened to those brushes? Candy Carlisle had access to the master bathroom the entire time. She could easily have returned to the house and taken those brushes out herself.

"Your Honor, we should let this go to the jury for them to decide. Let the defense finish their presentation, we will make our closing arguments, and then we will see what the triers of facts have to say.

"Thank you, Your Honor."

Judge Hopkins had been taking notes and continued writing after Frank had sat down. She looked up several minutes later.

"As to the timing of the request for a directed verdict, I don't believe that it is an inappropriate time to consider such a request." The judge looked at Candy Carlisle. "Ms. Carlisle, you are still under oath even though you are no longer on the stand. Did you remove your own hairbrushes from your bathroom?"

"No, Your Honor, I did not."

Judge Hopkins studied Candy.

"If I may, Your Honor," Frank said, "I do have one more thing I'd like to say. The defendant has just admitted to being party to several severe drug-related crimes. She has admitted in open court that they were using drug rehab centers to distribute drugs. How much more heinous of a crime can you think of? How much more vile—"

"Excuse me, Your Honor," I said, standing, "if I may interject. Things have been happening quickly today." I turned to Frank. "My apologies, I should have mentioned earlier that in conjunction with us providing evidence to your associates and promising testimony against Marc Guyton and his associates, we have secured a deal with regard to those crimes my client committed."

Frank went red in the face.

It looked like Judge Hopkins hid a smile. "I think that resolves that issue, and it makes what I'm about to do a bit easier.

"Ms. Carlisle, I believe you told us the truth today. I also don't find any reason to believe that these videos are anything but genuine. Therefore, I shall issue a directed verdict.

"The prosecution has failed to provide sufficient evidence to allow this matter to continue, especially in light of the new evidence brought forth by the defense."

Judge Hopkins leveled a glare at Ms. Carlisle. "Candy, you are getting off easy today. Your attorney has done a thorough job at finagling things for you. He has provided you a second chance. I suggest you don't waste it."

Candy glanced away. "No, Your Honor, I won't."

"I hereby enter my ruling. The defense request for a directed verdict is granted."

84

A murmur went through the courtroom. Most in attendance probably didn't understand what had happened.

Candy looked at me uncertainly.

"Your Honor," Frank said, standing, "I object."

"Your objection is noted for the record, counselor."

The judge slammed down the gavel. "Case dismissed. Court is adjourned."

And just like that, it was done.

I packed up my stuff.

"I'm free?" Candy asked.

I nodded.

She let out a sigh. "Then it's truly over, isn't it?"

"Yes."

"What happens to the poker boys?"

"Frank will soon charge them. He's not a bad guy. He's just wrong. He'll see that."

"Which one do you think shot Raymond?"

I shrugged. "They're all guilty, except for maybe Seth Roberts. My bet is that Bill Weaver shot the 9mm, and Kyle or Abe had the .22."

"How are you so sure about Bill?"

"Tammy Weaver's testimony about how her husband is a firearms enthusiast. She seemed a little smug, like there was an inside joke. She was trying to come off credible, but that's a detail that will haunt them now you're off the hook. That tidbit, with Bill's threats and the rest of it, should be enough to sink them all."

I walked with her down the steps of the courthouse, nodding at people as we descended. We soon reached the bottom.

I was about to leave but stopped.

"You're not going to throw this away?"

She shook her head. "What if Guyton comes at me from prison?"

"Witness protection was promised if that happens."

"Thank you, Mr. Turner."

I gave her a thin smile as I turned away. Normally, I would have taken the opportunity to release a statement to the press, but I wasn't in the mood.

I would let my work stand for itself today.

My watch vibrated, indicating that I had received a text message. I looked down, expecting to see that it was from Detective Stephanie Gray, who had just facilitated the arrest of Marc Guyton and his associates.

I was surprised it was a text from Barbara.

"Mitch, you have a second?"

I responded back. "Sure."

"Can you come?" She included an address I didn't recognize.

"I'll be right there."

"Hurry."

Books by Dan Decker

Dan Decker publishes books regularly in a variety of Genres. For a complete listing visit:

http://www.dandeckerbooks.com/books

For the most recent updates go to:

http://www.dandeckerbooks.com

Legal Thrillers

Mitch Turner Legal Thrillers

1. The Good Client
2. The Victim's Wife

Mitch Turner Legal Thriller Short Stories

1. The Mugger
2. The Hostage Negotiator
3. The Prosecution's Witness

And more!

Thrillers

Jake Ramsey Thrillers

1. Black Brick
2. Dark Spectrum
3. Blood Games
4. Silent Warehouse (Short Story)
5. Nameless Man (Short Story)
6. Money Games (Short Story)

Jason Maxfield Thrillers

1. Max Damage
2. Coming soon!

Science Fiction & Fantasy

Monster Country: Vince Carter Chronicles

1. Genizyz
2. Requiem

Monster Country: Parry Peters Chronicles

1. Recruit (Novella)
2. Delivery (Novella)

Dead Man's War

1. Dead Man's Game

2. Dead Man's Fear
3. Dead Man's Fury

War of the Fathers Universe

1. Prequel: Blood of the Redd Guard
2. War of the Fathers
3. Lord of the Inferno
4. Enemy in the Shadows
5. East Wind (Short Story)

The Containment Team

1. Ready Shooter
2. Hybrid Hotel

Red Survivor Mission Chronicles

1. Red Survivor
2. The Sawyer Gambit
3. The Assassin in the Hold

And More!

About the Author

Dan Decker lives in Utah with his family. He has a law degree and spends as much time as he can outdoors. You can learn more about upcoming novels at dandeckerbooks.com[1].

1. http://www.dandeckerbooks.com/

Author's Note

If you would like to receive notifications about other upcoming works, sneak peeks, and other extras, go to dandeckerbooks.com[1] and sign up for my newsletter. Finally, if you would like to reach out, please feel free to drop me a line at dan@dandeckerbooks.com. I always enjoy hearing from readers.

1. http://www.dandeckerbooks.com/

Published by Grim Archer Media, a publishing imprint of Xander Revolutions LC

Printed in Great Britain
by Amazon

74329425R00222